The Collected Stories of
William Humphrey

The Collected Stories of
William Humphrey

Delacorte Press · Seymour Lawrence

Published by
Delacorte Press/Seymour Lawrence
1 Dag Hammarskjold Plaza
New York, N.Y. 10017

"Quail for Mr. Forester" first appeared in *The New Yorker;* "The Hardys" and "The Fauve" in *The Sewanee Review;* "In Sickness and Health" and "Man with a Family" in *Accent;* "Sister" in *Harper's Bazaar;* "A Fresh Snow" and "A Job of the Plains" in *The Quarterly Review of Literature;* "The Ballad of Jesse Neighbours," "The Pump," "The Human Fly," and "The Last of the Caddoes" in *Esquire;* "A Voice from the Woods" in *The Atlantic Monthly;* "A Good Indian" (under a different title), "The Rainmaker," and "A Home Away from Home" in *The Saturday Evening Post.*
These and other stories in this collection were published in *The Last Husband* and *A Time and a Place* by William Humphrey.

Manufactured in the United States of America

First printing

Library of Congress Cataloging in Publication Data
Humphrey, William.
The collected stories of William Humphrey.
I. Title.
PS3558.U464C6 1985   813'.54
ISBN 0-385-29400-X
Library of Congress Catalog Card Number: 84-26046

TO DOROTHY

Contents

The Collected Stories of
William Humphrey

The Hardys

Mr. Hardy sat on the edge of the bed waiting for his mind to catch up, and told himself that today he ought to be especially nice to Clara.

He reached for his twist on the nightstand and, marking the spot with his thumb, carefully measured off his morning chew. He wrapped his teeth around it, then decided it wasn't quite what he needed and wrung off a man-sized plug. He gathered his clothes from the chair. In his sock feet, gaiters in his hand, he paused at the door and listened; Clara slept soundly.

Holding a kidney in place, Mr. Hardy bent to light the stove. He spat in the ash box and stashed his quid in the corner of his mouth so he could blow the fire. He set the coffeepot on the lid and put the biscuits in the oven and thought there was time to look the place over a bit before they started in on it, maybe tuck a few old things out of sight that Clara would cry over if she came across them.

The loose floor board just inside the dining room sighed under Mr. Hardy's feet. For the first time in he didn't know how long, he thought of Virgie. She was worn out from her trip, a new bride, new to Texas and scared, but trying to be brave and trying not to show how ugly and ramshackle this house seemed to her, and he said he would get to that board the very next morning.

When he rummaged around in his mind for a picture of her, Mr. Hardy found that Virgie's face and Clara's, like two old tintypes laid face to face in an album, had come off on each other. What would Virgie have come to look like, he wondered, if she had lived? The only way he could picture her was about like Clara looked now. The main thing Mr. Hardy recalled about his first wife was that she died and he married Clara. The three years that lay between had been lost in the shuffle. Mr. Hardy could thumb through his years like pages in a book, but looking up a certain one was like hunting a sentence he had come across years before. "How was it, Mr. Hardy, you took so long about getting married again?" he could remember Clara asking more than once, and of course he answered, "I was a while finding the right woman." It seemed now he hardly waited a decent time after laying Virgie in the ground. Being without a wife had made him feel queer. With three stepchildren to take on, and all boys so she couldn't expect any help with the housework, he was afraid no woman would have him. At the same time he feared some other man might see the day's work Clara Dodson could do and grab her up, she might just be waiting for a chance to lay down, he suspected, when she was mistress of a house of her own.

He needn't have worried about Clara, Mr. Hardy told himself, feeling guilty for standing off and thinking about her in such a cold-hearted way. As long as she was able she worked night and day, and often he wondered if even Virgie could have made a better mother to her boys.

Little by little, as Virgie's belongings got shoved further back in the attic of the house, Virgie had been pushed further and further back in the unused corners of Mr. Hardy's mind. He all but forgot they were Virgie's children, that this had ever been any but Clara's house.

Mrs. Hardy woke up just in time. Breathless, she lay listening to the thump of her heart, sure she had barely missed being taken, and thinking over what a terrible night she had been through. For each time she woke Mr. Hardy to rub her, there were ten times, she thought, when she bore her pain alone and in silence. If only Mr. Hardy would stay awake and talk to her a little while in bed at night. She would have rested ever so much better. Lying there in the quiet with her teeth out unnerved her, made her less certain of things, brought on bad dreams.

Each morning she felt glad all over again that never in thirty years had she once let Mr. Hardy see her with her teeth out. She trusted him not to look when he got up in the morning, and when she had to wake him she always took them from the tumbler first and eased them in. She smiled, thinking how Mr. Hardy always waited then, fumbling around as if he couldn't find the matches— in his own mind giving her a minute to wrap herself modestly— before lighting the lamp.

Mr. Hardy was nice in little ways like that, considerate, not like other men at all, and she ought not to complain if he was so quiet. Men just had little to say. She was used to all kinds, all funny in their own ways and no two alike except in one thing—men just never had much to say, and anything she couldn't put up with was one that did, you couldn't put any trust in them; she had never been much of a talker herself and couldn't stand gabbing women —still, being alone together as they were now, she did wish Mr. Hardy would try to be a little more company to her.

At least when he did find something to say it wasn't like other men, like the husbands of every other woman she could call to mind without exception, something sour-tempered or coarse, as if they begrudged you every word.

Being considerate by nature, Mr. Hardy would have opened out more, she felt, if he had been an American. But the English were close-mouthed and, to tell the truth, a little slow, she had long ago decided. Being English explained a lot of Mr. Hardy's quirks. Many times she had to make amends for his blunt manners to people he never really meant to hurt at all. He saved in niggling little ways. Nobody liked to see waste, but Mr. Hardy took it too far altogether.

It was being English had made him always work so hard, harder than he had to and harder than he need have let the neighbors pass by and see him at. There was nobody to blame but himself that now in his old age he had to sell his home; he had worked all the boys so hard it was no wonder each of them had enough farming by the time he was grown to last him the rest of his life.

Walking quietly, Mr. Hardy looked over the parlor until he saw on the mantelpiece the price tags the auctioneer had left. For weeks Clara had been telling everybody about the sale. She wanted them all to be sure it was not for money, but only because the house was too big, "now that the boys were all gone away," she said with pride, for she thought they had all come up in the world by moving into town. If there was anything that could come over him sometimes and make him feel he couldn't hold his head up before the neighbors, that was it.

It was terrible to have put in fifty years' hard work on a place and raised eight boys on it and there be not one among them willing to take up when you had done all you could and put in an honest day's work to keep it in the family. A great big bunch of conniving schemers with pasty-faced, shifty-eyed youngsters growing up just like them or worse. City slickers, that was what he had raised and whose bread he would have to eat from now on.

Clara, he expected, was looking forward to leaving, and he couldn't really blame her. It was a big house, and though they used little of it, hard to keep up. The very idea of a colored woman coming in to do the cleaning, handling all her stuff and dropping and breaking things, was enough to bring on one of her attacks. She would enjoy moving from one of the children to another in the time left them and he supposed that was how it would be. For a while he told himself they might take what money the old place brought and buy a little one with a couple of rooms and garden space, but Clara would never be happy in it, she would be mortified before the neighbors. A woman would rather have no home of her own at all than one without a big parlor with a sofa in it, and he had known all along it wouldn't turn out the way he wanted. A time came when you were too old for starting over.

Mrs. Hardy came into the kitchen rubbing her eyes and smelled the biscuits burning. She was in time, but if they had been burnt to a crisp, the idea of Mr. Hardy thinking to get breakfast would have made up for it. She thought of the day that lay ahead of her and how all sad things bring a little sweet with the bitter. Waiting for the eggs to boil she wondered what Mr. Hardy found so interesting he forgot about the biscuits. He was always mindful of such things, forever saying, "Now, Clara, don't forget about the biscuits," when to be sure she had forgot, her mind a thousand miles away.

When the eggs were done and still Mr. Hardy didn't come, she began to fidget. There were things about this day she had been dreading for weeks, and now she hoped he hadn't stumbled across a reminder of some old sadness and she not by his side to comfort him. Most such things had been done away with as she gradually made life easier for him, but some few, she always feared, might still be lying about.

She listened for his step in the attic. Could Mr. Hardy be sitting up there going through that box of Virgie's old things, too engrossed to stir?

He came in from outside, looking a little sheepish, it seemed to her. He had let the biscuits burn, she told him, and waited for him to say where he had been. She ought to try to get a bite down, he said, but the idea of food simply gagged her. Mr. Hardy felt he was not showing his own sense of the sadness of this day and pushed his plate back, but she said just because she couldn't eat he mustn't let that stop him.

She sighed and said she didn't know where to begin. It made no difference as far as he could see. He dug a pencil stub out of the silverware drawer. In the parlor they tried to choose what to hang the first tag on. She would have started in on little things and gradually got herself used to the idea, but Mr. Hardy went straight over to the player piano, the biggest thing in the room and the one over which she would have hesitated longest. Mr. Hardy stepped back and looked at it and thought it made the piano look suddenly very important. He imagined the auctioneer going through his spiel, "Now what am I bid for this fine player piano?" the bids going higher and higher, being called in from the front yard where the crowd had overflowed. He was beginning to enjoy himself.

"That player piano," said Mrs. Hardy, beginning to feel he was parting with it a bit too readily, "has been like a close friend to me. Many a night I believe I'd have went out of my mind if it hadn't been for that player piano."

"Well, maybe we could keep it," he said. "Isabel could find a place for it, I suppose, and you could listen to it whenever we went to stay with her."

She could listen to it; it meant nothing to him, all those fine old tunes she thought had stood for so much between them. No, she told him, they mustn't hang back over the first piece, they'd never raise any money. Well, now, they weren't that bad off; if she wanted it she would have it.

Mr. Hardy could not remember what he had paid for it and thought Clara was high when she insisted on a hundred dollars. Anyhow, they had used it a long time. Yes, but it was like new when they got it. They put down fifty dollars as the least they would take for it, and a note saying he could come down to $37.50 if that was all he could get; then Clara said to put down he ought to try to get fifty though, for it had the finest tone of any she ever heard. She stroked it. For one last time she wanted to hear "Over the Waves" and asked if he wouldn't like to, too. Really he thought they ought to get on, but he knew that tune meant a great deal to her.

She could close her eyes and hear it in her head any hour of the day and it was the night of her wedding when Mr. Hardy waltzed her till two o'clock in the morning. To look at him now who would ever believe it?

She hummed and swayed her head and tapped her foot and smiled to think she hadn't had two dozen words with Mr. Hardy when he asked her to marry him. No denying, he needed somebody to look after his boys, but there were others that he must have seen would do for that job just as well. At first she feared the change. But there was so little difference she felt at home right away, looking after Mr. Hardy and his boys instead of her father and brother and sister. For six months there was hardly time to think of anything; without a woman for three years the house, the boys, their shirts and socks all needed mending and darning, scrubbing and barbering. He told her to ease up a little, that she would kill herself with work as his first wife, Virgie, had done. No one had ever worried before how long or hard she worked. She had loved her mother and father, her brother and sister, but she grew to love Mr. Hardy so much more than all of them it made her ashamed. She came to think it had been sinful of her to marry him without feeling then as she did now about him. She thought of Virgie and dug out an old picture of her and, gazing at it, spent hours wondering if she had felt that way, too, about Mr. Hardy, which loved him the most, thinking up things she would do for him that Virgie, you could tell by her face, would have fallen short of.

The music stopped. If only there had been someone to pump the machine she would have asked Mr. Hardy to waltz with her, she was sure she still remembered the steps. He seemed impatient and she just wondered if he had forgot what tune that was.

When they were agreed on the davenport and the Morris chair, the marble-topped table and the chandelier, Mrs. Hardy took the photograph album, the mantelpiece clock, a couple of antimacassars her mother had crocheted, two or three pieces off the what-not, and the music roll for "Over the Waves" and went out to look at the buffet while it still had no price tag on it. She had tried for days to figure out some way of keeping it, but it was just too big. She could already see Cora Westfall going straight through the rest of the house until she came to that buffet; the woman had envied her that piece for years. Mrs. Hardy only hoped somebody else turned up who wanted it as bad and ran the bid up good and high.

She watched Mr. Hardy and the way he was putting that tag on the bedroom chiffonier anybody might have thought it was just any old thing instead of the present from the children on their twenty-fifth anniversary. Men never put much store in things, she knew, but that had not stopped her from hoping Mr. Hardy might be different. He never kept souvenirs. "Souvenir of what?" she could remember him asking at the end of days she would never forget as long as she lived. She must have a keepsake for everything that ever happened to her. She had come across a good many that no longer reminded her of whatever they were supposed to. All the same they meant a great deal to her. It would all come back to her in time.

By eleven o'clock Mrs. Hardy was tired, but he was the first to notice. He settled her with a pillow behind her head to rest in the Morris chair, but not before he had removed the price tag, for she said it made her feel she was up on the auction block. She eased herself out with a sigh and thought that even Mr. Hardy's attentions could sometimes cause her pain. He was tender with her, when he thought about it. He ought to know he could call on her to bear the sadness with him, that he needn't try to spare her any of it. Perhaps he was worrying what the neighbors might be saying, that he had failed her, left her without a home of her own in her last years. She didn't want anybody to hold anything against him on her account.

She was watching Mr. Hardy through the open door but turned her head so as not to see the trouble he was having getting up off his knees. She had had the best years of his life, she told herself. He had grown old by her side. But he had never been young by it and that was the thing she couldn't bear to think about. She said: A man's second choice was made when he knew better what he wanted, when he knew from experience what to steer clear of, when he looked deeper than a pretty face. It was only with a ripeness of years, as everybody knew, that true love came.

But as he worked he handled more carefully the things that had been Virgie's, held them longer in his hands as though he hated to give them up. A guilty feeling would come over him and what was it worth if he was gentle with her then? Watching him ponder over a lamp that had been brought out for Virgie all the way from St. Louis, then break off suddenly to come in and pat her head and say a word, she felt she was getting only the crumbs that fell from the table. Such a rush of old feeling for Virgie had risen in him, he would have said a loving word to anybody that stood near.

Mr. Hardy's little niceties were the only way he knew how to behave. She couldn't remember ever having seen him lose his temper. But so with Virgie, too, he must have been sweet and good and kind. She didn't enjoy thinking he had got on exactly badly with his first wife. In her own sure ways she had made life easier for him, but it hurt her to think he had ever been really unhappy. She hoped he hadn't stayed a widower for three years only because his first marriage had been unfortunate.

Sitting alone a feeling came over her that her whole life had been an accident. What if Virgie hadn't died? But she did and Mr. Hardy chose her, after looking the field over for a long time.

Mr. Hardy crossed the silver on his plate and tilted his chair back, feeling he ought to say something. He saw in a corner the pile of things Clara meant to keep from the sale. They had only been over the bottom part of the house and already she could start a rag and bone shop with the stuff she had put aside. He could ransack the rest of it, a suspicion came over Mr. Hardy, and not find in this house a single thing that was really his and his alone. Clara had so many things and got such enjoyment from each of them. He found a sixpence, worn smooth, and a rusty penknife from Sheffield; they were his and they were about all.

Clara had to stop and reminisce over everything she came across and persuade herself to part with it. If the job was ever to get done they ought to separate for the rest of the day. But he could not trust her to put sensible prices on things. Already he had spent a good half-hour talking her, first into giving it up at all, then out of asking five dollars for an old table that was not worth fifteen cents and ought, in fact, to have been chopped into kindling long ago, but was the one, she maintained, on which she had fixed the first meal she ever made for him. Then, things that were in perfectly good shape, unless they had some memory for her, she was liable to let go for nothing.

He struck a bargain with her—she could sort the things in the children's rooms if she would leave the rest of the house to him. How nice it would have been, she sighed, to go around with him and recall old times together as they turned up things, but as he didn't want her, she agreed. She worked her way up the steps and when she got her breath back, found she could not get up for the load of memories the girls' room laid on her.

If there was such a thing as being sorry and glad about something at the same time, thought Mrs. Hardy, she felt that way about leaving the house. Really her life hadn't been lived at all the way it was meant to be. It was a mistake to spend your life doing the same things day after day and she never got over feeling she was meant for something better, exactly what, she couldn't say, but she felt she would have been a great one for change, for setting out on new things, traveling. You could change the furniture around every week but it still all had to be dusted.

The trouble was, when a change happened to her it never really made much difference. Even the auction sale and leaving the home she had known so long she could barely remember any other, no longer seemed such a great upheaval, in fact, seemed already done with, accustomed to. Now, instead of her own, she would have a steady succession of her children's houses to look after, their children to bring up, just the same old thing when you got right down to it. It must be wonderful to look ahead and find in the days coming up a choice of ways to spend them. There were only the same old ways of doing the same old things, so she always fell back on the past; what else was there to think about?

She liked to sit like this and figure up how many diapers she must have washed in her time, how many times she had scrubbed this floor, how many strokes she had taken on the churn, and as the numbers climbed beyond her reckoning, she would sit back and rock inside herself in contented amazement. She liked best of all to recall suddenly that she had borne Mr. Hardy ten children.

Pregnancy had taken her by surprise. Mr. Hardy had to tell her she was in the family way. Her ignorance touched him. He thought it becoming; the truth was, as near as she could guess, it had not occurred to her. She had raised so many children not hers, children who had never known their own mothers, beginning at home with her brother and sister, then two cousins and then Mr. Hardy's boys, maybe she had forgot that children could have mothers of their own, that living women might have children.

Taken by surprise, she hadn't enjoyed that first confinement much, Mrs. Hardy thought. She had been scared. There was no time to store up memories of it, not time even to think up a name for the child, only time to think that if it was a boy she couldn't name it Charles Junior and, despite all she could do, to get to disliking the little boy who already bore that name through no fault of his own. The sickness and the pain she remembered and, as though it was yesterday, the feeling that came over her when they laid the child, raw and red, in her arms and she remembered that this was not new to Mr. Hardy, that he had gone through it for the first time with someone else. The doctor smiled and said she would be all right. She thought of how the other woman had gone through all this twice for Mr. Hardy and trying once again, died at it for him.

She made up her mind to live for Mr. Hardy. Out of bed a week her joy in the child grew such that she determined to have another as soon as possible. For twenty years she was never happy unless she was with child or brought to bed of one.

She had her favorites but didn't show it. Mr. Hardy had none and that had always made her feel he didn't like any of them well enough. He made a little joke, that, to be frank, she never had found so funny, of telling the children she was never pleased with any of them and would keep on having more until she was. Her pains were severe. She loved them all and the more she had the more she loved Virgie's as well, but her own she never forgave the travail they cost her coming into the world. "Lord!" she could gasp at one of them still, unable still to understand how she had endured it, unable to understand how the boy could spend his time except in making it up to her every minute of the day, "the trouble I had with you!"

She remembered getting up from that first one dissatisfied. How could she have let so many things slide or just stay the way they were when she came to Mr. Hardy's house? They made the upstairs over into rooms for the children. Mr. Hardy let her have every whim. He was glad, he said, to be able to give hers all the things that Virgie's children never had.

Mrs. Hardy went through the chests and halfheartedly made a pile of ragdolls and teething rings, baby slippers, a moth-eaten hairbrush, a gold-plated diaper pin, and found herself working up a quarrel against her children. They were so selfish. Hers no more than anybody else's, they were just all. As long as they were at home they simply took for granted you had nothing else to think about except them; once they were grown you weren't supposed to have any reason for living left at all. The way they were surprised if you came out once in a while with something that showed you weren't thinking only of them at the moment, that old as you were you might still have a few worries of your own, absolutely surprised.

She gathered her keepsakes into her apron and sat down on the side of the bed. She thought of her life, how little of it had been her own. Before she got half a start she simply bolted to seed.

After a while she went up to the attic. Mrs. Hardy pulled up a crate and sat down, and opening the big old packet trunk was like opening a door and watching herself, young and gay, walking down a long hall to meet her.

At the county fair they were alone together once for a change, with a neighbor woman in to look after the children. Mr. Hardy told her not to waste a minute worrying over them and she wasn't. She couldn't believe it was him; he was like a boy, shot the ducks and threw the baseballs at the bottles and wanted to ride her on the Ferris wheel. "The Ferris wheel, Mr. Hardy!" she declared—and you a man, she started to say, with four children—but he was the father of seven, and instead she said, "And us an old married couple." She won first prize in jellies and fourth in cakes and Mr. Hardy sold a bull for more money than she had ever seen in one lump sum. Mr. Hardy took a drink of whiskey with a man, something she had never seen him do before or since. She didn't scold him but said she was glad he took it; my goodness, everybody had to do something a little different from the workaday run once in their life.

Mr. Hardy bought her this mantle. It wasn't Mexican, it was real Spanish, the man said, but that you could tell by looking. It was heavy like wool but soft and smooth as silk with lace around the edges and must have had every color in the rainbow, but all blended and soft, not gaudy. The minute he laid eyes on it, Mr. Hardy said, he knew she had to have it. He smoothed it across her shoulders and put the ends down through her hands on her hips, saying that was how the ladies in Spain wore theirs.

Of all the moments in her life that had been one of the happiest. Mr. Hardy practically made her blush the way he looked at her in front of all those people. He said when the other women saw hers on her that man would sell every mantle he had.

In the wagon that night riding home, she laid her head on Mr. Hardy's shoulder smelling the good smell of him and listening not so much to his words as to the gentle sound of his voice. He was saying he had known beforehand she would like that shawl.

She felt it again while he rode silently for a while. Then he said he never forgot how crazy Virgie was over the one he had given her just like it. He hadn't seen another one and thought he never would. They buried Virgie in hers, as she asked to be. Smiling, he turned and told her that as if he expected it to make the shawl all the more precious to her.

While Clara washed the supper plates Mr. Hardy sat by the stove and chewed and spat in the ash box. He felt as if he had put in fifty years' work all over again today, but at the same time he felt good. Clara had not made the fuss he expected and the job was done before he thought it would be, wasn't nearly as bad as he had been dreading.

It was easier to believe he had lived in this house for fifty-six years. Today he had turned up whole pieces of his life like something he had lost and given up all hope of ever finding. Lately he noticed he was going kind of stale; now he would have a lot of new things to think about. Going to stay with the children didn't make him feel quite so bad any more.

Maybe he did have to sell his house—at least he had a good house to sell when the time came, with good things in it, well cared for. He never realized he owned so many fine things. There was nothing he need feel ashamed to have strangers see and handle and own. It was a feeling you couldn't get seeing the place day by day that came over him now. His mark was set on this spot; the work he had done was here for everybody to see. There were not a lot of things lying around half-finished. The man who bought this land would be lucky and would thank him for working it into such fine shape. A good neighbor for fifty years, he had never had any trouble with anybody, always minded his own business. People would miss him. They would point it out and say, "That's the old Hardy place," no matter how long the next man owned it.

Actually he had done twice as well as most men; it wasn't bragging of him to say it. For he had raised not one but two families here and raised them the best he knew how. He had done well by his first wife and what things he hadn't been able to give her before she died, he'd seen to it that his second wife got.

Without Clara, thought Mr. Hardy, he never could have done it.

Mr. Hardy collected the stray bits of tobacco in one cheek and squeezed them dry. He shot the wad into the ashes and ran his tongue around his mouth.

"You know," he began and paused, waiting for Clara to reach a stopping place in her thoughts. She had fallen into a way of not answering when he spoke. Her mind was so far away, forever thinking over some old party or the time she had the twins or some such thing. She didn't like to be interrupted in her thoughts and he could appreciate that himself. In a minute she would answer in a tone of voice that let him know she heard him the first time.

Mrs. Hardy stopped washing a teacup and dangled her hands in the dishwater, waiting for him to call her by name. Why couldn't he at least begin what little he had to say with, "Clara this, or Clara that," at least show he knew it was her he was speaking to, that he had something he really wanted *her* to hear, that it made some difference to him who listened. She stood remembering the early days when time and again he had called her Virgie. Oh, she couldn't count the times he had done that, and each time was like a slap in the face.

"You know," he tried once again, and she wondered if the fear of making that same mistake over and over had brought him to call her by no name at all.

Today must have taken him right back. Reminded in a thousand ways of Virgie who had died young, his own years had peeled in layers off his mind. He could see the two of them young and happy together, only to look up and find her there, stooped and worn with years of work and sickness, no teeth of her own, a thing that could never have been young. "Look at yourself!" she felt like telling him. "Do you think a young girl would look twice at you now?"

From the corner of her eye she watched him inspect the things she was putting aside. Was he afraid some of it was Virgie's? Wasn't it little enough for fifty years? You have yours; leave me to my own.

Mr. Hardy yawned loudly. He stretched and the effort sounded down his body like the snapping of many strings. Clara was tired and he decided to leave her be, when she turned and asked, "What were you going to say?"

He couldn't recall. "Nothing," he said. "It wasn't important." He smiled to show that she wasn't to worry herself, that she hadn't missed anything.

No, she supposed it wasn't. When had he ever had anything to tell her that he thought was important? She stood waiting.

"It takes you back, a day like this," he said, "makes you think. Brings back things you hadn't thought of for years. For instance—"

He looked up and there was Clara, her fingers pressed white against her temples. "Oh, what's the use," she cried, "of thinking over things past and done with?"

She started to say something more, then turned back to her dishes. Mr. Hardy got up and quietly stole off to bed. At the door he scratched his pate and thought to ask which of them was it that was always thinking over things long ago done with, but decided not to.

She had to sit; her backbone was like spools on a string. She rocked her head in her hands and wondered would all this misery never end. She thought of Virgie, Safe in Heaven these fifty years, safe in Mr. Hardy's mind, forever young and pretty. Surely, she thought, shuffling a finger across her withered lips, surely when the Lord called you you didn't have to come as you were. What else could Hell be?

Quail for Mr. Forester

WHETHER IT was the same all over Texas I do not know, but in Columbia there was quite a rigid caste system based on the kind of goods a person sold. To deal in notions was probably the lowest, and dry goods was pretty low. Groceries was acceptable, pharmacy quite acceptable, furniture almost genteel. In all this I mean retail. To be in anything wholesale, even in a modest way, was higher than to be in the highest retail. And yet no kind of wholesale was higher than retail hardware. For it was into that that the Foresters went, with that indifference to the conventions which only they could afford, when the last of the old family property was sold at public auction.

For a while after Mr. Forester bought the hardware store it had looked possible that the town might bankrupt him out of respect for him. No one could picture himself being waited on by a Forester. The first customer told how it seemed as if the world was coming to an end, and said that she had had to turn her head while Mr. Forester wrapped her package. Everyone had been touched and pleased to hear that it had been a very clumsily wrapped package.

But Mr. Forester had such dignity, and carried through with

such an air of remaining untouched, that people grew to feel it was not too insulting of them to trade with him, and he began to show a profit.

It was not a very big store and certainly Mr. Forester did nothing to bring it up to date; people like the Foresters did not put on show. Yet in ten years, while the town, so to speak, turned its head in order not to see a Forester practicing economies, he saved enough to buy back—just in time for his wife to die there—his family home, the largest house on Silk Stocking Street. That was the nickname of the street, but to show you how generally it was called that, I do not even remember its real name. It was where all the quality lived.

We lived on Oak Street and every morning at eight o'clock Mr. Forester passed our house on his way to business. My mother would let the milk stay on the porch until it was time for him to pass, and he always tipped his bowler to her, and sometimes he paid her a compliment in the old style.

My father was a hunter, one who never came home empty-handed, and we never sat down to a dinner of wild duck or woodcock or quail but my mother thought of the faded sovereignty of the Foresters, of the days when none of their many tenants would have dreamed of a trip into town without bringing some fresh game for them. In the lull after I had said grace, while we spread our napkins, my mother was sure to say, "Wouldn't poor Mr. Forester enjoy some of this."

She would have sent my father to him with presents of fish and game, except that she was sure it would be a perfect waste, for though she had never set foot in the house, much less eaten there, my mother had decided that Mr. Forester's Negro cook was not only a very poor cook, but that she took a vengeful delight in being so.

Time was, my father recalled, when hunters brought home towsacks full of quail, like to the present-day birds as a Brahma rooster to a bantam pullet; but when he and I, one fall Saturday in my twelfth year, brought home nine plump ones, we had had an unusual good day. When they were plucked and laid in a row my father said that, by Jim, you could almost recognize these as kin to the old-time quail. My mother seized this moment to suggest inviting Mr. Forester to dinner. Before she could take it back, my father said that that mess of birds was about as near worthy of a Forester as you would come nowadays, and, all right, we'd do it, by Jim.

He and I walked downtown. It was midafternoon and the square was filled with country folks. There were farmwives in poke bonnets, with snuff stains at the corners of their mouths, and bold country girls in overlong dresses who would say even coarser things than their brothers whenever they passed a town boy like me. Ordinarily I hurried past, pretending an errand of deafening urgency, while I tried to fix my thoughts upon some moment out of history. It was thanks to these girls that I had some idea what the word *violation* meant and I was fond of imagining that I had only lately saved these unworthy girls from violation at the hands of Union soldiers, and of enjoying the irony of their ingratitude. Today I was glad to have my father with me. I was even gladder to have him guide me past the corners of the square, where the narrow-eyed, dirty-talking country men collected, squatting on alternate haunches all afternoon and senselessly whittling on cedar sticks until they were ankle-deep in curly, red-and-white, tobacco-spattered shavings.

A crowd was in the hardware store and both Mr. Forester and the Saturday clerk were busy. My father and I stood out of the crowd near the coil of hemp rope, and by breathing deeply of the dry, clean, grassy smell of it I felt purified and removed. I felt acutely what disgust must fill a man like Mr. Forester to have to sell cow salves and horse collars to such men, and to have to refuse to dicker with their women over the prices of pots and mops and over the measure of a dime's worth of garden seed.

The crowd thinned out and I strolled over to look at the showcase of pocket knives, but seeing the clerk heading my way I rejoined my father.

It pleased my father to be able to tell Mr. Forester that he had not come on business.

"No, sir, I have come on pleasure. Not that it is not always a pleasure, of course.

"This is my boy, Mr. Forester. Son, shake hands with Mr.

Forester. He is a backward boy, sir, but do not take it to mean that he is not aware of the honor."

Mr. Forester's resemblance to General Beauregard added to the trouble I had remembering that he had not fought in the Civil War. At twelve, I had a very undeveloped sense of the distance of the past, and often, indeed, I found it quite impossible to believe that the Civil War was over. Certainly I could never believe that those remains of men, more like ancient women, who were reverently pointed out to me as Confederate veterans, could ever have been the men of the deeds with which my imagination was filled.

"Mr. Forester," said my father, "my wife has been after me I do not know how long to bring home some birds fit to ask company in to. Well, I went hunting today—me and the boy—and I will not say that what we brought home are fit, but as I said to my wife, I guess these birds are about as near worthy as I am ever going to come, for the birds do not get any better and neither do I."

I was aware of the solemnity of the moment by the lack of contractions in my father's speech.

"Now I would not know, myself," he continued, "but some say my wife is a pretty fair cook."

My father waited then, and in a moment Mr. Forester got the idea that somewhere politely concealed in that speech was an invitation to dinner.

Mr. Forester said, "Why now, this is mighty nice and thoughtful of you and your wife, John—of whose cooking I never would doubt. I don't mind saying that it has been a while since I had quail! Is it tonight that you want me to come? And what time would your wife like me to arrive?"

"What time do you generally take your supper?"

"Why, I generally take it around eight, but—"

"Then eight," said my father, "is when you shall have it tonight."

My mother suggested I be given my supper early and sent to bed. My father disagreed, as she had meant him to, saying that it was an evening I should want to remember, and that I was old enough to behave like a little gentleman now.

I was posted by the window to watch for him. Dusk spread in

the street and it began to be dark. The street lamps came on at the corners of the block and I saw my friends come out of their houses up and down the street and gather in the light to play, and I wondered if they knew why I was not with them. I was hungry from the smells of the kitchen and restless in my Sunday clothes.

At last I saw him round the corner. He wore his bowler and carried a stick with which he lightly touched the ground about every third step he took. My friends in the light of the lamp watched him and when he was past turned to whisper among themselves, for some of them dared to think such people as Mr. Forester old-fashioned and amusing. He carried something cone-shaped and when he was halfway down the block I saw that it was flowers wrapped in paper.

At the door my mother took his coat and thanked him for the flowers and said she hoped he had not had too hard a day in the store. I was embarrassed at her mentioning that he had put in a working day, and using the word *store*, but my mother's sympathy for Mr. Forester was deeper than the town's, and went beyond any hopeless efforts to keep up appearances.

Mr. Forester turned from my father and extended his fist to me and opened it palm up. It held one of the knives I had seen in the showcase in his store. It was a pearl-handled knife, and as we went into the living room he said, "I thought you might like that one because I was very fond of one just like it when I was about your age. It was given to me by a Mr. J. B. Hood. Did you ever hear of him, son?"

I started to shake my head, then I thought and cried, "Do you mean *John Bell* Hood?"

"Sir," my mother reminded me.

"Oh, you know about John Bell Hood, do you?" said Mr. Forester.

My father guided him to a chair, saying, "Does he know about him! Sometimes I believe he thinks he *is* John Bell Hood."

"Well," said Mr. Forester, "he couldn't want to be a better man. Now could he?"

My mother excused herself to look after the birds. My father mixed drinks.

"Yes," said Mr. Forester, "John Bell Hood was often in our

house when I was a lad. A great soldier and a great gentleman. *And* a cagey cotton buyer."

I laughed, but weakly, for I would rather he had not mentioned that last.

"You remember what General Lee said, son? 'In the tight places I always count on the Texans.' If they had had the sense to follow up Hood's victory at Chickamauga the South might have won the war."

"I can vouch for this mash, Mr. Forester," said my father. "I watched it made. It goes down like mother's milk."

Mr. Forester took a sip, held the glass to the light, cocked an eye appreciatively at my father, then for my benefit he put on a moral frown and, nodding the glass at me, said, "He was right about this stuff, too—John Bell Hood. You remember, when he was wounded at Chancellorsville they tried to make him take a drink of whiskey to ease his pain, and he said he would rather endure the pain than break the promise he had made his mother never to touch a drop."

I felt my face redden and I stole a glance at my father.

"That was not John Bell Hood, sir," I said. "That was Jeb Stuart at Spotsylvania."

It was one of my favorite incidents.

"Was it?" said Mr. Forester.

"Yes, sir."

I looked at my father. He was glaring at me.

"It was Jeb Stuart," I said.

"The boy is probably right," said Mr. Forester. "It's a long time since I went to school—and you, too, John, for that matter. Whoever it was, it is a good story. And in any case it was a Southerner who said it. But I am glad to see that they still teach them about the war in school."

"Oh, school!" said my father. "He reads all that on his own. I will say that for him. If you depended on what they teach them at school—!"

My mother came in. We rose.

"The schools!" she cried. "You wouldn't believe it was Texas, Mr. Forester, the things they teach them in the schools nowadays!"

"Now, now," said Mr. Forester, "things can't have had time to change much since your own school days."

My mother turned red with pleasure. "Oh, Mr. Forester!" she cried. And she was so carried away she forgot what she had come in for and my father finally had to ask was she hatching those birds out there before she remembered with a cry, "Oh! That's it! It's served!"

The table had the leaf in. It was lighted by three tall slender candles in a triple-branched holder. The shadows on the silver and glasses were deep, and the highlights seemed thick, the way the white paint is laid on in old pictures. The water flask seemed filled with trembling quicksilver. Side dishes of black and green olives and pearl-like pickled onions were stationed around the center platter, in which, nested in fried potatoes as yellow and as slender as straw, were the golden-crusted quail. Nearby was a basket of smoking rolls blanketed with a white napkin. There were bowls of deviled eggs, brandied peaches, creamed onions, peas, mustard greens, whipped yams topped with toasted marshmallows, and a bowl of green salad shimmering with oil. Stacks of dishes stood waiting on the buffet and a bank of apples on a dish there glowed like dying coals. I could hardly believe I was in my own home.

When we had spread our napkins there was a silence and everyone looked at me. I bent my head, closed my eyes, and said, "Bless us, O Lord, and these Thy gifts, which through Thy bounty we are about to receive through Christ our Lord. Amen."

"Amen," said Mr. Forester.

We were very hungry, for it was long past our usual suppertime. Mr. Forester was very hungry, too. So after everyone had servings of everything and Mr. Forester had praised each dish, for a few minutes there was no sound—not even the clatter of silver, since we were all mainly interested in the quail and this was eaten with the fingers—except, occasionally, the clink of a birdshot dropped on a plate.

When our first pangs had been assuaged my father signified the time for talk by leaning back in his chair, patting his stomach, and looking gratefully at my mother.

"I seem," said Mr. Forester, "to recall having heard these birds disparaged earlier in the day."

"Well, you may thank old man Walter Bledsoe," said my father. "We got these birds in his oat field. It seems he gave up about halfway through this year, and left more oats standing than he took in to the barn."

Mr. Forester shook his head sadly.

"And to think," said my mother, "what the name Bledsoe once stood for."

"They have gone even further downhill," said my father. "Me and the boy were up to the house today to ask permission to hunt. You ought to have seen the place. Gate hanging loose, weeds grown up, junk in the yard—just one step away from white trash now."

"And I myself," said my mother, "remember when old Miss Jane Bledsoe thought nothing of going over to Europe every other year and bringing back a boxcar full of souvenirs and treasures."

"Even then," said my father, "she was spending money she didn't have."

"Well, in those days you didn't expect a woman like Miss Jane Bledsoe to keep up with whether or not she had it to spend," said my mother.

We returned to our food, this time talking as we ate.

My father said, "Getting back, Mr. Forester, to what you were saying earlier. About the South winning the war if they had followed up the victory at Chickamauga. It is interesting, isn't it, to try to imagine how things might be now if it had turned out the other way?" He laughed a little from embarrassment.

"Well, I can think of a few things that would be very different," said my mother with a meaningful, sad look at our guest.

"Yes, yes," said my father.

"People may laugh at us for fighting it all over time and time again—even Southerners, the kind coming up now—but they just don't know," said my mother.

"Not that *you* remember any much better times," said my father with a laugh to her.

"No," said my mother, "Lord knows that's true. But I've been told. Well, but it's not for *us* to tell *Mr. Forester.*"

"Well now," said he, "I don't know. We have the electric lights now and the telephone, and now the automobile."

"Doubtful blessings," said my mother.

"And there is the motion picture," said Mr. Forester.

"Indeed there is," said my mother.

"Oh, I agree with you in disapproving them," said Mr. Forester, "as a general thing. But some of them, you know, are quite amusing, I must say. Very amusing," and he chuckled ever so softly over some memory.

"Light amusements," said my mother sternly, "don't seem becoming to people with what we have to remember. That's how it seems to me. Of course, you don't need any reminders, Mr. Forester. Not a person who has what you have to remember."

"Yes, our family lost a lot, of course," said Mr. Forester. "But then, every family with a lot or a little to lose lost it, and I am sure it was less hard on such as we than it was on those who may have lost less, but lost all they had."

There was a moment's silence.

"By Jim!" said my father. "Excuse me for being carried away, but that was well said, Mr. Forester!"

"Still, we don't have to be modest for you," said my mother. "And we know how much more it must have hurt the more you had to lose. Anyhow, it's not the money loss alone I mean. It's the whole way of life, as they say."

"Yes, yes," said Mr. Forester somewhat impatiently. "But times change and ways of life must change and we must accustom ourselves and make the best of it. Though I must say that this is the closest to the plentiful old way that I have been in a long while," and he indicated the table.

"Oh! Have more! Give Mr. Forester another one of those bird breasts. Here we have been talking and keeping him from the food!"

"Not at all. Not at all. You can see from my plate that nothing has been keeping me from the food! But I will just pick at another half of one of those birds."

With little urging he took a whole one, and he absorbed himself in it so completely that my mother could watch him openly. As his enjoyment increased so did her sadness over the decay of the Old South, as evidenced by Mr. Forester's appetite.

My father extended his plate and said, winking at me, "I vow, I believe I might work me up an appetite yet. Mr. Forester is ready for more, too. Give Mr. Forester that brown one there. That one was my best shot of the day—it must have been seventy-five yards, if I do say so myself."

"No more for me," said Mr. Forester. "I have disgraced myself quite enough already."

"Mr. Forester," said my mother, "you will hurt my feelings if you don't eat more than that little smidgin-bit."

"Well, ma'am," he replied, "I hope I am the son of my father enough not to hurt a lady's feelings," and he extended his plate.

"I just can't have any respect for a man with a finicky appetite," said my mother.

"Then you would have enjoyed making a meal for my father," said Mr. Forester. "There was a man who could eat!"

"We're none of us the men our fathers were," said my father.

The night had turned chilly and when we went into the living room after dinner my father lighted the gas stove. The gas lines had been laid in the town only that spring and the stove was a novelty still. It had pipe-clay chimneys and it was pretty to watch the red climb quickly up them from the row of sputtering blue flames. We had bought the stove at Forester's Hardware.

Mr. Forester said that they were just that week laying the pipes to bring the gas into his house. He would be glad to see the last of his sooty old furnace. It never had kept the big old house warm.

More and more, since his wife's passing, he said, as he watched the sputtering flames, he had thought of giving up the old place.

My mother said she hoped he did not mean that seriously.

Oh, said Mr. Forester, it would probably not come to anything more than talk. But something like we had, now—that would more than suit his needs, he, a lone man, without children—what use did he have for eighteen huge, high, drafty old rooms? The thing he could never understand was what had made him buy it back, how it was he hadn't known when he was well out of it. Probably simply because people expected it of him.

My mother said she supposed a certain amount of family feeling had been in it, too.

Mr. Forester said he supposed so.

My mother said she was sure of it, and that she did not think that it was a feeling to be ashamed of, surely.

No, of course not, said Mr. Forester. But when a person reached his age, for good or bad he began to think more of a little bodily comfort. Those old houses were all right in the days when people had big families and many guests always in the house, when relatives were closer than they were now and lived closer by and came often for long visits, and when people gave lots of parties and balls. But now—and what with the taxes . . .

"I declare it's a shame, just a shame," said my mother, "to make you pay taxes, Mr. Forester!"

Mr. Forester did not know whether this pleased him or not. "I don't understand," he said. "Why shouldn't I?"

"Taxes!" cried my mother. "On top of everything else!"

Mr. Forester colored.

"What short memories the people in this town have!" said my mother. "You might think that out of memory of old Colonel Forester and all he did for this town—you might think that just out of appreciation for your keeping up such a historic old home they might remit the taxes at least. What short memories! To me, Mr. Forester, you are a living reproach to them!"

Mr. Forester colored more deeply and turned to my father for help.

"Can't you just see them remitting the taxes!" said my father.

My mother shook her head sadly. But Mr. Forester laughed good-humoredly. He changed the subject. He and my father spoke of the cotton crop and of the coming state elections, while my mother got out her knitting and I sat listening, unnoticed. I was beginning to be disappointed in Mr. Forester. He did not seem different enough from us. And while I felt no particular shame of us, I did feel that Mr. Forester had lowered himself for the sake of his appetite to come to dinner at our house.

The clock on the mantel struck ten. Mr. Forester said it was time for him to be going. He was not good for much, he said, after ten o'clock on a Saturday evening.

Mr. Forester ducked his head to check a belch, then munched reminiscently a few times. He said he had not had such a dinner since—since he didn't know when. Since he was a boy. He ducked his head again, and when he looked up, his eyes, whether from gas or from emotion, were filled with tears.

"I can't tell you how much I enjoyed it," he said, first to my mother, then to all of us. "How nice it was of you to think of me and how—I—"

My mother was embarrassed and made a joke, saying he must come some evening when her cooking was really good.

Mr. Forester rose and we all followed him to the door. My father held his coat. When he had it on, Mr. Forester was overcome once more and again his eyes filled with tears.

"Really, I—" he began.

"It's only what you were brought up to expect!" my mother cried. "It's not as much as you ought to have every day! Don't thank us. The only thanks we deserve is for being among the few still about who realize that!"

Mr. Forester was taken aback. He smiled uncomfortably. He looked at my father and then at me. I could feel the tragic expression on my face, and the sight of my father's was enough to make me cry.

"It just makes my heart ache," said my mother.

My father gave a loud sigh. Mr. Forester slowly tapped his finger against the crown of his bowler. At last his face gave up the struggle, fell, and he, too, sighed deeply. I could stand it no longer, and I thrust his stick at him from the umbrella stand.

He bade us good night and we stood in the door watching until he passed through the light of the street lamp and into the darkness beyond. His stick, I noticed as he walked under the light, now touched the ground with each step.

My mother closed the door and she and my father turned. They became aware of me and stood looking at me. My father shook his head. My mother sighed her deepest sigh.

I felt that there was no hope for me in these mean times I had been born into.

Man with a Family

I

SHE LIFTED the lid and peered in the churn to see if the butter had come. Straightening, she saw him round the corner, carrying one of his hands in the other as if he were afraid of spilling it. She dropped the dasher and ran to the door. He thrust out his hands as if she might know what to do with them. She reached for them, then drew back sharply and stood watching the blood fall on the doorsill. What was it now? As bad as the other times? He licked his lips, shook his head, then took his hand over and laid it on the table as if he meant to leave it there while he looked for something to patch it with.

From the range she brought a kettle of water and filled the washpan, testing it with her finger. As the blood swirled sluggishly through the water she sat tensely, brushing a wisp of hair back into her bun, wishing he would say something. She sighed and went to the bedroom and took a tattered pillowslip from the cedar chest. She bit a start in the cloth and rent it into bandage.

"Well," he sighed, "it was like this."

She sat down and turned her face up attentively, trying to look as she did when he told some favorite story, as if she had never heard it before, as if this was the first accident he ever had.

"I was plowing." He waited a second until she had him placed. He held his hands out, gripping the handles. She had it—there's Daisy, here's you and those are the reins around your neck.

"There was a big stone," he said, looking at the floor. She looked down at it with a frown. "But I didn't see it because it was covered. Now who would have thought of a stone in that south twenty?" he wanted to know, bristling a little, giving her a defiant look. She tried to show it was the last thing on earth that would have occurred to her. "In three years I never took more than a bucketful of stones out of that field. And they was all no bigger than your fist." She made a fist and laid it on the table; she honestly wanted to help him. "Smack!" he cried, trying desperately to steady the handles and straining his neck against the reins. She reached out to catch him and he caught himself a moment to remind her that she was at home churning butter, so she settled back and helplessly watched him flung over the handlebar, shoot out a hand to catch himself and rip it to the bone on the moldboard.

The story finished, Dan snorted, looking around him for some explanation, some reason for it, and she looked, too, glaring blamefully at the air around her. The story finished, Laura roused herself and realized suddenly that he would never get the cotton planted.

As he held out his hand for her to wrap Dan said apologetically, "I figure it was that last heavy frost pushed that stone up so high."

"I suppose," Laura sighed.

He gave a laugh to show how little his fault it was.

"What is it to laugh about?" she demanded.

They talked about other things driving home from the doctor's office but Laura couldn't help being a little suspicious. Surely he had been more careless than he admitted. In this past winter he had cut one thumb, twisted his knee, broken a rib, sprained an ankle, and got a sliver of steel in his eye. To recall all that, why, who wouldn't be suspicious, and who wouldn't be aggravated with him? Of course he didn't do any of it on purpose and of course he was the one that suffered. When it reached the point where she just had to speak her mind about it, naturally she was not mad at him. But somebody had to insist he be more careful. She took her eyes from the road, trying to harden herself to speak plainly. Then she saw what he was hoping she wouldn't see, how much pain his hand was giving him and how carefully he was coddling it. She mumbled something about putting it inside his shirt and though he had heard her, he looked at the gasoline gauge and said he thought there was enough to get them home.

At four o'clock the school bus settled with a crunch before the gate and Harold came stamping in, yelling back from the door to friends and, without looking, flung his books on the table with a splash.

"What's he doing home?" He jerked a thumb toward Dan as he rifled the breadbox.

"He cut his hand," said Laura in a shooshing tone, trying to look a little respect into him.

He wanted to see. Laura said it might get infected. She added impressively, "It's got stitches."

"Stitches!" He gave Dan a look of respect. "Did it hurt much?" he asked.

"Lord, of course it hurt, silly!" Laura cried. "What do you think?"

He wanted to know how he did it.

"Oh," said Dan, "plowing. Hit a stone and fell against the moldboard." It sounded a little silly to tell it now and Harold looked as if he thought it did, too. "A big stone," he added.

"Why didn't you hold onto the handles?"

"What do you think I was doing, dancing a jig?"

"Here," said Laura. "Now you leave him alone. You go on out and play."

Harold drifted to the door and then wandered back. Coming close to Laura he said low, "You mean he's had another *accident?*"

There was rain every day for a week. Dan mended harness and puttered impatiently around the chicken yard. But rain could not have come at a better time, so he was not too downhearted. Laura was glad to have him home once she got used to the idea. She enjoyed shooing him out of the kitchen and showing him how to make fudge that always turned to sugar and had to be given to Daisy and reading the serial in the back numbers of the *Country Gentleman* aloud to him in the afternoons.

She finished milking on the third morning while he stood awkwardly by, then he grabbed the pail to take it to the house, took three steps, and a corncob rolled under his foot, twisted his ankle, and turned him end up in a puddle of milk. It was so funny they both rolled on the ground laughing but when he tried to get up she had to help him. But that was funny, too, and as she wrapped it up she said that pretty soon he would look like he had been hit by a truck and would need somebody to lead him around. He hobbled like an old, old man, but when Harold came home it would have been hard to tell he was limping even a little if she had not known it already.

Catching Harold's eyes on him, Dan decided to see what he could do with one hand about that old stump at the corner of the chicken yard that he had let stay there so long. He went over to it and spat on his hand, gave it a careless tug, then a heave, then nearly broke his back on it but it wouldn't budge. He looked around and decided to move that big stone he had let lay there for years, gave it a yank and it came loose. He raised it 'way above his head and threw it over the fence, then went casually back for his jumper, but Harold was gone. He looked back at it and had to admit it was not such a big stone at that.

II

Anxious as she was to have him get back, it did seem foolish for a man to think of planting cotton when his wife had to harness the mule. She was about ready to go to the field with him. Thank heaven, at least they were not that bad off yet, for the neighbors to see her walking behind a plow.

In low places in the fields, Laura thought, the ground would still be muddy. Neighbors who could afford to would stay home another couple of days; she hoped Dan didn't feel she was rushing him. She snapped the trace chains and settled Daisy's collar better. Dan gripped the handles and smiled at her.

As innocently as possible she said, "Now be careful, Dan," and he replied without resentment, "I will."

Laura might have canned a lot more peas but for looking up between every two she shelled, expecting to see him coming in with a limp or a drag or a stagger. Now that he had already lost so much time she feared he might be overcautious. Like Harold— leave him alone and he brought the milk in without spilling a drop, but just let him spill it once and then tell him to be careful not to, how much it cost and all, and he stumbled with it sure as the world.

A drummer came to the door and usually she simply couldn't turn one away, but today, as this one rounded the corner, she kicked over her bucket of pods, scared stiff, and almost slammed the door right in his face, he had given her such a scare. As the day passed she got jumpier. It was silly, she knew, but to think of any more delay in the planting made her run cold all over. Maybe she imagined it, but Harold looked around the place as if it surprised him, too, not to find Dan home with some ailment or other. She sent him out but he moped around the back door. Dan was late and to get Harold to bed and give herself something to do she gave him his supper early. He ate slowly while Laura fretted whether she ought to cook a supper of Dan's favorite things, or would that seem she was making an occasion of a day that ought to be passed over as nothing out of the ordinary?

Harold finished and went to the window. It was dark now and he sighed lumpily, "I wonder what happened?" Laura turned to snap something, but he was already in the bedroom and instead she sat down to cry when she heard Dan's step. If he noticed her red eyes he never let on and probably he didn't; he was blind tired. His arm was stiff and she guessed he had followed the plow bent double all day, one handle in the crotch of his arm to spare his hand.

As he got back into shape he came in less tired, able to sit up after supper and read a while, or try to read but not be able for watching Laura, seeing how worried she had been all day and how, through the evening, she tried to accustom herself to the notion that another day had been got past, able to see that some- thing, something he couldn't just put his finger on, but something peculiar had settled down in his house, and what was even more peculiar, even harder to find words to suit, something that seemed to mean to stay. He felt left out of everything. It was as if he had gone away for a while and come back before he was expected. It was such a queer feeling and it wasn't helped any by looking up sometimes and seeing Laura and Harold standing together like a photograph he hadn't got into.

The way they looked at him! Like they had really had something different in mind, but he had come and they had used him and now they couldn't send him back. Did they? Maybe he imagined it; he wasn't feeling good, anyway. Maybe his mind was all tired and bent over, too. But what could you think when your own boy looked at you like a horse somebody was trying to sell too cheap, and when he went to bed was thirstier than ever before and kept having to go to the pot to see if you had managed to keep on your feet once you had him out of sight?

III

Laura's mama came over as soon as she sent word that the washing machine had come. It was Saturday and Dan had gone into town to buy groceries, but Harold was too interested in the machine to go with him. Laura's mama drove her buggy over early. She loved machinery and was proud of her daughter for owning the shiny, mysterious washing machine and being able to run it. She loved the noise and loved having to yell above it to make herself heard.

"You might get that thing to churn butter," she urged in a shout.

Harold was disgusted but Laura thought it might work and promised herself to try it. Now the grandmother wanted to shut it off and give it a rest and rest herself. She rubbed a finger over it as tenderly as over a sleeping baby.

"A thing like that must cost a heap of money," she said.

Laura swelled with pride. "I should think it does."

Her mama stood with her question on her face but the amount was almost too much for Laura to be proud of. She said, "We bought it on the installment plan, of course."

"Well," said her mama, as though she had been taken for some kind of a fool, as though she didn't know a fine piece of machinery when she saw it, "I never thought you could buy such a thing outright," and in fact she couldn't really see how they had made the down payment. "How much was it?" she asked hungrily and cocked her ear around to receive some astounding figure.

She looked ready not to resent the price but to admire it. Laura couldn't think of another woman anywhere around whose husband had spent so much money on her at one time, so she told. Her mother flinched as if somebody had suddenly blown in her ear. She had prepared herself for the limit; now her face turned sour and she looked at the washing machine with distaste. She thought she had raised a more sensible daughter and one not nearly so trifling. She had washed work clothes and dirty diapers on her seventy-nine-cent washboard for forty-odd years and it was good enough for anybody. She began to take notice that Laura's dress had a hole under the arm and that Harold had on pants too small for him and needed a haircut. Well, she never thought she would see the day when Laura would let her family go to seed and put her man in debt for years because she was too lazy to wash his clothes, and she said as much.

Laura said, "Well, I don't know as it will keep him in debt all that long."

"However long it is, looks like you'll sure be ragged but clean."

"Well," said Laura, standing sharp, hands on her hips, "if I am it'll be no change from what I always was at home. Except maybe cleaner," and she turned the machine on with a clatter and stuffed it with practically every stitch the family owned.

Grandmother recalled the bag of candy she had brought and fished it out of her purse. She took one herself and called Harold over and gave him one.

Laura snapped off the washer and said, "Don't feed him that junk this near dinnertime."

"Let him have it," Grandmother insisted, and with a look at the washer, "I don't suppose he got much while you was saving up for that thing."

"I declare, Mama, I never thought I'd see the day," said Laura, "when you'd envy your own daughter a little comfort and not like to see her come up in life."

"Comfort," said her mama, "is for them as can afford it."

"Well, you just let me worry about affording it. And this is only the first. I mean to have a lot of nice things and I'm looking around now to decide what I'll get when the crop's in."

"Yes, I've seen a new player piano," her mama sighed, "and a new second-hand car come to our house and seen the men come and take them away when they was half paid for." She shot the bag of candy at the boy; it was giving her a toothache. "Probably the last you'll see for some time," she mumbled.

Harold looked at his mother to have this denied.

Laura snapped at him, "I reckon you get enough candy."

"I don't either," he appealed to his Granny. "I've never got enough candy in my whole life."

Laura sent him out the door and no buts about it. The old woman called after him, "You just come over to your Granny's. She's always got a little candy for her boy.

"You better send that thing back," she said. She was serious now. "You never know what's going to happen to keep it from getting paid for."

"You're just mad," said Laura, "that Dan wants me to have a few nice things when Papa never bought anything nice for you."

"Never mind that kind of talk. You just better get rid of it." She clamped her bonnet on and gave the washing machine a scampering look.

"I was going to say you could bring your wash over and use my new machine," said Laura, "and to show you how big I can be, you still can."

Her mama replied with a lift of her nose to show that she wouldn't be caught dead doing it, "No, thank you. Thank you just the same. I've come this far without it and I reckon my rub-board will see me the rest of my way. You as much as said I keep a dirty house. Besides we ain't got as much clothes as all that," and she gave Laura's wash pile a look that said as plain as day: But it's a good deal more than you all have.

IV

When the cotton was in the ground they all drew a deep breath. He was only a week or so behind with it, and then he started seeding his corn. That went so well that Dan spoke of taking off to go fishing. Laura looked forward to it and had it on her mind as she carried whey to the chickens. What a pity Harold was in school, she was thinking, when Dan came over the hill on Daisy.

Laura poured the whey in the trough and went out to meet him. He looked disgusted with something, so the fishing trip fizzled out.

"What happened?" she asked, holding the reins. Then she stooped under the mule's neck and she saw where Dan's leg dangled down and floated stiffly inside his bloody pants. Just above the knee his leg took a sickening jump to one side, like a pencil seen through a glass of water.

Laura crept out from under Daisy's head and started to look up, when she fainted. Dan slid off Daisy and got his good leg under him. But there he was stuck. He thought, Daisy might take it into her head any minute to make off for oats in the barn. Then what would he do? The nearest support was a fence post he could never reach. He couldn't possibly get on her back again. How long would she stand still? How long would it take Laura to come to? How long could he stand the sun without keeling over?

"Laura!" he shouted and Daisy shied. He licked the sweat from the corner of his mouth and called her more softly. Hanging around Daisy's neck, he inched his good leg out and gave her a shove, waited a second, and when she didn't stir he kicked her. Laura, with a groan, rolled over and buried her face in the dirt. Dan could feel himself going and decided it would probably be best to fall a little to his left and forward.

Laura got propped on her elbows and shook herself down and got to her feet. Dan moaned as she tried to raise him. Maybe moving him would make things worse. She looked around, half-expecting someone to see the trouble she was having and come over to give her a hand. She went to the house and got a quilt. She wrapped him in it and started for the car to go to the neighbor's phone.

Laura's papa sat at the table and steadily cropped the shreds of his cigarette, his coffee saucered and blowed, being careful to swill it quietly, stiffly respectful, which consisted in not hearing anything that was said to him and looking as if, under the circumstances, words just didn't reach him, trying to keep his own two good legs out of sight and not look any too well himself. Laura's mama worked quietly over the stove and Harold sat in the corner he had hardly left all day, trying to make himself as small as possible, scared to death. He would not go into Dan's room and Laura didn't insist. The sight of him could only have made Dan feel worse.

Laura pulled her hands out of the bucket of plaster and scrubbed them thoughtfully in the washpan. She picked up the heavy bucket and her papa looked like he would offer to carry it but he had had his own reverses lately and too much must not be expected of him. He rubbed a hand along a tender kidney and looked wistfully away.

The doctor plastered the leg. "Well," he said, "we might have waited till a little more of the swelling went down, but I don't think it will matter too much."

It didn't matter much to Dan. He looked at the leg with only the top layer of his eyes. He brought himself up with a bitter sigh and said, "He says I'll be in bed six weeks," and gave Laura a long defiant stare.

She had already told herself it would be a long time but now her surprise showed and so did her pain. Dan's tone hurt her. He didn't have to throw it up to her like that. She hadn't asked.

"That at least," the doctor said. "What I said in fact was six to ten weeks." He gathered up his tools and laid them neatly in his bag, taking out a bottle of pills. "Give him these to sleep but never more than three a day. I'll come out every day for a week or so. I don't know just what time of day but I'll get here."

"What I don't know," said Dan, "is when you're going to get paid."

"Well, I'll worry about that."

Out in the kitchen the doctor washed his hands, rolled down his sleeves, and drew on his coat while everyone watched. Laura's papa nodded sagely at his movements and her mama stopped setting the table to pat her hair in shape and smooth the ruffles of her dress.

"I wouldn't leave him too much alone," said the doctor. "Keep his mind occupied. Just don't make too much over it. Course you can't exactly act like nothing happened," he smiled broadly, "but remember, it could have been worse."

How? How could it have been any worse, Laura wanted to know. He said that to everybody without thinking. Her papa registered with a snort that he thought it was bad enough.

The doctor settled his things in his pocket and turned to the old man. "Well, John, how've you been coming along lately?"

It was no time to feel well when a doctor was talking to you free, so the old man dug out his cigarette and got ready to give details. "Well, when you get my age, you know, Doctor, ever' little thing—"

The doctor pulled up his watch and glanced at it impatiently. He has other calls to make, thought Laura with some surprise, other bones to set. She got a glimpse of her papa rubbing up his rheumatic knee as though to polish it for show. She saw the fright in Harold's eyes over all these broken bones and aching knees and cut hands. She saw her mother reach over and set the turnips aside to simmer and look at the doctor as though she would like to ask him to stay for a bite but was ashamed of what her daughter had to offer.

Laura slammed the door and buried her face in Dan's arm. He let her cry and then raised her to him. She hugged him and sobbed. He stroked her head gently and gently eased her back a little. She had shaken him and the pain in his leg was awful.

V

Mr. Johnson hung soggily on the barnyard fence while Dan stood stiff and uneasy before him, not knowing what to do with his hands that he was keeping respectfully out of his pockets. Not far away Mr. Johnson's car rested in the shade of a tree, with Mr.

Johnson's wife in the front seat. Mr. Johnson took out his cigar, shot a stream of juice onto a flat stone, and watched it sizzle.

"I ain't been mean, have I, Dan?"

"No, Mr. Johnson," Dan replied, "you been mighty patient and I appreciate it. But, Mr. Johnson . . ."

"Now, Dan," he interrupted, "you know as well as I do, not many men would have strung along with you as far as I have."

"I know it, Mr. Johnson. You been mighty patient."

"Well, these things just happen. I reckon everybody has a stretch like this some time or other." Mr. Johnson waved a large chunk of charity at him. "I don't want to be mean. I ain't forgot you done well here before all this begun to happen. I don't forget them things. But now, you see, prices is good. This here's a good piece of land and with proper work we'd have us a whopping big crop off of it. Everybody else is doing good this year. You got one of the best sixty acres in the county right here, Dan, and you and me could both be making a killing if it was going right."

Mr. Johnson removed his big lazy Panama and mopped his forehead and the back of his neck with a sopping handkerchief. Dan shifted the weight from his aching leg slowly, trying not to wince. What was the good of all this? Why stand out here in the sun and jaw about it? He hadn't done it on purpose, for God's sake. Didn't he know it was a good year, and who stood to lose the most, him or Johnson?

"You've got a good head on you, Dan," Mr. Johnson was saying. "You ain't wild. You're about as settled a man for your age as I ever seen. I knew your papa and I could see his boy would make a good farmer. I just mean to say I got faith in you, Dan. But you can see the fix this puts me in."

Dan nodded wearily and followed Mr. Johnson's eyes down along the length of his stiff leg.

"Jesus, it ain't your fault. But it ain't mine, either." Mr. Johnson was getting hotter and his eye acknowledged an impatient stir from his wife.

"Well, I don't know what to say. We'll just have to let things go on like this for a while, I guess. I don't see nothing else we can do."

Neither did Dan. He stood helplessly, wishing Mr. Johnson would go on and not stop at those awkward spots.

"I can bring in a team and make another alfalfa cutting. And we might get a stand of soybeans if the weather holds. But if anything else happens, God help us. Dan, you just got to be more careful."

Careful! It made him so mad he heard the insides of his ears pop. Careful! He raised his head, raised a forefinger, raised his leg to set it out before him in a stance, then thanked the Lord for the pain it caused him. Johnson would never know how near he had come to a good round cussing.

Mr. Johnson turned to go. Reaching into his pocket he brought up a lighter for his guttering cigar. At a gesture Dan went closer. Mr. Johnson, with a show of lighting his cigar, slipped a bill into his hand and signaled his wife that he was coming, that only the lighting of his cigar was keeping him.

VI

When Harold's summer vacation began Laura bent over backwards being nice to him. He'd been through so much, poor little fellow, had taken Dan's accident so serious and she had scrimped him on so many things he needed. Most of all she was ashamed of being sorry to have him home. She even refused to call him down when she knew he was bothering Dan with his racket. And Dan was being so nice, even softened her when once or twice she did fly off the handle at the boy.

Dan felt that his accident had done one good thing at least, brought him and Laura closer together than they had been since they were married, certainly a lot closer than they had been for a long time lately.

Not that he wasn't worried just about every minute. He worried over the look of things, what the neighbors were saying about Laura spading the vegetable garden and pitching manure out of the barn. They had seen her, all right, gone out of their ways to see her, and he worried most over how she felt about the loss of her pride.

One Saturday after she had gone to town he found the washing machine gone. How she managed to get it into the car by herself he couldn't guess and didn't ask. Someday he would get her another one, meanwhile it wasn't as if it was any comedown. It wouldn't hurt her to wash a few clothes.

Laura said, "How did you do it?" glaring down at the boy. She was worn out with chopping kindling and he had been going like a wild Indian since the break of day. She would have to leave off her cooking and trying to get in a few strokes on the churn and trying to clean up the place that had got to looking like a pigsty and having to move Dan around to sweep under his feet with him sitting there like he didn't even know she was in the same room, much less trying to clean up where he was, have to break off and leave things to boil over and burn and come out to drag Harold down out of the mulberry tree or off the barn roof or out from under the house where all kinds of spiders and snakes were liable to get at him, a dozen times she'd had to come out and yell at him for something and now this cut thumb was the last straw.

"Drawing the knife towards you, I bet, weren't you?" He made her mad the way he stood there so hangdog and she had a mind to grab him and shake a little of the nonsense out of him. Didn't she have enough to do without this now and didn't anybody care even enough to look after their own selves? "How many times have I told you never to whittle towards yourself? Huh? How many times? Well, just march over to that washpan and daub it good with iodine."

He twisted his face up at her with a plea. "Couldn't I use monkey-blood just as good?"

Dan put his paper down with a rustle and the boy looked at him with a slow flush of accusation, his eyes coming to rest on the leg stretched out under the table. He turned to Laura and began to whimper. She snatched him a turn and gave him a little whack, warmed up to it and gave him another.

"Stop it," said Dan. "He wasn't doing that a bit. I saw him and he was cutting away from him."

Laura shut her arm off midway and turned the boy to face her. He turned himself back and stared at Dan in bewilderment. Dan ducked back into his paper and when Laura looked down at Harold she knew instantly it was a lie. But what should she do?

Not ask him and have Dan shown up, or if he said it was so, why, she'd be just encouraging him to lie. He started to tremble and she knew he was thinking the same thing. Poor little fellow, what a fix to put him in. He shied away when she tried to hug him. Dan put his paper down and cleared his throat and limped to the door while they both stood and gaped at him. The thought in Laura's mind scared her and made her ashamed. Her husband, the father of her child, and for a minute she had stood there and just hated him.

Harold knew how bad he always got to feeling after he told a fib, so he thought Dan might use a little cheering up. He found him in the barn and said, "You know, that was a pretty deep cut I got," thinking he would give him a little company.

"It didn't look like much to me," said Dan.

"Yes, it was but I didn't cry a bit."

"Why should you have? It wasn't nothing but a scratch."

Harold thought deeply. "I'm not as big as you are and for my size it was just about as much as your cut hand was for you." After a moment he added gravely, "I don't think it needs stitches, though."

"You look like stitches," said Dan. "You couldn't even stand the thought of a little iodine."

"Do you think I ought to lay off with it for a few days?" asked Harold.

Why, the little smart aleck! Dan drew back his hand to fetch him a good one, then let it fall. "Get out of here," he said, "and leave me alone. And the next time I catch you whittling towards you I'll give you such a whipping as you never had."

VII

Dan had been on his feet about two weeks when Mr. Johnson brought over a riding plow and an extra mule. Dan could not really make out now, he knew it and had for a long time, but maybe he could keep from getting quite so far in the hole with some late-maturing truck crop. He had the land for it, three acres, black as coal.

"Now, Dan," Laura pumped herself up to begin, "I hope they

won't be nothing else happen. And probably nothing will." Lord, what else could? "But you never can tell and it's better to be safe than sorry. I was thinking, what if something was to happen and you wasn't able to get home. Here you are now still in that cast, I mean, and so you ought to have some way of calling me. Just in case, you understand."

Dan nodded. He couldn't afford to seem mulish.

She looked at him to see if it was all right to go on. "Now they's an old cowbell hangs in the barn. Suppose we wrapped up the clapper and hung it on your plow, then, just in case—"

She stopped. He was hopping mad.

It made him madder every time he thought about it all day long and he wouldn't have spoken a word to her when he came home if he hadn't come with a big blue bruise like a windfallen plum over one eye where he had fallen off the plow seat and just laid there, unable to believe it, for half an hour. So he spoke just about a word and Laura didn't urge him to any more. Herself, she hadn't one. Next morning, without letting her see, he took the big brass cowbell off its hook in the barn, wrapped the clapper in a strip of burlap and hung it under the plow seat. It made him feel like a fool, like a clabber-headed heifer that jumped fences, but when he reached down to yank the thing off and throw it in a ditch the blood pounded in the knot over his eye and he left it.

He plowed along and tried to forget it was there, but it might just as well have been strung around his neck. He couldn't be mad at her, she meant well and he was past pretending she didn't have reason for fear. He had got to feeling like he ought to have a bell, not to call anybody to him, but to warn them he was coming and they'd all better hide so they wouldn't catch whatever it was he had. People already looked at him like they would rather he didn't come too close, like he had caught something nasty, not to be spoken of. He didn't imagine it, no more than he imagined the look on Mr. Johnson's face the last time he was over, like he just couldn't see how a man could change overnight and go so completely to the dogs, shaking his head as much as to say, I don't see how you could do it, a man with a wife and family. Then again, half-awake in the morning, aching all over and dreading the clang of the alarm, he would see a long row of backs all turned his way and hear sniggers, "You know, he ain't no good to his wife any more. Ain't been for months. So just keep your eye on her for the next little spell."

He knew people talked about how tacky he dressed them, too, her and Harold. It looked like every dress she owned had a way of coming out at the seams under the arms and though he knew she had a lot to do, it did seem she could keep her things mended a little better. Not that she left those holes there to make him feel bad, but she ought to have seen they did.

Then her mama and papa would come over and the old woman would sit with her nose stiff and her eyes loose, looking behind and under and atop things as if what she saw before her, bad as it was, wasn't bad enough, and she was sure they had worse things hid away. And the old man would sit and rub his belly, ducking his head, pumping up a good long belch that rumbled like an indoor toilet, letting everybody know what a good dinner he had left home on and how little he looked forward to getting here for his supper.

The old man was the only one didn't think he had a nasty case of something. He just thought he was lazy and he had a sly steady look for him: I know what you're up to, tried it myself, but hell, they's a point to stop at and you passed it long ago.

And now, even Daisy, turning round with a long disappointed look at him. He pulled the team up, thinking he would eat, but he couldn't get a bite down.

He thought how Laura's mama shook her head over Harold every time she laid eyes on him. Dan couldn't see anything wrong with him. Kids were supposed to be a little dirty and wear old clothes around home. But to her he was such a pitiful sight, maybe he was just closing his eyes to all that was wrong with the boy.

He thought how long he had let that twenty-dollar bill Mr. Johnson slipped him stay in the cupboard, how he vowed to go over and give it right back the very next day but hadn't got around to it somehow, and instead come to say he'd let it lay there and never use it and return the very same one when he had enough for sure never to need it, and then, how he had turned it over to Laura and away it had gone. Gone fast, too, and he

wondered was Laura really being careful of her spending. How
he had stood around hemming and hawing and looking far-off
when Mr. Johnson came again, waiting for him to slip him another, and then being mad when he didn't. Being mad when you
didn't get charity—that was a pretty low comedown.

He leaned back against the tree, worn out, his leg thumping
with pain, and let the team stray off down the fencerow. He lay
down to rest a while but the sun shifted and bored through the
branches as if it wanted to get a look at him. He tried to doze but
he could hear that cowbell ringing in his head. Each of his hurts
came back to him and he tried to recall the day it happened,
hoping to remember something that might seem to deserve such
punishment. The details of his troubles began crawling up over
the edges of his mind and grew thick, like a gathering swarm of
bees. It was not his family nor the people on the street—he was
the one who had changed. Other men had troubles but they were
separate and unconnected, each came and stung and went on.
Something was wrong with a man when they came and did their
hurt and then stayed, waiting for the next, until they'd eaten him
hollow. He didn't have any troubles any more, he just had one big
trouble. For a moment that gave him a sad thrill. He had been
marked out. But why? He started to raise himself to see if the
answer didn't lie somewhere near at hand, and halfway up was
caught and held by the thought that nobody knew why, nobody
could tell him. He lay back heavily and said aloud, "I probably
have it all coming to me." It made him sad that he couldn't
remember whatever he had done to deserve it.

They sat down to supper with Harold quiet and cautious. He
had been punished for something and Dan felt like being sure he
had deserved it. "What's wrong with him?" he asked.

Laura looked at Harold, waiting for him to speak up and declare how bad he had been and just what he had got for it. "He
got a spanking," she said. Harold squirmed. Laura straightened
him up with a look and said, "He got hisself a bell and went
around ringing it all day. I asked him a hundred times to stop it
but he wouldn't. I was jumping out of my skin all day long every
five minutes thinking it was you and something bad had happened."

Dan threw his knife on his plate with a clatter. "Jesus Christ! Did you have it on your mind every minute that I was going to sound off on that damn thing!"

Laura bounced in her seat as if he had hit her; a slow hard pinch started in around the edges of her eyes. "Well, yes," she said, picking out all the bruises and breaks and bumps up and down him, "I did!"

VIII

Dan sat hunched up on the front porch, wandering wearily back and forth between the two minds he had about everything. He had sat there, just breathing, ever since they left, and now it was hard to believe that in the house behind his back anything had happened for years, or again, it seemed something had happened all right, the last thing that ever would, and now the house lay dead. Laura, she was down behind the barn, crying, he supposed, and one minute he would reckon he ought to stir himself and go out and try to comfort her, and the next minute figure he had just better keep out of her sight—not rousing himself to do either and not caring the next minute one way or the other, just wishing he could keep out of his own sight.

She was only going to take the boy over to her place until Laura had a little more time to spare him, the grandmother said, and Laura had taken no exception, even agreed with a tired nod that she hadn't given him much time of late and that Harold looked it every bit. It was not time she hadn't given him—though she hadn't given him that, either—and she knew it wasn't time or attention that his grandmother was thinking he needed. The old woman looked the boy over, tallying all the hollow spots that a few square meals would fill out. Her man was torn—strutting around throwing it up to Dan that he couldn't support his only child, pleased that *he* could, had figured for years that sooner or later he would have to, then suddenly fearing they might get to thinking he was better able to do it than he wanted them to think. Then he would pull a thin face to show how pinched he was going to be with his new responsibility.

Laura had followed them out to the buggy, wanting to say,

We'll have you back soon, Harold, don't you worry. And afraid he
would act as if that were the only thing that worried him. Suddenly she wanted to tell him that it wasn't any of her doing, that
she wasn't that way, that there wasn't anything wrong with her—
because he did look at her as though, since she was staying
behind, the same thing must be wrong with her. Instead, settling
him on the seat, not thinking, she said, "Drive careful, Papa."

She watched them move away and, turning, shoved the gate
shut and watched it fall back in exhaustion. As she walked up the
path her words scraped dryly in her mind: be careful, Papa. Be
careful, careful, be careful. She came to the front steps and stood
looking at Dan as she would at an old no-good hound dog lolling
on the porch, then turned and walked around the house.

IX

That three acres of truck was not going to make a stand; they
both saw that and so did Mr. Johnson. He hadn't got it in early
enough and hadn't been able to work it like he should have, it had
been too hot and dry or too cold and damp and it never got
proper spraying and the bugs got at it and it wasn't a very good
piece of land anyway and if anybody needed any more reason,
well, it was his, and that ought to be enough.

They clung as long as they could, holding out against what they
knew without saying was their only alternative. But a day came
when the last piece of salt pork spread its weak stain through the
last pot of beans, when the flour barrel was turned end up and
dusted out on a newspaper, when you could just about see the
blue flowers right through the pancakes on your plate, then, as if
he had timed it to the last mouthful, Laura's papa pulled up
outside the limp gate in his sway-backed wagon behind his
draughty mules and sat up on the high spring seat looking down
as though he might have revived things no end just by spitting on
that ruined soil and wouldn't do it—which was a lie; he was so
dried up himself he couldn't have brought up a nourishing spit.
His face looked eroded and was covered with a maze of capillaries
like exposed roots. On top of this a tangle of dry hair drifted like
tumbleweed.

Behind him, piled among their battered belongings, Laura and Dan rode away without a backward glance.

He was hard up all right, Laura's papa, always had been, always would be, but his actual condition was never so low as you'd guess from the meal he gave them that first night. You would have thought he expected a bill collector for company. And he was upset that Laura's mama had put on such a good expensive-looking dress to welcome her daughter home and he found a way to remark two or three times about it being her only one. What it was was her very best guinea-hen print and she sat puffed up in it all evening as if she had an egg but wouldn't lay it. As her husband offered the Lord his thanks for this and all His blessings—with a look at Dan—a scandalized look sneaked out of the corner of the old woman's eye and stole upward. She wanted Him and the others as well to know she hadn't forgot having had more in her day to thank Him for.

Dan guessed he'd never had more and they were all, it seemed, anxious to assure him that he never had. It looked as if her family had not only known him all his life but known him better than anyone else, better than he knew himself. They could recall accidents he had had and bring them clearly back to him, things he hadn't thought of for years, and now he supposed he had deliberately tried to forget them and had run for years from admitting this mark that was set on him, it seemed, the day he was born—and rolled out of his crib and got a knot on his head, the old man swore, and swore not to be mean, but you could tell from the look on his face, in genuine astonishment, it all added together so perfectly.

So perfectly it left not a minute's doubt in the mind of any of them that he was an absolute leper. Laura got tired of seeing him take it without any fight, but his time was taken up. Something would poke him awake in the morning, urge him to gulp down his coffee, so he could get started doing nothing and thinking nothing, and the effort of it had him worn out by evening. Everything everybody said or did was meant in some way for him, he felt, but it all had so little to do with him. Sometimes he felt like speaking up and getting in a dig himself at himself when they were all having such a good time running him down.

Laura believed he wasn't taking his position seriously enough. Instead of resenting her folks' charity as she had at first, she had come to feel they were being pretty nice to do all they had and that Dan might be decent enough to be grateful. He wasn't. They were getting their money's worth; they hadn't had anybody they could take as much out on in a long time. He had given them something more in common than they could ever have agreed upon amongst them. The bunch of them got along together now like fingers in a mitten.

At first Laura was always prophesying rain. If her papa was kept home then Dan wouldn't feel quite so bad that he wasn't out working. When it did rain she would pray for it to clear and get the old man back to the fields and out of the house where he couldn't torment Dan. The old man had the same problem rain or shine: Ought he to let them know how well the crops were coming for him—compared to *some* he could mention—or let them know what a lean winter they were in for around his table? He chose always to look worn to a frazzle; whichever way it turned out he had done his share and more.

Dan didn't care whether it rained or shone and he could see before long that Laura wasn't so worried one way or the other any more. Even with all she had to put up with from her mama, complaining about her cooking and the way she cleaned house and the grease she left around the sink and the way Harold dirtied his overalls so fast, with all that, Laura couldn't forget that she wasn't out forking hay or shaking out sods, couldn't feel any other way except that that was over now and she had come back home.

On the morning he was killed Dan woke earlier, struck with the thought he'd sooner spend the day with the old man than with the women. He went out to work a month before the date the doctor had set. He had expected it, but still it hurt when Laura didn't even try to stop him. She had seen him limp for so long she'd forgot there was a time when he didn't, couldn't believe a time might ever come when he wouldn't. He'd gone out too early before and the leg hadn't healed but it probably wouldn't have, anyway, and if it had something else as bad would have happened, if not worse.

How funny it was, Dan thought, that he didn't mind the old man now. It was clear that the old man despised him, and so it was no surprise to see that cowbell Laura had made him carry on Johnson's place hung under the mower that the old man meant for him to use. What did surprise Dan was that he didn't care. The old man stood by itching for a quarrel over it; Dan didn't have the energy.

He started in at one corner of the field and mowed three laps around. The steady clatter of the machine soothed him. With some surprise he had about decided that nothing out of the way was likely to happen when, near the end of his fourth time around, the mower bumped over a rock and he was thrown in front of the blade. The pointed runners held him spitted and the mules, taking fright, dragged him fifty feet before the spikes tore out and rolled over him.

He fought hard against coming to and half-conscious he knew he was badly hurt. He thought of what it was going to be like, dragging in bloody from head to toe, and he said to himself: Why can't I really have a good one once and for all and get it over with? He opened his eyes and looked at himself in disgust. Now, he thought, I'm going to catch hell sure enough. He started poking around in him for the strength to get up, but a wave of pain and sadness bent his will like the wind coming over the grass. If only he could just lie there and not have to go. But supposing they found him like this—that would be worse than if he dragged himself in. He tried to rise. But the grass came up cool and crisp, rustling like a fresh bedsheet, and tucked him in. What shall I dream about, he asked, and heard himself answer: You're already dreaming.

Then a voice like Mr. Johnson's said, "Are you going to lie there all day?" "No, sir, I'm going to get right up now and support my family."

He rolled over and groaned and opened his eyes. He could see the team a little ways off and was thankful for that bell hanging there. It cheered him so he got to his elbows and once he had he took a look at himself and laughed. If he could do that then he damned sure wasn't going to ring that bell. It would just be giving the old man too much to crow about. He looked again and wondered if he could have reached the bell anyhow, for there it went dancing all over the field.

Then Dan watched himself get up, get the bell and begin swinging it with all his might, pointing at the body on the ground as though he wanted everybody to come see what he had gone and done with himself now.

Sister

SISTER CAME down to the kitchen very early to attend Queenie through her labor. She found the other cats squatting in the shadows, solemn and stiff, while Queenie held the center of the room. Each of Sister's cats was temperamental; Queenie, the oldest, was the most difficult. Sister was touched by her moans and stricken looks, but she reminded herself that Queenie did like to have an audience. What a fuss she made!

"Queenie, Queenie," Sister chided. But her voice was soft as a purr. In each of her cats what she loved was just the weakness in its character.

The other cats drifted to the door where some sat and some paced up and down, waiting to be let out. Sister comforted each in turn. "No, no. There is nothing you can do to help. But don't worry—Queenie is going to be all right."

She offered her warm milk, ground beef, a raw egg. But Queenie wanted only to lie in the sunroom, wrapped around herself, down behind the potted oleander.

Yet Sister felt she wanted company. She regretted scolding her yesterday for stealing Zee-Zee's bone.

The whole house seemed to draw near to wait for Queenie's

pains to begin. Without the rest of her cats, Sister grew lonely and fretful. But she reminded herself of her responsibility. Queenie depended on her. Sister was always grateful for one more way in which she might be useful. It was gratitude—not pride—she felt in knowing that she could do more things than most girls of fourteen. She thought of her cousins Enid and Evaline and felt sorry for them; they missed so much enjoyment, being useless.

Queenie's labor soon began. Sister knew to keep away from her. The old cat clawed the floor; she grunted; she drew herself into a knot and rolled over and over on her back. With each of her spasms the fur stood up along her spine. Though Sister tried to sit still, before long she was biting her nails.

The first two kittens were each dark gray with darker stripes. But Sister soon found the ways to tell them apart. The third, which cried loudest, was paler. That one, like its mother, had a black ring around one eye.

"Well, that makes how many now?" asked Father as soon as he was told. His egg was boiling too long on the range, his toast burning, his coffee percolating too fast, and his corn flakes getting soggy, while in the guest bathroom off the kitchen he was nicking himself right and left with the razor. Busy with Queenie, Sister had forgotten his breakfast until he was already downstairs. Now, hurrying to make it, she also had to mix food for the mob of impatient cats gathered under the kitchen window.

The food for her cats had to be just so, neither too hot nor too cold. It made a heavy panful, which she balanced on one hand while opening the door with the other, trying at the same time to keep the cats back with her foot. But, as usual, two or three slipped in, and unable to find their food, went scampering around the kitchen.

Sister divided the food fairly among six plates, gently holding off the cats.

Father smelled the toast burning and rushed from the bathroom, his face covered with lather which here and there was stained pink with blood. The stray cats scurried. There was a howl; he had stepped on one's tail. Exasperated, he dropped his arms. He wanted to curse but denied himself; he started to complain but words failed him.

He had managed to calm himself when he sat down to breakfast. Sister was especially quiet to keep from irritating him. She set things before him with the least commotion possible.

"How many does that make now?" he asked.

Sister busied herself at the sink and pretended she had not heard.

"Hmmm?"

She studied the tone of his voice; it did not seem reproachful. He smiled.

But he could not help shaking his head when Sister said, "Nineteen."

All he could do was make his old joke. "With all these cats, there soon won't be room for a mouse in this house."

Father pushed aside his corn flakes and reached for his eggcup. The smell he had been trying to ignore overcame him. Of all animals, cats smelled the worst! He laid his spoon down in disgust. He turned to say, "Good heavens, Sister! If you must keep them inside, can't you at least try to housebreak a few of them?" But as usual he found her gone without a sound.

The dog barked at a car coming up the drive. Walter looked at his watch. The kitchen clock was slow! Paul, his brother, came in, pleased to find him late. They took turns driving down to the train. On mornings when Walter was upset and cross, Paul took pains to be jovial and loud; let Walter try to feel good and Paul was surly all the way to the city. I do believe, Walter told himself now, that Paul enjoys coming in here and smelling this smell. To think of my having spent all the money I have on this place, only to have it smelled up like this by a pack of cats, must give him a great deal of pleasure. He knows it's a better house than his, and otherwise better kept. No doubt he thinks I haven't the nerve to set my foot down and put a stop to it, for he expects me to be intimidated by Sister as he is by Evaline.

Thinking like this would sometimes drive Walter to speak harshly to Sister. But usually he behaved, when Paul came, as though he smelled nothing, and would find a way of repeating what a pleasure it was to have many cats in the house.

No one else, Sister knew, felt about cats as she did. Someone might come to, though, someday, if she kept trying to make them see how nice cats are. Of those for whom she had hope, Uncle Paul seemed the most likely. Not because he already liked cats somewhat—he paid less attention to them than many people, in fact—but because he was the only person who often called her Jane, instead of Sister.

"Jane," he said, "what is that?" looking into the sunroom and peering at the box from which came cries and the sucking sounds of Queenie's kittens. Cocking an eye, he looked at Sister as though he had caught her doing something mischievous, but was prepared to be amused by it.

"Would you like to see them?" she asked. If only he would hold one and watch them feed, she was sure he would love cats forever.

Father said, "Sister, don't annoy Uncle Paul with your cats. Everyone is not like us, you know, when it comes to cats."

Sister was left standing. Uncle Paul had turned away, his interest lost.

Preceded by a loud yawn, Edmond sauntered in.

"Ah," said Walter. "Look who decided to get up."

"Dad," said Edmond, "you won't by any chance be near a bicycle shop today in the city, will you?"

"So," said Walter. "So that's what got you out of bed before I was gone." He lowered his eyes and said resignedly, "I might have known."

For one of Walter's great pleasures was pretending that Edmond had no feeling for him. Sighing and rolling his eyes at Paul to show how mistreated he was gave him intense satisfaction. Paul would give the world for a son to tyrannize him.

"What is it you need now?" Paul was asking. He too liked to make himself out a victim of Edmond's selfishness.

Looking from one to the other, Edmond could see that each would like to be the one to get a new tire for his bicycle. It was a good time to ask for a speedometer, too. He chose Uncle Paul, sure that Father would then buy both.

Paul looked at Walter to be sure he did not resent his intrusion. Walter smiled tolerantly. It warmed him to be able to let Paul sometimes feel himself the father of a son. Feeling warm, Walter shook his head in admonition, saying, "I don't know, Paul. I don't know. Keep this up and you will ruin him." Paul glowed. How he enjoyed being told he was making a fool of himself over that boy.

Walter had long ago imagined a scene that was bound to occur one day. Sooner or later Nancy, Paul's wife, was going to burst out with all her resentment and say, "If that boy were mine—!"

And that was as far as she would get.

"My dear Nancy, that is just the point. He is not yours."

And with those words, Walter felt sure, he would be saying what Paul had wanted to say all these years.

Sister ducked her head and rubbed her eyes with the back of her hand. Father had got off. She had made Edmond's breakfast. The dishes were washed and replaced and the laundry ready for Mrs. Hansen. What was it she had not done? She had made her morning inspection of the garden and with great care reset two iris bulbs which the cats had dug up. Had there been something she was supposed to remind Father of?

It was in the morning when the house was still, and at night just before bed that this feeling came over her. She would think and think and not recall what it was, but grow more certain by the minute that it was something important she had forgotten to do, or something urgent that someone had said to be sure to remind him of.

She had no more time to worry over it. At eight o'clock she must begin cleaning up after the cats.

Her routine was to start in the dining room, just outside the right-hand kitchen door. There, under the table upon which the wines were ranged, was sure to be a mess. It was one of their favorite spots.

Certainly it was contrary of the cats not to use the sandbox. In four rooms newspapers had to be spread in every corner and collected once, often twice a day. Yet Sister could not think of punishing them. The training was so cruel. Poor things, they could not help themselves, and she had grown accustomed to it.

To get under the Swedish fireplace was a job, and that was where Huckleberry always went. No place suited Zee-Zee but

under the teakwood table upon which the samovar sat. Pinky
favored a spot behind the cabinet of blown glass, while Dots, his
sister, had a place behind the pottery cabinet.

No one could tell Sister that all cats were alike!

"Naughty Bo-Bo," she said each day as she went to clean
behind a certain copper urn, and, "Dreadful Yvonne," she murmured, crawling under the dining table.

And Clarabelle, Helen, Walter, Little Nell, Hildegarde and all
the rest, as she went behind the scented geranium, the lacquered
screen, the Franklin stove, the table with the Swedish bowl, her
voice growing softer and her smile broader as she went.

"Oh, naughty Leopold, naughty, naughty Harriet," she said.
"And Mr. Micawber!" she cried on seeing that a leg of the break-
fast-room table was being used again to sharpen claws.

The cabinets filled high with glass and china and the rows of
copper vessels glowed in the darkened room. Sister crawled
across the patch of sunlight spreading through the French doors.

She finished, straightened herself, and took a slow, thoughtful
sniff. She believed it was all right. She walked through the dining
room, pausing at the likely spots to test the air, warning herself
that she must be critical. Being so accustomed to the smell, she
could not trust herself to judge for other people's noses.

Poised on the doorsill, before she would step in, Mrs. Hansen,
the cook, stood sniffing.

Only once had Mrs. Hansen arrived before Sister finished
cleaning up after the cats. It was a revelation to her; she was
scandalized. She still grumbled about people with so much
money, a child so spoiled that she had not one, but umpteen cats
to mess wherever the urge took them all over a house costing
more than her dead husband, sweating day after day on a railroad
line, ever made in his life, plus the little she had earned since he
passed away, and often she would throw in all that her three
children were ever likely to make, for good measure.

One would think it was Mrs. Hansen who had to clean up after
the cats. Indeed, she believed that she did, and told her children
so, describing the task in revolting detail, to reproach them still
further for their everlasting ingratitude.

Always late, Mrs. Hansen, instead of apologizing, gave Sister to feel she ought to be ashamed, making a poor widow woman with three children of her own to get breakfast for, come then to attend her family.

All forms of quiet aggravated Mrs. Hansen. It gave her the creeps, she complained. She jumped and gasped each time she turned to find Sister standing near. When Mrs. Hansen had no one to talk to at the top of her voice, she hummed as loud as she could.

Mrs. Hansen began her day with a good loud complaint. She could settle down to work only when she knew that her grievances were in ahead of everyone else's. "Well, here I am," she declared.

Outside, cats bounded up in alarm and slunk off out of range of Mrs. Hansen's voice.

How was she to break the news of Queenie's litter, Sister wondered. She did not feel apologetic about the new kittens; but if she seemed to be, perhaps Mrs. Hansen would give in with a smile and a shake of the head. She had seen people pass off their whims and weaknesses in a way that made others humor them.

"Oh, dear," she sighed. "Queenie had a new litter this morning."

"Well, if it's got you worried," said Mrs. Hansen, "I can tell you just what to do. Now, we have cats at our house. But," she said, "there's cats—and then, there's cats." The water for her tea was boiling. She turned to set it off the light. "I'm glad to see you've realized that it was getting out of hand. Now, if you'd like, I'll just put them in a sack and on my way home as I'm driving over the bridge—"

Mrs. Hansen drew herself up, listening suspiciously. She had the feeling that she was talking with no one to hear her. She turned. The child was gone! What a creepy feeling that gave her.

Sister was dusting in the library. Out in the garden Leonard knelt, patiently untwining the runners of the strawberry plants. The old Negro's face gleamed in the sun; it was the color of eggplant. Sister watched him rise and greet her mother when she came upon him from around the hedge, the special smile she had for him already on her lips. Leonard's ways gave Martha Taylor much amusement; she imagined he disapproved of most everything she did; she walked in the garden in pajamas.

Leonard's quaint uprightness made him a character. Guests were charmed by Martha's anecdotes in which she did something frivolous, and Leonard extinguished her with his solemn scorn.

She suggested work for him, sure that once she was gone he would fall back to snipping runners from the strawberries, declaring to himself that he knew what needed doing.

Martha took a turn among the flower beds, kneeling here and there to pluck a weed. At the herb beds she lingered to enjoy the sunshine and the fresh air and the smell of sweet basil and tarragon. She glided over the cobblestones of the court, ran her fingers through the Dutchman's-pipe that hung over the dining-room door, and went in.

"Good morning, Mrs. Hansen," she said. "Ah, there's my boy."

Edmond came forward for his hug. He was beginning to wish to have it some place other than in front of Mrs. Hansen.

"Tell Mother what you've been doing, Sweet."

"Nothing," he said, meaning, nothing wrong.

"Did you have your breakfast? Was it good?"

"It was all right. Well, I have to go now. I'm going down to Billy Morgan's."

"Did you finish that birdhouse you were building?"

"Long ago. It wasn't so good. I threw it away."

"Oh—too bad. But then why not build another?"

"I have to go down to Billy's. He's got a pair of guinea pigs."

"You have had guinea pigs. You were never interested in your own. Wouldn't you like to stay and help me in the garden?"

"I'd rather go down to Morgan's."

"Aunt Nancy is coming this afternoon. Perhaps she will bring something for you."

Edmond shrugged. He knew the sort of things Aunt Nancy brought.

"Well," said Martha, "I know a little boy with a birthday coming up soon."

His birthday was twenty-four days away. Already she had begun teasing him. She enjoyed making him guess what he was getting and where it was hidden. As the time neared she worked him into a frenzy of impatience. Then, as on the day before Christmas, at the last minute she would tell.

"Oh, well," he said, "I'm not expecting much this year. Besides, it's not the gift that counts."

She could interest him in nothing. He was determined to go. Martha yawned and rose.

"Where is Sister?" she asked.

"Here."

"Good heavens, child!" Martha cried.

Sister stared. What had she done now?

"The way you slink up on people! Just look what you've done to poor Mrs. Hansen!"

Sister began accounting for herself since getting up.

"I watered the plants," she said, "and dusted the library. I took out the trash and burned it and put some rugs out to sun."

"Did your father leave any message for me?" asked Martha.

Sister thought for a moment. "No." She hurried to tell the other things she had done this morning. "I scrubbed the bathtub."

"Are you sure?" Martha asked.

"Yes. Edmond left a ring."

"Who, me?"

"No, no, no," said Martha. "I mean, sure that Father left no message."

She had been sure; now she hesitated.

Martha sighed wearily. "Well, I just hope it was nothing important."

"I swept the back steps," said Sister hopefully.

Martha said that that was thoughtful of her.

Sister smiled her bashful smile. She blushed. She felt encouraged to tell that Queenie had had her kittens.

"How nice," Martha said.

Sister watched her closely. "Would you like to see them?"

"All right."

"They're in the sunroom," Sister said. "I put them in a box. They're behind a plant. There are three of them. One has a ring around its left eye, just like Queenie. I've already named them.

But if you can think of better names . . ." Her words trailed off as she realized that Martha might be annoyed with so much chatter.

The kittens were asleep. Sister stroked Queenie. She was proud of her. Martha knelt and cautiously put out her hand. Queenie growled.

"Queenie!" Sister cried.

When the tips of Martha's fingers touched her head, Queenie snarled. Sister gave her a hard slap. Growling softly, Queenie drew back in bewilderment. Sister, too, was astonished at what she had done.

"Come back, Mother," she cried. "She won't do it again, I promise." But Martha was gone. "Oh, Queenie," Sister moaned. "Why did you have to do that—just when things were going well."

Queenie sulked; she refused to make up, and it seemed to Sister that she looked misunderstood. She considered Queenie's side of the affair. A cat, she reminded herself, can tell when a person is only pretending to like it.

"Hot, isn't it?"

"It is, miss," said Leonard, barely looking up. The thin gray fuzz on his head was like pocket lint.

"It's the humidity," Sister suggested.

"That's what they say."

Sister wished she could find something to say that others were not always saying. Leonard was known not to like to waste words on the same old things.

"Now, missy, if you'll just stand out of my light I can tell which is the weeds and which is the vegetables."

She started. She was dreadfully embarrassed.

After a short wait, Sister softly cleared her throat. Leonard went on carefully teasing out a clump of crab grass.

"My," she said, "there are a lot of them, aren't there—weeds, I mean." She meant to sympathize with him.

But he thought she was saying that he had neglected his job. "Where they's dirt," he said, "they is bound to be weeds."

"Do you have a very big garden of your own?"

Seeing that he must talk, Leonard drew off his gloves and brought his pipe out of his jumper pocket and fitted it in the one place where he had teeth strong enough to support it.

"My old woman raises us a few things," he said. He looked puzzled as to how that could interest anyone.

He made his living raising other people's gardens, yet his wife raised theirs. Sister was tickled. Leonard smiled, too. Then he straightened his smile, as though he had caught his lips doing something without his permission.

All the same, Sister believed he was in a good humor.

"Do you have chickens?" she asked.

They did, and ducks and one old gander.

"And a cow?"

She could not quite catch whether or not they had a cow.

But dogs they had. Three. And they had cats, she supposed? No? No, the last cat they had had had got run over on the highway, it must be—oh, six, seven years ago.

Its name was Citronella. Or maybe he had that one confused with another that was a little bit lighter in shade.

And had they never had another since?

Never another. No'm.

Sister said she hoped that was not because they had lost their liking for cats.

Leonard stopped sucking on his pipe and looked at her out of the corner of one eye. Was she working her way around to trying to give him one of them measly kittens?

"Well, to tell you the truth," he said, "we ain't much on cats. Dogs, now . . ."

Sister assured him that she was fond of dogs, too. Many people who loved cats were not, but she was.

"Now if it was puppies you was trying to get shut of, why, that'd be something else again," said Leonard.

For a moment Sister did not understand. Then, "Oh, dear," she cried. "You thought I wanted to—" She could hardly think of it. "Why, I'd never give one of them away. Not for anything." And certainly not, she thought, to a man who had just said he did not like cats.

Leonard chuckled. "Well, miss, now I knew that was just what you'd say. I was just testing you. I knew you wouldn't part with one of your kittens. And to tell you the honest truth, I do like cats. Like 'em fine. Yes, indeed—cats."

Sister smiled faintly.

Leonard knocked out his pipe. When he turned from picking up his gloves he found her gone.

"I'm sure it's very good of you to say so, Nancy—but it's perfectly inedible. And soufflé, you know, is a dish that Mrs. Hansen is so good at ordinarily."

"No, no, Martha," Nancy Taylor said. "It's fine." And Enid and Evaline spoke up, "Yes, yes. It's fine. Really."

Their table was in the grape arbor. Shashlik was slowly doing to a turn over a charcoal brazier within Martha's reach. The juices simmered from the meat and fell on the coals with a sizzle and a puff of smoke. The smell of sweet basil and fresh earth drifted in from the garden. The day was warm and still. Cats slumbered on the rocks.

"You are kind, all of you," said Martha gratefully. "Poor Mrs. Hansen. She worked so hard on her soufflé, too—knowing you were coming. You can imagine how badly she felt. After what happened, she wanted to make another one, you know, though the poor woman could hardly get a grip on her nerves."

"After what happened?" said Evaline.

"She saw a dead mouse," said Edmond.

"Edmond. Dear. Not at the table," said Martha.

"She always spoils the dinner when she sees a dead mouse," said Edmond.

"Or a live one," said Martha. "Which is considerably more often."

It was true that Sister's cats were rather slack at mousing. She fed them too much, Martha said. Loving cats had not made Sister hate mice. She loved her cats all the more because they did not molest them.

Martha gave a toss of her head. "Madness!" she cried gaily. "Plumbing that never works, a horse no one can ride, a gardener who won't let you near your own garden—and a houseful of cats that won't catch mice. Where else but at the Walter Taylors'?"

"But really, Martha," said Nancy, "I find the soufflé . . ."

"What that poor woman must think about this fantastic household!" cried Martha. "The stories she must tell in the village about the Taylors!—*us* Taylors, I mean," she added with a smile.

"Oh, Lord!" cried Nancy. "And our Mrs. Porter about *us* Taylors!"

Martha smiled down the table upon her sister-in-law. And that smile dealt with all attempts to match her singularity.

Being poached upon by nineteen cats who caught a mouse a year was one of the most delightful of the Taylors' whimsicalities.

"Nineteen!" visitors exclaimed. They were answered by Martha's smile, bashful and guilty, a smile that said: I know it's a weakness in me, but isn't it an adorable weakness.

"Well, I'm afraid we shall simply have to call the soufflé a bad job," said Martha, and pushed hers away. So did the others, their appetites for it fairly gone by now.

"May I have some more, please?"

This came from the end of the table.

Everyone turned and found it was Sister. A queer child.

Martha took the skewer of meat from the brazier. Cats stirred, yawning and stretching, sniffing the air.

Serving the plates, Martha said, "I suppose Sister has told you that three more were born this morning."

"Why, no," exclaimed Nancy Taylor, turning to smile at Sister kindly.

Perhaps she might have asked to see them, had not Huckleberry's paws appeared just then over the edge of the table. He jumped and landed near Evaline. Sister leaped from her chair. But Martha was already lifting him by the scruff and putting him on the ground.

"Do sit down, child," she said. "I can lift a cat."

When it happened that a cat could not escape punishment, Sister tried always to be the first to reach him. If it must be done, she would rather do it herself. There was never a person who could congratulate a cat while apparently scolding it, as Sister could.

A silence fell on the table. To break it, Aunt Nancy said, "What have you been doing with yourself since we saw you last, Edmond?"

"Oh," said Edmond casually, "just running true to form." He loved to spring phrases on them like that. There was a large family stock of the funny things he had said, and he was always hoping to add to it.

"Poor Mrs. Hansen had not quite collected herself, it seems, by the time she got to the pudding," said Martha.

Roast for dinner was in the oven, and in the quiet, clean kitchen where the clock on the wall ticked contentedly, Mrs. Hansen sat at the table sucking her teeth. Before her was spread her tabloid. Her eyes were wide and her lips indignant as she read; she held her breath while fumbling for the page in the back section where her story was continued. When she finished it she had to sit back, breathing heavily, and pat her chest to soothe the outrage in her heart. She saw herself coming home from working late to support her three fatherless children on a cold night down a dark deserted street. Suddenly, out of the shadows a figure loomed, reeling drunkenly. It made a guttural sound. It was . . .

Queenie—prowling in from the sunroom.

Mrs. Hansen yelped. Little did those three children Mr. Hansen left her with appreciate all that she went through for their sakes.

Sister, coming down the hall, heard Mrs. Hansen's gasp, and having some idea what might have caused it, turned and stole off to the library. She curled up on the sofa and found her place in a book. But the windows were open; there was a breeze in the maple tree and the steady rasping of Leonard raking the gravel walks. Soon she was asleep.

"Sister," said Martha, "bring me a pincushion."

Evaline's party dress was almost finished. She stood with one arm raised for Martha to let out a seam.

"Can't you find one, Sister?" Martha called.

"Here's one, Aunt Martha," said Enid.

"Thank you, dear. Never mind, Sister."

"She isn't here, anyway," said Enid. "She went downstairs long ago."

Martha smiled. "Worried over her cats, I suppose."

"Nineteen," said Nancy Taylor.

Martha gave the dress a final tug, and settled back in her chair. The studio had been filling with gentle, late-afternoon light, and Martha was moved to think of her own gentleness, her patience. She let Sister keep nineteen disgusting cats, with never a thought for her lovely home.

"It is a lot, isn't it," she said. She was filled with wonder at herself. "But you wouldn't want me to make her give them up?" She sighed. "I suppose it's what any other woman would do."

"But, Aunt Martha," said Evaline, "don't they make you—" She broke off with a shudder.

Martha said, "Yes—I forget, don't I, that they are disgusting to many people. That's selfish of me, isn't it? I mean, to allow my child to offend others." She sighed and said, "Perhaps, my dear, you will understand better when you are a mother yourself. You know what they say about a mother's love."

"There is more than one kind of blindness," said Nancy, her voice grown suddenly hard.

Martha did not like her tone. She found herself getting excited. She said, "Well, I'd like to know of another woman with a house as fine as mine who let nineteen cats simply ruin it to please a child."

"Or to please her conscience," said Nancy. But she had not been able to say it as loud as she had meant to. The whine of a cat, beginning low and growing to a howl, had hushed them all. Nancy gave a shudder. Enid came to her and sat on the arm of her chair. Nancy hugged her reassuringly. Evaline came, too, a little jealous perhaps.

"Why," said Martha with a little laugh, "it's hard to imagine Sister without her cats."

They all sat trying to do it.

Dusk was turning to darkness. In the garden, under the balconies, among the plants in the rocks, cats were waking, yawning, and stretching. They prowled in from the woods, from the drive, from the stables. One cat licked the table in the grape arbor, growling at all comers, while another searched beneath the table, sniffing for scraps.

They gathered in the courtyard. They perched themselves on benches, on tables, in the dirt of potted plants. One old cat found a vase in his way, knocked it off the table, and settled himself comfortably. They all sat waiting intently, each securely in possession of his spot.

Sister yawned and rubbed the sleep from her eyes and raised herself to her feet with a mighty stretch.

She made her way down the dark hall, stepping over a pail someone had left in the way. Passing the windows, she could see the cats listening to her approach and gathering in the moonlight near the door, purring all together.

Sister held the door open. Huckleberry was the first one in, and Sister, with a smile and a nod, watched him make straight for his spot under the Swedish fireplace.

The Shell

THIS WOULD be the season, the year, when he would have the reach of arm to snap the big gun easily to his shoulder. This fall his shoulder would not be bruised black from the recoil. The hunting coat would fit him this season. This would be *the* season —the season when he would have to shoot the shell.

It was a twelve-gauge shotgun shell. The brass was green with verdigris, the cardboard, once red, was faded to a pale and mottled brown, the color of old dried blood. He knew it intimately. On top, the firing cap was circled by the loop of a letter *P*. Around the rim, circling the *P*, were the two words of the trade name, *Peters Victor;* the gauge number, 12; and the words, *Made in USA*. The wad inside the crimp of the firing end read, *Smokeless;* 3¼; 1⅛-8. This meant 3¼ drams of smokeless powder, 1⅛ ounces of number 8 shot—birdshot, the size for quail. It was the one shell he had found afterwards that had belonged to his father, one that his father had not lived to shoot. So he had thought at first to keep the shell unfired. But he knew his father would have said that a shotgun shell was meant to be fired, and he, Joe, had added that any shotgun shell which had belonged to him was meant to hit what it was fired at. For four years now it had been out of Joe's pocket, and out of his hand fingering it inside his pocket, only to stand upon the table by his bed at night. For four years now he had been going to shoot it when he was good enough, but the better he became the further away that seemed to get, because good enough meant, though he did not dare put it to himself in quite that way, as good as his father had been.

He had been in no great rush about it during those first two seasons afterwards, then there had been time—though now it seemed that even then there had been less time than he admitted. But on opening day of the third, last year's season, he had suddenly found himself sixteen years old—for though his birthday came in May, it was in November, on opening day of quail season, that he really began another year—time was suddenly short, and then overnight gone completely, after that day when he returned with the best bag he had ever taken and, in his cockiness, had told his mother about the shell, what he had saved it for and what he meant to do with it.

He had not allowed himself to forget that at that moment he could hear his father saying, "Do it and then talk about it." He had argued weakly in reply that he was telling only his mother, and then it was not his father but the voice of his own conscience which had cried, "Only!" Because whom alone did he want to tell, to boast to, and because already he knew that that was not what his father would have said, but rather, "Do it and don't talk about it afterwards either."

She had seemed hardly surprised to learn about the shell. She seemed almost to have known about it, expected it. But she handled it reverently because she could see that he did.

"Aren't you good enough now?" she said.

"Hah!" he said.

She was turning the shell in her fingers. "I always knew nothing would ever happen to him while hunting," she said. "I never worried when he was out with a gun . . . Well," she brought herself up, "but I worry about you. Oh, I know you're good with a gun. I'm not afraid you'll hurt yourself."

"Not with the training I've had," he said.

"No," she said. "What I worry about is the amount of time and thought you give it. Are you keeping up in school? The way you go at it, Joe! It hardly even seems to be a pleasure to you."

Pleasure? No, it was not a pleasure, he thought. That was the name he had always given it, but he was older now and no longer had to give the name pleasure to it. Sometimes—often times when he enjoyed it most—it was the opposite of pleasure. What was the proper name for it? He did not know. It was just what he did, the thing he would have been unable to stop doing if he had wanted to; it was what he was.

"I see other boys and girls your age going out to picnics and parties, Joe. I'm sure it's not that you're never invited."

"You know that kind of thing don't interest me," he said impatiently.

She was serious for a moment and said, "You're so old for your age, Joe. Losing your father so young." Then she altered, forced her tone. "Well, of course, you probably know exactly what you're up to," she said. "It's the hunters the girls really go for, isn't it? Us girls—us Southern girls—like a hunting man! I did. I'll bet all the little girls just—"

He hated it when she talked like that. She knew that girls meant nothing to him. He liked it when she let him know that she was glad they didn't. He liked to think that when she teased him this way it was to get him to reaffirm how little he cared for girls; and yet she should know that his feeling for her was, like the feeling he had for hunting, too deep a thing for him to be teased into declaring.

He took the shell away from her.

"You're good enough now," she said.

"No," he said sullenly. "I'm not."

"He would think so."

"I don't think so. I don't think he would."

"I think so. You're good enough for me," she said.

"No. No, I'm not. Don't say that," he said.

He was in the field at daybreak on opening day with Mac, the speckled setter, the only one of his father's dogs left now, the one who in the three seasons he had hunted him had grown to be his father's favorite, whom he had broken that season that he had trained, broken, him, Joe, too, so that between him and the dog, since, a bond had existed less like that of master to beast, more like that of brother to brother, and consequently, he knew, he had never had the dog's final respect and did not have it now, though the coat did fit now.

He had not unleashed the dog yet, but stood with him among the bare alders at the edge of the broom grass meadow that had the blackened pile of sawdust in the middle—the color of fresh cornmeal the first time he ever saw it—to which he, and the big covey of quail, went first each season, the covey which he had certainly not depleted much but which instead had grown since his father's death.

The coat fit now, all right, but he wore it still without presumption, if anything with greater dread and with even less sense of possession than when it came halfway down to his knees and the sleeves hung down to the mid-joints of his fingers and the armpits looped nearly to his waist and made it absolutely impossible to get the gun stock to his shoulder, even if he could have lifted the big gun there in that split second when the feathered balls exploded at his feet and streaked into the air. He had not worn the coat then because he believed he was ready to wear it nor hunted with the big gun because he believed he was the man to. He had not been ready for a lot of things, had had to learn to drive, and drive those first two years seated on a cushion to see over the hood; he had not been ready to sit at the head of the table, to carve the meat, to be the comforter and protector, the man of the house. He had had to wear the coat and shoot the gun and rock on his heels and just grit his teeth at the kick, the recoil.

Maybe there had been moments later—the day he threw away the car cushion was one—when he was pleased to think that he was growing into the coat, but now, as he stood with Mac, hunching and dropping his shoulders and expanding his chest inside it, it seemed to have come to fit him before he was at all prepared for it to. He heard the loose shells rattle in the shell pockets and he smelled the smell of his father, which now, four years later, still clung to it, or else what he smelled was the never-fading, peppery smell of game blood and the clinging smell of gunpowder, the smell of gun oil and the smell of the dog, all mixed on the base of damp, heavy, chill November air, the air of a quail-shooting day, the smells which had gone to make up the smell his father had had for him. Reaching his hand into the shell pocket he felt something clinging in the seam. It was a faded, tangled and blood-stiffened pinfeather of a quail. It was from a bird his father had shot. He himself had never killed so many that the game pockets would not hold them all and he had had to put them in the shell pockets.

He took from among the bright other ones *the* shell and slipped it into the magazine and pumped it into the breech. He would have to make good his boast to his mother, though he knew now that it was a boast made no more out of cockiness than cowardice and the determination born of that cowardice to fix something he could not go back on. He would have to fire the shell today. He had known so all the days as opening day approached. He had known it at breakfast in the lighted kitchen with his mother, remembering the times when she and himself had sat in the lighted kitchen over breakfast on opening day with his father, both in the years when he himself had stayed behind and watched his father drive away into the just-breaking dawn, not even daring yet to yearn for his own time to come, and later when he began to be taken; he had seen it in the dog, Mac's eyes as he put him into the cage, the dog cage his father had had built into the car trunk though it was the family car, the only one they had to go visiting in as well, that he would have to fire the shell today, and he had known it most as he backed out of the drive and waved good-by to his mother, remembering the times when his father had been in the driver's seat and she had stood waving to the two of them.

Now he felt the leash strain against his belt loop and heard the dog whimpering, and out in the field, rising liquid and clear into the liquid air, he heard the first bobwhite and immediately heard a second call in answer from across the field and the first answer back, and then, as though they had tuned up to each other, the two of them fell into a beat, set up a round-song of alternate call and response: bob bob white white, bob bob white white, and then others tuned in until there were five, eight separate and distinctly timed voices, and Joe shivered, not ashamed of his emotion and not trying to tell himself it was the cold, but owning that it was the thrill which nothing else, not even other kinds of hunting, could ever give him and which not even his dread that it was the day when he would have to shoot the shell could take away from him, and knowing for just that one moment that this was the real, the right feeling to have, that it was the coming and trying that mattered, the beginning, not the end of the day, the empty, not the full game pockets, feeling for just that moment in deep accord with his father's spirit, feeling him there with him, beside him, listening, loading up, unleashing the dog.

As soon as the dog was unleashed his whimpering ceased. Joe filled the magazine of the gun with the two ordinary shells and stood rubbing the breech of the gun, watching the dog enter the field. He veered instantly and began systematically quartering the field, his nose high and loose, on no fresh scent yet, but quickening, ranging faster already. They claimed—and of most dogs it was true—that setters forgot their training between seasons, but not Mac, not the dog his father had trained, not even after three seasons, even with no better master than him to keep him in training. He watched him now in the field lower his muzzle slightly as the scent freshened and marveled at the style the dog had, yet remembered paradoxically that first day, his and Mac's, when each of them, the raw, noisy, unpromising-looking pup and the raw, unpromising-looking but anything but noisy boy, had flushed birds, the pup a single but he a whole covey—two of which his father had bagged nonetheless—for which the pup had received a beating and he only a look, not even a scolding look, but a disappointed look worse than any beating he had ever had.

The dog set: broke stride, lowered his muzzle, then planted all four feet as though on the last half-inch of a sudden and unexpected cliff-edge, raised his muzzle and leaned forward into the scent streaming hot and fresh into his nostrils, leaned his whole body so far forward that the raised, rigid, feathered tail seemed necessary as a ballast to keep him from falling on his face. You could tell from his manner that it was the whole big covey.

He called as he set out down the field. "Steady, boy. Toho," he called, and on the dead misty air his voice did not seem his voice at all but his father's voice, calling as he had heard him call, and he was struck afresh and more powerfully than ever before with the sense of his own unworthiness, his unpreparedness, which seemed now all the more glaringly shown forth by the very nearness he had attained to being prepared; he felt himself a pretender, a callow and clownish usurper.

Now the birds were moving, running in the cover, still banded together, and Mac moved up his stand, so cautiously that he seemed jointless with rigidity. Stock-still, trembling with controlled excitement, his eyes glazed and the hair along his spine bristling—you could have fired an artillery piece an inch above his head and still he would have stood unflinching for an hour, until told to break his stand, and so Joe let him stand, to enjoy the sight, as well as to give his pounding heart a moment's calm, before going in to kick them up. He held the gun half-raised, and the shell in the barrel seemed to have increased its weight tenfold. Alongside the dog he said again, "Steady, boy," knowing that this time he spoke not to the dog but to himself.

It was as if he had kicked the detonator of a land mine. There was a roaring whir as the birds, twenty of them at least, burst from the grass at his feet like hurtling fragments of shell and gouts of exploding earth, flung up and out and rapidly diminishing in a flat trajectory, sailing earthward almost instantly, as if, though small, deceptively heavy and traveling with incredible velocity.

The gun went automatically to his shoulder, snapped up there more quickly and gracefully than ever before. He had a bird in his eye down the barrel and knew that he had got it there quickly enough to get a second shot easily. But his breath left him as though knocked out by the burst and pounding rush of wings. Fear that he might miss, miss with *the* shell, paralyzed him. He lowered the gun unfired. Turning to the still-rigid dog, he saw—as one in such case is always liable to see on the face of a good bird dog—his look of bewildered disappointment. In that instant it seemed to Joe that the fear of finding just that look was what had unnerved him, and though he was ashamed of the impulse, all his own disappointment and self-contempt centered in hatred for the dog.

As soon as he was given leave, Mac went after the singles. He set on one instantly.

Joe kicked up this single and again the anxiety that he might miss, such that sweat filled his armpits and he felt his mouth go dry, overcame him, and with trembling hands he had to lower the hammer and lower the gun unfired, and was unable to face the dog.

He tried on three more singles. It got worse. He knew then without looking at him that Mac had given him up and would refuse to hunt any more today. He did not even have to put him on the leash. The dog led the way out of the field. Joe found him lying at the rear of the car, and he did not need even to be told, much less dragged, as usual with him on any shooting day but especially on opening day, to get into the cage to go home.

The lemon pie was in the refrigerator, the marshmallow-topped whipped yams in the oven and the biscuits cut and in the pan and on the cabinet waiting to go into the oven the moment the birds were plucked—all as it always was when his father returned in the evening of a quail-shooting day, and as it was later when he and his father, and still later when he came home alone and laid the dead birds in her lap, as he had laid the first dollar he ever earned.

She said, cheerfully, that it was a lucky thing she happened to have some chops in the house. She added that she had learned that long ago. A woman learned, she said, never to trust to a hunter's luck—not even the best hunter. He was both grateful and resentful of those words. He knew she had never bought meat against his father's coming home from a hunt empty-handed.

He rested a day, went to school a week, and practiced, shooting turnips tossed into the air and hitting five out of seven, then he went back. The quail were there, you could hear them, but when he looked at Mac as he was about to loose him and felt himself quaking already, he snapped the leash on again and went back to the car and home.

And so what it turned into, this season for which he finally had the reach and the size, the endurance, in a word the manliness, was the one in which he fired no shell at all.

The Thanksgiving holidays came and he spent every day in the field with the shell in the barrel of the gun—a few bright brass nicks in the dull green now where the ejector had gripped pumping it in and out of the breech—and the magazine full behind it of his own waiting shells and with Mac. He hardly spoke to the dog now, gave him no commands and no encouragements, nor did the dog give tongue or whimper or even frisk, a kind of wordless and even gestureless rapport between them, the two of them hunting now in a grim, cold fury of impotence.

The dog had gone past disappointment, past disgust, past even bewilderment, and seemed now to have divined the reason or else the irresistible lack of all reason behind the coveys kicked up, the boy—almost the man now—raising and cocking his gun, but shaking his head even as he raised it, holding it erect and steady on his mark, then lowering it slowly and soundlessly and releasing him from stand and hunting on. His mother gave up trying to keep him at home, and seemed to have sensed the desperate urgency in him.

And now as the days passed and closing day of the season neared he could feel the whole town watching him, awaiting the climax of his single-minded pursuit, their curiosity first aroused by what they would have been most certain to observe: the lack of interest which they would think he should have begun to show in girls. The boys had noticed, had taken to gathering in a body on his shift at the Greek's confectionery at night, ordering him to make sodas for them and their dates, and ribbing him.

"Haven't seen much of you lately, Joe. Where you been?"

"Around."

"Yeah, but around who?"

Guffaws.

"I've been busy."

"I'll bet you have, old Joe."

Titters.

"Busy. Yeah."

Then he would blush. "I've been hunting," he said.

"I'll bet you have!"

He blushed again and said—he could never learn to avoid that kind of double meaning—"Quail."

They roared. "Getting many?" they said, and "Aren't we all?" and "Watch out for those San Quentin quail," they said.

Everybody knew everybody else's business in town anyhow, and moreover he was a kind of public figure in his way—they could not have helped but watch the coming-of-age of the son of the greatest wing shot the town ever had—so that he felt now that the ear of the whole town was cupped to hear the report of the shell, a sound which to him it had come to seem would have no resemblance whatever to the noise of any other shotgun shot ever heard.

At nights he studied the shell, trying to discover the source of its charm. He had come to fear it, almost to hate it, certainly to live by and for it.

How can you, he asked himself—no, he could make the question general, for he asked it not self-ironically but just incredulously—how can a boy want to be better than his father? Not better. It was not that. Not even as good as. That was not what he wanted at all. What was it? It was that you wanted to *be* your father, wasn't it? Yes, that was it. That was more what it was. And you weren't.

But wasn't there just a little bit of wanting to be better than mixed in with it? Wasn't there, in fact, just a little bit of thinking you *were* better than mixed in with it? All right, yes. Yes, there was. Why? It was because you believed that being half him you had all he was, and being half your mother you had that much again that he wasn't, that he did not have. And you knew that he would have agreed with this, which did not make you believe it entirely, or stop believing it.

Then it was closing day. The big covey was long gone from the broom grass meadow now, ranging from the swamps and brier patches to the uplands and the loblolly pines at the thicket edges. You had to work to find them now and any shot you got was likely to be a snap shot, through branches or brush. But this was how he wanted it. Let it get hard enough and it would be *the* shot and he would take it.

There were no waiting shells in the magazine of the gun today. He wanted no second shot, at least not on the same flush.

It was about eight in the morning when Mac got a warm scent. Did he know it was closing day? You would think so from the way he had suddenly taken cheer—or hysteria—determination, certainly. His spirits were not dampened even by the lowering of the unfired gun at the first single he found. He seemed in agreement that this one had been too easy.

They were hunting in uplands, in blackened stover bent to the ground and frozen, so that it snapped against Joe's boots. Then Mac headed down out of the cornfield, crossed a fencerow and was in a swamp, in sedge, tall and dead and bent. Joe could follow Mac, as 'way ahead of him the tall stiffened grass parted and closed heavily behind the dog's passage. Then he could not follow him any more and he whistled, and when he got no answer he knew that the dog had set and could not give tongue.

He began to rush, though he knew that Mac would hold or follow the birds. Feeding time for the birds was almost over. They would be drifting toward the thickets now and in another hour would go deep into the pines and then the dog could not hunt them, no dog. Then the hunting would not be good again until nightfall and that was the very last chance. It had better be now.

The bog continued for as far as he could see in the milky mist and he stood for a moment wishing the dog would give tongue just once, knowing that he was too well trained, and then he decided to go left, south. The land soon began to rise and the sedge got shorter and soon he could see where the swamp gave out at a fencerow and beyond that he soon could see a clearing rising out of the fog and rising up into pine woods. He could see no sign of the dog, but that was where he was sure to be.

He climbed over the barbwire, still looking ahead up into the clearing, and bent to get through the briers and came out with his head still raised looking up and almost stepped on the rigid, unbreathing dog, his nose in the wind, pointed as stiff as a weathervane.

He cocked the gun and stepped into the brush and kicked. They roared out toward the pines. He swung on his heel, holding the gun half-raised, picking his bird. He swiveled a half-circle, twisted at the waist, and saw the big cock, big as a barnyard rooster, streaking for the pines. He shot. The sound seemed to go beyond sound, one of those the hearer does not hear because the percussion has instantly deafened him, and he felt himself stagger from the recoil. But down the barrel of the gun he saw the bird, pitching for the ground at the thicket edge, winging along untouched, without a feather ruffled, and he knew that he had missed. From old habit he was already pumping the gun, and it was when he saw the big shell flick out and spin heavily into the brush that he realized he had heard no sound but a light dry click. The shell had not gone off. The shell was a dud. He had kept it too long; it had gone dead.

He said it aloud. "I have kept it too long. It's a dud."

Then he felt himself soaring as though in a burst of wings like the cock bird, as though he had been shot at himself and gone unscathed, free.

He dropped the shell into his pocket. It would rest permanently on his bureau now, he had time to tell himself. Then he was fumbling for fresh shells, his own shells, and dropping them all over the ground at his feet and getting one into the chamber backwards and saying to Mac in a voice he could just recognize as his own, "All right, don't stand there! Go get 'em! Go get 'em, boy! Go get 'em!" And he could tell that Mac knew it was his master's voice speaking now, a hunter's voice.

Report Cards

INSTEAD OF calling the roll, Miss Carpenter peered over the rims of her glasses and said, "I suppose everyone is here." The groan that arose satisfied her that everyone was. There was a rustle of adjustment; the girls sighed and smoothed down their skirts; the boys coughed and squirmed and shuffled their feet. Only Thomas Erskine sat quietly, knowing he had nothing to fear.

"Grace Adams," Miss Carpenter called.

When Grace, on the way back to her seat, looked at her report card, she could not help smiling. Everyone was pleased for her.

Miss Carpenter bore hard on Jackie Barnes. Coolly, he put his into his pocket without a glance; that was showing her how much he cared.

Even Miss Carpenter had to give a smile for John Daniels. It was not how well he had done, just that he had passed was more than anyone expected. He grinned modestly from ear to ear.

Thomas only wished his mother could have heard the change that came into Miss Carpenter's voice when she called his name. He went up for his card, trying to look solemn and as though he did not understand the looks of hopeless envy on all the faces.

Then everyone looked busy or thoughtful to spare Miss Carpenter being watched at an unpleasant chore—it was time for the Hazeltines. Luther clomped up the aisle with his head hanging, took his card without looking up, and clomped back to his seat. Then, without waiting to be called, as though she knew people preferred not to have to speak her name, Sal Hazeltine sidled up the aisle. She took her card and started back, then could not resist a look at it. She stopped. Her cheeks turned red. She began nibbling at the shreds of her chapped lips and blinking her eyes. Finally she remembered where she was, blushed a deeper shade, then hunched herself together and hurried back to her seat.

Thomas Erskine listened to her snuffling and thought with a shudder of the beating she would get when she got home. After today her parents need never give her another thought; she had lost her right to their affection. From now on even Luther, her own brother, would be ashamed to be seen with her. Her life here, he believed, was ruined; he could think of no way to make up for such a thing as Sal had done. That was what it meant to fail. At last he had seen it happen to someone. He might have known it would be Sal Hazeltine.

Yet, would such people as the Hazeltines care whether their child passed or failed? They would beat Sal for failing, but only because they never missed a chance to beat her, not because they really cared. Nor would they have cared very much if she had brought home straight A's. Imagining himself, for a moment, with such parents, seemed to Thomas the worst thing that might have happened to him in life.

He remembered coming home from school one afternoon and telling his mother, when she asked what happened in school that day, about Sal hemming and hawing and winding her skirt in her hand over a question so simple that probably even Luther knew the answer. They laughed together over the way Thomas imitated her. But one ought not to laugh, and straightening her face, Mother said, "Well, somebody loves her, I suppose." From the way she looked you could tell she thought it was hard to understand why.

While Miss Carpenter checked their books, examining the corners and giving the pages a quick but careful going-over, then checking off a name in her roll book, Thomas sat thinking about going to the country in just two days.

Virginia Tate was going to Hot Springs, Arkansas. Josephine Morris said her folks might go to New Orleans or maybe to Mexico. Everybody was going somewhere. Thomas was going to his grandmother's. They had talked about it before the bell rang, gathered on the school steps, the girls seated neatly on their handkerchiefs, the boys standing, everybody taking pains with clean linens and white shoes. A few feet away sat the Hazeltines. Everybody knew where *they* would spend the summer. Everybody could remember turning down the dusty road past the gravel pit, beyond the city-limit sign and driving past the Hazeltines' and seeing the scrawny razorback pig rooting wearily under the porch, the dusty, weathered old coonskins stretched on the walls of the house, and the Hazeltines stretched out on the front porch. Five or six or seven little Hazeltines would stop playing in the rusty old body of a Model-T Ford to stare at you through the thick white dust.

Richard Taylor was going to Carlsbad Caverns, and, oh, someone said, they were not so much. Just a lot of stalagmites and stalactites. And those who knew what those words meant took half a look and half a snicker at the Hazeltines, and so did those who no more knew than they.

Surely, thought Thomas, one day they would wake up, take a good look at themselves and then a look at the other children, and give up coming to school for shame. But they never missed a day. You might come ever so early, there they were—Sal in a molting straw hat and all that was left of a dress that once belonged to Jane Tucker, Luther in a floppy old leather chauffeur's cap and coveralls that had faded almost completely away.

Through the winter Luther smelled of stale Vick's salve, Antiphlogistine, Mentholatum. In the spring when all this lifted he was left smelling strongly of something that town people never ate—hominy. And Sal, because of the asafetida she wore in a little bag on a ribbon round her neck to keep away the croup, no one could get near Sal. At school they hung back and hung around and moved cautiously into a spot after the others had left it.

The Hazeltines. How could they not see all the things that were wrong with them?

Now they sat on the bottom step listening with their mouths hanging open while each told of the wonderful things he planned to see and do this summer. Finally, each trying to outdo the rest, everyone had told. A lull came, and the danger was that someone might mention report cards. Bobby Johnson nudged a couple of fellows and edged over toward the Hazeltines.

They looked up to see what was coming.

Smiling sweetly, Bobby Johnson said, "And where-all are you Hazeltines going to go this summer?"

The boys all simply yelped. The girls sniggered politely behind their hands. Some half got ready to run. Bobby Johnson looked like he wished he hadn't done it. For something down inside him gave a tug on Luther's Adam's apple. With his great callused hands, Luther could have wrung Bobby Johnson like a rag. But slowly a smile spread over Luther's face. He thought it was as good a joke as the rest. Then everybody really whooped. Sal grinned wider and wider; everybody was having such a good time; she was proud of Luther.

Oh, the Hazeltines! They were so dumb you simply could not insult them.

Thomas Erskine was miserable, though. No one hated the Hazeltines as much as he; the very sight of them embarrassed him. But he was miserable whenever they were tormented. He prayed that the Hazeltines might simply disappear. He hated the others for drawing attention to them, even if it was to make fun of them. He found himself hating their tormentors so much that he was almost sorry for Sal and Luther. To feel in himself a moment of sympathy for them made him hate the Hazeltines all the more the next moment. On top of everything, he was terrified that someone might notice him not joining in the fun, might think back and realize that he had never joined in, then suspect him of liking the Hazeltines.

The bell rang. Thomas's relief was so great it left him feeling weak.

The Hazeltines' lunches always looked like something wrapped in newspaper to be disposed of. Across Sal's thin little bottom as she bent to pick hers up, you could read in faded letters, *Bewley's Best.*

Miss Carpenter opened the door and the children fell in line. Alphabetically the Hazeltines were entitled to march in behind Thomas Erskine. Everybody else had better fall in where he belonged. The Hazeltines, though, always marched at the rear, and Miss Carpenter never corrected them.

Luther sat behind Thomas, breathing noisily through his mouth. Behind him sat Sal, gulping softly with every breath. Thomas tried to get his mind on the country, on his bicycle, on his last birthday party. Finally he could hold off a certain thought no longer, a thought so painfully embarrassing that he could feel the blood rising up his neck and making his ears tingle. There would be many boys like Luther, openmouthed, overgrown country boys, and many weasel-faced little girls like Sal coming to Grandmother's farm during the summer to spend the day. Thieving along at their mothers' heels, they would be jerked forward to gawk at him and then be introduced by Grandmother as cousins of his.

They were very, very distant cousins, said Thomas's mother— so far removed nobody would think of counting it except old folks like Grandmother, who liked to keep track of such things.

Grandmother believed in owning all your kinships, but sometimes even she did not want to own to any more than she had to. "This is your fourth cousin Effie Hightower, Thomas," she would say. "And this is her little boy Ferris and that makes him your fifth cousin, I suppose." And she would smile at Effie's boy, glowering up at her like a gopher down a hole, as though he was lucky to be able to claim that much.

It was hard to smile all the way across a fourth cousinship.

Thomas lived in fear of the day when one of those children might turn up at school and claim kin with him. It was bad enough already, with Aunt Jessie's boys there.

Aunt Jessie was Mother's sister, the one who had moved into town. She thought she dressed her boys in very townish clothes. Their great red hands hung out of their sleeves, their tight shoes squeaked with every step. Giles, Jess and Jules were their names.

Aunt Jessie was always thinking up things for Thomas and her boys to do together. It never seemed to bother her that Mother always found some way to get Thomas out of it. Aunt Jessie said she, too, had decided she didn't like her boys to play with any of their other cousins, and she was sure Harriet would understand what she meant.

"They are your nephews, you know, Jessie," said Mother. "The sons of your brothers and sisters."

"They are *our* nephews, Harriet," Aunt Jessie replied. "But I'm afraid there is nothing we can do about it."

To get his mind off all this, Thomas thought how proud his father would be of his report card. He would be bragging about it for weeks. He loved to have Thomas in the shop to show him off to friends, to have him near whenever he told a story. Then he would choose his words carefully, working his way around to some big word that Thomas had taught him lately. Sometimes, Thomas suspected, he used a word wrong deliberately, just so he could correct him. Then Father would turn to his friend with a look of wonder, as much as to say: Would you just look a-there! You and me, Joe, have been using that word wrong all our fool lives, and would be still if it wasn't for this boy of mine. He would say, "There. What did I tell you? I declare, Joe, this boy'll educate me yet."

When Father was eleven years old—and a little backward maybe, for even then he was only in low third, a big gangling boy and always in trouble, to hear him tell it—though Mother said he laid that on somewhat—he was taken out of school and put to work where there was cotton to hoe, sorghum to cut, and wood to chop.

Thomas would have advantages, a headstart such as Father never had. Thomas knew very well how lucky he was; it was nice to visit the country, but what a wonderfully lucky thing that he had been born in town! His birthday came on June the eighteenth. One day more, they told him when he was little, and he would have been born black, for that was Emancipation Day. That was silly, of course, but the feeling he once got whenever they told him that was like the feeling that came over him when he thought what a lucky accident it was that he had been born in town.

Grandmother was just the other way. When she came up to town once every year or two, it was hard to get her to stay even overnight. "Don't coax me, Harriet," she would say peevishly, "I know very well I don't belong here and you don't need to worry that I'm going to stay very long." She would not wear the clothes Mother sent her for just that trip, but came in her country bonnet and her shoes with the left one slit for her bunion. And each such visit was her last. Never again, she would tell Thomas time after time through the summer he spent with her. She was going to sit right under the grape arbor where she belonged. Those that wanted to see her, if anyone did, could come out here, where she wouldn't be any embarrassment to them.

He would certainly come, Thomas said.

"Why?" she demanded. "To keep me from coming to your place?"

But she was not really as cross as she sounded. He knew, for Uncle Ben would wink at him when she got going like that, to remind him that that was just her way.

Uncle Ben made little boxes for Grandmother to cover with quilting and tassels and braid, making footstools one after another as she sat in her rocker in the arbor. He brought her milk bottles that she covered with plaster and into that set pretty stones and sea shells and bits of colored glass. He collected tin cans for the thing she liked best of all to do—cut the sides halfway down into thin shreds that curled up and made a ruff collar around the top. Wrapped with crepe paper and tied with ribbon, they made the prettiest flower pots. When Ben was too busy to find things for her she sent Thomas out to scout for snuff boxes that she decorated for holding collar buttons, though nobody used collar buttons any more. People who came to visit brought things for her that no one else, they said, could find any earthly use for, but that she would know how to make something pretty of.

Uncle Ben had an old car, but when his stay was up Thomas liked to be taken home in the buckboard. His things would be all packed in, Uncle Ben would climb up on the seat, Grandmother would kiss him and Grandfather shake his hand, then at the last minute Grandmother would make up her mind to send some little thing for Harriet. Thomas and the two men would wait while she went into the house, and all three were embarrassed. She would come back loaded down; she had so many and she had been unable to decide between three or four.

Riding in, Thomas held the reins while Uncle Ben enjoyed his tobacco. He chewed. And sometimes he spat long streams of juice, which was disgusting enough, but most of the time he swallowed it. Around ladies, to be polite, he swallowed. But around Harriet he never chewed at all, so as soon as they came in sight of Thomas's house he would clear his throat and spit out his wad and wipe his mouth. Then, reaching behind him, he would cover over Grandmother's gifts with a towsack or a tarpaulin. He pretended not to be doing anything and Thomas pretended not to notice, for they both knew that Mother always threw those things right out.

Wasn't that Katherine Spence? It was. She had left her car and was coming over to chat until the children were let out. Harriet found her left shoe under the clutch pedal and forced it on. She fluffed out her hair and gave Katherine just two minutes to work her way around to Our Walter. Had she told what our Walter came out with the other day? Did your Thomas ever do what our Walter did last week?

Harriet smiled. Didn't it go to prove something, the way women were always coming to her to talk about their children? It reminded her of an old colored woman who used to sit up on her front porch and explain the meaning of their dreams to darkies that came to her from miles around. For Katherine was only one of many. Harriet had noticed how the bridge women, and before them the forty-two club women, could talk among themselves about other things, but turning to her they invariably got off on the subject of children. She could not help feeling they wanted to check and see how theirs were coming along compared to Thomas Erskine at a certain age.

Katherine Spence came and stood with her foot on the running board, chatting away and trying to be carefree, but really nervous and hot and tired. The poor thing was Harriet's own age and looked five years older.

"Harriet," she said, interrupting herself in the middle of something to which she herself was not paying any attention, "I don't know how you manage to always look so cool and collected. All I can say is, you're lucky you don't have three of them." Which was her way of saying she felt lucky that she did. Katherine was known to think that having had three children showed she had been well able to afford them.

Katherine Spence was from a good old family, long settled in town. And here she was now, envying Harriet for being so cool and collected. Who could have predicted it, to see them when they were in grammar school together, where Katherine was one of the cruel little town girls, all cool and prim and sweet-smelling in their stiff Kate Greenaways, that grimy little Harriet Purdy wanted so much to be like? Harriet began to feel rather warm toward Katherine. To ask after her children gave her a charitable glow. Were they looking forward to vacations? Mercy yes, *they* were—but as for herself—

How awful, how guilty it must make you feel, thought Harriet, to know that you would feel relieved to be rid of your children for the summer. She said, "Well, if Thomas was like other children so you could get his nose out of a book once in a while and send him out to run and play, then I wouldn't let him go to the country for the summer. But he always comes back looking so good, it seems selfish of me not to want him to go." She smiled at the sight of him in her mind, so fresh and rosy and filled-out.

"Well," Katherine sighed, "all I can say is, you're lucky to have a place to send him and know he's safe without worrying every minute."

Without worrying! As if she would get a wink of sleep all summer! All she had been able to think about lying awake at night for the last two weeks was all the terrible accidents she'd seen happen to her brothers when they were boys. She would never have said such a thing, of course, and even to think it seemed wrong, but that did not keep her from feeling that Katherine, nor any other woman, did not know what it was to worry over a child!

Harriet was pleased when Katherine Spence left. She soon

grew tired of listening to women talk about their children. She found it hard to follow, never having in mind a very clear picture of their children. That was because to think of children automatically got her mind on Thomas.

At seven months he had talked. Immediately he knew eleven words and from the very first there was never a baby flavor to his speech. Often as Harriet called that to mind, it never failed to surprise and please her. The reason for it was, she had never spoken baby talk to him and never allowed anyone else to, so much as a word. At eight months and three days he said, "Oh, look at the dog."

What a shame it was, thought Harriet for the hundredth time, that the classes were attuned not to the quickest, but to the very slowest pupils.

At last the doors were opened and the children tumbled out. How loud and rough they were! Harriet hardly saw them, but looked over them, around, and through them impatiently. Then, there he was! Each time she saw him was a surprise. He is mine, she told herself; I am responsible for him. But she felt she would never get quite used to the idea.

He walked down the steps with his shoulders square, very dignified and grown-up. Before long he would be changing to knickers, then long pants before you knew it. He did look sweet in short pants, his knees were never scuffed, his stockings never sagged.

The compliments she had had on him would fill a mail-order catalog. His fine nose, his high clear forehead and long lashes were like no one else's in her family, thank goodness, and certainly not like anyone's in his father's. He was fair, almost pale. Not sickly-looking, but not a big freckle-faced bumpkin. He never had a cowlick. Everybody wondered how she kept his hair always so neat. In fact, in every way he was something to wonder over. In fact, thought Harriet, he was the absolute despair of every other mother in town.

Thomas said, "Miss Carpenter wants to see us both in her office."

Miss Carpenter's office was a dark room with a wall map and an old globe. It was a room which once held terrors for Harriet and it gave her a funny feeling now. She was amazed how little it had changed since the day she came there to tell old Miss Briggs that she was being taken out of school. Harriet had been through four grades, which was four more than anybody else in the whole connection, her father said, and as many as he could afford. She had expected Miss Briggs to see how cruel that was and to say that she would speak to her father. She had broken down and sobbed. And then Miss Briggs had said, in what she meant to be a soothing tone, "Well, Harriet dear, I guess it *is* enough, really, for living on a farm." She wished it was Miss Briggs sitting there now so she could see the change in things.

"Mrs. Erskine," said Miss Carpenter, "I, and Thomas's other teachers, have been watching him closely this year, and we feel that he is decidedly in advance of his class."

Harriet sat quietly and tried to look solemn. But she had to grin. The next minute she felt a pang of disappointment that no one else was there to hear.

Miss Carpenter brought out her roll book. "Erskine, Thomas," she read. "Class response—at random: 99, 98, 97, 99, 96, 98."

Miss Carpenter never gave 100's, Harriet reflected. No one was perfect, she maintained.

"Music 96, Geography 98, English 98—but you know all this, of course," said Miss Carpenter, and Harriet nodded, though she would not have minded hearing more of them read out. Miss Carpenter closed the book. "So we feel, Mrs. Erskine, that with your permission—for we don't want you to feel we're rushing him —we might give Thomas a try at high fifth next year."

From now on, Harriet sat thinking, he would do three semesters in every two. Think how young he would be to enter college!

"Well, how do you feel about this, Thomas?" she said.

He was thinking back through the year, trying to find what he had done to deserve this. He had studied every night and raised his hand for every question. But he had done all that before, too, and not been double-promoted. What more could he do to be sure of getting double-promoted again next year?

"Perhaps," said Miss Carpenter kindly, "perhaps Thomas feels sad at the thought of leaving all his little friends behind."

Tommy smiled faintly. Harriet smiled broadly, delighted with the thought of his leaving them behind.

"Well," said Harriet, "Thomas will soon make new friends in high fifth."

"Then it's all settled," said Miss Carpenter rising.

She asked them to wait one moment. She lifted the wall map that hung in front of a bookcase. She fitted her glasses and peered into the dark shelves until she found the book she wanted and brought it out, blowing dust off it.

"Here," she said to Thomas, "something to keep you busy for a while." For Miss Carpenter barely tolerated summer, a season of laziness good only for making children forget all that she had taught them the year before.

Walking down the quiet halls Thomas thought how neither his father nor his mother had ever got as far in school as he was now. He could understand Harriet's pride in him. But he wished she wouldn't show it so plainly. It was not modest and it was not refined. He hoped she was not going to make too much over this in front of other people. Whenever she did that it made him embarrassed for her and angry, afraid that people thought he enjoyed being shown off. For her to make so much over it seemed to reveal that she herself had never had much schooling.

One minute Harriet was glad that no one else knew about this, so she could have all the pleasure of telling it, and the next minute it seemed impossible that the news was not already all over town.

As they reached the steps she threw back her head and laughed. "Just wait till I tell Jessie!" she cried. "Can't you just see the look on her face!"

To Thomas this sounded exactly like the sort of thing Aunt Jessie herself might have said, and a tremor of shame ran through him.

Harriet thought of the letter she would write her family. She could see her mother and father and Ben and all the rest of them sitting, reading it aloud, growing madder by the minute, until one of them said, "Well, you know Harriet. She would say anything in the world just to be different from the rest of us."

"I guess you're mighty proud of yourself, aren't you?" she said, feeling actually that he did not seem nearly as proud as he ought. "Why, when I was a little girl," she said, and her voice began trailing, growing far away and sad, as it did whenever she spoke of her childhood.

They passed the lonely seesaws and the swings hanging deadened and stiff. Down at the far corner of the playground, leaning against a slide, the Hazeltines sat waiting for somebody to come get them, chewing on their peanut butter sandwiches, watching the cars go by.

"Why, when I was a little girl," she said, "if I'd got double-promoted, why, I'd have been so proud of myself nobody could have come near me."

The Fauve

MR. EMMONS the butcher no longer smiled or shook his head in sympathy, and certainly he never brought down his price on anything when Rachel Ruggles said, "Oh, dear . . ."

It embarrassed Rachel to have to sigh over the prices of things. She dreamed of a time when she would be able simply to pay what was asked for things. But each time she went shopping she found prices a little higher.

Mr. Emmons shifted from foot to foot while Rachel stood looking at the meats in the counter. It took her a long while, not to choose, but to resign herself to another week of lung stew.

While Mr. Emmons wrapped her order Rachel allowed herself to gaze at the lamb chops. James craved lamb chops. So, although lamb chops had been beyond their means for years, Rachel felt sad each time the price of them went up. And the more expensive they became the more she admired James for his expensive tastes.

From Emmons' Market Rachel went down the street to the Universal Union store.

For years Rachel had wished for a supermarket in Redmond. When the baker first quit giving baker's dozens, when the butcher began charging for marrow bones, she sighed, "If only there were a supermarket in town." Finally a Universal Union was built. Rachel had been astonished to find that the prices there were still more than she could afford.

But hope was always strong in Rachel. Before each shopping trip she convinced herself that this time she would find prices within her budget. Then she would come upon soup which had been nine cents a can last week and now was eleven. Other women begged her pardon, reached around her and took two, three, four cans of soup while she hesitated. Sometimes she felt she was the only woman in the world who had to watch her pennies.

Today, however, at the Universal Union Rachel found day-old bread at half-price, a one-cent sale on soap, and a special on sugar—so many bargains that she decided to buy some little treat for James. He loved artichokes. She picked out two. As the clerk was putting them into a bag she said:

"Oh, wait. That one is bruised."

The clerk said, "I'll get you another instead."

"I suppose part of it is all right," she hinted. "If I just took off the top leaves."

The clerk said nothing. He stood waiting. She was about to suggest he let her have it for half-price. Suddenly she imagined James watching her. She said hurriedly, "Never mind. Just give me the good one."

The clerk shrugged his shoulders. Rachel took the bag, wondering what she was going to do with one artichoke. The clerk picked up the bad one, looked at it, then, as Rachel was turning away, tossed it into the wastebasket.

Rachel almost gasped. A perfectly good artichoke! Her next thought was of James. What if he knew she had haggled over something for him which a clerk considered fit for the trash!

Standing there, Rachel could not help thinking that if she asked him, the clerk would probably give her that artichoke. James need never know. It was selfish of her to rob him of such pleasure merely to spare herself a little embarrassment.

Rachel shook her head to get such thoughts out of her mind, and wheeled away her carriage to put herself out of range of temptation. She shuddered to think of serving James that artichoke, and him finding out. And she was convinced that with his fine taste he would know. She was even afraid he would be able to tell that she had had these thoughts.

But Rachel could not worry or remain unhappy for long. She walked down the street enjoying the air and the early sunlight, and even seeing onions cheaper than she had just paid could not put her out of humor.

Many of the shops were just opening. The blinds went up in the bakery and the door was opened to let the smell of fresh bread settle heavily on the street. Mrs. Burton, her hair in curlers, leaned out of the window of her apartment over the variety store and shook the breakfast crumbs out of a red-checked tablecloth. On the sidewalk in front of the hardware store the clerk was setting out spades and turning forks and flats of pale tomato plants. The sun moved from behind the spire of the church and lighted the new glass onyx front of the drugstore, and the china, the milk glass, and the brassware in the window of the antique shop.

Suddenly from around a corner rolled a truck loaded with men in overalls. It pulled up in front of the old Redmond Inn. The men piled out and began unloading tool kits, while a fat man from the cab of the truck stood surveying the building with his hands on his hips. The men rummaged in their kits and came up with hammers, chisels and wrecking bars.

A young man shinnied up a porch pole to the weather-beaten sign of the Inn, and motioning those below aside, raised his hammer. But the sound of a blow was heard while his hammer was still poised. The men turned to look up the street. The crew hired to demolish the old Putnam Tavern had beaten them to the job this morning.

Soon, thought Rachel, all the old landmarks would be known only in pictures. In the early days there had been so many things in Redmond to paint. That was why it had been chosen as a colony. One of the most popular subjects was the Inn. James was perhaps the only painter in town who had never done a picture of it. Among the artists the saying was, you can alway sell a picture of the Inn. Rachel herself had painted it many times. It was ironical that all those pictures of the Inn and the Tavern and the old mill had brought so much money to Redmond that now it had no room for old unprofitable buildings and was tearing them down two or three at a time to make way for movie houses and tea rooms and ski-supply stores. It was becoming hard for Rachel to remember Redmond as it looked when she first came. And according to James a great deal of the charm was gone already when she got there.

"Good morning, Rachel."

"Oh, good morning, John."

"Fine morning."

"It certainly is. How are Mary and the children?"

"Fine, thanks. Just fine."

Rachel had not gone five steps when she recalled that she was not supposed to be friendly with John Daniels. What a nerve he had, saying Mary was fine! What could one trust? Rachel asked herself. John Daniels was known as a great family man—and all those years he had been beating his wife every Saturday night! Oh, it seemed that every day one discovered fresh wickedness in the world. And what she knew was only a fraction, even, of what went on in Redmond, for James protected her from the knowledge of so much more. It was for her peace of mind that he never told her about John Daniels until last week, though he had known it for years. James was so considerate. I, too, Rachel told herself, might have got a man who beat me. The more she lived and the more she saw of the world, the more sure she was that hers was the best man alive.

"Rachel, you're looking mighty cheerful this morning." It was Martha Phillips.

"Martha!" cried Rachel. "Just the person I was hoping to see. I've been dying to tell you what happened with James and me the other day."

"Don't tell me you've left him," said Martha.

"Martha!" said Rachel. "Now what I wanted to tell you was about a little misunderstanding we had the day before yesterday. It was in the morning. Then . . ."

"You're welcome to come to my place, Rachel. I've got an extra . . ."

"Wait, let me finish. It was nothing important, you understand."

"Well," said Martha, "just remember, if he ever . . ."

"Let me finish, Martha. Listen. I don't even remember what we
disagreed over. The important thing is what happened in the
afternoon. James said he knew he had been short-tempered with
me lately, and asked me to forgive him. 'Don't say I haven't,' he
said, 'because I know I have.' And he said that now at last he
could tell me the reason."

Rachel paused to get her breath, then emphasizing each word,
"He said that for the last six months he had been tormented with
the fear that he loved another woman!"

"What!" cried Martha. "Who?"

"Wait, wait. Then he said, 'Well, I know better now. I thought I
was in love with Jane Borden,' he said, 'but now I realize it was
only her money I was in love with.' "

"Ah-hah," said Martha. "And now that all of a sudden she
hasn't got any any more he knows it wasn't love."

"Oh, Martha, imagine him living in that torment all that time!
Not knowing how he felt, doubting himself at every turn, not
wanting to hurt me." Rachel's eyes moistened, she was silent for a
moment, then she sighed, "And when I think how it is with some
couples."

"You have," asked Martha, "some particular couple in mind?"

"Martha, would you ever think to look at him that every Saturday night for the last ten years John Daniels has beaten Mary!"

"What! John Daniels! Oh, Lord! Who ever told you that one?"
cried Martha. "Why, if anything, Mary beats him!"

Rachel was confused. She changed the subject. She said,
"Martha, I've got a little laugh on James. I didn't tell him, you
understand, but I hadn't noticed he was being short-tempered
with me lately. Had you, Martha?"

"Oh, Rachel, Rachel," Martha laughed, and went off down the
street shaking her head.

Rachel liked to spread her shopping over all the stores in town.
It made her feel she was buying more. She spent ten cents here,
twenty-five there, and thought that in so doing she kept a good

name with each merchant. It was eleven o'clock by the time she finished. She started home.

Rounding the curve in Main Street she was delighted to see James strolling into town. His migraine must have passed. She set down her packages and waved to him. He came on at the same pace. He sparkled in the sunshine, with his pink cheeks and his orange curls. "James Finley Ruggles," said Rachel to herself.

He was a big man with a slow stride. He wore red mustaches trained into a cheerful twirl. His tweed jacket was ancient; fuzzy and gray, it seemed to have sprouted a mold. The sleeves came down no further because they had grown frayed and been turned back more than once. His trousers had once been some other color, now they were more pale pink than anything else. Too short, they revealed Argyle socks of red and yellow.

Gathering up her packages, Rachel hastened to meet him.

"James," she called, "I got an artichoke," and fumbling in the bag as she walked, she found it and brought it out and bore it before her. "See?"

"I never knew you liked them," said James.

She came to a stop. "It's for you."

"*All* of it?"

Rachel looked at it. It seemed to shrink.

"With lung stew?" said James, clearing his throat.

She had not thought of that. She looked again at the artichoke. Then she found James smiling tolerantly at her, as though having asked himself how she could be expected to know any better.

She did not say how glad she was to see him up. James never liked to have it observed that he had got over an illness. Rachel was pleased with herself for having discovered this little quirk of his. She had a little hoard of such insights. She admired him for being complicated.

James said there was a meeting of the Artists' Association, and set off. Rachel hitched up her packages and followed, taking two steps to his one.

Rachel thought that when they walked together they made quite a handsome pair. She thought she set James off well. She was dark as he was fair. Her eyes, set in slanted lids, were as intensely black as his were blue. Her hair, glossy black and straight, parted in the middle and gathered into a heavy bun, was the perfect complement to his mass of orange ringlets. It was with an eye to James's clothes that she had made her low-cut flowing peasant blouse with its rich embroidery, and her long skirt of thick blue flannel.

As she walked Rachel was trying to think of someone to talk to James about. He had standards so high that few people could come up to them. Rachel was aware that she had no standards at all; but for James she would have let herself like just anybody. So she mentioned names to him, hoping always to have luckily hit upon a person really worthy. She said cheerfully, "I saw Martha Phillips this morning, James."

He sighed. "Drunk as usual, I suppose."

"Drunk?" cried Rachel. "Why, I never knew Martha drank. Martha Phillips, James?"

"Phillips, yes. That's what she calls herself now."

"Now? What do you mean 'now'? Why, I've known Martha Phillips for . . ."

"Yes—many people have known Martha. Many people—and many places."

"Martha *Phillips*, James? Why . . ."

"Well," he said, "you've got to give the old girl credit. She's managed to keep her many lives pretty well apart all these years. Not many people know about that old Mexico City business."

"Many lives?" gasped Rachel. "Old Mexico City business? Why, James, you simply take my breath away."

"So what did she have to say?" asked James. "If it's fit to repeat."

"You've got me so confused I can't remember. But she laughed when I told her about John Daniels."

"One is bound to laugh, Rachel, at anything about John Daniels. Exactly what do you mean?"

"Why, Martha said if anything Mary beats him."

"You didn't know that?" asked James.

"But, James," she cried. Her head was reeling. "You told me . . ."

"Why, on Saturday nights you can hear them all over town. She ties him to a bedpost and beats him with a coathanger and shouts filthy names at him while he cries, 'Harder! Harder!' "

Rachel stood shaking her head and gasping.

"If she didn't satisfy him that way," said James, "God knows what he'd be out doing."

"Really, James?" said Rachel. "*Really?*"

James sighed. "Rachel," he said, "do you have to believe every word I say?"

"You mean it isn't true?"

"Of course it's true," he said.

They walked on, Rachel still trying to think of someone worth mentioning to him, but afraid to mention anyone now.

James was thinking about himself. He pictured himself walking into the Artists' Association meeting. During the three months between these meetings he saw little of the other artists in town. Since the last one many things had happened. David Peterson had won five thousand dollars at the Carnegie International. The Cleveland Museum had paid two thousand dollars for one of Carl Robbins's watercolors. Most everyone had had exhibitions.

The faces of the people he was about to see came into his mind, and as they did he seated them one by one around a banquet table. It was a surprise party. On the walls of the room his pictures were hung in thick gold frames. A toast was proposed. To James Finley Ruggles! Everyone drank. Then the table fell quiet. A page boy entered and approached James, bearing a tray on which lay a book. The title was *James Finley Ruggles: A Tribute.* He looked around the table, remembering the struggle he had had, the years of working and waiting. Yet he felt no rancor toward these men, each of whom had been so slow in recognizing his superiority. A lump came into his throat. "Open it!" a shout went up. He read the table of contents: "My friend Jim Ruggles" by Pablo Picasso; "To JFR from H. Matisse: Greetings"; "James Finley Ruggles, the First Thirty Years" by the Staff of the Museum of Modern Art; "Ruggles and Cézanne" by Sheldon Cheney. . . .

In the book was a biographical sketch.

James Finley Ruggles, the fourth to bear that name, was born in Wellfleet, Massachusetts, on the night of September 22, 1904.

The doctor gave no hope for him. The nurse, not so easily discouraged, blew into the infant's lungs time after time. That nurse blew the breath of life into American painting.

The Finleys were descended from a charter member of the Harvard Corporation. They were a family of doctors and brokers, shippers and tea importers. General Isaiah Ruggles was with Washington at Valley Forge.

To the public school teachers of Wellfleet the future artist seemed backward. He drew pictures on the pages of his arithmetic text. Plate 10 is a copy of a Raphael drawing that Ruggles made at the age of eight.

His was the classic story of the misunderstood artist. His father insisted that he enter the family insurance firm, badly in need of new blood. James was sent to Bowdoin, where all the Ruggles had been educated.

His legacy upon the death of his father in 1925, though not as large as he had expected, was enough to take him to Paris, where he studied for two years.

Upon returning to this country he lived for a while in New York, then went to join the artists' colony at Redmond. There he entered upon his Modified Fauve period, producing his first major works.

In Redmond, fame and money came to the third-rate all about him while Ruggles struggled against poverty and neglect. The epoch-making *Still Life with Pineapple* was rejected by every major exhibition jury in the country. But though accustomed to ceremony and tradition, to ease and gracious living, Ruggles bore his poverty lightly. A gay and colorful figure, he brought to Redmond the charm and gallantry and the cultivation of his aristocratic background. His wit was legendary and—

"James," said Rachel, "where are you going? Here we are."

His wife Rachel, née Ravich, was the eighth child of Solomon and Sarah Ravich, of Delancey Street and Brownsville, Brooklyn.

The doors of the meeting hall were not yet open, so everyone was gathered in the gallery lounge to chat. A heavy layer of smoke hanging just above their heads rocked lazily each time the door was opened. People drifted from one group to another as though they, too, were stirred by the wind from the door. The talk rose and fell.

How fat they were all becoming, thought James, how bourgeois. The men in double-breasted suits and suede shoes, the women with Florida suntans gave it the look of a convention of fashion buyers.

The Ruggles stood while James singled out someone to approach. An aisle fell open revealing David Peterson at the end of the room. But before they could reach him they were stopped by Mary McCoy.

"Mary, you've done something to your hair," said James. She certainly had, and Rachel was alarmed at his drawing attention to it. "You always did have the prettiest head of hair in town, and now it's even nicer."

The truth was, her hair was probably the least attractive of poor Mary's features. It was James's way with women always to flatter them where they most needed it. No harm was done if, on the side, it amused him to do it.

"It's a regular rat's nest," said Mary.

"Well, of course," said James, "you may be right. I'm no expert," and having spied an opening to Douglas Fraleigh he left her to regret not leaving well enough alone. When he offered to flatter someone he did not like her to try to draw more out of him. Besides, he really enjoyed flattering only people who did not need it, who were indifferent to flattery.

Douglas Fraleigh finished the story he was telling and left his listeners to laugh while he turned. "Oh, hello, Ruggles," he said.

"That's a nice suit," said James.

Fraleigh thanked him, making little effort to suppress a smile over James's garb. But it was lost on James. He was fascinated by Fraleigh's suit. He reached out his hand and Fraleigh suffered him to finger the cloth of the lapel. It was soft, dark flannel, glowing brown with a tasteful light stripe. The sight and feel of fine cloth brought to James's eyes a glossy, vacant look. As he fingered it he could feel the cloth upon his own skin. He was born for soft, luxurious fabrics.

There came to his mind the image of himself in the rags in which he stood. James had suffered at being Bohemian when everyone in Redmond was. Now that he was the only one he suffered intensely.

Douglas Fraleigh gave a twitch, a cough. James recovered himself to see one of Fraleigh's knees twitching with impatience inside his trousers. There was a tolerant, bemused smile on Fraleigh's lips.

James drew himself up, proud of his rags. He had known the best. He would rather know the worst than this tawdry in-between. Thank God he didn't look like Fraleigh and the rest of these parvenus! He promised himself to dress even more outrageously from now on. He was the only one in the room you would have known for an artist. And what suits he would have someday! So tasteful, of such elegant simplicity.

"Nice," he said with a gesture at Fraleigh's suit. "Just be careful not to let it get wet."

James drifted about. Time was running out and here he had alienated somebody, when he had meant to do just the opposite. He could not settle on the one person most worth his efforts.

It was growing hot in the room and the restraint wearing off. The little groups were dissolving, melting together, and the conversation becoming general. It took a while for these people to warm up to each other. No doubt they had all known each other too well in their days of communal poverty and Bohemianism. More than one was resentful that to those close to him he was not as legendary as he had become to the world at large.

They had had too many things in common ever to trust one another. Too many women, for example, such as Bertha Wallace. Bertha had posed for them all, and been the mistress of many of them. She was still far from unattractive. But Bertha was resentful of the men who had painted all those famous pictures of her, and who wanted to paint her no longer. Now that the Redmond Inn was being torn down she needed a place to live. She felt it was up to the painters she had helped make famous to find one for her. She must have been drinking heavily all morning and now as she circulated among them she had worked herself up into the conviction, never far from her at any time, that they owed her not only a roof but a living as well. "Where would you be," she demanded of Carl Robbins, hanging on to his lapel and thrusting her face up into his, "I'd just like to know where you'd be if it wasn't for *Portrait of Bertha, Bertha in a Yellow Gown, Bertha Reclining*"?

"You're right, Bertha, you're right," Carl Robbins tried to quiet her. He looked about him for help, and all the men who owed Bertha just as much, or as little, as he did, turned away and became suddenly absorbed in their conversations.

James found himself being vigorously shaken by the hand of Sam Morris.

Morris was the town doctor. But he refused to let anyone call him Doctor. "The name is plain Sam," he insisted. When Morris came to Redmond a few years back he painted only on Sundays. Now, the joke went, he was a Sunday doctor. At first a timid man, impressed into silence by his slavish respect for the artists, he had grown more and more talkative until now he started babbling the minute he stepped up and never let the other person say a word. He had been brought to this by one of the great disillusionments of his life. He had read all the great critics, subscribed to all the art magazines and read each from cover to cover, knew more about the history of Impressionism than any man alive—only to find that the artists never mentioned these things, but insisted on telling him of their migraines, the traces of albumen in their urine, their varicose veins. Now he had come to be suspicious that when they praised his painting they were only working their way around to wheedling some medical advice.

No one praised his art more extravagantly than James Ruggles, nor did Ruggles ever seem to have an ache or a pain. His other reason for liking Ruggles was that he *looked* like an artist.

"You're busy I know," he said, "but you must take just an hour someday to let me show you what I've been doing lately. I flatter myself that my late work is not without some sign of your influence. It's in the way you handle three-dimensionality."

As he talked he kept admiring James's clothes with one eye. One could tell he was thinking that but for his wife he, too, would let himself go like that, be really unconventional, really look like an artist. James could not help feeling somewhat flattered, but not enough to overcome his annoyance. James hated anyone who painted, but he hated more someone who spent only part-time at it. Moreover, he considered it a pitiful spectacle, a man who was a member of a solid respectable profession taking up painting.

When Morris finally left him the first person James saw was Max Aronson. Aronson stood to one side, neglected, a sad-faced, nervous little man with his hands to his mouth, gnawing a fingernail. He beamed when he saw James approaching.

"That was quite a spread you got in *Life*, Max," said James.

"Did you like it? The color reproductions were good, didn't you think?"

James said he thought they were.

"You really liked it, then?"

This little man, one of the most famous painters in the country, did not distinguish among the people who praised him. He lived on praise. Now, praise was the thing that came easiest to James Ruggles's lips. He liked to be amiable that way. But he thought everybody understood that it was to be taken for amiability and nothing more. To find somebody taking his flattery seriously shocked him. He was not giving out art criticism when he praised you. He was being a likable fellow.

"You really liked it, huh, James?" Max implored. "Tell me the truth now. I'd like to know what you really think."

James could not bear the sight of such naked hunger for praise. "I liked it," he said, tugging at his mustache. "You understand, of course, that I'd say so whether I thought it or not."

Max laughed, trying to make a joke of it.

The doors of the meeting hall were thrown open.

Scanning the room, James found the seat next to David Peterson empty. He grabbed Rachel's arm, and apologizing in advance as he pushed people aside, elbowed his way down the aisle. A man was just stepping into the row where Peterson sat. James got behind Rachel and shoved her into the man. Rachel blushed and began stammering apologies. The man glared, then gave a strained smile and stepped aside to let her enter. She started to, but James laid a hand on her arm. With a smile at the gentleman and a nod of thanks, he went in first and walked serenely down to the seat beside Peterson. Rachel followed, upsetting the hats of the ladies in the next row down as she smiled apologies back to the gentleman on the aisle.

"Dave!" cried James. "I thought it was you. Well, this is luck. Hello! Haven't seen you since the big news. Congratulations." He nudged Rachel.

"Yes! Congratulations!" she said.

"Yes, indeed," said James. "The Carnegie International! How does it feel to be world-famous?"

Peterson wound his watch, smiled uncomfortably and crossed and recrossed his legs, trying, as James knew, to keep his eyes off James for fear of bringing attention to his clothes.

"It must have come like a bolt from the blue," James went on, growing louder.

Peterson smiled agreeably. But he did not think it had come quite that unexpectedly, to him or to the world.

"Well, well, well," said James. "Old David Peterson! And I knew him when. Who would ever have thought it?"

People were beginning to turn to look. Peterson grew still more uncomfortable.

"I suppose the money's spent by now," said James. He gave a hearty laugh that made Peterson squirm. "That's not a question," he added hurriedly. "I'm not prying." He slapped Peterson's knee. "But you understand that, of course, Dave." He was sickening himself with his loud, back-slapping familiarity. "Well, all things come to him who waits."

Peterson obviously felt that he had hardly waited all *that* long. He was not so old. "How has your work been coming, James?" he asked.

"Oh! Don't ask after *my* work!"

"Don't be modest," said Peterson. "I'm sure you've been doing fine work, as always."

This was sincere. David Peterson had always admired James Ruggles' painting, and had put in a good word for it in places where he knew it could never be popular, even in places where he was not likely to make himself more popular by praising it. But James would never know that. James did not mind giving praise, but he hated to receive it. It never occurred to him that praise could be sincere.

He smiled, but such a savage smile that Peterson drew back,

wounded. He felt he deserved some credit for being one of the very few men in Redmond who appreciated James's work.

"It must be hard now," said James, "for you to remember the days when we . . ."

David Peterson remembered all too well the days when he resembled James Ruggles. He did not like to be reminded and he curled his lips to say something cutting. Then he felt ashamed. He had risen and he had a lot to be thankful for. His face relaxed. James followed all these feelings of Peterson's and he foresaw his next. The man was about to take pity on him, to offer to pull strings. James began to twitch. He stuttered, trying to find something to say quickly. "Well, how's—ah!—hmm—well, where are you— Oh! there's the chairman!" he almost shouted, and breathed a sigh of relief.

The chairman pounded the table with his gavel and when the crowd became quiet he announced that a letter had been received from the trustees of the Walter Fielding estate offering to the Redmond Gallery a fund of three thousand dollars annually to be awarded to the winners of the Redmond Exhibition.

There had never been any selection of winners in the annual exhibition. It had been simply a time to show one's work, with no jury, no prizes, no awards. The rule of the Gallery from the day of its founding had been to show everything. Anyone who lived in Redmond and who had ever painted a picture could hang it in the annual exhibition.

Now, if the Redmond Gallery wanted to accept the fund from the Fielding estate a jury would have to be chosen. It should have been done long ago, said the chairman. For, said he, the Redmond Gallery had come to have a responsibility to the country, indeed, to the world, and could not afford to hang pictures that brought laughter and ridicule to it. He threw the matter open to the floor. Two or three men got up to voice their approval. Someone put it in the form of a motion. It was quickly seconded.

"Further discussion?" asked the chairman.

"Mr. Chairman." This voice was deeper, more authoritative than the others. Everyone turned. James was on his feet, his arms folded across his chest. The chairman's eyes grew wide with apprehension. An embarrassed silence fell on the audience and people looked avertedly at one another.

"Mr. Chairman," said James, then turned his gaze upon the crowd. "Friends and fellow artists. At the risk of repeating what many of you have heard me say too often already—" He paused to allow them to chuckle. The silence was intense. "Well, anyway, let me say that it is indeed time that the Redmond Gallery came of age."

A man from the audience tiptoed up to the chairman and drew him close, and as he whispered in his ear they both watched James from the corners of their eyes.

"The walls of this gallery are sacred space," James said. "I have observed with alarm the increasing amount of that space given over in past exhibitions to the work of—well, let us speak frankly —to the 'work' of amateurs and dabblers."

While catching his breath James observed Sam Morris nodding in agreement.

"It begins to seem," said James, "that everyone thinks he is a painter."

The silence was broken by a snigger unmistakably ironical.

"The walls of the Redmond Gallery," James was becoming passionate now, "are being taken over by retired schoolteachers, superannuated bank clerks and unemployed schizophrenics."

He gave a laugh, which fell upon the silence with a dying ring, like a coin dropped on a counter.

"Now I have nothing against these classes of people," he said. "Some of my best friends, you know. But I hardly think their daubs deserve to hang alongside the work of serious painters, men who have given their lives to painting. There must always be room in the Redmond Gallery for painters of different persuasions, but the painters of Redmond have suffered enough laughter and ridicule and indignity by hanging alongside the dabblings of amateurs and neurotics! And so, ladies and gentlemen, I wholeheartedly endorse the recommendation to elect a jury, and I am sure you will all follow me in supporting this much-needed reform."

Conscious of the silence, which he took for a hushed admiration, he closed on a rising note, then lowered his gaze to the audience to receive their smiles of approval. Instead, he saw upon their faces looks of uneasiness, and embarrassment, blank stares. His smile began to give way to confusion. The silence deepened. He brought his eyes to focus upon the faces nearer him. As he stared at them and one by one they turned their eyes from him, his confusion changed to dismay. An impatient coughing, a nervous shuffling of feet, a general stir broke in upon him. His own voice hung in the room, mocking him. "The painters of Redmond have suffered enough laughter and ridicule and indignity." Each word stung him like a lash. He was the one they wanted out! What a fool he had made of himself. He forced himself to face the audience once more. All at once there passed from face to face a frown of indignation. It had come over them that he was to blame for not having sensed their feelings without exposing them to this embarrassment.

Then he suffered the most crushing realization of all. He was not special, a solitary martyr, but only one of many they wanted out. They lumped him with all the undesirables. He raised his elbows and let them fall against his sides. He lowered himself into his chair.

"You were wonderful, James!" Rachel whispered.

When the meeting was over they left quietly and unobserved. A little way outside the Gallery James stopped and turned. "Give me those packages!" he said. "Are you trying to make me look like a fool?" Rachel handed them over and again fell two steps behind. In this way they trudged up Main Street, around the curve and down through town. When they passed the last house Rachel came up and took the packages, fell back two steps, and they walked on home.

The Ruggles had lived in each of the six shanties one passed in going to the one they lived in now. They were built for chicken houses. When the artists began coming to Redmond in the 1920s an enterprising native turned them into homes. Twenty-odd more were scattered in the woods behind the road but only three were inhabited now with any regularity, one by a trapper, one by a hermit and one by the Ruggles. When one house began decaying faster than Rachel could repair it the Ruggles moved to another. They had been living in number seven for about a year.

Whenever they moved Rachel got a bucket of paint and spent weeks prettying the place. To James it seemed she could take pride in anything. She transplanted the rose bush and lined the path to the door with colored stones. She straightened the palings of the fence and gave it a coat of whitewash, while James groaned and begged her to let him enjoy his poverty, his discomfort, instead of trying so vainly to hide it.

On opening the door one was not in the hall or the living room or the kitchen—he was in the house. The bedroom and the studio were meagerly set off with screens; the kitchen and the living room and the dining room flowed into each other. Yet nothing seemed cramped or incongruous or makeshift. One was struck by the repose of the room, the balance of light and dark, the pleasing arrangement of rich colors. Light from the windows was directed to fall upon old-looking, rare-looking things. Softly glowing, suggestive objects rested in the shadow of the corners. It was like stepping inside a Vermeer.

But the Hepplewhite chair was a fake. One had been disturbed by it on first coming in. It was handsome, though, genuine or not, so handsome that one stole further glances at it—whereupon he realized that it was never meant to pass for a Hepplewhite. It was the Ruggles improvement on the Hepplewhite design. Then there was that small hanging glowing on one wall—it turned out to be a scrap of cloth. Still, what beautiful cloth, and who else would have dared hang it there?

When one had decided that nothing was what it seemed he found that the Persian prayer rug hanging on another wall was thick, rich, old but unfaded—genuine. The plates hanging over the mantel, then—were they genuine Spode? And the Steuben glass? But by this time one no longer cared whether the things were authentic. They were real. And the realest thing was the care and taste with which they had been assembled.

Sooner or later, if one strolled about the room, he saw through a back window the outhouse, painted Chinese red, set at the edge of the woods.

It was in that bright red outhouse, ten days after the gallery meeting, that James sat thinking, "What if I were to send a picture of mine—say, *Still Life with Plaster Bust*—to Matisse? One look, and he'd see to it that I didn't stay in Redmond any longer. Or, send one to him and one to Picasso at the same time, and let them fight over the credit for discovering me."

Rachel called him in to lunch.

While he sat at the table waiting to be served he talked half to himself, half aloud. "Of course the man who would really appreciate my work is Matisse. Hmmm. What is there to lose? A package comes from America. He opens it. He is annoyed at my presumption. But he takes one look at the picture. Suppose he didn't like it?" This James asked himself, though he did not believe for a moment that it was possible. "Well, he would send it back." He thought about that for a moment, then decided that he could trust Matisse; he would send it back. "So what is there to lose?"

"Yes, what is there to lose?" asked Rachel. She was beside him, setting a plate of stew before him. "I heard you, James, and I think it's a perfectly wonderful idea. Why didn't you think of it before?"

The light died out of James's eyes. The hand with which he had been reflectively stroking his chin fell and he said, "For Christ's sake, Rachel! How can you be so childish!"

They ate silently. After lunch Rachel thought of a way to cheer him up. She said, "James, why don't we invite the David Petersons over this evening. It's been so long since I've had any company." Rachel always took upon herself any longing for company.

"What!" he roared. "Invite people to this!" He waved an open palm around the room.

Rachel ran to straighten a doily under a lamp, then the lamp shade, then a picture on the wall.

"Oh, Lord!" James moaned.

Rachel darted her eyes around the room, trying to find what else offended him. She stooped and smoothed out the rug, she adjusted a chair.

"Oh, oh, oh," James moaned.

Rachel gave up. She stood in the center of the room, her arms hanging helplessly. James gave her such a look. "You think I'm complaining about your housekeeping!" He rolled his eyes beseechingly. Then he began an elaborate exercise of self-control.

"I must be charitable," he said. "I must keep in mind your background. How could you be expected to know what's wrong here? Even this is better than anything you ever knew. In fact, I expect you think you've risen quite a ways in the world. And indeed you have, you have."

So now, instead of the room, Rachel tried to straighten herself. She smoothed her hips, patted her bosom, her hair.

"Guests!" he cried. "What do you know about entertaining? You'd serve them lung stew, I suppose. But first a *vorspice*—a little *lox* maybe? Jesus! When I think of my Aunt Patience Summerfield! James Russell Lowell called her the most charming hostess in the state of Massachusetts. Not that you ever heard of him. There was a woman who knew how to entertain. What would she say to see me today? No wonder I can't get anywhere in the world! Suppose I ever did make a name for myself—could I invite anyone to this? I don't know where I get the courage to keep trying. Guests! You!"

Rachel's anguish during these harangues was not for herself but for him. She knew how tormented and disheartened he was to make him say these things. She knew James did not care one way or another about Jews. He had invented his anti-Semitism to lacerate himself.

And that was what he was doing as he tried to look scornfully at her black hair and broad cheekbones and slanted eyes. But upon her heavy breasts and wide hips his eyes began to soften, to linger. They came to rest upon her great firm thighs.

"Rachel," he said, and at once all his defenses, his anxieties, his sham fell from him, leaving him frightened, deflated, almost physically smaller, but for a moment relieved, "Rachel, without you what would ever become of me?"

"There, there," she said, rubbing her cheek against his mustache and stroking the nape of his neck, "don't you even think of it."

She helped him unbutton her, then as she unbuttoned him she smiled to think, without any spite or feeling of triumph, that her Jewish looks were just what he loved—it was, despite him, poor dear, his style of beauty.

The slight chill of the room only excited them further.

They were getting into bed when there came a knock at the door. They looked at each other and silently agreed to make no sound. The knock came again. Still they made no sound. The fourth time they gave up.

Only Homer Austin could be that persistent. He knew that the Ruggles were always at home. Besides, only Homer ever came to see them. Only Homer could be sure to be so ill-timed.

Homer's certainty that he would always find them there and that he was always welcome annoyed James. Today it infuriated him. Scantily dressed, he stood at the door with his hands on his hips and demanded, "Who is it?"

"It's me," said the voice; the tone was: Who else?

"Who is me?"

The door opened and Homer peeped in. "I was just passing by . . ."

"On your way to the city dump?"

Homer laughed and came in. Since no one ever seemed glad to see him he did not notice that James was not. He said:

"So the Gallery has expelled you. Art is now the tool of the artist class."

Homer watched eagerly for every sign of the imminent death of art, individual freedom, human values. His mind was filled with anticipations of persecution. He was ready to go underground any day, though with no hope that he would not very soon be caught and shot, or buried in a prison. He bestowed on James Ruggles, as his friend, the distinction of being the second victim after him of the coming totalitarianism. Occasionally this view of him suited James's own mood.

So far as James was concerned, Homer's radicalism, indeed all radicalism, was nothing but a defense. Since Homer couldn't fit into society, he damned sure wasn't going to. But James enjoyed the flow of Homer's political jargon. He did not want to see society done over—the very notion seemed comical to him—but he loved to hear its condition criticized. As James in one of his lucid moments had said, he and Homer ate sour grapes together.

Today, however, James was in no mood to have his misfortunes treated as incidents in a general disaster.

"Of course," said Homer, beginning to relax into his chair and clasping his hands behind his head, "of course you can't blame the men personally. It's the age. They merely manifest the decay of mutual aid and the general vulgarization of taste that has followed the dissolution of the Left."

"Can't blame them personally! Listen," said James, "I'm not so broad-minded as I like to seem. When I think of David Peterson with his Brooks Brothers suits and sturgeon on his table!"

"You can have all that," said Homer. "All you have to do is paint pictures that make you sick at your stomach. Of course, then you get ulcers and your sturgeon doesn't do you any good. You see, in a society like this you're beat any way you turn. Maybe you think David Peterson is a happy man? He'd change places with you in a minute."

"And Carl Robbins," said James. "Did you see that new Buick? I remember him when he didn't have a sole to his shoe. Did you see that Buick?"

"Yes, and someday he'll kill himself in it driving drunk. Not that he won't be better off. Alcoholism, ulcers, hypertension—that's the price you pay. The wages of sin. Or the wages of virtue—they get you either way."

Rachel came in from behind the screen doing her hair into a bun. With a tender look at James, she said she was going down to the mailbox.

"Well," said Homer, "let me tell you . . . ."

"No," said James, "let me tell you." He got up and paced down the room and back. "Do you know why they want to get rid of me? They're afraid. The only reason for hating anybody is because you're afraid of him. And it's not me so much as what I stand for in their minds. They live in terror of anything new. They're afraid of young men coming up."

Suddenly, as he was getting his breath and about to go on, it stole over James that he had been saying that for a good while. He thought of Robbins, Peterson, Fraleigh. He had come to Redmond only a little later than they. It struck him for the first time that they were not much if any older than he; the difference was that they had arrived.

He had to sit. Homer went on talking. For the first time James began assigning the actual dates to the events of his life. He realized that 1919, 1925, even 1937 were no longer just a little while ago, no longer in the last decade. "One of the young Redmond painters," he called himself. It must have been sounding mighty foolish for quite a while now.

Gradually, without the loss of any of its poignance, the humor of it began to appeal to him. He did not mind sounding foolish so long as he was aware of it. In fact, then he enjoyed it.

"As I was saying," he brought himself back. His mustache assumed an amused tilt. "As I was saying, young men have to live, too." He waited for Homer to reveal that he saw the humor in this. Had Homer seen through him at that moment James would have been delighted with him. Homer merely arched his brows and nodded his head wearily. Homer, James decided, still thought of himself as a young man.

The door flew open and Rachel scrambled in. She caught herself up, tried to appear controlled, hoping to spring a surprise, but her excitement was too much for her. Flushed with her secret, she stood trying to build up James's suspense. But she was the one who could not stand the suspense. She thrust a letter at him. "From the Gallery," she gasped.

Hope and suspicion mingled in his face. But Rachel's certainty and enthusiasm decided him. They had changed their minds, were writing to beg his pardon. Phrases from the letter raced already through his mind: "a grievous mistake . . . a hasty faction . . . by no means representative . . . forgive any anxiety . . . an ugly misunderstanding. . . ." He had ripped open the envelope, when he stopped abruptly. He gaped at it. His face went blank, then filled with disgust. He handed the envelope slowly back to Rachel.

She stared fully a minute at it before it began to dawn on her— the letter was addressed to her. Still she could not believe it. She was sure she had read it three or four times coming back from the mailbox; it had read, "James Finley Ruggles." It seemed she had even read the letter it contained, begging James to forgive them. She gave an embarrassed little laugh. She drew out the letter.

She unfolded it and lifted out a narrow strip of yellow paper. "It's a check," she whispered. "For five hundred dollars!"

"Dear Miss Ravich, we take great pleasure in informing you

that your picture *Mother and Child* has won . . ." She stole a glance at James.

He was stunned. The thing he could not grasp was that the time had rolled around for the awarding of the prizes. He had waited, convinced each day that the Gallery Board would appear in a body to tell him that he had been accepted. He had not realized that the time was past for any possibility for that. Of course he had submitted a picture; he had never been able to believe they would really exclude him.

Rachel found herself spun around by her shoulders. "This is wonderful!" cried Homer. There were tears of joy in his eyes. "Rachel, wonderful! I'm so proud of you!"

"Yes," said James in an unsteady voice, "congratulations," and he got up and walked out of the house.

Breakfast the next morning was hardly finished when James said, "I'll do the dishes," though he did not stir from his chair.

"What!" cried Rachel. It was the last thing he might have been expected to say. Not since Rachel had known him had he ever offered to dry a cup. He scorned men who shared their women's work, and Rachel agreed with him.

"I said I'll do the dishes. I'll do all the housework from now on. It's only right. You must paint. You're a success now. You mustn't let your public down."

Rachel winced at every word. He went on, disregarding the plea on her face. "Move my easel and put yours under the north light. And use my brushes. Yours are getting pretty worn down for a famous painter." (They were pretty well worn when he passed them on to her.) "Yes, you'll have no time for housework from now on. If you keep on like this, though, maybe we can have a maid, and let me get a little painting done, just for the sake of amusement."

"I've been thinking," she said timidly, "of giving up painting altogether."

"What!" He was infuriated at her thinking her success hurt him. "Have you gone out of your mind?"

So, although he had no intention of doing the housework, he gave her no peace until she left it off. He sent her in to paint. He squeezed out her colors for her—generous gobs of each, and sat her in front of a canvas of terrifying dimensions. "Now paint!" he commanded.

Of all James Ruggles' irritations the worst had always been the notion of women painting. And more of them were taking it up every day. It was getting so any self-respecting man was ashamed to go in for it.

He went to see how Rachel's picture was coming. The canvas was blank. "You'll never get anywhere that way," he said.

By noon she still had done nothing. He gave her about ten minutes to finish her lunch, insisted that she leave the dishes and sent her back to the studio. By this time his feelings were mixed. He had come to want her to paint. Visions of the money she would bring him filled his mind. He could see himself painting all day on the Riviera, in Mexico, on some tropic island. Her painting was only woman's painting anyway. If it could bring in money for him to do serious painting then he had the laugh.

James Ruggles had strict theories on the proper way for women to paint—if paint they must. There was a time when he began to detect the influence of his own work on Rachel's. He took her to museums and stood her in front of pictures in sweet fuzzy colors of plump girls and pretty children. That, he told her, was the way for her to paint, that was woman's painting. She never doubted him; she was grateful to him for setting her right. He tried now to enjoy the irony of this, but he was forced to admit his vexation.

In the middle of the afternoon he startled her by asking how she meant to spend the money.

She came into the kitchen looking puzzled and pained. "Why, James," she said, "I hadn't thought about it. Of course there are a good many things we need. I thought we might talk it over and decide. I thought we . . ."

"We?"

"Oh, I wish I'd never seen that check!" she cried. "I'll send it back!" she whispered in a shaky voice. "I'll refuse it. We were so happy before it came. Oh, James!"

"Just think of the things you can buy yourself that I never got you," he said. "Vacuum cleaner, electric washer, television set. You could get a Persian lamb coat and look like a real *yenta.*" And he went on like this all afternoon, growing more bitter and outlandish.

As they sat down to supper, "It seems to me," he said, "that this calls for a celebration. We have to throw a party."

Even in her present state of torment, the word "party" could not help but bring a smile to Rachel's lips. The storm was over, she thought; this was his way of making up. But the smile which lingered on his lips, even she could see, was unmistakably sardonic. A shudder of apprehension ran down her spine.

The first guests to arrive were the Sam Morrises. James met them at the door.

"Good evening, James!" Sam shouted.

Just to walk into the Ruggles' house was a delight for Sam Morris. Such unconventional beauty! He stood beaming, inviting his wife to respond to the charm of the place.

Edith Morris made no effort to conceal that she had expected something very different from life as a doctor's wife from what she had got with Sam.

"Good evening, Mr. Ruggles," she said.

A smile began to play in James's mustache. "Just call me Mister Ravich," he said. Rachel was just coming from the bedroom. Her hands flew to her cheeks in horror.

Fortunately more guests arrived at that moment. Rachel led the Morrises away. The new ones whom James greeted were the John Woosters. Whether out of guilt over their share in expelling him from the Gallery, or anxiety to show that they were not among those responsible, they had not dared refuse his invitation. Their discomfort inspired James with cruelty. His way of punishing them was to abase himself before them.

"So very good of you to come," he said. His tone was savagely obsequious. "Do come in," he urged.

By this time Rachel was hurrying to extricate them. When she saw who it was she grew flustered. Faye Wooster was a person she could never see without blushing. Faye used to be a model, and James had told her something simply unheard-of about Faye, something horribly funny, though it was cruel to think so. These thoughts reminded Rachel that she would also see Martha Phillips tonight. How would she manage to greet Martha, knowing all the things she now knew about her? Then there would be Carl Robbins, about whom James had told her recently. How did James manage all that coolness before these people that he knew such scandalous and personal things about?

She came to herself to hear James saying, "And please let us not stand on ceremony. Just call me what everyone will from now on—call me Mister Ravich."

Rachel led them away.

James could not understand himself. For earlier in the day he had come actually to look forward with pleasure to the evening. He had known it would be somewhat painful to him, but he had also admitted to himself that he was lonely, and had resolved to be pleasant. He had even craftily imagined that Rachel's success might open a path to his own recognition.

Rachel flitted among the guests, keeping them talking and laughing. James stayed at the door. The face of each new guest filled him with loathing and anger. Rachel ran to greet each new arrival, but not before James had managed to shout to him that he was to be addressed as Mister Ravich. The room filled and the talk grew louder, louder still as the guests, out of their mounting embarrassment and indignation, tried to drown out his shameless, painful joke. But he managed to make himself heard each time.

Finally he gave up his station at the door to join the party. He came examining the face of each guest, anxious to find one of them revealing that he had come out of pity, or for amusement, or that he was feeling uncomfortable.

But everyone was enjoying himself quite innocently. Sixteen guests had come. The John Woosters clung together, and Mrs. Wooster regarded James with apprehension. Edith Morris had a corner of the divan to herself, much to her satisfaction. But everyone else was gay. The David Petersons had come and James remarked that Dolly had not seen fit to wear her silver fox stole or one of her Paris originals. Max Aronson was there and had lost all his usual nervousness. Max was known to feel that people who had just had good news were happier to see him, being then no longer quite so envious of him. But his joy in someone else's good fortune was as great as in his own, so he hovered over Rachel in a perfect dither of happiness.

Martha Phillips had shown up, bringing with her a visitor, Mrs. Kunitz, who had been better known in Redmond as Muriel Johnson, but who corrected no one's calling her Mrs. Kunitz. For Mrs. Kunitz, then, it was old home week. She once lived next to the Ruggles and never bothered pulling down her shade at night. In those days she always looked as though she had just got up—eyes puffy and ringed, hair blowzy. Obviously it had been meant to show that she was too taken up with her art to bother. She even won some kind of prize, James seemed to recall. She had quite suddenly married Mr. Kunitz, a widower in wholesale groceries, who was in Redmond for a vacation, and a cure, ten years ago. Now she was greatly amused at the distance she had come. It seemed to astound her afresh each moment that people still lived like this, still took seriously the things these people did.

As was his way at gatherings, Carl Robbins had abandoned his wife the moment they came in, and though the room was small he managed to keep a great deal of distance between them. She was pregnant with her third effort to keep Carl at home. The evening had turned off warm, the windows were up and Carl Robbins, like everyone else, was helping himself plentifully to the beer.

Despite himself, James felt beginning to steal over him a warm satisfaction at being a host, having people drink and laugh and enjoy themselves in his house. Rachel's spicy little liver knishes were a great success, they brought tears to Max Aronson's eyes and set him reminiscing over the famous cooks in his family, and when they were gone Rachel suggested games.

Games? Two or three of the guests exchanged significant glances. What were they in for now?

"Or, David," Rachel said, "give some of your impersonations!"

Peterson flushed and looked sheepishly at his wife. Dolly had got him—how many years ago!—to give up making a fool of himself in public. He felt guilty also that it showed how long it was since he had been friendly with the Ruggles. No one had reminded him of his impersonations in years. And yet, he thought, with a look of some defiance at his wife, they were damned clever impersonations. Especially the one of Chaplin (but again, how long ago was Chaplin!) and he was pleased with Rachel for remembering them. All the same he demurred; he, too, thought that impersonations were no longer becoming to his dignity. Besides, no one was coaxing him but Rachel. And besides, Dolly's look was quite threatening.

"Then let's play games," Rachel insisted. She supposed that games were no longer quite so popular at Redmond parties, but she wanted to revive some of the spirit of parties she remembered.

"What sort of games?" asked John Wooster.

"A community picture!" Rachel cried, and ran off to the studio where they heard her scrambling about.

How long was it since any of them had painted a community picture! In the old days it was a party stand-by. Now the ladies exchanged smiles of pity and condescension for poor Rachel. How long it must have been since she had given a party! How much longer even since she had been invited to one, not to know that community pictures were *passé.*

Rachel came back bearing the easel and on it was a large canvas. She made another trip for brushes and a palette and all was placed in the middle of the room.

No one would go first.

"Then I'll choose," said Rachel. "And David is it, since he wouldn't give us any impersonations."

She handed Peterson a fistful of brushes and led him to the easel. Everyone enjoyed his discomfort.

But Peterson was a good sport. He regarded the canvas, took a few tentative swipes at it, then began wielding the brush with dash, with obvious relish. Vague, but already recognizable and already funny forms began to take shape on the canvas. For everyone knew what he had to put there before he began. In painting a community picture each person contributed the little mark of his style, his *petit sensation*, the little mannerism or the subject by which his work was known. Soon it became apparent that David Peterson was doing one of those hollow-eyed, nebulous nudes for which he was famous, but one even more gaunt and soulful—a delightful self-parody. Peterson had been taken right back ten years and was having a marvelous time.

Peterson stepped back to regard his creation and everyone was hugely amused. There was no lack of volunteers for second; they fought to be next, and Rachel had to choose to keep order.

Max Aronson started in a little above and to the left of Peterson's lady and from his first stroke everyone began laughing uncontrollably. In no time at all there took form one of those bleary-eyed, long-faced, ancient rabbis for which Max was known all over the world—only this rabbi, while looking just as burdened with *Weltschmerz* as ever, even more ludicrously so, was regarding Peterson's lady with a sly and lecherous glint in his eye. Everyone held his sides laughing.

Then Carl Robbins and Martha Phillips took brushes and began painting at the same time, racing each other while everyone cheered them on.

At this point Mrs. Kunitz drained her beer glass and set it down, looked searchingly into every corner of the house, got up and peered around the studio screen, and still not finding what she wanted, came over and bent to Rachel's ear.

"You'll find it," said James in a voice that made everyone hush and turn, "about thirty yards behind the house. Just follow your nose. Would you have believed it possible in this day and age?"

They were pressing Rachel to add her bit to the painting. "Get James," she said, "get James." The tone of his voice had alarmed her, and she breathed a sigh of relief for this distraction.

"Here, James," said Carl Robbins, holding out a brush to him.

James made no move, but left Robbins standing, awkwardly holding out the brush. The others stirred uneasily. James raised his palm in a gesture of overwhelmed unworthiness. "Let me not bring laughter and ridicule and indignity to this work," he said. A hush fell on them all.

But on her whole trip nothing had so delighted Mrs. Kunitz as the outhouse. "Well! That's the first time I've seen one of those things in a while!" she said as she stepped in.

"Yes, we keep it for sentimental reasons," said James. "Not to mention other reasons." The prolonged, stunned silence of the guests made him more audacious. "We try to keep up the old traditions. People come expecting to see the real thing, the artist's life, you know—and where else are they going to find it in Redmond? Though now," and he gave a glance at Rachel, a deferential smile, "now I suppose we too will begin to slip and backslide and forget the simple life. In fact," his voice rose to a shout, "in fact, we have already begun. Indeed yes!"

He relished their embarrassment for a moment, then said, "I'm sure you're all dying to know what's been done with the money. Well, let me just show you. None of you is quite as, ah, thin, as you once were. But just draw in a breath and perhaps we can all squeeze into the, ah, the bedroom."

He strode over and folded back the bedroom screen with a flourish.

"There!" he exclaimed. "Our prize money bedroom suite!"

The little room looked positively embarrassed. In it stood a huge highboy, a vanity with an oval mirror tinted blue, a padded vanity seat covered with glossy satin and a bed with a gleaming headboard, covered with a bright blue chenille spread.

The silence was broken by the ladies' exclamations. "Lovely. Charming. How nice." The men assented in embarrassed grunts.

Rachel had seen it yesterday in the window of a shop in Redmond, where she had gone to get away from James and to look for something to get rid of the money on. Her mother had had one very like it. Rachel thought it was beautiful.

How was it, then, that otherwise the house was so tasteful? Was that all James's doing? Far from it. In fact, aside from his contribution of a few heirlooms—some of them among the few ugly things in the house—he had no part in it. He was indifferent to his surroundings. So long as they could not come up to his notions of what they should be, he preferred to go to the opposite extreme; it would have given him pleasure to live off orange crates and hang dime-store chromos on the walls. No, the charm of the place was Rachel's doing. But Rachel had taste only so long as she had no money. When her resourcefulness was demanded, when she had to make shift, she made beauty. When she had money she bought the things she thought other people bought with money, the things she remembered money as being for.

"Lovely, isn't it?" James demanded of Mrs. Wooster.

"Yes—yes, lovely!" and she cringed against her husband.

"Isn't it lovely?" he shouted at Edith Morris.

"It certainly is," said Edith. She meant it.

James included them both in his look of utter contempt. "Maple, you know," he said, looking at the furniture with nausea. "That is, pine with a coat of maple syrup."

Those who were not too embarrassed for Rachel even to look at her sent her looks of sympathy and support. John Wooster said, "We had better go."

James was taken aback. "Go?" he said. He had humiliated himself for them. Weren't they enjoying it?

The Woosters began moving toward the door; others followed. James saw all his crafty plans collapsing. He grew panicky to keep them there. His urgency gave a repulsive oiliness to his smile and the affability of his tone was repellent as he said, "Come now. You're all used to staying up later than this. The evening's young." He realized he was saying the wrong thing. This pleased him and goaded him on. "Why, there's no telling what may happen yet," he said.

He stood in the middle of the room and watched them leave. He half-expected them to return, to slap him on the back and say that he was better than all of them put together. He could think of nothing startling to say, no show to make which would detain them. He wanted to say something disdainful, something contemptible even, yet have them admire him all the more for it.

The last ones were stepping out. James thought how as they walked down the road Sam Morris would take it upon himself to explain him to the rest. "It's James's nature," he would say knowingly, "to be volatile and impulsive, always to be different and conspicuous." Sam was certain he understood James. How James hated that kind of understanding! For if he acted extravagantly, made himself conspicuous, it was all because he had such a great wish to do just the opposite, because he had such great respect for convention and the proper form.

Rachel stepped outside and detained the last few. "James doesn't mean anything by it when he goes off like that," she said in an intimate tone. "You needn't feel sorry for me, because he is always terribly sorry afterwards. It's only his own unhappiness."

They gaped at her. Was she then as bad as he? Had she no more sense of privacy than he had? It was shameless, such confiding eagerness.

Not all the prize money was spent on the bedroom suite. Thirty-six dollars went for the suit in which James stood admiring himself on a morning two weeks after the party. It was the first one the clerk had shown him, and he had liked it right off. When he tried it on at home he found the pinstripe too broad and too light in color, but that no longer bothered him. He stroked the lapel lovingly.

Another seven dollars went for the shoes.

James turned and looked at himself from the back, particularly at his haircut. Then he faced himself once more and looked at his mustache. His mustache had been clipped and trimmed and his curls lopped off so that now his hair lay in tight kinks against his skull.

He wore a white shirt with a starched collar so cruelly buttoned that his great red neck hung over it in a roll, and after swallowing he had to duck his head to get his Adam's apple up again.

Every few seconds he was worried that the suit was not what it should be. It had been so long since he had bought one. Then he would again decide that it was grand.

The thing which amazed and delighted him most was that he looked just like anybody else. He might be in advertising or the law.

Rachel came in rubbing the crown of a new brown hat with her elbow. But when he put it on it fell down over his ears. He had bought it before Rachel cut his hair. She took the blame for that, but said that a little tissue paper in the sweatband would fix it.

While she went to get some, James polished the emblem in his lapel and pictured himself at the fraternity house tomorrow evening after the Reunion Dinner. He was amazed that he had gone so many years without attending Reunion Day. He saw himself sitting back in his chair with his legs crossed, sipping Benedictine while he talked with Pee-wee Moore, now Charles Moore of Ohio, Michigan, Ltd. or with Walter Beck of U. S. Steel.

Men like Moore and Beck would, of course, know nothing of

the art world. But they would simply assume that he had done well. Especially when they saw him in this suit. He looked at it again to be sure, and he decided once and for all that it was not so much what the suit did for him, as what he did for the suit.

Besides Beck and Moore there were men like Joseph Caspar and William Malcolm Cooper in the class of '26. That was his class. Or rather, the class he would have been in if he had stayed another year.

"Rachel," he said, "these men I'm going to be with the next couple of days are my kind of people. They come from the best families. They were brought up to respect ceremony and tradition. They know what culture is. And don't think they won't remember me. They know what the name Ruggles means."

The taxi that was to take him to the train pulled up outside the door and honked.

Rachel carried out his grip and the bundle of paintings. He had decided first to take five, then eight; now there were eleven of them and it was arranged that Rachel was to send ten more tomorrow by express.

He looked at them and smiled shrewdly.

"I can ask any price from men like those," he said. "What's money to them?"

In Sickness and Health

MR. GROGAN'S bald head broke through the covers. He experimented with his nose; it rattled like steampipes warming up. He was so stiff he felt that all the veins in his body must have froze and busted. He opened his eyes and wriggled painfully upwards, feeling, after only one day in bed, stiff and strange as an old snake crawling out of hibernation. Now, if only he had stayed on his feet, as he had insisted, he would have been feeling hearty again this morning.

He could hear his wife down below walloping up his breakfast, doubtless assuring herself that he was so near dead he would never hear her, murmuring soft little Viennese curses whenever her big hulk smacked into the cabinet corner. Mr. Grogan licked a fingertip and scrubbed the corners of his eyes. When she came up he would look long awake, though he had not been able to get up.

Mr. Grogan was an early riser. You couldn't tell her otherwise, and his wife had the notion he did it to make her look lazy. He just wanted to get out of a morning without the sight of her. Maybe she was brighter than he took her for, and just as spiteful as he knew she was, and wanted to rob him of that pleasure. One reason or another, she was to be heard scrambling and puffing in the mornings, trying to get down before he did, and now he could just imagine how pleased with herself she was today.

He knew just how her mind was working. Had she stopped to consider that he just might be better this morning? Not for an instant. She was too cheerful down there now for such a shadow to have passed even momentarily across her mind. An hour at least she must have lolled abed this morning, thinking to herself how, even after time for the alarm, she might go right on lying there as long as she pleased, and still be the first down in the kitchen. No racing down this morning, no colliding in the hall, no frowzy hair nor unlaced shoes, all to see which one—and he it was just about always—could be sitting there already polishing off his coffee with a distant, foregone glance for the stay-a-bed. Yes, she had that kind of a nasty mind.

The breakfast she came up with would have winded a slender woman.

"Ah, *liebchen*, no better, hah?" she grinned, and when he opened his mouth to remonstrate, she drew a concealed thermometer and poked it in him.

Mr. Grogan lay there with it poked out defiantly at her, making it seem there was so much of her that he had to look first around one side of it, then around the other, to take her all in. She stood over him regally; she did every chance she got. Mrs. Grogan carried her head with great pride of ownership, as though she had shot it in Ceylon and had it mounted on a plaque.

She must have thought that the longer she left the thermometer in, the higher it would go. He started to take it out, but she beat him to it.

"Ah!" she sighed, regarding it with deep satisfaction. "Ah-hah!"

Nothing could have made Mr. Grogan ask her what it said. Not even if he had believed she knew how to read the thing.

"That's what you need," she said. "Plenty sleep and decent food," and the way she said it you would think she had found him in a doorway in the Bowery and given him the only home he had ever known.

"Well, you don't," he replied, but she was gone. Amazing,

truly, how fast she could move that great body of hers when it meant getting out in time to have the last word herself.

He could hear her vast sigh as she stood at the head of the basement steps. He could hear her settle slowly down the steps, then scrape her way over to the coalbin. There was no subtlety in her, and that was what he resented most. There she went now, rattling the furnace. She might be Mrs. Beelzebub opening shop. Soon she would come up to demonstrate her pains, complaining of the heat, the dirt, the waste of coal. Were he to dare remind her that *he*, certainly, required no fire, why, she would burst. What would she have done for heat if he hadn't come down like this? Last winter she had practically turned blue before she would ask him to build a fire. But that had not taught her, and this time she would have moved out sooner than admit she was cold—though how she could get cold through all her insulation was more than he could guess. But cold she was, stiff as untried lard, while here was himself with his hundred and twenty pounds, and that old and ailing, and all along he might have been a teapot in a cozy, he told himself—while the yellowed old teeth danced in his mouth like popcorn in a pan.

She stood at the door, grateful for having made the stairs once again. She had been sure to get good and smeared with soot and coal dust, and not stop to wash any of it. Mr. Grogan had thrown back two of his blankets and was smoking the pipe she had forbidden him, though he did not dare inhale for fear of a coughing spell. So smug she looked, turning up his radiator, her sleeves rolled back, just stifling for the sake of his health. He could not resist asking, "Would you mind just raising up that window there while you're close by?" She turned on him such a smile as she might have given a child she was holding for ransom.

After that she left him alone. Maybe she was thinking that alone he would come to enjoy a nice warm room, a day in bed with meals brought up, realize how much he did owe her to be sure. But even if it were pleasant would she let a man enjoy it? And on that sour thought his pipe drained in his mouth and started a coughing fit that very nearly choked him in trying to keep her from hearing. Ah, Grogan, he chided himself, wouldn't it have been better now to have built a fire back in November and worn the muffler like she said? A stubborn, wheezing "no!" shot through him. But wouldn't it now? Didn't he regret the false front of good health and didn't he wish he had confessed to sniffles three days ago and staved off what was sure to develop into pneumonia?

Come now. Were things that black, truly? Well, he was not exactly what you would call hale, but nobody but himself would ever know it, and better by far than she gave him the credit for. He still cut a pretty sturdy figure and nobody ever heard him complain. In fact, he had been maybe a little too uncomplaining. Well, if so he could point out where to lay the blame. What else could a man do only swallow down his aches and pains, never mention them nor so much as let them be guessed, when he knew that if they were her face would light up at every hole like a new candle had been put in it. Many the time he had felt so bad that younger men than he by years would have spent the week in bed and he had got right up—first, too, more like than not—made his own breakfast, it went without saying, and gone to work with a smile and a tipped hat for everybody on the street.

Meanwhile she had been giving him a standing with the neighbors that she never dreamed was noble. "Oh, *I'm* very well, Mrs. Harriman, very well indeed. It's *Mr.* Grogan, you know." This she would sadly volunteer over the back fence. She had to volunteer it, for no one ever thought to *ask* after such a chipper man. In those days Mr. Grogan got no end of delight in knowing that to Mrs. Harriman and to the rest of the neighbors, his wife was making of herself either a liar or a lunatic. For whenever he caught sight of her on the back fence speaking with Mrs. Harriman and looking sadly up at his window, then he would rush out and start weeding his garden in a flaming fury. Or he would trot down the street and catch flies as the kids played baseball, wind up and burn the ball home. He just wished she could have seen the neighbors' faces then!

But people are always anxious to believe the worst about someone else's health. The neighbors then respected him, stood aside on the walks, offered little services and some of them went so far as to consult him about their own illnesses, he being such a fine example of how to bear so many. Then he may have peacocked it a bit; he supposed he did. Not that he wanted their attention. If he played up to all this ever so little it was because it was pleasant to see her program turning out so different from the way she had planned it.

Soon, though, it got to looking like they were saying among themselves, "Well, here comes that poor half-dead fool Grogan, with no idea of all that's going on inside hisself." There did seem to be such a conspiracy against him, he had thought more than once of taking a loss on his equity in the house and finding a new neighborhood. Hereabouts just to walk down the block of an afternoon made him feel the morgue had given him a day off his slab.

Now another situation held among Mr. Grogan's friends and it was only this that kept him going. Mr. Grogan was a great one for broadening himself with new friends and he was attracted naturally and by principle to young men. The few friends his wife had managed to keep were as old and mostly older than herself. Her claim was that he palled around with his young friends in a vain and unbecoming attempt to imagine himself their age again. But this, he knew, was to cover her own guilt for avoiding all younger women that she might not appear any older by contrast, and comparing her own fine fat state daily to the failing energies of her old crones.

Mr. Grogan prided himself on the job he had done of keeping his friends away from his wife. They, then, had no reason for not taking his word that he enjoyed excellent health. Not one of them but would have had trouble believing otherwise of anybody, and when he was with them Mr. Grogan never felt an ache or a pain. So, it was shocking to slip like a ghost down the three blocks nearest his house, turn the corner and enter McLeary's tavern like the playboy of Western Long Island.

Just the kind of a shock Mr. Grogan would have welcomed when toward eleven o'clock there came up to him the sound of substantial steps on the back stoop and he heard his wife greet her friend Mr. Rauschning, the baker. Into the kitchen they would go, where she would stuff him with the marzipan she bought from him at cutthroat prices, so Mr. Grogan expected, but instead he heard them on the steps up to his room and the two of them rumbled in like a Panzer division.

Mr. Rauschning took one look at him. Then he removed the cigar from his mouth and turned it over and over, squinting at it as though he could read his temperature on it and was satisfied that it could never be as alarming as Grogan's. "*Ja,*" he said, and to this Mrs. Grogan nodded gravely.

Neighborhood kids said that Rauschning soured his dough by scowling at it. But to Mr. Grogan he was no surlier than the rest of his compatriots. To Mr. Grogan it seemed his wife's friends wore a look of petty insolence, to which he contrasted the noble defiance of generations of Irishmen oppressed by the same grievance.

"Since yesterday morning," his wife commented on his condition, and Rauschning nodded; he could have predicted it to the hour.

"And the *Herr Doktor,* what does he say?"

"Hah! What doctor?"

Mr. Rauschning said ah-hah. Between them his fate was sealed.

"Well, how's the bakery business?" Mr. Grogan inquired amiably, and wished he hadn't as Rauschning nodded faintly to a man who would soon have little concern over the staff of life.

"Well, Grogan, I hope you get better," he said, and turned back at the door to add, "soon." He turned then to Mrs. Grogan to indicate that his anxiety was for her, as well as his condolences —for hopes, before such evidence, were vain, ending with a smile of agreement that she would be better off afterwards, of course, for a good strong German woman would always get by.

Now they were gone and Mr. Grogan thought he would just forget they were ever there, doze off wishing the two of them off on one another. But that would suit her too well. Ah, how often had she wished aloud for the likes of him herself, him or her first husband back again, whose speckled portrait sat on her bureau fading a little more each year as though still fleeing the vigor of her tongue.

The two dearest friends Mrs. Grogan owned came around noon to have the invalid exhibited to them. His wife must have phoned everybody she knew the night before when she had him drugged asleep, urged them all over for a laugh. But there stirred in him suddenly a fear that something unmistakably desperate in his appearance that was plain to all but him, something that they figured would this morning come to an inevitable crisis, something that had escaped him while draining away his very life, something horrible had summoned them all this morning with no help from her necessary. Was it possible? Had she been right all along, sincere, and the neighbors, had they honestly seen it coming?

They came up while he was feeling himself frantically for ailments he might have overlooked. They were Miss Hinkle and Mrs. Schlegelin and it was easy to see how even Mrs. Grogan could feel secure in their company. Miss Hinkle came in with a twitter at being in a man's bedroom and Mrs. Grogan was astonished that she could feel that way in the bedroom of a man with so little of his manhood left him. The sight of Mrs. Schlegelin could make Mr. Grogan feel there was hope for even him, for who ever saw such a thing so skinny from head to toe?

"Like the flu looks maybe," she diagnosed. "Just like *mein* Helmut exactly when he came down mit flu."

Mr. Grogan snorted, thinking how much more than flu he would have to have to look at all like her Helmut.

Miss Hinkle, terrified that she might catch sight of a bedpan, squealed, "Elsa, smells here like in Germany in the epidemic, ain't it?"

"Hush, Hedvig, no," shooshed Mrs. Schlegelin, her nose climbing up her face, and Miss Hinkle sniggered.

And they said other things, even after Mr. Grogan slowly flourished from the drawer of his nightstand two abandoned wads of chewing gum—really two waxen cotton plugs—and screwed them into his ears.

A tactic he had developed some time back. Mr. Grogan disliked using it, it made for all sorts of trouble, but was surely called for now. Wax-treated cotton they were, soft, easily got in, and they set like cement. Twenty-five cents a month bought a private little world all his own. Herself resented the price. With a display of thrift and resourcefulness, she bought a roll of cotton big enough for quilting, a tin of tallow, and made her own. She looked to be troubled with his voice for even longer than he ever hoped. For a while it piqued him. Now he simply had to laugh. One of many examples it became of her racial penny-wiseness—because he could make himself heard to her with but the tiniest elevation of his ordinary tone, while she had to shout herself hoarse.

You could not insult them. They left, but not before they were ready. But they might have spent the night for all of Emmett Grogan. He was sealed in, with smiles rising up like bubbles in new wine. But try as he might there was no convincing himself that this solitude was at all what he wanted. He was lonely in there. And he feared that these last two were not the last by any means. A long list of Mrs. Grogan's acquaintances rolled across his mind, the two down in the kitchen being welcome compared to some. He uncorked one ear and a dull whistle of Plattdeutsch rushed in.

Mr. Grogan gave himself a shake to unstick a joint or two, threw the covers back and carefully watched himself get up, afraid of leaving something behind. Sadly he wrenched himself out of his nightgown. Once in his pants he knew how much he had shrunk. Breaking up, he could see it in the mirror. But it was never a clear glass, and the light poorly, and moreover it was a man had spent a day in bed. Lying there that way the flesh slid of its own weight off the bones in front and would take time to get properly rearranged. He would know in McLeary's tavern. Someone would be sure to remark, "Grogan, you're not looking yourself"—which he was bound to admit, that is, not looking *himself*, meaning that a slight change in a ruddy face was enough for decent well-meant concern that never for a minute overstated the case.

Down the steps stealthily went Mr. Grogan that his wife would not hear the labor it cost him, his eyes steady on the landing where he planned a rest, but as he reached it his wife brought her guests from the kitchen to see them out the front door. From somewhere he dug up the energy to trot briskly by.

"Don't wait supper on me," he flung at her without so much as a glance over his shoulder. And his little spurt of exertion turned out to be the very thing he had been needing. He knew all along it was.

Housewives were indoors, children in school, dogs in kennels, Ireland still in the Atlantic and Germany in ruins and Emmett Grogan was in the street. Natural phenomena all. There was a list to his step that passed for a swagger as he crashed the door at McLeary's. The place was deserted. McLeary hung over a scratch sheet at the far end of the bar and he tucked it grudgingly away while Mr. Grogan ascended a stool. Somebody had surely pickled McLeary as a foetus, but he had kept growing, had been lately discovered, spilled out and set going. Little half-opened eyes were getting a start in his squashed face, he was adenoidal, pot-bellied, but to Mr. Grogan he looked good.

"Leave the bottle?" he asked after pouring a shot, to which Mr. Grogan nodded carelessly. McLeary went back immediately to his scratch sheet. Mr. Grogan tamped another down, and felt his insides warm and expand. He got down from his stool, looked annoyed with the sunlight at his end of the counter, and moved with his bottle down nearer McLeary.

"Something else, Mr. Grogan?"

"No. No, nothing further, thank you, McLeary. This will do it if anything will, I suppose."

"Something amiss, Mr. Grogan?"

"Ah, nothing serious, you understand. Nasty little bit of a cold."

"Ah, yes. Too bad. There's an epidemic, so I understand."

That was conserving your sympathy, spreading it pretty thin. Starting on another tack, he asked, "Where could everybody be this fine day?"

"Not here," McLeary observed sourly.

"What can it be, do you suppose?"

McLeary shrugged; he was unable to imagine a counter-attraction so strong.

Grogan pushed away his bottle. "And I'll be having a beer to help that on its way, if you please, McLeary." He was determined to stick it out until some friend came in. But he had had whiskey enough and more, and he always did get a guilty feeling sitting empty-handed in a bar.

To go home again would have robbed the venture of all its worth. But he did not like to think of it as a venture. He would like to feel he could go home when he pleased, for after all he had done nothing unusual—got well, got up. No point to be proved to anybody. All too subtle for her, however. She would get the idea he hadn't been able to stand on his feet any longer. She would have something there, too, but his unsteadiness came from good healthy rye whiskey.

Grogan, a voice pulled him down by the ear, you're not feeling well and you know it. Naturally, he replied, I've been sick, what do you expect. You're sick and getting sicker. No, drunk and getting drunker. Mr. Grogan decided to take his stomach out for an airing. Would drop in later when some of his friends were sure to be there before going home to supper. McLeary would solemnly not let them out until Emmett Grogan had seen them.

It was fast getting dark and the night air settling down. Five steps Mr. Grogan took and sobered so suddenly it was like bumping into himself around a corner. He had better get home, he decided quickly. If he could make it, he added soon. With one block he was apprehensive, two and he was scared, three had him terrified. Something had him by the throat, no air was getting in, he was turning hot and cold, his joints were rusting fast. Holy Mary, Mother of God. Holy Mary, I'm not ready. His mind cleared long enough to wish this on his wife—take her, Lord, she's mean.

Mr. Grogan lurched up the steps of his house and found the door locked. It wasn't possible. Could she have gone out, thinking he might collapse? He fumbled in all his pockets at once, could not find his key, tried them systematically. No key. He wanted just to slump down on those stones and die crying. Maybe the back door was open, if only he could hold out that long. When finally he shoved it in she was sipping tea at the kitchen table and looked up as if she was seeing a ghost. That was when he really got scared. She was not shamming, probably never had been.

"Well, Mr. Big," she brogued, "I hope you enjoyed yourself."

"Oh," he managed to groan, leaning on the table edge, "sick. Terrible sick."

Mrs. Grogan drained her tea, picked a leaf off her tongue.

"Hah!" she snorted. "You? Grogan, the Iron Man? You've

never been sick a day in your life. Told me so yourself many a time."

"Oh, I'm dying, woman. You were right. I admit it. I'm a sick man. A dying man. I admit it. Do you hear? What more do you want for your pleasure?"

"Get on with you, Grogan. Sober up. I've no time to be bothered with you."

Mr. Grogan licked his lips. They were hot and crinkly. "Will you just help me up the stairs a bit?" he whispered.

"Now don't let me have to tell you again, get out of my kitchen and leave me to my business. You're well enough to swill with the pigs at McLeary's, you're well enough to bring me up a scuttle of coal from the cellar."

Mr. Grogan turned and dragged himself out in an agony of terror and pain. He crawled up the steps, pulling himself with rubbery hands, and into his room. He struggled out of his overcoat and shoes, laid his cap on the table and crawled under the covers as the phone began ringing.

"Hello," she said. "Who? Oh, Mr. Duffy, is it? Young Mr. Duffy," and she raised her voice to a shout. "Well, yes, he was a little under the weather earlier in the day, one of the same old complaints. No, no we didn't. I always just look after him myself. Serious? Well, you ought to know Grogan well enough for that. Bring yourself out on a night like this? For what? Why, he's just come in from McLeary's where he spent the whole afternoon. I'm surprised you didn't see him."

The Last Husband

I

OUR HONEYMOON was over one bright warm Monday in late November when Janice drove me down to catch the 8:02 and I became a commuter.

There was a fine invigorating pinch in the air and standing on the station platform with my new wife and new brief case and my unpunched commutation ticket, I was conscious of looking like a young man of whom a lot was expected and who expected a lot of himself, and I did not care who saw. I did not need to care, I soon began to feel, for no one noticed me.

They did notice when Janice kissed me good-by. I was the only man whose wife kissed him, and I waited with Janice to be the last on the train. Then I saw why no other man got a kiss—nearly all their women got on the train with them; they were going to work, too. Janice was almost the only person left on the platform as the train pulled out.

Needless to say, while honeymooning we had been content not to know anyone in Cressett. But now we were eager to meet people. It was not by chance that we had come to make our home among them, for while not everyone in Cressett was an advertising artist like me, enough of them did things similar to give the place a name. But though people in the streets had smiled and some had said hello, they smiled more as if they were afraid they knew you and said hello as if they feared perhaps they ought to know you. I'd had to admit to myself that I'd not seen a really friendly face, and after walking down the aisle of the train that morning, down that double row of grumpy, unrested faces—the few, that is, that were visible, for most of them were protected by newspapers—my hopes of seeing one were at their lowest.

Then I encountered the smile of Edward Gavin. He was sitting by the window beneath which Janice stood to wave to me. He was not the only man my age, but he was the only one who looked as if he felt himself to be. It was when I asked if I might share his seat that he gave me his smile. Such politeness as mine, or perhaps it was my desire to share a seat with anyone, apparently confirmed my innocence, for several people turned and smiled. But my man's smile was a friendly smile.

He nodded toward Janice and asked, "Married long?"

"Two months," I said.

He spared me the pleasantries. In fact, after telling me his name he said nothing. I told about myself, pausing often to let him say something, but he didn't, and finally, growing ashamed of my egotism, I said, "Married yourself?"

"Twenty years," he said wearily.

I smiled. But I was at that stage of my own when to hear a man joke about his marriage was not funny to me. "It doesn't seem to have hurt you," I could not help saying.

To my surprise he got to his feet. The train was slowing for Webster's Bridge, the first stop after Cressett. That was where this man Edward Gavin got off, having commuted just three miles.

Being the last stop on the line, barely within commuting distance, Cressett was the starting point for the morning train, the 8:02. The coach was empty when we came in and each man and woman took a seat to himself, like a herd of milch cows trained to go to their separate stalls. Oh, I noticed pairs who sat together daily, but I noticed also that after a grunt or two they settled down to as deep a silence as those who sat alone until their seats were shared by strangers getting on at stops down the line; indeed, I decided that those pairs had agreed to sit together just to keep each from having to sit with anyone he disliked even more. And so for me the coach came soon to have the atmosphere of an elevator ride prolonged for nearly two hours. The evening train, which had a lounge car and which set out from Grand Central loaded full of people going home from work, promised to be more sociable. But I learned quickly that if anything can make a person more ill-tempered than having to go to work in the morning, it's having to go home in the evening, and so the occasional gusts of sociability from the gin rummy games on the evening train only intensified the general incivility.

I found myself thinking again of the man Gavin's smile. I looked out for him and saw that he sat regularly with no one but that he did not seem to resent it quite so much as others if someone sat with him. He lived in Webster's Bridge, I knew now, having seen him board the train there every morning since the first, so when we stopped there one morning, the seat next to me being empty, of course, I invited him with a look to take it. He seemed to recognize me with something other than pleasure; in response to my look he frowned deeply, and he took a seat up the aisle.

Coming home that night, as we drew up the line, I left my seat and worked my way up to the head coach. Edward Gavin was there. The sight of him then was something of a shock. Slumped in his seat, abandoned to his exhaustion, he resembled nothing so much as an elder brother of the man I had seen before. But when he saw me he drew himself together and his smile performed the most amazing transformation on his face, as when a photographic print lies in the developer and the washed-out features of a face suddenly collect themselves into life. I forgave him completely his unfriendliness of the morning. Tell yourself there's nothing personal in it, that anyone else could do just as much—still it does something to you, makes you feel good, to have your approach bring that much change to a person's face.

I said, however, that if he did not feel like talking to anyone . . .

He rejected vigorously the implication that he was tired, commanded me to sit, and talked with animation. Then the conductor
came in and announced Webster's Bridge. I gathered up my
topcoat and brief case and stood in the aisle to let him out.

He made no move.

"This is only Webster's Bridge," he said.

I was about to reply when I saw that his eyes had narrowed
strangely, narrowed with something very much like suspicion.
Then I saw that upon his lips had come a playful, almost sinister
smile. He seemed to be daring me to ask for an explanation.

"Oh," I said. "Oh, yes," and sat down.

My bewilderment quickly gave way to fear. He seemed to know
this and to be enjoying it. We rode silently for what seemed a long
while. When he finally offered to talk it was not to ease me. For
the time left he chatted gaily and forced me to answer his questions, and all the while he kept smiling his playful, sinister smile.

When he boarded the train next morning at Cressett he did not
share my seat because I'd made sure he couldn't by sharing
someone else's and because I was hiding behind a newspaper.
But I distinctly felt that he knew I was behind that paper; I could
feel his smile coming right through it. Nor did I ride out with him
that evening. Again, sitting behind my paper, I felt he knew I was
in the same coach; in fact, though I had waited until I saw him
seated and then gone to another coach, he had come into my
coach when we were a few miles up the line. And his knowing I
was there did nothing to keep him from getting off—and with an
air as careless, as regular as you please—at Webster's Bridge—
only Webster's Bridge!

I watched him for a week. One morning he would get on one
place, the next morning the other. One night he would get off at
Webster's Bridge, then take the train at Cressett the next morning, and another time it would be the other way around. Sometimes he'd take the train at neither place, yet be in Grand Central
and take the train out that evening.

I would often look around me to find if any of the others
noticed these goings-on, or to find if any observed my interest.

Everyone was busy or tired from a busy day, everyone was too self-absorbed, and I felt silently reprimanded for my idle nosiness—which did nothing to check it, as you may imagine. I may say, though, that after a few looks around at my tired and busy and self-absorbed fellow passengers, I was ready to give Edward Gavin my sympathy if his only reason was to have a little variety in his life and be different from them, who got on and off at the same stop every day.

After three weeks something happened, but for which I suppose I should have lost interest and should have forced myself to find some perfectly logical and prosaic explanation for him, and have forgotten the man altogether, especially if I could have found someone who looked at all pleasant to ride with. It was this:

One night the person sitting in front of me got off at the stop before Webster's Bridge, revealing Gavin sitting in the head of the coach. I fell to thinking of him and his two train stops and I became so absorbed in it, said the names of the two towns to myself so many times, that when the conductor came in and announced Webster's Bridge I got up, put on my coat, took up my things, and got off the train.

As I was walking down the platform still puzzling and looking for Janice in the crowd, I realized my mistake and felt so foolish that instead of chasing after the train as it pulled out I stood stock-still. When I did begin to run it was too late and at the end of the platform I gave up and stood panting for breath. Then I saw a man standing in the red platform lights, his hand on the door of a station wagon inside which sat a woman. It was Gavin, and he was staring at me wildly.

The next afternoon as I hurried up the platform in Grand Central I found myself overtaken by him. He smiled as though nothing had happened, asked if I was riding with anyone, whether I had got into a rummy foursome yet, and when I finally managed to say "no," suggested that we ride up together. "After all," he said in a side-of-the-mouth way as he gave me a hand up the steps, "we'd might as well be as friendly as possible under the circumstances, hadn't we?"

We were barely seated when he said, "Strange, isn't it, what jealousy can do to a person? Read a story the other day about an old couple who'd been married fifty years and all that time the woman had lived in jealousy of the husband's dead first wife. Now, the author takes you inside the husband's mind early in the story and you know that he had completely forgotten that first wife. You see the irony. Woman might have had a full life. There it was just waiting for her. If it hadn't been for her jealousy. For which she had no reason at all. Isn't that just like people? Women especially. Take my wife now—"

I must have blushed at this sudden, tasteless confidence.

"You know my wife," he said, and it was not a question.

"Not at all," I hastily replied.

He smiled at me knowingly, intimately. "Come now," he said. "You an advertising artist and new in town and don't know my wife?" His tone was quite insultingly incredulous. Apparently those two qualifications of mine were enough to make his wife certain to know me. He then gave me another long, sly, familiar smile, which, to my amazement, I saw was meant to convince me that there was no use trying to deny that I knew his wife.

"Alice, you know, has this one fixed idea," he said. "The same as the woman in that story. Comes from sitting home all day with nothing to do, so her imagination gets somewhat—hmm"—he leered—"inflamed."

Imagine telling this to a stranger!

"Poor Alice," he said, and he shook his head sadly. "Of course, I guess I *haven't* been always as model a husband as the one in that story," he added slyly. "*Poor* Alice," he insisted. "No-o, no, I guess you couldn't say I've always been *that* model," and in the tone of this was considerably less of genuine repentance than of fond reminiscence. Then he seemed to have caught himself saying too much. "It's got so bad, Alice's jealousy, I mean, that I can't even keep a secretary. I have to keep one on the sly in Webster's Bridge and work with her in the evenings. I don't have to tell you what Alice thinks I'm out doing those evenings. You may wonder why I risk keeping her just three miles down the line from home. But doesn't that prove how *innocent*"—he laid a broad emphasis on the word, and as though that weren't enough, accompanied it with a wink—"it all is? Would I be so stupid if it was something more?" He had thought this out carefully and was obviously pleased with it. He wanted to avert my suspicions, but at the same time he was obviously too proud of his prowess to resist letting me in on the truth, so that it all added up to the most proudly guilty protestation of innocence you ever saw.

Well, it was all so strange that I did not immediately realize its implication for me. Then the night when he had said that this was only Webster's Bridge came back to me, and his wild glare beneath the station lamp the night before, and I realized that he thought I had deliberately watched and followed him. I was insulted and about to tell him so, and then I had to ask myself what else could the man think on seeing me, breathless from running, on the platform of the station where he knew I did not belong, where I had tried to lure him into getting off before. No wonder he was sure I knew his wife. He probably thought, and well he might from the look of things, that I was in her pay.

I said, "Mr. Gavin, if you've got troubles with your wife, I— well, I'm very sorry." My stupidity infuriated me. "But, but I assure you"—and here I got infuriated at my pompousness— "that I do not know your wife. I don't even know you! Last night —well, last night I, I got off the train at the wrong stop, that is at Webster's Bridge, out of pure absentmindedness. Pure absentmindedness. And when I realized my mistake I ran after the train and I missed it, as you know." I could have kicked myself for that "as you know." I was conscious also that people were turning to stare, for I had grown a bit loud. Now I whispered, "If you think I had any other reason, why, then, why you're wrong, that's all. And, really, you ought to look into things a little further before you come up to a man and begin accusing—well, forget it!" And with this I left him and found a seat in another coach, cured of my loneliness for a train companion.

II

Imagine my astonishment when after this the man seemed to go out of his way to bump into me on the train, in the stations and on the street in Cressett. I chose a different coach each morning

and evening but he always found me and on the evening train if
the seat beside me was taken he took the nearest seat and waited
until the person beside me got off. He made no mention of what
had passed between us, but he seemed to feel it had given us the
basis for a close friendship, close enough for him to wink at me
now when he got off the train in the evening at Webster's Bridge
and to show me with a leer what an exhausting night he had had
of it when he got on in the morning. He boasted so much I began
to have suspicions.

He was pretty crude, and so I was not eager to accept his offer
to drive me home from the station one night. Janice had phoned
in the afternoon to say that our car was in the garage. Gavin saw
me getting into the taxi and hurried over and was so insistent that
I had to give in.

On the way he slowed at a side road and suggested stopping in
at his place for a drink. I did not protest. I wanted to get a look at
his wife.

"Like you to meet my wife," he said grimly.

Beneath the name Gavin on his mailbox was the name Metsys.
"Any relation to—"
"Sister."
I was thinking, as you have no doubt guessed, of Victoria
Metsys, the woman who, by drawing upon Picasso, Klee, and
Miro for her subway posters, had started a whole new trend in
advertising art twenty years ago. Gavin seemed nonchalant
enough, I thought, about having her in the family. This I could
understand better when I saw his house: he had not done badly
himself.

A man bringing you to meet his wife could not very well pre-
pare you by saying, "Oh, by the way, you must expect her to look
twenty years older than I." But if Gavin had, he would have saved
an awkward moment when I said to myself, "Why, she must be
fifty!" and what I was thinking showed all too plainly on my face.
This must have been painful enough for Mrs. Gavin, but the next
moment I made things worse by turning involuntarily, as though
I needed to recheck his age, for another look at Edward. What I

saw in his face then explained why he had not prepared me; it was not the first time he had enjoyed this trick.

We sat, and while Gavin told her about me I studied his face. I could believe now that he was her age, but the way he had chosen to show me was the only way I could have been convinced of it. It was the way his face was made that gave it its youthful look. It was thin and small, there would never be much flesh on it to sag, and the overall impression it gave was one of such boyish fun that the lines around his eyes and the corners of his mouth would for a long while yet be thought to come from laughter rather than from years.

Gavin left the room to mix drinks and the first thing Alice said to me was, "I'm older than my husband, you know." It took coolness to come out with it like that. I had wondered already how she met this problem—it was too big for silence—and I admired her way. Then, "Two years," she said, and though I didn't doubt her, this specification somehow robbed the thing of its daring self-assurance.

I said, "You're Victoria Metsys' sister, aren't you?"

It had not occurred to me that she might be something in her own right and that *Alice* Metsys was a name I ought to know, or pretend I knew, as well as Victoria. Her smile showed me my mistake. It was a smile that had had a lifetime of service in answer to that remark, "Oh, *Victoria's* sister!"

She knew my work, it seemed, and talking about it served as the excuse for showing me some of hers, hers of a certain period, she said, which mine reminded her of—not, she added, that she meant to accuse me of copying her. She thumbed through some magazines kept under the end table, though they were, at the newest, five years old and two of them defunct, and found some "little spot fillers she had tossed off, just to help out the editors," and a four-inch ad for a short-lived breakfast food which I'd forgotten all about but now remembered trying once and then a year later, when I was packing to move, discovering the box on the shelf alive with weevils. Her work bore no resemblance whatever to mine. What it was like, embarrassingly like, was the highly individual work with which her sister Victoria had burst upon the world twenty years ago. She might not enjoy being Victoria's sister, I thought, but if she hadn't been, those drawings would never have been published.

Gavin reminded me of the time and said he didn't want my wife mad at him for holding up dinner. But Alice said she had to show me the house. She seemed, in fact, to feel she had to show and tell me everything about herself in the few minutes before I went home.

I praised every room we passed through on our way to the conservatory, and I praised that, though not quite strongly enough, it seemed. She was wild about flowers herself, she said, and I could believe it, for in this room it was as if the spring and summer had been brought in out of the cold. So I waxed appreciative and said of a peony that I had never seen such a lovely chrysanthemum. She seemed to have extravagantly high hopes for our similarities and sympathies, and this disappointed her unreasonably. But it appeared that one way or the other she was not going to permit the least difference between us, for she then said in a confidential tone, "To tell you the truth, I don't really care a lot for flowers myself."

What she did care about was setting me right on one point without delay. She was afraid I thought something was being put over on her, and she wanted me to save my pity.

"You might think I don't know what's going on, living back here in this wilderness—immured, as you might say. But I manage to know pretty well, considering that I never learned to drive a car. Edward, you know, always discouraged me from learning. And I used to think it was because he enjoyed having me dependent on him. Well, I just want you to know that I know all about Edward."

"All about—"

"All about his philanderings, of course," she said impatiently. "Don't pretend you don't know about them. Everybody knows about Edward's philanderings. Poor boy, he thinks he is so careful and so clever and he gives himself away every time he turns around."

I remembered our encounter in the train and I could not help laughing.

"Yes, it is amusing, isn't it?" she said. "And at the same time rather touching. I think that's why I like him, you know—he is such a poor liar. He's always working up some little affair for himself and he can hardly enjoy it for fear I'm going to find out. In fact, I sometimes believe that his real pleasure is in thinking he's putting something over on me, and not in the poor girl herself at all. Just now it's some little beauty parlor operator down in the city."

I supposed she had not been as recently posted as she thought. Then I decided that she simply hadn't bothered to keep up to date.

"I can't tell Edward this, you understand. It would hurt his pride. He'd hate to know I had known all along despite his elaborate pains, and he would die to know I didn't mind. I just didn't want you to think I was a perfect fool. So," she concluded in an intimate tone, as though we were both long accustomed to pampering him, "don't let on to him that I know. Let him have his fun."

Naturally, her anxiety to set me right so quickly made me suspicious. It hardly seemed likely that she could care so little, that her vanity should not have been at least a little wounded by her husband's escapades. But by the time I left I was pretty well convinced that none of her vanity was invested in her husband. As soon as she got over this one hurdle she could think of nothing —certainly not of how late she was keeping me—except her "work," and I gathered that it left her no time to care what Edward did with himself. Moreover, I got the feeling about her that she was just as happy to have Edward busy himself in that way elsewhere.

III

All afternoon I watched the snow swirl past my office window and at three I phoned Janice to ask how much had fallen in Cressett. I was thirty minutes getting a line through and I learned that there it was worse than in the city, that it had given way now to a steady rain that was turning everything to ice.

In Grand Central it was announced that frozen switches would hold the schedule up all night. A single train might get through around 1:00 A.M. I decided to stay over in town. I was turning away with the rest of the crowd by the gate when my arm was caught.

"Staying over?" asked Gavin. "Ah. Haven't had your dinner, I don't suppose. Since we're stranded down here why don't we make the worst of it together?"

I said I would have to call Janice and Gavin stood with me in the long line of conscientious husbands waiting for the telephone booths and when my turn came I said, "Like me to tell my wife to call yours and tell her?"

"Don't bother," he said. "She wouldn't believe it."

Out in the street the snow had stopped and it was hard to believe that it was not possible to get home to Janice tonight. We decided on a hotel and registered for rooms and then Gavin knew a restaurant on Forty-first Street. They knew him, too, for the waiter said, "I thought you might be turning up here tonight, Mr. Gavin."

We ordered drinks.

"Well, here's how," said Gavin. But he stopped his glass at his lips, a shrewd smile formed on them and his eyes went hard. I looked at him questioningly, as he seemed to be waiting for me to do. "Hmmm," he said. "The waiter wasn't the only one who thought I might be turning up here tonight."

He left this quivering on the air, then, "See that man over there —don't look now."

I waited a decent interval, then bent to pick up my napkin and stole a glance at the little bald man at the bar. "Don't tell me he's anyone worth knowing," I said.

Gavin gave me his smile of mystery and left me to wait.

"No-o," he mused, looking up suddenly from his drink, "just a private eye."

I was touched, and so I used a gentle tone in saying, "Well now, I believe you once thought I might be a detective hired by your wife, too."

This did not have the effect I had intended. "Yes!" he cried, much amused. "Things were going very badly just then, and I must have been seeing detectives everywhere I looked." Then he nodded towards the bar and said, "He knows I've spotted him, so he'll pay his check and leave in a minute. Poor guy. What a job. And on a night like this."

"Then how do you know that man is a detective any more than I was?" I asked.

"Oh, I can tell," he said earnestly. "I really wasn't very sure about you, you know."

"Oh," I said, "not very sure. Just sure enough to—"

"Look," he said. "See? He's paid his check and left, just as I told you."

"Yes," I said. "I suppose that's proof enough."

He nodded.

"Let me tell you something," I said.

"I'll bet I can tell you what you're going to say," he said. "You're going to tell me I have nothing to worry about from my wife."

He must have seen from my face that he had hit it right. He went on, "I'm sure that's what she gave you to feel the other night when you had your little tête-à-tête. I suppose she told you something like this: 'Poor Edward. Really, it's pathetic. He's just like a little boy who thinks he's putting something over on his mother.'"

He mimicked her with amazing accuracy, and looking at that boyish face of his it was hard to keep in mind that he had lived with her voice for twenty years.

"Don't you see," he continued, "it's proof she needs. Whenever she meets a new person she tries to get some by pretending she doesn't care about the whole thing."

Well, this was possible, of course, and for a moment I wavered. Then I recalled his wife's obsession with her career. I said, "Don't you see that your wife is too interested in her so-called work to care—"

"Hah! Her so-called work!" He laughed so loudly that the couple in the booth across the floor turned to stare. "And you ought to know!" he cried. "I've always said so, of course, but you're a real professional. Pathetic stuff, isn't it? But tell me," he leaned across the table and whispered, "you didn't give anything away, did you? You didn't mention Webster's Bridge, I hope. It's very handy for me having things set up like that. And besides its being so convenient, I can't help being just a little proud of it. The last place she thinks to look is right under her nose. The very nearest town. In fact, right over the mountain behind her house! You didn't, did you?"

"I didn't! What do you think—"

"Of course," he said, "it wouldn't have made the least difference if you had."

This was exactly what I myself had been going to say. It was disconcerting, this way he had of lifting phrases out of my mind and putting them to his use.

"Because she has such pride," he said, "that if you told her it had been right under her nose all along then she *couldn't* let herself believe it. I wish you had told her. I ought to draw her a map to the place and tell her the best hours to find me there. Then she could never let herself believe it. Next time she asks you, tell her!"

"Let me tell you an easier way to put an end to your fears," I said. "You don't have anything to—"

Suddenly he looked weary and apologetic and he gave a sigh. "Charley, forgive me," he said. "Forget it all. I'm sorry to have dragged you into this mess. Why, we're almost strangers. I appreciate it, don't think I don't. But don't let yourself get involved. Don't let me talk to you about it. It's been going on like this for years and—here. Here's the waiter. Eat your dinner and forget it."

After dinner he suggested a show. We strolled over towards Broadway. We stopped to shelter a light for cigarettes. We moved on and Gavin jerked a thumb over his shoulder. "To think," he said, "it's my money that guy's getting for trailing me."

"Why, that's not even the same man!" I cried. "Are you blind as well?"

"Of course it's not the same man." Gavin was being patient with me. "The first one knew I'd spotted him, so this one relieved him. They always work in pairs."

"Look," I said, pointing to where the man stood innocently examining the billboard of a musical revue. "He's just somebody out looking for something to do with himself. Listen, you'd better get a grip on yourself. You'd better—"

"Well, so long as I'm paying for it," he said grimly, "I might as well have fun."

He edged up close to this pudgy little man and stressing his words for his benefit, said, "Hell, Charley, do you mean to tell me that the best you can do on a night away from the wife is a girlie show? Now come with me and I'll show you a real hot time. (See him take that down in his notebook?)"

"That's his wallet and he's counting his money!" I whispered.

It was one of those standing sandwich boards with pictures of the chorus girls and this tired little man had moved around to the other side for a look at the rest of them. He was rubbing his hands because of the cold and this gesture gave him the look of an old-fashioned lecher, an impression of which he was aware. His timid excitement shone on his face and I took him for a salesman in town for the night, whose main enjoyment of this show would come from thinking all through it of his unsuspecting wife sitting at home in Weehawken or somewhere. He had heard what Gavin said—he could not have helped hearing—and he leered at me around the sandwich board to let me know that he, too, was out on a spree.

Meanwhile Gavin was rattling on. "Listen, Charley, this is kid stuff." (This, too, the little drummer or whatever he was, heard, and frowned; Gavin was belittling the fun he had planned for himself.) "I'll get us a couple of hot numbers to warm this winter evening. How do you like yours, married or single? I like mine already broken in. I once knew a little woman in White Plains. Her husband was a salesman, always out on the road, and that made things very nice. He's probably caught out on the road somewhere tonight. She was all right, let me tell you. Those salesmen's wives, they don't get much and they're always ready for—"

Now the little man flung a look at Gavin and strode away from the marquee in dignified outrage.

"Listen, Charley," he said, projecting his voice after the retreating figure, "let's rent a car and go up to Webster's Bridge. I'll phone my girl and tell her to get in a friend for you!"

"Ssh!" I hissed. "If the man *was* a detective—" Was I going as crazy as he?

"Well, that'll give her something to think about," he said, standing with his hands on his hips and watching his detective slip off to make his report.

I would try one last time to disabuse him. "Now, Gavin," I began, patiently, sympathetically, "believe me. You have nothing to fear from your wife. Nothing. She doesn't care what you do with yourself so long as—"

He was beginning to smile tolerantly at me again.

"Listen. Do you know what she said to me? 'Let him have his fun,' she said."

"Now, Charley," he said, "think a minute. Does that sound likely to you?"

IV

Gavin did not feel it was disloyal of me to go to Alice's teas. He assumed that I shared his judgment of Alice and her circle and he thought my duplicity a good joke on her. In the beginning I went often. Gavin was never there; he hated the men who came even more than the women; and that desperate and phantom fear he had of Alice became all the more pathetic when I observed that I never once heard her mention his name.

Perhaps Gavin's judgment did influence me, for from the start I felt myself obscurely unsuited to that crowd. This seemed unnatural, for they were the people with whom I ought to have felt most in sympathy, so I kept going there in an effort to overcome it, or at least to determine whose fault it was, theirs or mine. And finally I went back because Alice was so importunate.

Alice was always eager to ingratiate herself with a new person; she was especially so with me. Perhaps because I had met Edward first she felt she had to work to overcome a certain prejudice in me. When she learned, as she somehow learned all her sister's movements, that I had met Victoria, she had, she thought, and she was not far wrong, another prejudice to overcome in me. She was even more anxious for my company when during the winter it became known that I'd landed a fair-sized contract.

The price of admission to one of Alice's teas was a slow, worried shake of the head in answer to her question, "How is your work going?"

Now Alice had the best ear in Cressett for whisperings that some person was on his way up, or on his way out, and it was only because your work was known to be going very well that you had been asked to her house. But . . .

"Oh, that's too bad," she would say sympathetically, and the more successful you were known to be the more her face beamed with satisfaction. "But then, what do you expect?" she would say. "If you keep on doing the same old things year after year they love you, but just try something a bit new and they're afraid to risk it." This was directed at her sister Victoria, who was doing very well indeed on the same old thing. Alice herself was forever changing her "style" abruptly and trying something new, "experimenting" as she called it. Her final words of consolation would be, "Well, we all seem to be in a slump just now, but we'll come out of it, won't we?"

Her having chosen me as the special object of her attentions had the effect of making Alice all the more uneasy with me. Her fear of failing to impress me made her urgent and shrill. She always had a look of being too concerned with what she was going to say when I was done talking to pay any attention to me. This made conversation with her rather a sequence of non sequiturs. On top of this, when she did begin to talk she forgot what she had been so carefully planning to say, and chattered desperately, frowning with anxiety over my opinion of her. If I had not observed all these things on first meeting her it was because, unlike most people, who grow more relaxed with you with time, Alice was at her best in the first five minutes of your acquaintance.

She was worried about the invitation, she said, the way she had worded it, afraid she had written asking me please *not* to come to tea Friday at five, and would not let me assure her that she had made no such mistake, but kept me ten minutes at the door while she told of the many embarrassments this habit of hers of being positive when she meant to be negative and vice versa had got her into, how she once lost a dear friend through the constraint between them after she had written and then not been sure whether she said she was glad to hear that she was now home from the hospital, or glad she was not home.

By the time she came to the end of her speech she was frowning with irritation, for she always feared that in her urge to be intimate she might have let something slip that showed her unfavorably. But mostly she was annoyed with the time it took her. Words did take time, and—strange as it may seem in a person who rarely stopped—Alice hated to talk. One ought to appreciate her nature, she felt, without her having to explain it to him, through silent, sympathetic feeling.

When at last she let me join the guests I saw at once the reason for her unusual discomfiture. Her sister had come—uninvited, I was sure, just as I was sure that Victoria's sole reason for coming would be to make Alice uncomfortable.

My acquaintance with Victoria had begun when I turned to find her standing behind me in the Cressett gallery one day, asking me please to tell her why I had avoided her. She was not used to being snubbed for three months by new young artists in town, she said, and when I tried to say something she stopped me with, "Why not say right out that my little sister has told you what a witch I am? Then I can prove what a false notion you've been given." When she left me I realized that she had not felt it necessary to tell me who she was.

Now Alice left her station by the door and joined us and did just what I had told myself she would if she ever got her sister to one of her parties. To be known as Victoria's sister had been the burden of her life, and yet in front of others she was willing to take the credit they gave it. So now she was exhibiting her to her guests and loudly praising her latest work, a series of billboards that had been plastered all over the nation and which among us artists had caused a lot of talk. And joining in with Alice's praises was Robert, Victoria's husband.

Even in writing it, it is hard not to call Robert Mr. Metsys. But already this afternoon Victoria had loudly let a new person know that her name was Mrs. Hines. It amused me that she, who had made the name Metsys famous, was superior to it, while Alice, who had suffered from being the sister of the woman who had made it famous, and who had certainly not done much to enlarge its fame, clung to it to the point that she signed checks and invitations and laundry lists with it. But if it amused me, it amused Victoria much more. She also enjoyed belittling poor Robert by using his undistinguished name. A subtle pleasure, but Victoria's pleasures were.

Now she had taken all she could of Robert's and Alice's praises. "*Kitsch!*" she said. "That's the word for what I do. At least *I*"— she looked pointedly around at the members of her audience— "know it."

Alice smiled to her guests to indicate that this was Victoria's modesty. I had once made the same mistake. Now Victoria's eyes flashed as they had flashed at me. She had no more mock modesty than she had genuine modesty. She was genuinely irate. She wanted everyone to know that she was superior to the way in which she made her money.

She spoke of the men from whom she had stolen, of Picasso and Klee and Miro, and of her guilt for what she had done to them—"What I have done to them in the process of converting them into this," she had said to me my first night at her place, waving her hand around her sumptuous drawing room, and I had remarked to myself that nothing could have better shown how very expensive the room had been. It was an unexpected attitude and gave her, if I may so express it, a marvelous extension of personality. In fact, before that evening was over she had made it seem almost purer in spirit to have done what she had and *know* it, than to have refused to do it, and I had felt myself beginning to appreciate the moral pleasure she took in this role.

Now one of her listeners made the second of the mistakes I had made that night, and said that he, too, could probably, if he searched himself for a moment, find a few such thefts on his conscience, whereupon in the look she gave him she revealed her belief that nobody had a conscience but her. Then she turned to abuse her husband with the gusto with which I had seen her do it.

"*Kitsch!*" she flung at him. "Bad enough to dirty your own good ideas, but to steal and pervert the ideas of others—and when those others are the big men of the age!"

Oh, she was at least a big thief. We others stole from her; she stole from the source itself.

"*Kitsch!*" she flung at him one last time. Poor man, she had left him nothing but his wife, and she would not let him have even a belief in her.

I remembered the first time I saw him. We had left our car at the foot of the steep snow-covered drive, Janice and I. We had not walked far when up at the house a dog barked, and then piano music had started up and floated down to us on the still winter air. It accompanied us all the way, a passage from *The Well-tempered Clavier*, terribly difficult and very well done. After knocking at the door we had had to wait through half a dozen measures for the end. Then Robert, whom I actually did call Mr. Metsys and he did not correct me, greeted us in sneakers, faded corduroys and a tattered denim jumper, which, as he was well aware, made a striking contrast to the splendor behind him as he stood in the door.

I pointed to the piano and said, "Please go on."

"He can't."

It was Victoria who had come gliding into the room unheard. "He can't go on, that's all he knows."

Robert had smiled modestly, as though that was her way of bragging about him. As a matter of fact, it was true. Those thirty-odd measures of Bach were literally all the music he knew. Every time we went there the same passage began when our arrival at the foot of the hill was announced by the bark of the dog, and at the door each time we had to wait until it was finished in a final burst of triumphant virtuosity.

Robert knew music about as he knew sculpture. There was one promising carving in the hall off the drawing room which he modestly owned to. When I asked to see more I was told by Victoria that there weren't any more, he had done that one and then given up. It was not the first such mistake I'd made in the course of our acquaintance, having asked why he never went on with playwriting or anthropology, so to Victoria it seemed time for a general explanation, though I tried desperately to suggest that I didn't want one. Robert looked penitent while Victoria, in a tolerant scolding tone, a tolerant tone which was the most withering contempt I ever want to hear, explained that Robert's weakness had always been a lack of persistence.

I myself had by this time watched him take up hand printing and fitfully resume the playwriting, and I had seen why he never got anywhere with anything. He was licked before he got a start, Victoria so minimized any effort he made—or, I ought to say, she hardly felt it necessary to minimize them now; his own memory of his past failures was enough to foredoom any new undertaking. Robert still cherished visions of himself succeeding at almost anything, but like those photographer's proofs one takes home to choose among for the final print, they had faded and blurred from being kept too long.

"I'm just lazy," he said.

Yet he worked around the house and grounds ten to twelve hours a day. They pretended their liberal politics as the reason for keeping no hired help, but actually they did not need any. "I'm just lazy"—I supposed he would rather feel he could blame some weakness of his own than admit the true reason for his failures.

I strolled over to talk to Hilda Matthews. Hilda was the woman at whose bidding the country's skirts had once risen an incredible six inches, who had brought back the shingle bob, who had originated the horsetail hairdo. A part of me stood abashed before a woman who could change the look of a whole country like that.

We had talked a while when through the door across the room a new man entered and Hilda said, "Oh, it's my husband. I must go over and say hello."

"Has it been that long since you saw him?"

"I can still recognize him," she said.

"Business, I suppose," I said wisely.

"That's the word we use for it," said Hilda gaily. Whereupon I, who thought I'd been holding up my end of one of those knowing talks about the husband's absences and his excuses, realized how very wrong I had been. It was *she* who had been too busy, or told her husband so, to get home nights. She had assumed I understood it that way.

And perhaps I should have. For the next moment I was joined by John Coefield, who said, "Charley, where's your wife? I haven't seen her in ages."

"Neither have I," I said. "She isn't here."

"Not sick, I hope?"

"No," I confessed, "she's at work."

"Work? Why, I never knew Janice *did* anything."

"She didn't 'do' anything until we came here," I told him. "Now she leaves breakfast for me and takes the early train." I found myself using the half-humorous tone for this which I'd observed in other men, and it irritated me.

Arthur Fergusson, who had come up in time to hear this last, said, "Oh-hoh. Becoming one of us, eh, Charley?"

"No," said John Coefield. "That will be when *he* gets the breakfast and *she* takes the later train."

This had an edge to it, and Arthur Fergusson smiled coldly.

Coefield wore such thick glasses that he seemed to be looking into them rather than through them, but even so he made me understand with a look that he had been trapped once already this afternoon by Arthur. Nothing would ever mean much to Arthur after wartime Washington, his captain's uniform and his desk in the OSS—to say nothing of his African trip. At first, right after the war, while others talked of their experiences, he had made his impression, so I was told, by being silent. Now that that war was a good ways back and people spoke more often of the coming one, he talked incessantly of "his war." He had tried every way in the world to go, had lied unsuccessfully about his age and suffered the humiliation of having a recruiting officer scan his employment record and ask what earthly use he thought he might be to a war effort. But it was one of the things in that record that got him in. He had worked once for an American advertising agency in Morocco, writing copy for soap in three native dialects. So he was sent to recruit natives for spying against the Germans.

Surely he remembered one or two of the many times he had told us about it.

His wife remembered not one or two but all the many times he had told everybody, so she came over soon to extricate us from him.

"You off on Morocco again?" she said, giving us an indulgent shake of the head over Arthur, and giving Arthur a less indulgent look.

Arthur drew himself up and it seemed for a moment he was going to answer back and cause a scene. Then he subsided and gave a sheepish grin.

Coefield said, "Go on, Arthur. You were about to say?"

I thought it was very considerate of Coefield to do that, and quite convincing the look of interest he put on. After a hesitant glance at his wife, Arthur smiled his appreciation.

"You are much too polite, John," said Mary Fergusson.

John Coefield's determined answer surprised me. "Not in the least," he snapped. "Charley and I were absorbed in what Arthur was saying."

Mary shrugged her shoulders and retreated.

A sigh escaped John Coefield as he settled down to Arthur's war again.

We men had gradually drifted together in one corner, and whenever that happened the subject of gardening was bound to come up sooner or later.

One man was a recent convert to organic gardening and he was telling of the dangers to one's health, to the soil, to the national economy, to the very rhythm of nature that came from using chemical fertilizers. They killed earthworms. Now earthworms, he said with much enjoyment of the words, dropped castings that were simply incredibly rich in trace elements, besides keeping the soil aerated by boring holes, networks of holes in it. The great thing about fertilizing with compost was that it was natural. This was admitted by all to be a weighty argument. The word *natural* was a magic word. Moreover, it was felt that the use of artificial fertilizers was not very sporting somehow.

All this made one man who had been prodigal with superphosphate rather uncomfortable. "Well," he demanded, "who had the biggest tomatoes last year, Tom, and the earliest? You or me?"

Bigger, Tom was willing to admit. A day or two earlier perhaps. But as nourishing? What chemical fertilizer did to a tomato was blow it up, force it. But the food value was nil.

Then there was the matter of insecticides. Who wanted to eat arsenic and lead and nicotine with his vegetables?

This man was fifty or so, rather fat, and proud of his callused hands. They showed honest toil and he enjoyed the way they fitted so ill with his job of producing radio programs at fifty thousand dollars a year. I got a vision of him out in his garden before going to the train in the morning raking Mexican beetles into a tin can full of kerosene with a little paddle.

It was growing dusky outside and Alice had turned on no lights but allowed the room to steep in soft grayness. But now it was time for the two groups, the women around one fireplace and the men around the other, to come together for a last exchange before breaking up to go home. To signal the arrival of that moment Alice switched on a lamp.

A change of mood had been coming over me which this sudden light and rustle of activity quickened. The amused, half-contemptuous detachment with which I had been listening to the men now struck me as false and I felt myself filled with a vague dissatisfaction. Suddenly I felt the emptiness of their lives and knew that my own life was no better, no more vigorous. I turned from them.

When I turned I saw Gavin standing in the farthest door, smilingly surveying the room. He had never looked so young, so gay and reckless. From the door he held open came a draft of cool air and to me at that moment he looked like a bringer of fresh air.

Some kind of look was passing between him and the ladies' end of the room. I turned and saw responding to him, unnoticed by all but me, a woman whom I had often seen at Alice's teas. Gavin caught sight of his brother-in-law and pursed his lips with disdain. Then he cast upon the men's corner where I stood a look of utter contempt but reserved a smile for me, and for that I forgave him his insanity. I was glad to be his friend and I recalled with shame the times earlier that I had avoided him.

He strolled over and joined the women. He greeted each one smoothly, concentrating on each that smile of his and all his attention. But when he came to Leila Herschell he blushed, stammered, looked caught, and did a job which a ten-year-old could have bettered in covering up his slip. Now I knew where I had seen the woman before, in Gavin's station wagon the night I got off the train at Webster's Bridge. I looked at Alice. She was talking with somewhat hysterical unconcern to her brother-in-law. How *she*, Leila, was taking it, I couldn't tell—I never got to know her very well—but it is possible that she was enjoying it.

The thing I couldn't understand was why he had seemed so terribly put out at finding her there, when he had recognized and winked at her from all the way across the room.

By now the men had all gathered round and Gavin went to the portable bar and offered to mix drinks. I think they all sensed the possibility of a scene, for everyone accepted eagerly. He asked each of us—except his brother-in-law, and he pointedly asked Victoria how he wanted his—how each of us took it. But he did not ask Leila Herschell. Hers he mixed automatically. And it was a very personal kind of a drink with a rare combination of ingredients, which Gavin measured and mixed with an all-too-practiced hand. I was spellbound. It took him a long time and in the process he seemed to forget the existence of everyone in the room except her. By this time I was not the only one spellbound. In fact, the only one who was not was Alice, who was trying with desperate chit-chat—the only sound in the room now—to divert the bewitched attention of her neighbors. The last touch was Gavin's tasting the drink himself very deliberately and smacking his lips judiciously, and, satisfied, handing it to Leila with a flourish, all of which seemed to declare an absolute identity of taste between them, developed over a long and intimate period. All this, plus the husky tone in which he spoke to her, was quite enough, but to add one final touch he straightened himself from bending close over her, and, as though sensing the quiet, the stares, suddenly coming to and discovering the enormity of his indiscretion, he hardened his neck and looked around at Alice in wide-eyed alarm. It was the best job of bad acting I ever hope to see, and I understood then that was what it was meant to be.

I realized that Gavin had never been trying to conceal his philanderings from Alice, but to make her take notice of them. How I must have wounded him that night when I said she was too wrapped up in her career to care what he did with himself!

I saw him suddenly as a kind of inverted sentimentalist, a believer in marriage—the old-fashioned kind—a man with pride enough left to care if his wife ignored him. He was out of place and out of time, with a pride not to be bent and pacified by the memory of one glamorous, martial, male moment of escape from his routine of meaningless work which any other man could do as well as he and any woman as well as any man, nor in finding something—like gardening—which he could do and his wife couldn't. He took entirely too much pleasure in the mere fact of being unfaithful to his wife, though, who knows, I asked myself, but what in perverse times like ours, perhaps the only way left to honor a thing is in the breach rather than in the observance.

I went home and made my wife promise to give up her job.

V

The next day on the train Gavin and I began playing our game. I was his spy and on mornings after seeing Alice I reported her latest wiles to catch him. He knew it was pure invention and that his "slip" about his mistress had made Alice not a whit more interested, but this called forth our creative abilities and made the game all the more exciting. I quite outdid myself to help him feel hounded and harassed and to feel he was causing her acute distress. Times, I was in some peril of believing it myself.

I pointed out that she was beginning to show wear. She had grown dark circles under her eyes and become careless of her hair and there were days when she looked quite distraught. But the reason, I knew, was the continued failure of her work. She had brought herself at last to come to me for help and this necessity made her almost insulting before she was done. But it was not that which made me so halfhearted in pushing her work. The spectacle of middle-aged love had always appealed to my sentimentality, and though I don't think I quite hoped to bring the Gavins to a state of belated bliss, still I certainly was not going to do anything to help things stay as they were between them, and if Alice were finally discouraged about that career of hers, why, who knew, perhaps she might return to him, become a wife. Stranger things had happened. The Gavins as they were now had happened.

He kept me posted daily, too, on his running skirmish with her, appearing on the train some mornings looking harried and hollow-eyed and hinting darkly how close upon him she was, then the next morning smiling and crafty and pleased with himself at the way he had outfoxed her this time.

He would get off the 6:36 at Webster's Bridge and have dinner with his mistress. Then maybe he would stay, maybe he would go home to Cressett. When he went home he took one of about seven different roads, never allowing himself to decide which until the last moment. He changed cars often, buying each time a different make and color so that none should become familiar to the workers whose houses lay along the back edges of the towns, nor to their children who played in the streets until late at night. After leaving Webster's Bridge all roads climbed above the long valley where in the distance the lights of Cressett lay like scattered coals, and Gavin tried to describe the pleasure it gave him in coming home from his rendezvous to look down on those lights, to glide powerfully through the night past darkened, unsuspecting farmhouses. He felt himself freed from all likeness to the people in those houses, and at the sight of a fox stealing across the road one night with a chicken in its mouth he had felt a thrill of fellowship.

It was clear to me that love was dead between him and Alice. I doubted that there had ever been any. It was not his heart that was wounded by unrequited love, but his pride that was wounded by her ignoring him. I knew it was pride with him, and, if you take my meaning, *male* pride, when he told me that he made a point, even if "Webster's Bridge" (the only name I ever heard him use for his mistress) bored him, of not getting home until after midnight, and that when he came in he made as much noise as possible, for unlike most men, who try to keep their wives from learning how late they've been, Gavin wanted to be sure Alice knew how late he was. There had been times, he told me somewhat shamefacedly, when he had sneaked in so she would not know how early he was.

He was proud of his record of never offering her any excuse for his nights away from home. She was too proud to ask, he said, so she just had to stew in silent fury. He had a variation on this of sometimes offering her an excuse so transparent it would have insulted the intelligence of a ten-year-old. Now *that*, I could imagine, *would* irritate Alice.

He told me of evenings he had spent away from home and not in Webster's Bridge either, but wandering all night in New York. Once, around five in the morning, he had found himself near the Battery and he never forgot the sun coming up over the East River and the gulls rising out of the mist. He had stayed away from his mistress deliberately, so that his torture of Alice would be abstract, pure. I wondered whether, sitting there on the pier that dawn, he had been able to convince himself that Alice was lying awake in an agony of jealous suspicion. Or had he lost by that time all sense of the reason for his act?

He had his own doubts now, and wondered sometimes if all was right with him in the head. His memory was going bad, for example. Or rather, the worse it got for recent things, the more vividly he recalled things that had happened to him fifteen and twenty years ago. Things returned to him in dreams, painful scenes for the most part, in which he had played a foolish role or done something despicable. He was depressed often and he assured me solemnly that he was a much less happy man than I no doubt imagined. He was always restless and dissatisfied lately and had even caught himself asking himself such silly questions as whether he was a success in life. More and more he found himself, he said with self-contemptuous amazement, *thinking* all the time. He was dissatisfied with his mistress, for one thing, tired of her; she no longer excited him. Or rather, he added hastily and with a leer, other women excited him more. He told me one morning of having had a woman up at the Cressett house the night before, having got Alice away on an elaborate pretext (a simple one would not have satisfied that strong sense of drama which I was beginning to recognize as perhaps his main characteristic) and the delightful thing was that the woman was not his mistress. Oh, she had once been his mistress, but that was long ago, and, as he said, what woman hadn't been his mistress one time or another? He laughed to fill the coach when he thought of not only Alice away on a wild-goose chase, but his regular mistress sitting at home in Webster's Bridge, both being deceived at once. There he had had, I said to myself, two wives to be unfaithful to at the same time; was there ever such respect for marriage?

His escapade excited him tremendously, and all the more because he did not understand why. There was something about his enjoyment of such things that mystified him, and more than once he asked me to explain it to him. "Now what makes me do things like that?" he would sober suddenly and say. Yet when I tried to tell him he shut me off at once, just as he always shut off his own self-questionings. He preferred to act on impulse, to be wrong if necessary in what he did, but not to be deliberative. And yet, he said, he had not always been the kind of fellow who, for example, could decide without investigation that I was a detective hired by his wife, and he confessed to just a shade of doubt that the little man in the city that night had been one. But what if he wasn't? What the hell! Deliberation robbed things of excitement. He was too old now, he said, to start looking back over everything he had ever done to find out whether he had been right or wrong.

But, like everyone, he had an urge to understand himself which even he could not always deny. He liked me to ask him questions about himself. So I said, "Whatever made you marry her?"

"Money," he said. But he said it too quickly. There was something in his tone which assured me that this disarming, frank admission was a lie. It was not that he seemed to expect me to doubt it, but that it seemed not to satisfy him entirely. His true reason must be something pretty shameful, I thought, if to claim this one was less painful to him. And then I knew what it was—to him far more shameful—he had married her because he loved her.

"She had a lot?" I asked.

"It seemed a lot to me at the time. It was during the crash, you see. I'd always made good money and when the crash came I laughed. We all did. Things would pick up in no time, so why worry. But things didn't and so—"

"So she came along with her gilt-edged securities and you saw your chance and took it."

"I married her," he said, and with those words the false tone was gone. "I think she had pretty well accustomed herself to the idea of staying single, being a career woman—or trying to become one. Only one man before me had ever had the nerve or the ignorance to buck her sister and propose to her. And you should have seen him. He was a florist. She showed me his picture once after we'd been married a while. In this picture he's on the board-walk at Coney Island in an old-fashioned bathing suit down to his knees. He was about five feet tall and already bald all the way back to his ears. His name was Adelbert something. I think she meant to make me jealous by showing me his picture. Well, she didn't marry him because her sister objected, and she *did* marry me for the same reason. It was the first time in her life she ever crossed Victoria and for a while it made her feel she had done something heroic, defied everything for a great love."

He took a breath, then went on. "I spent the night before our wedding with this girl I was keeping. I guess you might say I'd decided to convince myself with one last fling that I had no regrets at leaving the single life behind. Anyhow, this girl had sort of dared me to do it and I did. Her name was Dolores. Dolores Davis. I still remember her quite well." (Evidently he thought this quite a feat of memory, considering, I supposed, how many had come since her.) "Alice believed I was out at a stag party too drunk to get to her place. To punish me she announced on our wedding night that she'd determined not to let me 'share her bed' for three months. She even marked down the exact date when I could begin to on a calendar—to torment me. That's the thing that's always got me. Alice never liked the business in bed, but she thought she ought to. It was the modern thing.

"In those days," he informed me in an aside, "people were beginning to talk about repression and all that sort of thing.

"I don't know how many women I've had since Dolores Davis. If you want to know," he said, "ask Alice. I'll bet she can tell you!"

. . . And so the spring wore on and the strange, perverse troubles of the Gavins wore on and I thought how many changes of the season had brought no change to them and I wondered why I thought it ever would.

One night Gavin took me to dinner to the house he kept in Webster's Bridge. There was something—something unpleasant, I grant—but at the same time something rather touchingly inno-cent in his way of reminding us every few minutes that we were all doing something we oughtn't to be. I felt embarrassed for Leila—

not for the obvious reason, but because she seemed unaware how insignificant a place she, as a person in her own right, had in Gavin's heart, and I remember trying to help her out by arousing a spark of jealousy in him with questions about the husband she still had somewhere, though if he had been jealous of her he would have seen the eyes she was making at me.

VI

It must be hard, in keeping up an illusion, to be helped by the one person who has seen through it, no matter how sympathetic he may be. One morning, towards which I'd seen signs accumulating, Gavin allowed me to do all the talking, thereafter he responded but feebly to my reports of Alice's maneuvers, then I missed him for three days running and after that his participation in our game was no more than perfunctory and I began to miss him regularly every other day or so, both in the morning and in town at night, then for four or five days at a stretch, and at last for as long as two weeks together. I could imagine him picking up another newcomer, first accusing him of being a detective if not something more outlandish, and training him for my role.

Meanwhile Janice's father continued to ply me with gifts of fine cigars and rare books and old brandies, until she told him he would spoil my taste. He seemed to have had his answer in readiness. "No," he said, "I'll whet it." He must have. I got ambitious in the late spring and spent nights working overtime, and on one of those nights on the late train when I left my seat in the deserted coach and went out on the platform for a breath of air, I found Gavin. We must have stood for five minutes not three feet apart in the yellow light, he looking out one window at the night rushing past and I out the other, and then he recognized me first. Had he not I don't believe I would have known him at all. He was so changed that I know no way to express it but to say that now he looked his age. And though he was pleased to see me, his smile failed to enliven his face much, as it had done on a former occasion.

Our meetings had been ritualized before, and now I took his weariness and his pleasure at seeing me as a cue to begin again where we had left off. I said, "My, she must be really out to get you this time."

His reaction was slow. He thought for a moment with visible effort, apparently not knowing what I was talking about. Then he cried, "No!"

"No?" I echoed weakly.

And, seeing that I was not sure of it, that I had said it only to cheer him up, he laughed and said, "That old business is all over, Charley." There was a maturity in his tone which saddened me.

I remembered telling him once that like Dorian Gray he looked younger with each sin. Obsessed, desperate as his life had been, it was just what he had thrived on, it was what had kept him going. I felt guilty for having allowed him to tire of me. I said, "Hah! You're playing right into her hands. That's just what she intends —to lull you into complacency."

For a moment I thought I had reawakened him. For a moment the old fear came into his eyes. Then he said, "Nonsense. You're just trying to scare me."

We returned to the coach and when we were seated he turned suddenly and caught me looking aggrievedly at the changes in his face and he said, "You're looking older, Charley."

It was not the irony of this which made me thoughtful. He had always been too self-absorbed to notice my looks or anything else about me. Our mutual interest had been him. Strange, to think that becoming less selfish could be a sign of a man's breaking up. He was all solicitude now and he presumed upon our friendship to hope earnestly that my marriage was working out well. And then he asked rather determinedly what I was doing out so late.

I said I had worked late.

Janice was a fine girl, he said.

I agreed.

He hoped I appreciated her, he said, with more than a shade of doubt in his look.

Now, just what had those few weeks since I'd seen him done? I asked after Alice, to which he replied in a tone from which I guessed that she was still alive, or that if she was dead that he hadn't heard about it, then I asked after Leila and he replied in the very same tone. I waited for an explanation.

"Oh, yes," he said. "You didn't know about that, did you? How long has it been since I saw you? Well, she and I broke up, oh, it must be, oh, five or six weeks ago." He was amazed, apparently, to realize that it was no longer ago. He wanted then to tell me something more, but something that he did not know how to lead up to, and finally he decided to dispense with any lead-up. "Well, about her," he said. "I've told Katherine about her, of course, but all the same—"

He paused and I nodded to show that I had explained Katherine to myself. But this did not altogether please him. I had placed her, perhaps, a little too categorically.

"You get off with me at Webster's and come in for a while. Have dinner," he said.

It was no use my protesting the time. I had to see Katherine.

She was waiting for him, standing in the light of the doorway, waving. He stopped the car and she started out to meet him, but when she saw me get out of the car she stopped and, to my astonishment, grew quite flustered. Awkwardness was the last thing I expected—I can't tell you how long it was since I had seen a woman blush—and it was still less to be expected in a woman who looked like she did. For she was one of us, all right; such things as her relation with Gavin were not unheard-of to her; perhaps, indeed, she was what the women I knew only thought they were; there were depths of sophistication in her eyes and she carried herself in the approved way; she was knowing, chic— despite her innocent calico dress and her frilly little apron—but, as the evening taught me, there had remained an incorruptible simplicity in her and she filled her position with a refreshing unease.

No, she was not naturally the earnest, simple young matron sort, nor was their union, hers and Gavin's, the rocking-chair and reading-lamp and hassock-y kind which I saw through the open door. Things had changed here since Leila's time, and the thought of a life of sin in such ultra-middle-class respectability had me ready to laugh aloud—until I caught Katherine's look as it came to me over Gavin's shoulder when he hugged her. That look told me what I should have known—that he, not she, was responsible for that room, that dress and that apron, and it warned me not to laugh.

She was that way, fiercely protective—even after he told her that I was his only friend—of his dream of domesticity, the sentimentality of which was simply incredible. He had to show me all of it, and it was like a trip through a Sears Roebuck catalog: the kitchen, a vision of decalcomania and chintz, the silver service (Orange Blossom pattern), the newly redone knotty pine breakfast nook for two and the dining room for eight, the gadgets which were enough to make housekeeping a chore for Katherine —and throughout our tour I noticed her shy but determined affection for him and I approved her not letting my presence keep him from feeling it.

I was their first guest, so they treated me to all their accumulated hospitality. They treated me also to all the traditional foolery which newlyweds feel called upon to amuse older people with. There was a little skit in which he burlesqued his own easy householder air, one in which she demonstrated her wifely interest in his business day and her inability to understand the devious workings of the masculine world; then he tried to fix the iron which he must do if he were to have a clean shirt for tomorrow, and there was, of course, his disastrous attempt, in the costume of her apron, to mix the salad dressing.

While she prepared the dinner and he and I sat in the living room, he tried not to let me see how completely she absorbed him, tried to pay some attention to what I said, would engage me in earnest talk—only to break off and dash into the kitchen to get down from the shelf something for which she had only just begun to reach. And once he had to call me out there to show me that she had been about to put cinnamon on the asparagus, thinking it was pepper.

"She's nearsighted!" he said rapturously. He thought this the most attractive, the most delightfully quaint, the most wondrously lovable quality any woman ever possessed—he had even made her feel it was something to be modest over—while she, it was apparent, thought herself inhumanly blessed to have got a man with twenty/twenty vision.

After dinner, over drinks, while they spared me only the minimum polite attention, I began to feel quite rosy. I was touched by the innocence and the sincerity of it, but more than that, by its being for Gavin so climacteric. I was beginning to feel quite paternal towards them, when suddenly . . .

"Mommy!"

It came from upstairs. It was all that was lacking. It was too much. I burst out laughing. Gavin looked at me reproachfully and he and Katherine exchanged stricken glances.

"I'll go," said Gavin.

It was the moving, Katherine explained. It still frightened Shirley to wake in a strange bedroom. "She's used to having me sleep with her," she said—then blushed violently.

Gavin, embarrassed at so much happiness, came down bearing a little girl who hugged him tightly and, ashamed of being seen in a crisis by a stranger, buried her face in his neck. When at last she was ready to be presented, Gavin introduced me as her Uncle Charley. Skeptical as she was of this sudden connection, even she, it seemed, had resolved to humor him.

He passed her to Katherine and sat looking at the picture they made and then suddenly his hospitality was at an end. "Your wife will be worried," he said in a tone which admitted no argument, and I supposed that in his new state this was a thing he did not want to be responsible for.

As he drove me home I watched his face in the glow of the dashboard light. Perhaps it was only that I noticed it for the first time then, but his face had undergone another of those transformations of which it was so capable; it lost years as the man in the ads loses his headache on taking the pill. He was almost deliriously happy and he couldn't get rid of me fast enough to carry out his determination. And yet, he told me later, he had thought at one point of taking me with him, to have someone to share his joy —that was how little difficulty he foresaw and how little need he felt for privacy when he asked Alice for a divorce.

He found a car in the drive, Victoria's car. This put him out of his stride for just a moment, then he realized that he could count upon her presence as a help. After all, what had Victoria said for twenty years but that Alice would do well to get rid of him? And if it occurred to him to reckon the effect of Robert's presence, he dismissed it, as anyone who knew Robert—or perhaps I should say, as anyone who knew Victoria—was bound to do.

He was disappointed to find the fully lit drawing room empty and it annoyed him to have to search for them. I think he actually was impatient to share his enthusiasm with them and when he burst into the studio where they sat I believe he half-expected them to guess his state and congratulate him.

He did not even pause over Alice's question, "Where have you been?"

Then he began to notice with some surprise that the looks on their faces were not friendly.

"Where have you been?" Alice repeated. "These ten days."

He had actually forgotten how long it was since he had been home. In his late joy he had forgotten that he had another home in Cressett. Amazement over this was his first thought, then the full impact of Alice's question struck him. The irony of it was too much and he laughed. To gain a moment's time he strolled across the studio to the window, where, to look more at ease, he tapped out a rhythm on the drawing table. His fingers came back to him capped with dust. He looked at them slowly, then at the three faces. He saw Victoria smile faintly and he saw Alice flush. He knew then why Victoria was here and in Alice's face he saw what it had cost her to ask her sister to come.

Little was said by anyone. Their faces spoke for them. Gavin stood with his hopes still in his eyes and Victoria sat surveying him and Alice sat looking, as he told me later, very much as she had the first time he ever saw her. All Alice's professional dreams had at last deserted her and she had been brought sharply to face the fact of her age. She was bitter. All her resistances had been lowered and so when Gavin had not come home for ten days she had found herself vulnerable in some small but vital organ of female vanity that she never knew she had. She had become the helpless little spinster that he had married and she knew she had no one to fall back upon except Victoria. That was not going to be any soft cushion to fall back on, but something more like cold stone, and she was determined that if her rest henceforth was to be uneasy, Edward's would be, too. Victoria, she knew, had waited a long time for this; one whipping post, Robert, had never given her the workout she needed daily, and Alice was determined that for every lash she felt she would make Edward feel two. He had something now that he really wanted, something through which she could hurt him.

She did not want him back. Marrying him in the first place had meant for her that she no longer needed a husband. He had never suited her anyhow. She would have liked a husband like Robert, one who allowed himself to be made over into a kind of decorative, thoroughbred-looking hearth dog.

It was Robert's face which said the most to Gavin. For Robert had always hated him and Gavin knew it and knew why and now he saw that he would have to pay for his difference, those twenty years of independence, for Robert meant not to leave him a shirt to his back.

VII

I see Gavin now and again on the train and sometimes we ride together, but I can't be much company to him now, he doesn't need anybody to stimulate any mock fears in him anymore, and he feels bad that he is no more company to me. He is aging badly and the strain of trying to lead a double life—that is, to include his legal one—is beginning to tell. He never tried to make his excuses convincing before, so now when he does steal a night away for himself, for Katherine, he has trouble thinking up what to tell Alice. He has softened a great deal towards Alice. No doubt this is partly tactical but mostly it is genuine. He knows now how much she missed in life and he is tender with her. But no matter what he does it's wrong; when he comes home nights she is more suspicious than when he stays away, his excuses confirm her suspicions and his kindness leaves her no doubt at all.

I tell him every time I see him to get out of that house in Webster's Bridge and he agrees vacantly but does nothing about it. Lately I've even seen him get off the train there again and just last night I was sure I saw Robert Hines follow him off there. He likes the place. It is the scene of all his happiness. He likes to recall what it was to him before Katherine and to contrast that with his present love. Perhaps he still tries to convince himself that they won't think to look so near home. But at bottom it is hopelessness that keeps him there. What he had found at last seemed to him from the start too good to last and he is convinced that to move would merely postpone the inevitable end of a happiness which is more than he deserves.

Dolce Far' Niente

AT THE banquet in honor of the Donatis after Giorgio retired from business, as old friends drank to them and recalled their early days, Gina felt as though they were the stars for the night of that television program *This Is Your Life.*

Joe Carlucci, in his toast, recalled Giorgio when he was just off the boat. Hard times those were. Little work for anybody, much less for a carpenter, which was what Giorgio had been born, back home in Borgo Santo Spirito. Lines of the jobless stretching around streetcorners in the city, and even in a small New England town, even one full of immigrants from your own part of the old country, only odd jobs for one who spoke no English. Aged twenty-nine, Giorgio apprenticed himself to the language.

His English in those days was that of the lumberyard and the hardware store—still was, pretty much. Word by word, how hard they came, how slowly they added up! As if he had had to make each one by hand using dull tools. *Colla:* glue. *Chiodo:* nail. *Legno:* wood. *Cacciavite:* screwdriver . . . And the curse of inches and feet, ounces and pounds, pints, quarts, and gallons. Hearing little children rattle off the tongue-twisting sounds, a grown man felt like a cretin.

Lou Whitehead (born Luigi Capobianco) remembered Giorgio scavenging for scrap lumber and hauling it on his back through the streets at night, laden like a mule.

Giorgio had been astounded to see good wood going to waste. Back home in Italy, that land of stone, every splinter was used and used again for generations. Here fine lumber was to be found discarded in vacant lots, in alleyways, on loading platforms at the backs of stores—packing crates, pallets, boxes: yours for the hauling away. So, on his back at first, then later with a cart he made using the wheels of a bicycle he found on somebody's dump, Giorgio collected wood at night, roaming all over the town, and brought it to stack in his back yard.

What to make out of it? In those days nobody—meaning none of *us, noialtri*—was building much of anything. The only thing *we* were doing with any dependability was dying. So from his scavenged lumber Giorgio began making coffins. Poor coffins, pieced together out of scraps, but suited to the times, cheap, what the people could afford.

Most of the guests at that testimonial dinner were members of the burial insurance plan which, remembering them from the old country, Giorgio had started. In the beginning, subscribers paid, depending upon their age and upon Giorgio's appraisal of their health, their habits, the hazards of their jobs, twenty-five cents, fifty cents a week, and for this Giorgio undertook to bury them when the time for it came. The scheme had almost ruined him at the outset. He could afford to laugh now, but remember Paolo Vacca? Stout as a staff, a bachelor without habits, a tailor, just thirty-two years old, that sly one outsmarted Giorgio by cashing in from a prick of his needle after paying just seventy-five cents in premiums.

Times were bad but even so people could not put off dying until a better day. When the filling station just down the road from the main gate of the Catholic cemetery went out of business, Giorgio rented the building. The location was ideal for a coffinmaker. With the war, times got better. People could afford to bury themselves in finer style. What Italian could resist having the last word with his friends by piquing their envy with a big expensive funeral? One such was a challenge to an even bigger one. Giorgio made a down payment on the building. Before long he was the boss of two men and two women. The women padded and quilted the satin linings that his coffins now featured.

Giorgio began to think of taking a wife and starting a family. For that he had to wait for the war to end.

Because when Giorgio thought of a wife he thought, naturally, of home. No American woman for him, it went without saying. Like bred to like. American women were all right for American men, but for *noialtri* they were too independent, spoiled, lazy, extravagant, prone to infidelity, lax in bringing up their children. Nor could Giorgio marry just any Italian girl. For example, one from the Piemonte would never do for him. The Piemontesi lived on *gnocchi*. On Giorgio's stomach *gnocchi* lay like a tombstone. In the Veneto, now, they ate *polenta*. Ah, *polenta!*

What Giorgio must have was a woman of his own strain. One who spoke the dialect. Who knew and could gossip with him about the people back home. A poor girl—though that went without saying: there was no other kind in Borgo Santo Spirito— a peasant girl, a *contadina*, a worker, one who knew the value of money, who would be grateful to him every minute of her life for lifting her out of that *miseria* and bringing her to America. A robust, obedient girl like they made them nowhere else, to bear him robust, obedient sons to help him in the business.

He went home to choose a wife in the autumn of 1947. He said in the village that he had come to visit his family. Nonetheless, unmarried girls—five, six to a family in some unfortunate cases— hung from their windows and balconies like canaries in cages whenever the rich Americano passed beneath.

He had seen Gina when she came down from the mountain where she had spent the summer tending the herd and making cheese. Brown as a chestnut she was and with muscles on her like a man's.

"Daughter," said her father, "Signor Donati here wants to marry you and take you with him to America. You are young. It is a long way to go. We will miss you. What do you say?"

She would have said yes to the Devil if he had come from America. What she said was what she had always said, although she was then a woman of seventeen: "It is for you to decide, *babbo,* "but knowing she would get her wish, that her father was as happy to have a child of his escape to America as she was glad to go, though it should mean they never saw each other again in this life.

They were married in the parish church of Borgo Santo Spirito. Gina still had as a memento one of the *confetti,* a candied almond, its silver coating long since blackened by time. They came home to Phillipsville where she bore Giorgio one son and two daughters, worked the farm he bought for her to work, tended her herd and made cheese, kept chickens, grew vegetables, raised rabbits for the table, ranging over the land with her sickle and her basket for the plants they favored, kept her barn neater than most women kept their kitchens and, expecting from them labor that no American was willing to give, lost one hired man after another so that when it got to be too much for her, with the children now gone from home and the house too big for the two of them and she alone in it all day, the farm was sold to city-folks for a good profit and they moved into town where, a country girl all her life, Gina felt lost and, without her animals to tend and to talk to, useless and lonely, in all that time never wearing anything but black while attending every Italo-American funeral in the town and county.

All the funerals! How many souls lay awaiting the Day of Judgment far from the place of their birth in coffins built by Giorgio Donati!

"A nice funeral," he would say as they rode home from the cemetery. "They chose our best model. Nothing too good for them. It shows respect. Judge a man by the funeral his family gives him."

Now she had nagged him into retiring and turning over the shop to son Frank and for the last month she had had him at home "with his hands in his hands."

"*Sono stanca morte della morte!*" she said. "*Viviamo un po' mentre viviamo, per pietà!*"

She always had to say everything to him twice, the first time in Italian for his benefit, the second time in English for herself. He never understood her English, although it was far better than his. It was as though, the language having cost him such effort, having, in fact, defeated him, he could never believe that she had been able to learn it.

She was proud of her English. Well she might be! God knew what labor it had cost her, *lingua bisbètica!* She had come over speaking not one word of it. When she tried to pronounce a word it was like having a tombstone on her tongue. And that was just one word. There was one to be learned for every word she knew in Italian. That thought had many times made Gina hold her head in her hands and cry. Whenever she found a word that was a cognate—a cousin—she rejoiced as though having found a life-and-blood American cousin she never knew she had. Yet he insisted on their speaking Italian. As though to keep her in her place. She came to think of English as the language of emancipation, an emancipation other women had won, not she. Sometimes, God help her, she resented her mother tongue, as though it were a mark of subjection, of inferiority.

But if she chafed at being made to speak Italian with Giorgio, and took it out on him by making him listen twice to everything, she had to pay for it with the children. With them the case was reversed. She would have liked sometimes to speak Italian with them, but they had forgotten all that she had taught them.

When they were little she had spoken both languages with them, correcting them in English, reserving Italian for intimacy and affection—it was a language so well suited to motherhood! She knew of course that it was bad manners to speak a language that another person did not know; before she learned English she herself had suffered the pain of that slight many times. It was only when they were alone together that she spoke to the children in the old tongue. As infants they lay in the straw or in the grass and she crooned to them as she milked or gathered fodder for the rabbits, old songs from the old country and from times long ago.

Then the girls came home from play crying and were ashamed to say what had made them cry, the boy came home bruised, bloodied, and was ashamed to say what he had fought over. After that, whenever she spoke to them in Italian they were uneasy, embarrassed. They would answer her only in English. In time it came to be their only tongue. Then Gina spoke Italian with only one person, the one with whom she would have preferred to speak English.

"I am tired to death of death! Let us live a little while we are alive, for pity's sake!"

Bewildered by her outburst, Giorgio asked, "What is it that you would like to do?"

A tombstone on her tongue, in neither language could she find a word to say. How was she to know what she would like to do? What opportunity had she ever had to learn what diversions life offered? She knew only what she did not want to do. Not work every minute of the day. Not be always a funeral mute, always dressed in black, always in the presence of grief, of relatives of the dead. Until she was put into her own, never again to go near another coffin.

Afterwards she felt foolish and chided her unruly old heart. Fearful of being punished for her ingratitude, she counted her blessings along with the beads of her rosary.

Now, looking about her at the banquet table, at her children and her grandchildren, Gina awaited a feeling of contentment. She had earned it, that she knew. This if ever was the time for it. Instead she asked herself was it for this that she had left home and come to a strange country? Was it for this that she had worked so hard, so long? Was it for this that she had been so self-denying, so *risparmiatissima?* The huge savings that Giorgio and she were wildly rumored to have laid up had earned them the envy of their friends, and to be envied was sweet; what was bitter was the knowledge that it had earned them the contempt of their children. What they despised was not just their parents' frugality but all the old-world ways it represented. When, shocked at some extravagance, Gina lectured them and told how life had been back in Borgo Santo Spirito, they sighed wearily and said, "Mom, this is the U.S.A. You only live once and you can't take it with you." Using her childhood as a lesson in the need to work and to save, Gina had succeeded in teaching her children to be bored with her childhood and ashamed of their background of poverty. Towards the three Americans to whom she had given birth, Gina had the feeling that they were of a different race, one that held itself superior to hers and despised her native tongue, her memories, the history and the customs of her people and her place. In the land where she had spent most of her life she felt herself to be a stranger.

The evening ended with the presentation to Giorgio by his former employees of a watch, now that he would never again need to know the time of day. It was passed around the table for all to admire, ending with Gina. It was a heavy gold pocket watch with a heavy gold chain. The watch was silent, its hands still. That was because it had yet to be wound and set going, as Gina quickly realized; but for a moment it seemed to her that time had stopped, had never begun, that in her gnarled and workworn fingers she held the emblem of her joyless past, her joyless future, her approaching end. Attributing her tears to gratitude and a sense of fulfillment, the guests all smiled at her.

As for Giorgio, never one for *dolce far' niente*, he had lately found a way to pass the time. In his basement workshop he was busy nowadays making little wooden chests. Of scrap lumber— there was an endless supply at the shop. Nice little lidded chests. For keeping things in.

The Patience of a Saint

WHENEVER THE villagers of Tracytown sighed and said, as they had been doing for some thirty years now, "What will become of poor Ernest when old lady van Voorhees dies?" they were thinking not of Ernest's dependence upon his mother but rather of his dependence upon her dependence upon him. Ernest van Voorhees lived for his mother. Poor soul, he had nothing else to live for.

The van Voorhees for generations had been subsistence farmers. While all about them mechanization came and small farmers like them sold out to bigger holdings, moneyed outsiders for whom farming was a profitable loss, they kept on with their few dairy cows, sold eggs, hay for the saddlehorses of the ever-growing number of summer and weekend people up from the city. They netted herring in the Hudson on their spring spawning run and smoked and salted down a year's supply as their pioneer forebears had done. They canned the produce from their kitchen garden, stored roots, apples. In the fall they regularly put their couple of deer in the village's cold-storage locker.

But even for Ernest, who lived only to work, and no bigger than it was, the farm was too much for him alone. So, his younger brother having been killed in Korea, when his old father died it had to be sold. Since then Ernest and his mother had lived in a trailer some five miles outside the village, not far from their old farm, for whose new owners Ernest worked part-time. He supported himself and his old mother by hiring out to do odd jobs. He mowed my lawns, raked my leaves, cut my firewood, and I was but one of several for whom he did these and other chores. No better mower of lawns could be found, not even among golfcourse-keepers. Each time a different pattern so that the nap would not be pressed in any one prevailing direction but would always stand up like that of a fresh-laid carpet. With a chainsaw he was as skillful as a professional logger. A workhorse. Non-stop. Tireless. And for this the wages he charged were such that when I moved to the area and Ernest came to work for me I made myself unpopular with his other employers by insisting upon paying him more. A non-smoker, non-drinker, non-gambler, non-womanchaser—a non-everything was Ernest van Voorhees: a model of the negative virtues. The respect felt for him in the village was not unmixed with pity for all that he was missing out on in life and with a sense that such self-abnegation as his was possible only because he was "not quite all there," though what more those who said that about him had that Ernest did not have, I for one was never able to discern.

But the outstanding thing about Ernest, the thing that earned him the village's universal, unstinting, and unqualified admiration was his dutifulness toward his old mother. He tended her like a baby, which was about what she had now become, was never without her, and his devotion was even more exemplary because his mother was not an attractive nor a sensible woman, never had been, and now that her mind had failed her, was enough to try the patience of a saint. All this not to mention the odor. Giuseppina, our cleaning woman, whenever she paused in her work and glanced out the window and saw Ernest mowing the lawn or spading the flowerbed while his mother dozed in the pickup truck, would say, "Poor soul! What will become of him when she is gone?" And from Giuseppina's ample bosom, which had known what it was to nurse, would issue the contented sigh with which the sight of filial selflessness can inflate a mother's breast.

Yet it was not Ernest but rather the other, dead son, who had been their parents' favorite, or had become so by dying, and Ernest knew it, for no effort was made to conceal it from him; he knew it and he never resented it. I did, and not having the patience of a saint myself, I showed it.

"It's a terrible thing, Mr. Robinson," the old lady once said to me, "to lose your son."

She sat on my right, Ernest on my left at the wheel of his pickup truck. It was as though he were not there, as far as she was concerned.

I said, "Yes, that must be a terrible thing, Mrs. van Voorhees. I just hope you appreciate how lucky you are to have left to you a son like yours."

There was certainly nothing about her deserving of such devotion as Ernest's. I found her spoiled by his attentions, a chronic malcontent and complainer, tiresome, foolish even before her brain began to go soft, misshapen by age, and to sit beside her in the cab of that pickup with the windows shut tight and the heater going full blast was to feel—well, as if you were in, and not alone in, an outhouse.

It was Ernest who did the shopping, the cooking, the housekeeping, the laundering. It must be said that at none of these tasks did he excel. Their diet was monotonous, the house not the neatest, the clothes drying on the line rather dingy. But he did them all, uncomplainingly, in addition to his outside work, and on top of all that he looked after his elderly neighbors along the road, shopping for them whenever they were down sick, shoveling them out from under the snow whenever the man of the house had a bad back, doing for his neighbor no more than his neighbor would do for him, though none ever did because Ernest never got sick, never needed help. Not quite all there!

The years passed, so many of them that even the notable ones, those marked by storms, floods, droughts, were repeated time and again and lost their distinction, sank in the mass and faded from memory. The snows melted and the grass grew and had to be mowed, the leaves fell and had to be raked, the snow fell and the paths had to be shoveled. Our summer afternoons were filled with the steady drone of the mower as Ernest's plodding figure, as regularly as a shuttle in a loom, passed back and forth outside the windows. He raked the leaves as though he were motor-driven and when this seasonal chore was done we heard the snarl of his chainsaw day-long down in the woodlot or nearer by when, out behind the shed, he chopped the logs into fireplace length, the pile of sticks and the mound of sawdust patiently growing mountainous. And in these latter years, always, in the heat of summer and in the cold of winter, when the engine was left running and the heater on, Mother sat in the cab of the pickup truck for hours while Ernest worked. She had grown deathly afraid of being left alone and now accompanied him everywhere he went. She was afraid of falling sick or of simply falling and not having Ernest there to help her and of dying alone in the house before he got home.

In the beginning of this final phase, to pass the time, she read. Or rather, she looked at the pictures, or merely turned the pages, in the same half-dozen old tattered magazines—magazines of special interests as remote from hers, had she had any interests, as hunting, travel, fashion. Later on she dozed away the hours. I woke her from her sleep whenever I took Ernest and her a glass of lemonade or a cup of hot chocolate, until the time came when I found the glass or the cup hardly touched and after that I left her alone. Passing the truck where it sat in the drive on my way to the mailbox across the road I would see her slumped asleep, shrunken, frail, barely breathing, and it was an object lesson in the irony of existence. There was no such thing as a long life and yet there was such a thing as too long a one. Her gold brooch, her diamond engagement ring and her wedding band, now as loose on her dried-up finger as the band on a game bird's leg, were the only reminders of the woman she had been. She had shriveled to skin and bones and her hair had thinned to the scantiness of the fur on a coconut. The effort to pin it up looked as though it were Ernest's, not hers, and indeed, the mind balked at imagining the bodily functions of hers it was now his duty to attend to. The features of her face had lost their symmetry and gone awry. She was half blind, half deaf. Yet she lingered on. Rigorous natural selection, over a long span of time, had made of the old original Dutch stock of these Berkshire Hills a hardy race. Every township had its centenarian. And the same people who longed to live forever themselves saw in old lady van Voorhees what it was to live that long and heaved a sigh for her and for poor Ernest. He would have her on his hands for years yet to come, and then when she died he would owe it to her that he had many a long, lonely year to live on without her, with nothing whatever to live for.

To my question, the one time I ever put it to him, how old was he? Ernest's reply was, "Old enough to know better." Having had his little joke, he did not retreat from it; I got no answer. I was surprised at this vanity about his age in a person otherwise totally lacking in vanity and to all outward appearance content with his lot, without regret for time lost or any sense of its having been misspent. Longevity is often the boast of those whose lives have been the emptiest.

He looked both aged and ageless, bent as though to his lawn-mower or his snowshovel even on the streets of the village and moving with that plodding gait made even more elephantine by the clothes bought always too big for him, big as he was, at church bazaars, thrift shops, a figure out of a drawing by van Gogh or a painting by Millet, and yet with the bland, seamless face, unworn by worldly emotions, of the celibate, the anchorite.

Always narrow and confined, the lives of Ernest and his mother contracted further with the closing in of time. Both had loved to play bridge, their one entertainment, and had long been regulars at the Tuesday night bridge parties at the village Grange Hall, where Ernest often won the door prize. But as the old lady's mind began to fail her she became increasingly undesirable as anybody's partner. Her confusions, her mistakes, and her gaffes grew more and more frequent. Finally she became an embarrassment to Ernest and, hard as it was to believe, a story got about that on what turned out to be their last attendance at the Grange Hall he had actually been publicly short-tempered with her. For some village gossips nothing was sacred and there was even talk of an ugly, a shocking scene between them as he hustled her to the cloakroom and out to the truck to be taken home. In any case, that was their last appearance there.

Now they never went anywhere, except for lunch daily to the diner in the village where they had been regulars for more years than anybody could remember. They had their own table there. That, however, was not entirely owing to the proprietor's gratitude for the van Voorhees' loyalty to him, though that was the fiction kept up. It rather spoils a touching story, but the plain truth of the matter was that the van Voorhees were segregated from the other customers at the diner because the old lady had become incontinent and close proximity to her would have spoiled anybody's appetite. That same unfortunate infirmity may have been partly the reason why their few friends, the few of those whom time had spared, visited less and less often and finally stopped altogether. Their friends excused themselves on the ground that they did not want to embarrass Ernest. As for him, the best son a mother ever had, he never gave a sign that he noticed anything.

I could sympathize with those friends. I did not have to imagine the atmosphere in the stuffy, overheated living room of that tiny trailer. I was obliged to ride between Ernest and the old lady in the pickup truck once a week to the town dump to get rid of my trash. I had gotten started doing that years ago, before the smell began, and now could think of no way of getting out of it without raising questions and causing pain. Distasteful to me as they were, those trips were a pleasure to Ernest, a break in his monotonous routine. It was hard to deprive a man of his enjoyment when that was so meager a thing as driving you weekly to the municipal garbage dump. So I went along, breathing through my mouth and trying not to hear with either of the two heads I felt I had at those times.

Some people have tape decks in their cars; in Ernest's pickup, on our weekly trips to the dump, we had Mother, our one cassette. Poor old soul! Nearly blind and nearly deaf, painful to behold, foul-smelling, she was now quite dotty as well. It was as we passed the Bohnsack place, just a quarter of a mile from my house, that she switched on.

Already by then she was lost and had asked Ernest at least twice where we were. Little do I know about saints, though given this chance to study one, but I suppose that even their patience can wear out, and having been asked that question now times out of number, Ernest chatted on without answering.

"Ernest! Ernest!" the old lady, getting no reply and growing panicky, would squawk. "I'm talking to you! Where are we, Ernest?" Born just five miles from there, never in her life having traveled farther than fifty miles away, she was lost in the fog, in the featureless and unfamiliar terrain of her own decaying mind.

The sight of the Bohnsack farmhouse calmed her. It also unfailingly evoked the story of how the Bohnsacks had come home from church one Sunday morning long ago to find their hired man on the roof of the house stark naked and stark mad and how he had stayed there for two whole days before being coaxed down and being tied up and sent off to the insane asylum.

Between that one and the next of her long life's landmarks she would get lost at least twice more and would squawk at Ernest demanding to know where we were, and also that many times if not more would insist that he drive slower because the bumps in the road hurt her stomach and had ever since as a girl she jumped out of the hayloft and threw it out of whack.

The Jehovah's Witness church brought out the story of how they had come to her door, two of them, and tried to convert her and how she had sent them packing. Lost again, she was restored to calm by the sight a bit farther down the road of what was now The Highway Inn. A farmhouse then, it had been one of the many homes of her childhood, and what a time they had had trying to get rid of them bedbugs! One hundred and four times a year I heard about the bedbugs, how many times Ernest had heard about them—well, in fact, Ernest had long ago ceased to hear it. As a defense against hearing this and the other set pieces, such as that prompted by the Garrison place, where his younger brother had come close to getting caught by the no-good daughter of the house, Ernest kept up a running chatter of his own. This went into my left ear while Mother's went into the right. If sometimes I felt I had two heads, other times I felt I had none at all, that into my one ear, as into a speaking tube, and out the other passed her questions to Ernest and his answer, when there was no longer any getting out of one, to her. The trip home was a re-run, in reverse, which accounts for my hearing all this twice as many times annually as there are weeks in the year.

What would Ernest do without his mother to look after?: the

question came to seem an idle one. Indeed, you now heard it asked in the village, what would she do without him to look after her? Which would have been a harder case materially but not of course emotionally. However, it never came to that pass. For though it looked as though she were destined to outlive him and go on forever, during the bitterest stretch of last year's bitter winter old lady van Voorhees died, aged God only knows what. Ernest came very near dying along with her. Some were convinced that was what he had been trying to do. And nearly everybody thought he would have been better off if he had.

We were away on vacation at the time, gone south to escape the rigors. I heard about it by letter. It was Jay Campbell, my friend and neighbor, another of Ernest's part-time employers and the doctor in the case, who wrote informing me, knowing I would be especially concerned, I being the nearest thing to a friend that Ernest had. But it was not until our return in the spring that I heard the details.

Ernest was then still in the hospital but his mother was already long in her grave, a last mark of his respect and of the self-sacrifice he was prepared to make for her. For, be it understood, in these parts the dead cannot be buried in winter, not, that is, without considerable expense, the ground being frozen so hard and to such a depth that only the heaviest earth-moving equipment can open it. With the return of the robins and the wild geese and the spawning runs of the herring and the shad in the river the ground can again be worked and one of the crops for spring planting is the dead; over the winter they are kept in cold storage. Last winter was, as I have said, a hard one even for us.

But although it is accepted as a fact of life, the local people dislike this usage forced by the climate upon them, and the family that says, "Never mind the cost, Mother is going into her grave now, without delay," is one that is looked up to. It came as a surprise to nobody that even from his hospital bed and chronically hard up as he was, Ernest van Voorhees had directed that his be laid at once to her eternal rest.

A virulent strain of the flu, made worse by the weather, had swept the region, bringing life to a virtual standstill. It was the sort of epidemic that drew Ernest, always immune himself, out on his errands of mercy for his stricken neighbors. Not this time. His absence from his accustomed rounds was noted only quite belatedly, so unused was everybody to thinking of him, or his mother either, for that matter, being sick. Both were, as the neighbor discovered who knocked on their door, sick enough to alarm the man, to make him call in Jay Campbell.

Ernest looked every bit as bad off as his mother, which was to say he looked worse, taking into account their respective ages. A glance at them was enough to tell Jay that both had pneumonia, but to his recommendation that they enter the hospital Ernest returned a flat "no." This did not much surprise Jay. He was used to that irrational fear of hospitals so common among country folks, and to this Ernest added the false sense of security of never having been seriously ill, the false confidence of having for so long nursed his mother himself, and his jealousy in the possession of that filial obligation. Disclaiming further responsibility, Jay did the only thing he could do: he phoned in prescriptions for drugs to the pharmacy and had them delivered to the house. Ernest agreed to let him know should either of them take a turn for the worse.

After that Jay was busy doctoring so many victims of the epidemic he had little time for thought of any particular ones. Patients of his who were neighbors of the van Voorhees, seeking at last to repay the many favors Ernest had done for them over the years, reported being thanked but no-thanked, which, considering the old lady's indestructibility and Ernest's own lifelong ruggedness, worried none of them overmuch. "Smoke still coming out their chimney. Reckon they must be alive in there," they said. "Take a lot of killing, them van Voorhees." After a week or so of hearing nothing further about them, Jay concluded—insofar as he gave the matter any consideration at all—that they were recovering on their own.

When the phone call came Jay could hardly make out who the man was on the line, much less what he was struggling to say. How, in his condition, Ernest had managed even to get to the phone was a wonder. He said he reckoned the time had come for them to be taken to the hospital. The time had not just come, it had come and gone, several days before.

After being brought in by ambulance, the old lady lasted just twenty-four hours. Meanwhile Ernest was responding to treatment in the intensive care unit no better than his mother had. His condition worsened hourly. His pneumonia was the least of Ernest's troubles. It was discovered that in addition to it he had peritonitis from a ruptured strangulated hernia.

"He must have been going around with that hernia for years," Jay said to me, and I groaned to recall the hours of raking leaves, pushing the lawnmower, shoveling snow, lifting logs that Ernest had put in for me. Heroically neglecting his own condition to look after his old mother, Ernest had very nearly killed himself.

Emergency abdominal surgery was performed on Ernest although even the doctor who did it considered the case hopeless.

"Made of leather," that was Jay Campbell's comment on Ernest's miraculous survival.

I found him emaciated, pale, feeble, and still in a mental daze when I went to see him in the hospital. I thought the locals were right, that with nothing left to live for he would have been better off dead. His listlessness and absence of mind were owing to shock and grief, loneliness and lack of purpose more than to his own close encounter with death. I forebore to condole with him on the loss of his mother, afraid even to mention her name.

Visiting hours were almost over and I was preparing to leave when Ernest asked me to find and hand him his mother's purse from his nightstand. He then entrusted to my keeping her gold brooch, her engagement ring, and her wedding band. But not without first an incident affecting in the extreme. As he was fumbling in the purse for the jewelry something flew across the bed and struck the wall with a clatter. At the same moment Ernest let out a screech.

"Get those out of here!" he cried.

I looked on the floor and under the bed I found the object, or rather the two objects: his mother's dentures. It was deeply affecting, this pain at the sight of something so intimately associated with his mother, with which she had sustained life itself, and now would never again have use for.

I disposed of them in a trash bin out on the street.

It was to a house from which his mother was now absent but

which was filled with mementoes of her that Ernest came home. Old lady van Voorhees had been one of those people who never throw anything away. Into that tiny trailer was crammed everything brought there from the big old family farmhouse. To clean it all out would be an enormous undertaking, one that I urged Ernest to let wait until he was stronger. But reminders of his mother and of their long life together were too painful to him. Just as his first act on being discharged from the hospital was reclaiming her jewels from me and selling them, he now insisted on cleaning out the house as soon as he was inside it. For the next week he and I in his pickup truck, its bed heaped high, plied back and forth from his place to the dump. Very different these trips were from the former ones, with silence now on either side of me. When we were done not a relic of Ernest's mother remained. Every least trace of her sojourn on earth, lengthy as it had been, was gone.

On our return from the last of all those trips I sat down with a sigh in the recliner, more than ever the dominant piece in that now bare little room. The place smelled of disinfectant. The time seemed to me momentous, the turning point in poor Ernest's life. The past was past, the future had arrived.

Ernest, too, sat down with a sigh. Looking about him at his altered arrangements, he, too, was evidently conscious that the moment marked a milestone. "Well," he said, "it come awful close to backfiring on me but I seen my chance and I took it. Lord knows it was long enough in coming!"

It took me some while to grasp what I was being told—after all, it isn't every day that somebody lets you in on his having murdered his mother. So long, in fact, did it take me that I detected in Ernest some confusion, some regret for having misgauged my acuity. It now appeared that mine was the same incorrigibly sentimental view of him as the one the villagers all had. From them he knew he had nothing to fear; he might have shot his mother dead at high noon on the main street and they would have sworn to a man that the killer had been somebody else. Me he credited with more imagination, or maybe with less imagination and more common sense, more knowledge of life as it is, and I had disappointed him.

I nodded, and with my gesture regained Ernest's confidence. Nobody could have looked more impenitent. He positively radiated the certainty that he had done what anybody else would have done in his place. While hoping to succeed in his desperate gamble, he was quite prepared to fail, to go out with the old lady rather than go on with her any longer. To be sure of her not recovering he had waited until the last possible moment before calling for help, risking his life and coming within an inch of losing it.

He had come through. Ernest van Voorhees was free, his own man, at long last. Not much time was left him, perhaps, but that made it all the more precious, was all the more reason to seize it. A family of his own he would never have, no wife, no children, no grandchildren, but at least he would have himself to himself for however long he lasted.

I thought of Oedipus the King, of his horrendous self-punishment for his awful crimes, of Prince Orestes and the bloodthirsty Furies that pursued him. Or, rather, I tried to think of them but in their larger than life size, their exalted station, their superhuman suffering, those legendary figures eluded me. Unlike those of Oedipus, Ernest's bright blue eyes, still in their sockets, shone with the innocence of a child. Sister-sufferers though they were, I could not, here in this tiny tin trailer with its color TV and its La-Z-Boy recliner, equate Clytemnestra and old lady van Voorhees. The high-flown word *parricide* that had entered so clamorously through the front door of my mind, finding itself woefully out of place, slunk quietly out the back. My brain spun but not with horror and shock, rather because it all seemed so simple, so down to earth.

The Ernest who comes now to work on our grounds is a new man and it shows in his new, sprightlier pace. He has not had to tell Mother half a dozen times on the way over where she is nor listen yet again to the tale of the man on the roof of the Bohnsack farmhouse. She is not dozing in the cab of the truck as he works. He will not have to spoon-feed her this evening nor go to the Laundromat tomorrow morning with the bedsheets she has soiled in the night.

Meanwhile both his fortitude and his weakness equally excite the admiration of the villagers. To the one they ascribe his reappearance at the Grange Hall, where one night recently he won the door prize, and to the other his frequenting the local bar, breaking a lifetime's abstinence, in an effort to drown his sorrow. Typical is our Giuseppina, who, pausing in her work and looking out the window and catching sight of Ernest, fetches a sign and says, "He may not be quite all there, as they say, but he has feelings the same as anybody else and he's a brave soul to carry on as he does all alone in this terrible cruel world with nothing left to live for."

A Fresh Snow

IT WAS silly and a waste of time. School was not even out yet. She could not expect him for half an hour at least. Still she sat at the window watching the corner of the block.

Snow, dingy with soot, lay thick upon the window ledge. The street ran with slush and through the gray light hovering in the street the mass of buildings opposite looked black and close.

As she watched, a few large flakes began to fall. They lighted on the window ledge, and bending forward to look at them, her breath condensing on the glass, she thought of the thrilling, rare snows of her childhood.

She had been five years old when she was wakened in the night to see her first snow. Wrapped in quilts, she and her brother had stood at the window wiping away the steam of their breaths and peering into the blackness, while their father told of the snows he had seen. Two inches fell that night, a good fall, and in the morning the grown-ups were gay and happy for the children's sake. After breakfast everyone went out with soup bowls. Each looked for a drifted spot to fill his bowl; even so, they had to scrape lightly to keep from picking up dirt. They ate it sprinkled with sugar and flavored with vanilla extract. Her brother came home in midmorning, for school had been let out to celebrate, and through the afternoon they watched the snow disappear. By night it was gone. She was eight before she saw her next.

Otherwise the winters there were fitful times, days of pale sun followed by days of slashing rain. How often she had sat looking out at the dripping trees and the colorless, sodden fields. Seven years before she had sat all day for weeks at the parlor window in her brother Leon's house. Then she was waiting for Donald to be born. Leon had taken her in when she grew too big to work in the confectionery or climb the three flights of the boardinghouse in town. She had had to stay behind when George was transferred from the camp. There was no housing in California and George was expecting to go overseas any day. Donald was three years old before his father saw him.

She had met George in the confectionery where she was the cashier. The soldiers from the camp were mostly Northern boys and the town mistrusted girls who went out with them. She always rang up their bills and counted out their change with a quickness which discouraged conversation. But George never tried to say more than "thank you." Perhaps it piqued her that her distance suited him that well. In time he grew friendly and she did not remember his former silence against him. One thing right off stood in his favor: he was not an officer. She mistrusted even Southerners who were officers. And once you got to know him George turned out to be a regular tease. She had always enjoyed being gently teased, and when George mimicked her accent, saying, "Yawl fetch it an Ah hep ye tote it," she felt she was being appreciated in a pleasant new way. He teased her also with outlandish tales about the North, but she was more impressed when he told her the truth, such as when he described the bolt factory where he worked, which employed more men on each shift than there were in her county seat. She began to compare him to the local boys whom she knew she might at times have had, and she was glad she had done nothing hasty. To have been forced to settle down with never a glimpse of the world beyond came to seem a dreary life.

What foolish notions she had formed then, and how long ago it seemed. Now she was a regular city dweller. If her kinfolks could see her would they think she was much changed?

A sudden darkening of the light made her turn to the window. The snow was thickening. Down in the street an old bent man was groping along. He was pulling a child's sled on which rode a small carton of groceries. His rapid breath condensed in feeble whiffs and he swayed a little from side to side.

Cities, as she had thought so many times, were no place for old folks. No one had time to help or notice them. Whenever she saw an old man waiting helplessly on a street corner or risking the traffic she was thankful that her poor father had lived and died down South. She was glad she had been with him that last year, glad that he had lived to see Donald and glad she had let him believe that when George came back they were going to settle on the old homeplace. He had liked George. He liked a man, no matter where he was from, who looked you square in the eye, who put something into his handshake, who was not a damned smart aleck. Of course he had felt bound to say something about the Civil War. She remembered well his surprise and her own when George said he did not know whether any of his ancestors had fought in it.

She closed her eyes and saw her father's grave lying under a steady gray rain. She could see the whole family plot and she named them off in order in her mind, with their dates and epitaphs. Another month and it would be graveyard-cleaning time. Surely that old custom had not died out since she went away. It had been such a good time for all, a little melancholy, but not solemn, as you might think. Everyone came early bringing garden rakes and worn-down brooms. It would be the first nice day in spring, still cool enough to work comfortably and make it pleasant to smell the fires of rotted leaves. The children ran and played, being careful not to tread on any graves, of course. It was not thought good taste to clean the graves of your own kin. You cleaned other people's plots and trusted them to clean yours. The children's special chore was to clean and decorate the graves of little children. Each brought a "pretty"—something weatherproof—a china doll or a glass doorknob or a colored bottle, and with these they decorated the graves while they told again the sweetly sad story of each dead child. Then came dinner on the ground. Each woman brought the dish she was famous for and everybody knew without asking whom to compliment on each dish. Her mother always brought pecan pie. It was a time known for forming friendships among the children and courtships among the young. By night the graves had been raked and swept and the headstones straightened, and by then all the men had gone a few times out to the woods where a bottle was kept, so everyone went home feeling tired and happy, pleasantly melancholy, and good friends with the whole community. It seemed you were born knowing the names of every member of every family and when they were born and died, and after a while it came to seem that you had known them all personally all your life and their loss was a personal loss to you.

Often she had wondered where the city dead were buried and how they were looked after, but a feeling of propriety came over her and she hesitated to ask. Surely they could not be as forgotten as they seemed to be. In George's family they never mentioned their dead. You would think they had no kin beyond the living ones.

She saw in her mind the unfinished stone beside her father's grave. It could not be long before her mother would lie there. Would she see her again before that time? What would the date read on that stone? Donald seemed to be losing his memory of his grandmother. Would he see her once more so he could have a memory of her? George would have let her have her mother with her, but her mother would not come. It was just as well, she supposed. It pained her to think how helpless and out of place and lonely her mother would feel, cut off from her old ways, her relatives and old friends. She would feel so lost and frightened, caught in the shrill, jostling store crowds. She would have sorrowed all day to have been yelled at by the butcher in the chain store.

"Mek up yer mind, lady, mek up yer mind!"

Would her mother find her much changed? She had tried to be a good wife to George. She had believed she ought to try to forget the ways she had been brought up to when they were different from her husband's ways. But there were things she felt she would never get used to. She remembered George's mother asking her right off what nationality she was. If you asked anybody that question back home then you were already sure he was some kind of foreigner, and beneath taking exception.

She looked out for some sight of Donald, but the street was empty. She lay back in her chair and saw herself and him stepping out of the bus in the depot back home. Should she let them know she was coming, or surprise them? If she wrote ahead they would go to a lot of trouble, but, she must admit, that would not have displeased her. They would exclaim over Donald and disagree about which person in the family he looked most like. Strange to realize that many things, so familiar to her, would have to be explained to Donald. In the afternoon they would have people over, relatives and old friends, to sit on the porch and talk. They would tell of births and deaths and talk of the weather and crops, of the things they had always talked about, of life and the afterlife, and stretched out in the porch swing she would feel herself soothed by the warm breeze and by the slow warm liquid flow of Southern voices.

She was startled from her thoughts by the sound of running on the stairs. She had forgotten what she was waiting for and for a moment the sight of the boy in the door awoke no memory in her. She looked at him without recognition. He wore thick snow pants and a padded jacket, heavy rubber boots and a fur cap with large muffs from which his face peeped out red with cold. He was covered with snow. He had dashed in so quickly from outside that flakes still clung to his cheeks and in his brows and lashes.

He closed the door and stamped in, shaking himself like a dog and giving off the smell of cold wool and cold rubber. When he neared her she felt the cold which surrounded him and it seemed to penetrate to her heart. She stood up in an impulse of fear.

"I gotta get my sled. Me and a gang of boys are going to the park," he said. "They're meeting me on the corner in five minutes."

Even his voice seemed stiff with cold. What kind of talk was that, so sharp and nasal? That was not the voice she had given him! She heard the voice of her kin reproach her for bringing up her son in forgetfulness of them.

"No," she cried. "You can't go. Stay with me."

Her strangeness frightened him. He said weakly, "But I told them I would. They've all gone to get their sleds."

But she would not let him go. She made him take off his things. She put cocoa on the range to heat and when it was done she sat him on her lap and rocked him softly, his head against her breast, while she told him all about the South, where he was born.

The Ballad
of Jesse Neighbours

FEW MARRIAGES were being made in Oklahoma in 1934 and Jesse Neighbours didn't have a pot nor a window to throw it out of, but Jesse just couldn't wait. Things might never get any better! He had to have her—Naomi Childress, that is. What were they going to live on, love? Well, they would have each other and they would scrape by somehow. Things couldn't go on like this much longer. Meanwhile, two can live cheaper than one. And Naomi didn't expect any diamond rings.

Jesse was just twenty, though he looked older, and Naomi just eighteen. In the road of their courtship there had been one bad bump. It was the old story: poor boy, heiress, and her father. Jesse's people had never owned one red acre to sit back now and watch being blown away in dust. Will Neighbours had raised, rather was raising, seven children, Jesse the eldest, as a share-cropper. And so from the first Jesse had had to come to the Childresses hat in hand. For old Bull Childress had a house and clear title to twenty-seven acres of hardscrabble. The deed was unencumbered through no fault of Bull's. He had tried, but no-body would loan him anything on that patch of Jimsonweeds and cockleburs.

Bull's consent to the marriage had been given only on condition that the bride be taken to a home of her own, and not to live with her in-laws. And indeed to have gotten another into Will's place they would have had to hang her on a nail at night. Bull's provision might have proved an insuperable obstacle. But fortunately Jesse was the son of a man known for hard work and honesty; and though only twenty, Jesse himself, after some ten years now, was beginning to earn a name as a steady worker. And so Mr. Buttrell, Will's landlord, agreed to try Jesse on shares on a place that he happened to have standing vacant.

Not a very big place, and maybe not the best thirty acres left in Oklahoma, but a place of his own and land which a strong young fellow not afraid of a little work could make out on—always barring Acts of God, of course—with a two-room dog-run cabin, a well, a barn, a toolshed, and a chicken house. Jesse had a heifer due to freshen around September and Naomi was raising a dozen layers that she had incubated underneath the kitchen range. There would be a pair of shoats as a wedding present from Will. The two of them were spending every spare moment fixing the place up. It would have curtains made from the pretty flowered prints that chicken feed came sacked in, and all that winter a quilt on a quilting frame had hung above the dining table in the Childresses' parlor, and the neighbor women came over every Thursday afternoon and quilted on it, and made jokes about it that made Naomi's round and sweetly fuzzy cheeks glow like a ripe Elberta peach. And she was canning all that previous summer and fall as if she had three hands. If nothing else they would be able to live on cucumber pickles. Jesse had an old car. Something was always going wrong with it, but luckily Jesse had a second one exactly like the first, except for the lack of wheels, which squatted out in the front yard, a sort of personal parts department, very handy. He had given up smoking and instead was putting his tobacco money in a jar, and by fall he hoped to have enough to make a down payment on a mule. He was the saving kind, saved tinfoil, twine, saved rubber bands, making large balls of all three items which he stored in cigar boxes.

Naomi knew what a catch she had made. She had first taken serious notice of Jesse Neighbours one night at a country dance for which he supplied the music. He hired out around the section as a one-man band. He had a rig which he was buying on installment from the mail-order catalogue. Once in it he looked like a monkey in a cage. With his hands he played guitar while with his feet he worked two pedals on which were drumsticks that banged a pair of snare drums; one stick was bare wood, the other was covered like a swab with bright-orange lamb's wool. A French harp was held to his mouth on a wire frame with earpieces. The boy was a musical fool. In his pockets he always carried some kind of musical instrument: a jew's harp, a French harp, an ocarina. He played the musical saw, the washboard, water glasses, blew a jug. He could draw music out of anything. And on the guitar or the banjo or the mandolin he picked notes, not just chords but whole tunes. His singing voice was like a bee in a bottle, a melodious, slightly adenoidal whine, wavering, full of sobs and breaks, and of a pitch like a boy's before the change of voice. That night when he laid aside the French harp and sang:

> "I don't want your greenback dollar;
> I don't want your watch and chain;
> All I want is you, my darling;
> Won't you take me back again?"

it seemed to Naomi that he was singing to her alone. And when with his next number he showed the other, light side of his nature with *Sal, Sal, Sal, oh, Sal, Sal, let me chaw yore rozin some*, then Naomi was hooked. And Naomi was not the only one, as she very well knew.

But the music he courted her with was none of his lovesick ballads. Seated on her front porch on a Sunday afternoon, in his fresh-ironed khakis so stiff they squeaked, his chauffeur's black leather bow tie fluttering on his Adam's apple as he sang, like a black butterfly, he would throw back his head and bawl:

> "I heard the crash on the highway.
> I knew what it was from the start.
> I rushed to the scene of destruction.
> The picture was stamped on my heart.

I didn't hear nobody pray, dear brethren,
I didn't hear nobody pray.
The blood lay thick on the highway,
But I didn't hear nobody pray."

For it was bad enough already, him being landless. If on top of that he had come around strumming and crooning ballads and ditties old Bull Childress would have shooed him out of the yard like a stray dog. Bull would think, any fellow that played all that well, not just chords but notes, must have spent a lot of time sitting in the shade learning to pick them out, and that was not the kind a man wanted for a son-in-law. The truth was, Jesse had spent very little time learning; it just came naturally. But of course he could not say that. The pious wail of "The Crash on the Highway" was meant to overcome a prospective father-in-law's misgivings.

And Jesse was not shiftless. He was a most unusual combination of music and prudence. His music meant a little extra money. He liked to play and sing, and in fact his foot was always tapping to some tune running in his head; but he liked to be paid for it too. He was ambitious. He meant to get ahead. He was already thinking of a family of his own, thinking of it with a passion beyond his years, and notwithstanding her blushes, he broached the subject very early to Naomi. He spoke of it with such earnestness that she had to say at last, she hoped he was not thinking of quite as big a one as his own. It had not occurred to her that, however many there were, he meant to bring them up in a very different way from the way he and his brothers and sisters had been brought up.

Though it might be hard to understand why a young fellow should want to follow in his father's footsteps when his father's only followed in those of a mule, and why he should want to do it in order to own something which the wind blew away in clouds of red dust before your very eyes, Jesse Neighbours meant to own land of his own one day. Not that he couldn't wait. Not that his longing made him discontent with what he was starting out with. But stumbling along behind the plow among the blocks of dirt like chunks of concrete paving, straining against the handles, grunting, his face caked with dust, he would let himself think of the future. He was of an age and a seriousness to have a place in the councils of family men, farmers, and on the corner of the street in town on Saturday afternoon Jesse had heard it said time and time again that this land was cottoned out. Well, he meant to rotate his crops. He would have a margin of land over what he needed in order to just get by, enough to quarter his acreage and leave one quarter to lie fallow by turns each year. Then there was the weather. A man might have a good year, but then one of drought could wipe out all that he had saved. The weather, they said, was one thing you could do nothing about. But there was one thing you could do. You could grow one crop that did not depend so heavily on the weather. Jesse had heard those same men say that this land, once the range of the buffalo, was best suited to grazing. He meant to have a little herd of beef cattle one day. He knew already what breed. Bramers. Funny-looking things, they were, with that white hide like a scalded hog, that hump on the back like a camel, and those great flopping ears. And mean! But they were from India and could stand this Oklahoma heat and dryness like no others, and fever ticks never bothered them. Jesse didn't fool himself: he would never own any big herd. That was for men with capital, not for the likes of him. He would always be a dirt farmer. But a few he would have; then in a year when there came a drought or a hailstorm, or worst of all, when the crop was so good the bottom fell out of the market price, then you wouldn't have to go crawling to the bank and lick spit and put yourself in hock right up to your very eyeballs.

And though he would be a clodhopper all his days, if he started a little herd his sons wouldn't have to slave like this, daylight to dark, seven days a week, just to keep body and soul together; they could be cattlemen, breeders. Patience, he would need patience to save and then save more, until he could buy good stock, blooded, purebred, pedigreed—it paid off in the long run. And, sweat pouring from his face like rainwater off a hatbrim as he hunched himself, he drove the plowshare back into the stony ground and swore at the wheezing mule, thinking as he lurched down the row, if a man started out with one heifer, bred her and was lucky and she had twins and they were both heifers, and each of them had a heifer . . . So that he never heard his little sister until she was at his back, though all the way down from the house she had been screaming at the top of her lungs that they'd struck oil on the Childress place.

Oil-well derricks on those Oklahoma plains were a commoner sight than trees. New ones sprang up, old ones were drilled deeper, with every fresh discovery of oil anywhere within a hundred miles. Bad times and bad soil bred them like weeds, where no edible plant would grow. The lucky ones struck water, and the derrick was converted into a windmill. Even Bull Childress had long since given up hope of anything from that one down behind his house. Jesse had forgotten it so completely that for a moment he hardly knew what his little sister was talking about.

"They claim it's a real gusher, Jess," she said. "The Childresses are rich! Naomi's going to be one of them millionairesses, like you read about in the newspapers."

Even as she spoke her voice ran down like a phonograph, seeing the look in her brother's eyes, blank holes in the terracotta mask of his face. Her mouth gaped, snaggle-toothed, as it dawned on her that the news she had brought might not be good news, after all.

Jesse leaned for a moment on the plow handles, breathing hard, his head sagging between his shoulder blades, sweat dripping from the tip of his nose. He spat thinly and of the color of blood and wiped the back of his gritty hand across his lips. Then he straightened, and settling the reins about his neck, grasping the handles and pointing the plowshare downward again, he said in a dry husky voice, "Come up, mule."

The story told was that the well blew in while old Bull was in the outhouse looking at the pictures in the unused pages of the mail-order catalogue, and that when she let go he shot off the hole and out the door with his flap hanging open and his britches down around his knees, tripped and sprawled flat on his face, rolled over, looked up, and then lay there moaning with joy and letting the slimy, thick, foul-smelling black rain spatter in his face and into his open mouth like sweet California wine. The roar was a steady explosion and the stink enough to make you gag. Air to breathe there was none and the sky turned black as in a dust storm. And as he lay there Bull's moaning turned insensibly into a whimper, a sob, as he thought of the years of his life that had gone into that hard, unyielding soil, the sweat from his hanging brow that had watered every inch of it, of the furrows he had broken, the cotton sacks he had dragged across it, bent double beneath the broiling sun, the seed he had sown in it and which had rotted there, never sprouting. Of this dry red dirt he had eaten his allotted peck, and more. His head was bent to it like an ear on an undernourished stalk; his skin had taken on its very color like a stain. And all this while deep underground lay this black treasure. And rolling over he commenced to beat the earth with his fists for having hidden its riches from him all his life until now. Then when he had exhausted himself beating it, he flung his arms wide in an embrace and kissed the ground again and again.

In the house he found his daughter trying to pull down the windows and his wife cursing over her wash that had been hanging on the line and that now looked like a heap of mechanic's rags. Aghast at her blasphemous complaints, Bull roared, "You'll wear silks and laces from now on, you old fool! Shut your mouth and thank the good Lord! Don't let Him hear you grumbling!" And grabbing up the laundry he flung it to the floor and danced on it with his bare black feet, bellowing jubilantly.

All afternoon it rained down and Bull hopped from one window to the next, crowing, "Spew, baby, spew! Oh, honey, don't never stop! Flood us! Drown us in it! Oh, Godawmighty, blow her sky high! Let it come down for forty days and forty nights!" Three times in the course of the afternoon he dashed outdoors like a boy in a summer shower and baptized himself anew, letting it dance in his open palms and blacken his upturned face, and in that state he would return, tracking up the floors, and demand a hug and kiss from each of his women, chasing them screaming through the house.

All night long it fell like a spring rain on the noisy sheet-iron roof, and the stench grew hellish. But Bull lay unsleeping in his bed, smacking his old woman's flat bony behind whenever he suspected her of dozing off, listening to the patter overhead and crooning, "Oh, keep it up, sweet Jesus. Oh, pour it down. Don't never stop till I tell you."

Towards daybreak the next morning the crew succeeded in capping the well, and they ventured out to have a look around. The world looked burnt, smelled burnt too. From the eaves of buildings, from the handles of tools long abandoned about the yard, from the limp leaves of trees and plants the black syrup hung in long slow-swelling drops. From the sagging fence wires they were strung in ropes like beads and amid the leaves of bushes they resembled small poisonous black berries. From every blade of grass, like a viscous black dew, hung a single unfalling drop. A dying songbird staggered about the yard, his wings heavy and useless. Upon the pool in the bottom of the cast-iron washpot lay insects in a thick, still crust.

"Won't nothing ever grow here ever again," Mrs. Childress wailed, seeing her dead peonies and the earth around them that looked as if it had been tarred and asphalted.

"I hope to God not!" cried Bull. "I done raised all the crops I ever aim to off of it!"

Breakfast (oily biscuits, coffee that tasted like it had been drained from a crankcase) was hardly over when Bull said, "Well, gals, yawl take off your aprons and paint your faces. The Childresses are headed for the big city. Don't bother packing nothing. We won't need none of this trash"—the sweep of his arm comprehended the sum of their previous life—"never no more."

So they piled into the cab of the truck (a pickup, cut down from a La Salle sedan) and took off. In town they stopped just long enough for Bull to go to the bank, from which he returned carrying two bulging canvas sacks, and after that they never even slowed down for Idabel, nor even Paris, but drove straight to Dallas, with old Bull sitting on that horn all the way. And when they got there they drove straight to the Adolphus, pulled up out front, and though they had not brought one piece of luggage with them, sat there honking until the whole corps of bellhops and porters had been sent out to receive them. When they got out, so did the broody hen who had made the trip with them unbeknownst. She staggered off her nest among the corn shucks and croaker sacks in the truck bed, and out into the street, and there she died, in a shower of feathers and with a bloodcurdling squawk, underneath the wheels of a new red Ford V-8, right on the corner of Commerce and Akard.

Without turning his head, jerking his thumb over his shoulder at the old jitney, Bull said to the head greeter, "Get shut of that for me, will you? Maybe you know some poor devil that can use it."

They were not turned away. They were welcomed like royalty. After Corsicana, after Spindletop, after Kilgore, Dallas had developed a keen collective nose for crude oil, and rolled out the red carpet for their kind of barefoot millionaire. Bull drew his *X* on the register as big as a level-crossing sign.

And at Neiman-Marcus that same afternoon they seemed to have been expecting Naomi. To her request for a permanent wave and "a beauty treatment," they smiled, and showed her in. She was undressed and popped into a box with her head sticking out like a turkey's at a turkey shoot, parboiled, removed feeling as if she had been peeled and her quick exposed, stretched out on a white table and kneaded like dough until her bones jellied and her brains melted and ran. She was put into a white gown and whisked into a second chamber, seated in a dentist's chair, and mud, or what certainly seemed like mud, piled on her face. To soft music wafted sourcelessly in, a bevy of sibilant attendants busied themselves about her, one to each foot, one to each hand, plying, chafing, clipping. The mud was removed, then came lotions icy and astringent, a brisk facial massage, a shampoo. The head beautician materialized, a gorgeous young sorcerer of intermediate sex with bangs and plucked brows, a pout, fluttering hands smaller and whiter and far softer than Naomi's own, a voice like molasses in January and a pettish toss of the head. From a palette of rosy tints he chose, and with brushes and swabs applied them to Naomi's cheeks, frowning, standing back from time to time to squint at her like an artist before his easel. Her head was anointed with the contents of various vials, her hair cut and curled.

At last it was finished and she was permitted to look. One glimpse and she looked about for confirmation. They nodded. She looked again, sidelong, scared. She reached out a hand (once, or rather always, red and cracked from lye soap, cold water, broom handles, the bails of buckets—now white, soft, a row of small pointed flames burning at the fingertips) and shyly touched the vision in the glass. Her lips parted in wonder, her lips that had blossomed, sweetly sullen, moist, quivering. Wonder, not self-infatuation, was what she felt, for that was not her, it was a creature from another world, out of the pages of *Silver Screen*, beautiful as a dummy in a store window. Her hair was a platinum cloud. Her eyes had doubled in size. Beneath lids elongated and shaded with blue, the whites sparkled, the pupils swooned within themselves, liquid with promise and cruel caprice. Her brows had been resettled; they arched of themselves. Sophistication had been shadowed into her hitherto round and girlish cheeks.

To maintain this new beauty of hers, regular and frequent return visits would be necessary. Meanwhile there were certain ointments and extracts of which she herself was to make nightly application, according to a ritual which she would be taught. This cream, from the beestings of wild Mongolian she-asses. This, with ambergris secreted by afflicted whales and found floating upon tropical seas. A hair rinse of champagne and plovers' eggs. This jelly rich in the hormones of queen bees fed on the nectar of Alpine wild flowers. This lotion, to prevent dry skin, containing morning dew from the Sahara. Miracles of modern science and ancient recipes, the guarded secrets of Cleopatra and the Queen of Sheba, precious as virgin's milk, reserved for the world's privileged few fair women.

When she had been metamorphosed Naomi was shown the raiment she was to wear in her new station. In a mirrored room carpeted like spring grass haughty models paraded for her private pleasure. Naked ones—no, not naked, clothed in lingerie so diaphanous as to seem to be. Then dressed in spidery lace, silk as fine as smoke, scratchy tweeds to tickle the skin and suave satins to soothe it. Leathers supple and scaly, of reptiles and birds and unborn calves. Furs from every corner of the globe, Andean chinchilla that shrank shyly from the touch as if still alive, sleek otter, marten, mink, and sable, ermine fluffy as thistledown, velvety clipped beaver, smooth leopard, kinky karakul. Around their svelte necks they wore ropes of pearls, chains of icy-green emeralds, around their thin wrists that had never wrung out a mop, bracelets of diamonds and rubies and gold, tiny watches that imprisoned time and kept them eternally young. The bills were to be sent to her daddy, Mr. O. B. Childress, care of the Adolphus Hotel.

"The Hotel Adolphus?" said the lady.

"That's right," said Naomi; and that night she was able to correct her mother's pronunciation: the accent in "hotel" fell on the second syllable.

They stayed a week, saw the zoo, the aquarium, went to a nightclub, and took all their meals in restaurants.

The new Packard was delivered to the door at the hour of their departure. It was mustard-colored; the seats, upholstered in red leather, looked like davenports. And though it was as long as a hearse, when the porters had brought down all the hatboxes and shoe boxes and boxed dresses and coats and suits and piled them on the sidewalk and started packing the car, it was evident that they would never get it all in. So Bull telephoned the dealer and another Packard, identical twin to the first, was brought over. As he was the only one in the family who could drive, Bull turned to the manager, who had come out to bid them good-by, and said, pointing to one of the porters, "What'll you take for that boy there? And throw in his uniform?" The porter couldn't drive either. He could steer, though, and that was how the Childresses returned home, one car hitched behind the other.

Jesse did not expect any word from Naomi, and it was not just that he believed her father would forbid her to send him any. The lore of his class, the songs he sang, were rich in cynical commentaries on such situations as his. He cursed her and dismissed her from his mind. Or told himself he had. But the first time he saw her on the street, and she passed him by as if afraid of dirtying herself by looking at him, though he tried to despise her new clothes they frightened him instead, and her new hairdo and those little refinements of carriage that she was already exhibiting all made her so beautiful that he was smitten as never before. The scent she left behind her in the street broke his heart. And he might as well have been dead for all she cared. Not a word. Not a glance. Not even for old times' sake.

Meanwhile, following Bull Childress's strike, the oil fever hit the section, and it seemed to poor Jesse that everybody except his folks had a piece of ground big enough to drill a hole and sink a pipe; only they had none. Land prices began to skyrocket, and there went the other dream of Jesse's life. Land that always, until now, had gone begging at twenty dollars an acre, land that had sold for unpaid taxes and gone unsold even for that, was suddenly fetching thousands of dollars. He alone owned none. Now he never would.

Clyde Barrow and Bonnie Parker were dead, the Texas badman and his gun moll. The town, one Saturday just past noon when Jesse joined his gang of buddies on Main Street, pullulated with the news. Dead. Clyde Barrow and Bonnie Parker. It had happened some days before (the previous Wednesday, in fact) but it was news, for if like Jesse and most of the others on the streets you spent Monday through Saturday morning behind a plow talking only to a mule, it was in town on Saturday afternoon that you caught up on the week's events. Clyde and Bonnie. Dead. The groups of men collected on the corners were both subdued and excited, with an air at once conspiratorial and challenging, as if defying a ban on public gatherings; and as with the people of an occupied country, when a partisan hero (and heroine), one of their own, had been caught and executed by the authorities, the flag of their traditional, classless, blood sympathy with the outlaw flew at half-mast.

The folk hero, in yet another avatar, was dead, and already the prose of their lament was growing cadenced and incantatory, half on its way to being verse, and soon would be music, and then, in the cotton fields, to the rhythm of the chopping of a hoe, on records in café nickelodeons, on street corners sung by blind, legless veterans to the whang of a steel guitar, young men would be adjured to take warning and listen to me, and told his story. How he was a poor boy—and thus already, even before his first recorded infraction (which had been to defend his sister's honor against a rich lecher, or the theft from hunger of a dime loaf of bread, or through impatience with the law's delay in righting a wrong which he, a poor boy, had suffered) on the outs with the law. A poor boy, alone, against the world, and orphaned. Orphaned of a father, that is; for a mother there would be, old and ailing, to visit whom in her illness he regularly slipped through the cordon of deputies and marshals posted around the family homestead with the loose insolent ease of a nocturnal panther. A poor boy who died young; handsome it went without saying; with women by the score ready to die for him, and one who gained immortality by dying with him. And a man (already in the barber shops and around the marble machines in the cafés they were wondering how the law could have known that Clyde would come down that road at that hour that day, he whose every move had been as stealthy and as sly as a hunted coyote, they who for two years he had made look like monkeys), a bosom friend, the one man he had ever taken into his confidence, whose life perhaps, which is to say undoubtedly, he had saved, ready to kiss his cheek in public for a handful of silver.

The actual place it had happened was in Louisiana, where, as their car passed through a narrow and bushy defile, they had been jumped, ambushed, by a party of local and out-of-state lawmen, who opened fire with shotguns, pistols, and automatic rifles. The car in the picture looked like a colander and the bodies of a thin, undersized young man and a thin young woman, who even in death retained the lean and sinewy wariness of an alley cat, looked like wild game, the lawmen standing over them with their guns, posing with stiff proud smiles, as in those photographs of hunting parties with the day's trophies lying at their feet. "I hated to bust a cap on a woman," the gallant leader of the posse was quoted as saying. "Especially when she was sitting down. But if it wouldn't of been her it would of been us."

And so at last it had come: the end to a reign of terror throughout the whole Southwest of some two years, as the newspapers put it. The end which had been expected daily and its every detail long foreseen (he would go out blazing, would take as many with him as he could, if they gave him a chance, which they didn't, and her too, old cigar-smoking Bonnie too, would never surrender, not Clyde, but would, should it come to that, save one last cartridge, or rather two, for themselves) had been foreseen and almost already lived through, yet never for one moment believed in, and secretly prayed against, even by those holding what they considered the sure number in the betting pools that had been made on the date.

And already, in the barbers' chairs beneath the turbaned mounds of towels, on the shoeshine stands, to the click of snooker balls, in the otherwise unused (except as a kind of local Salvation Army shelter for the town's two incorrigible and hopeless drunks) waiting room of the depot, hanging around waiting for old 88 to howl through and fling off the mail sack, they were saying: a dozen of them, and after two years of being made to look like a pack of fools, against one man and a girl! And without even giving them a chance to surrender (when what they meant was, without giving them a fighting chance to return fire). And saying that when the bodies were taken from the car (he had been at the wheel) she was found to have died in the act of drawing her pistol—not no lady's purse popgun but a real sonofabitching honest-to-by-God old .45 government-issue Colt automatic— from the glove compartment. And maybe her kind was what had led that poor boy astray in the first place, but she had stuck by her man, I God, through thick and thin, you had to say that for Bonnie Parker, she had stuck by her man.

And then—a note of state pride in the voice then, and a dry cackle of a snort—"I God, they ain't caught Purty Boy yit!" Meaning Oklahoma's own Pretty Boy Floyd. And how there was a man —not mentioning no names, but if you was to, why, it wouldn't be the first time they ever heard it, and he lived not so very far away —that answered a knock on the farmhouse door late one cold and rainy winter night and called *Who's there?* and got back for answer *A friend,* and opened the door and held the lamp up to a handsome young face that he had never seen before except on the wall alongside the rental boxes in the post office, but had said *Come in, friend,* for he had been honored by the title, been proud to give him the night's lodging he asked for, and had turned the kids out despite his protests and made them down a pallet on the floor, and next morning had found, or his wife had, pinned to the blanket a one-hundred-dollar bill. And that man was not the only man in Oklahoma that such a tale might tell. Not none of these biggety new oil-rich that up to six months ago had always wiped on a cob and now tried to look as if they never wiped at all, but them that still knew what it was to be a poor boy and on the outs with the law—which two things came to the same.

And someone wondered, for sooner or later someone was bound to, if it really was Clyde and Bonnie in that car. For the law shot first and asked questions later, and never confessed afterwards to any little mistakes of theirs. And they had been made to look mighty foolish for a long time. And they could use the bodies of a young man and a young woman, too shot up to be really identified, for public consumption. And that led to talk of the greatest badman of them all. How a man, an old-timer, had turned up in Oklahoma City, or maybe it was Tulsa, not so very long ago, claiming he was Jesse James and could prove it, and that the dirty little coward who in the song had shot Mr. Howard and laid poor Jesse in his grave had done no such thing, only it had been convenient at the time to let it be thought so.

And our Jesse listened, smiling bashfully, the black leather bow tie riding up his Adam's apple as he ducked his chin, reddening a little, as one must when a hero is being spoken of who shares one's name.

And they talked of other storied outlaws past and present, of Baby Face Nelson and Dillinger, of Sam Bass and Billy the Kid, and always, here among Jesse's crowd in particular, the word *poreboy, a poreboy,* sounded, like the bass string which the hand must always strum no matter what the chord, on a guitar. A poreboy who had got himself into a little trouble, and was maltreated and made mean by the law because he was a poreboy with nothing and nobody to buy them off, whom they might club and rubber-hose with impunity, a poreboy with no one to go his bail. For the gang that Jesse squatted and whittled and spat with in town on Saturday afternoon was different now from his former companions. Instead of the older, steadier (and as he now thought of them, cowed and beaten) family men, he hung out now with a group of young men of all ages, bachelors married and unmarried, hired hands and tenant farmers' sons from off the land and young mechanics and day laborers from the town and those without any fixed address nor visible means of support nor traceable origins who spent the days between Saturdays sitting along the loading platform of the cotton compress or in the domino parlor, those left out of the current oil boom, who made vague threats every now and then of running off and joining the Navy. And always in their telling there was a woman in it, too, at the root of it always some woman, one for whose sake a poreboy had gone wrong, and who, if she had not actually sold him out, had deserted him when the chips were down. As in the ballad, merely one of the most popular of hundreds on the theme, which had become Jesse's favorite among his repertoire:

> I got no use for the women.
> A true one can never be found.
> They'll stick by a man while he's winning;
> When he's losing they turn him down.

Except for passing showers lasting half an hour, and leaving upon the parched soil a crust like dried blood, it was six weeks since rain had fallen. The sun swooped lower by the day, singeing the stunted cotton like feathers in a flame. There was not even dew by night to settle the dust that choked the air. Men's heads were commencing to shake. It looked as if they were headed into another summer like the last, and the one before that.

In all of Oklahoma there was probably just one farmer whose mood this weather exactly suited, and that was Jesse Neighbours. He was spoiling for something, he himself did not know what. Now that he had nothing and no one to work for, he was working harder than ever, in the field before daybreak and out until after nightfall, unable to straighten his back, stalking down the rows (it was cotton-chopping time) with his hoe rising and falling as though motor-driven, neither speaking nor spoken to for twelve to fourteen hours at a stretch, so that his mind was furrowed by his thoughts as regular as a tractored field, throbbed to a beat as insistent as the rise and fall of his hoe. You chopped three acres a day and what did it get you? A plate of greens at night, enough to just keep you going tomorrow. You picked two hundred pounds, dragging the heavy sack after you like a wounded animal its entrails, bent double, blinded by your own salt sweat, no time to mop your brow, other hands quick to pick whatever you missed, half a cent a pound, take it or leave it, and at the end of the season what did you have? Enough to not quite pay your bill at the company store. Convinced now that farming was for fools—fools like him—Jesse delighted in every affliction that beset the crops: the fitful blossoming of the cotton, as if discouraged by the price it was fetching on the market, the coming of the boll weevils and the leaf hoppers and the corn smut, the blackbirds in clouds, the dust storms, the scorching sun that wrung a man out like a rag. He despised his condition and despised himself for acquiescing in it. And it was not long before that talk of desperadoes which had been dropped like refuse in a corner of his heated and airless brain burst aflame through spontaneous combustion.

People were robbing banks again, now that they had reopened following their little holiday. In town every Saturday there was talk of some bold new stickup. Then on Monday back to the fields, up and down the long weary rows, swinging a hoe or dragging a sack, and Jesse dreamed of fast cars, a new one stolen every week, always on the move, always in the money, spend it fast before it burned a hole in your pocket, plenty more where it came from, of living by the gun, quick on the trigger, feared and adored by multitudes, your exploits followed in the daily newspapers, good-looking women at your feet, fancy clothes, fast company. And when his name was on everybody's lips, then wouldn't Naomi feel sorry! Suppose you got caught? That was the risk you ran. Suppose you got killed? Suppose you did. Death by gunfire, quick, clean, a pistol bucking in your hand, at the end of a few glorious years, dying young and leaving a handsome corpse—compared with that was long life, spent in a cotton field, such a precious thing? Before long Jesse had begun to save up his money.

His earnings at picking went to the support of the family, but what he picked up playing Saturday-night dances was his. After being jilted he had recklessly gone back to smoking; now he quit again and once more began putting his tobacco money in a jar. It was no mule this time that he was saving for. He had to have a pistol; and before she would be reliable as a getaway car the old buggy needed a set of rings and at least one new tire to replace the one on the right rear with the boot and the slow leak around the valve.

Which bank Mr. O. B. Childress kept his money in Jesse did not know, but he wanted to be sure not to rob that one. Not that Jesse had any love for Bull. But Bull's money was, or would be, Naomi's; and if it should come to pass that having robbed just one bank and gotten away with it he decided not to make a career of it but came back home rich and they got married after all, he would not want it on his conscience that some part of his money was his wife's. The surest way to avoid it was to go outside the state.

Across the river over in Texas, in the county-seat town of Clarksville some forty miles away, was a bank which had been the object not long since of a spectacularly unsuccessful robbery attempt. The three robbers had been shot down like fish in a barrel as they emerged from the bank by lawmen posted on the adjacent rooftops. That gang had failed because they were too many—including a fourth who had informed the law of their plans. No one would be able to tip them off on him; and according to Jesse's calculations, swollen with self-conceit, the Clarksville sheriffs would be incapable of imagining that their bank might be struck again. And when things had blown over and he returned home in the chips, he would explain how he came into it by saying he had gone wildcatting in Texas and struck oil. And if he got caught? He was not aiming to get caught. And if he got killed? Who was there to care if he did?

The old buggy turned out to need more than a new tire or two, as Jesse found when, cotton picking over, he went to work on her. He gave her a valve job, up to his elbows in grinding compound, cleaned the plugs, put in points, regulated the timer. Then came the crowning touch, installation of a second carburetor, taken from the companion car, the adapter engineered by himself. The result: pickup that left new cars sitting, as he proved on the road to Tishomingo, where he went one day in October in quest of that pistol.

And on a subsequent trip shortly thereafter, thanks to those two carburetors, she hit seventy, shaking like a shimmy dancer, but she did it. That was a practice run down to Clarksville, where under an assumed name he opened a savings account at the bank with that fruit jar full of pennies and nickels and dimes, which took the teller a long time to sort out and count, giving Jesse a chance to study the layout.

He chose Halloween. You could wear a mask then and be just one among many, and the noise of firing, should it come to that, would be lost among the firecrackers and torpedoes. The night before Jesse wrote a letter to his folks, to be mailed from somewhere when the job was finished (it was found on him afterwards), explaining that he had left home to seek his fortune and would come back when he had made good, that he had left without saying good-by so as to avoid tears, and not to worry about him.

He left the car in a side street in back of the bank, as planned, engine running, a thing that attracted no notice in those days when old cars were often left running at the curb for fear of their not starting again. In an alleyway he slipped on his witch's mask. The square was filled with masked revelers and there was noise of fireworks. At the door of the bank Jesse faltered for just a moment, then boldly stepped in.

It was all over in seconds. Jesse went to one of the cages, pulled his pistol, and said, "This is a stickup." The teller ducked, bells clanged, Jesse panicked and ran, straight into the arms of a bank guard, who held him in a bear hug while a second guard slugged him senseless with a blackjack.

A young man who identified himself as his attorney, appointed by the court, came round a few days later to visit Jesse in his cell. He was still new to his trade and nervous as a young intern with his first cancer patient. In exasperation he said at last, "Fool! If you just had to rob a bank, why didn't you pick one near home? Or don't you even know that here in Texas armed bank robbery is a capital offense?"

No, Jesse said, he never knew that.

At the trial the lawyer pled his client's youth and previous good character and lack of criminal record. But there had been a rash of bank robberies of late, and it was felt that an example must be made. Being from out of state went against the defendant also.

The jury was out one hour and returned a verdict of guilty, and the judge sentenced Jesse Neighbours to die in the electric chair.

Appeal was denied, and in answer to their letter to the Governor of Texas, Jesse's father and mother received a form reply regretting that nothing could be done, the law must take its course.

Execution was fixed for a day in February. Will and Vera went down to Huntsville the day before to bid the boy good-by. They were given an hour together, but three quarters of it passed in silence. They spoke of things going on around home, as they had agreed beforehand they would. Once or twice they laughed over something, and once started all three laughed loudly. All through the interview his mother kept glancing nervously at her boy's hair despite herself, thinking of it being shaved off, as she had heard was done. Nothing was said about Naomi Childress. When the time was about up Jesse said he was sorry for the troubles he had brought on them, and they said not to think about that. He said tell his little brothers, and especially Doak, not to be proud of their outlaw brother and want to follow in his footsteps, but to be sensible boys and stick to farming, as crime did not pay. His mother would have liked to ask if he had made his peace with the Lord but was afraid of embarrassing him. When it came time to say good-by they kissed and she managed to stay dry-eyed, as Will had admonished her that she must. It was he whose eyes filled with tears as he and Jesse shook hands.

They were told they could come for him anytime after seven the next morning. Money being a little tight, and neither of them feeling much like sleep, they passed the night sitting in the waiting room of the depot. They did not know the exact hour of execution. But when at shortly past five the lights in the station dimmed they reached for one another's hand and sat holding them until, after about four minutes by the clock on the wall, the lights brightened again. At seven at the penitentiary gate they found a truck waiting with a casket on the bed. They were given Jesse's effects, his guitar, his clothes, and a bale of tinfoil from the inner wrappings of ready-rolled cigarettes, each sheet rubbed out smooth as a mirror, at the sight of which his mother could not keep back a tear.

They were given a ride back to the depot in the cab of the truck. There the casket was put on the scales and weighed and Will paid the lading charges. Then it was put on a cart and rolled out to the end of the platform. They went back to their seats in the waiting room. There remained in the shoe box which Vera had put up for their trip some biscuits and meat, but neither felt hungry. When the train came in they watched the casket loaded into a freight car. Their seats were in a coach in the rear. The overhead rack being too narrow for it, the guitar rode across their laps. And still though they sat, in four hundred and fifty miles it happened now and again that one or the other would brush the strings, drawing from them a low chord like a sob.

A Good Indian

WHEN I WAS a boy I was ashamed of the color of my skin—
ashamed for my family, for the whole white race. From that red
Oklahoma earth which we walked upon and called ours had
sprung the red man; we palefaces were aliens and usurpers. On
our farm you could not plow ten feet, especially not after erosion
had laid the soil bare and the dust storms had flayed it rawer still,
without turning up a flint arrowhead, and while I treasured them,
they were a reproach to me. The name "Sooner," so proudly
worn by our state, to me was an emblem of infamy; and although
at school we were taught to glorify that day in 1889 when our
forefathers had gathered on the borders of what was then called
Indian Territory, poised themselves, and at the crack of the starter's pistol swarmed in and staked their claim to however much
they could pace off and fence in, I was not a bit proud of my
grandfather's part in that adventure. My father might sigh and say
he wished Papa had gotten more while the getting was good; to
me it was evident at an early age that Grandpa must have stolen
our fifty acres from some poor Indian brave, perhaps the very one
who, in leaving, had sown the earth with dragon's teeth in the

form of his arrowheads, and whom I pictured as proud and noble and sad, like the one on the head of the nickel.

Whenever I had a nickel, and bought myself a magazine, I sided with them—the Apaches, the Blackfeet, the Cheyennes—against my own people, and excused their cruelties. And when we kids played cowboys and Indians, I always took the part of Geronimo or Quanah Parker, and sometimes I came near to drawing blood with my stone tomahawk in trying to lift the scalp of my fallen paleface foe.

That tomahawk, by the way, was the genuine article. Like everybody else in our parts, we had an Indian burial mound on the property, and over the years ours yielded me, in addition to the tomahawk, stone grinding pestles and scraps of painted pottery, knucklebones, a skull, skinning knives of flint and obsidian, worn-down bits of antlers, and always arrowheads of all colors and of sizes for every variety of game, from tiny ones hardly bigger than a grain of corn, to great broadheads which I liked to think had once brought down two-ton buffaloes.

Feeling always something of a renegade (for stories of the Indian Wars were still told during my boyhood), I read all I could lay my hands on of the history of the Indians. The record of the white man's greed and perfidy was hardly to be believed. From the very beginning, in Jamestown and Massachusetts Bay, those original owners of the entire American continent welcomed the invaders as friends and neighbors, and where they did not make them outright gifts of land enough to live on (the Indians all had a very backward and undeveloped sense of individual land ownership and did not believe that one man could own what belonged to all men—what belonged, in fact, to no man, but instead to the Great Spirit), they sold it to them at fair, not to say overgenerous, prices. And then the whites (I thought of them in those days as like white mice, with the quick, grasping paws and the sharp, busy teeth and the greedy little red bug-eyes of white mice) overran the Indians like a plague. In every state of the Union those who had once owned all saw it nibbled away and gobbled up until they were dispossessed of their ancient hunting grounds and herded into pens called reservations. Where they resisted they lost, and were punished for defending what was theirs. Where they conferred, and went voluntarily, with treaties guaranteeing the bounds of the reservation in perpetuity, they saw, in the same generation, in the same decade, often by the very signatories, every treaty mocked and broken. Mice do not know how to share; what's yours is theirs—all of it. And so the Indians were moved off these reservations to others farther west, on land belonging to yet other Indians, and given a treaty guaranteeing that it would never happen again.

Then positively the last resettlement was proposed—at gunpoint—to them. All the Indians, from all over, would be brought together in one large tract, and this land would be theirs for as long as the sun should shine: here was a treaty to show for it, hung with red ribbons and seals like tassels. And from the shrunken reservations which were all that remained to them of the land of their fathers, in Alabama, in Tennessee and Carolina and Mississippi and Florida, they were herded like winter cattle, and thousands left dead along the trail, to Oklahoma. It was not much good, this land; but it was theirs. The treaty was signed by the Great White Father in Washington, D.C. But Great White Fathers come and go, and that one was no sooner gone than the mice were running in the walls and boldly scampering out to thieve by night, and breeding and clamoring to get in; and the sun went down in the land which was to be theirs for so long as the sun should shine, and the red men were herded onto the last reservations, little pockets of the leanest land where the best was none too fat, and all the rest declared to belong to whichever white man got there "sooner" and staked his claim.

When you are a kid, you can get so carried away that those olden times seem more real to you than the times you live in.

I was scarcely able to look an Indian in the face whenever I met one on the street in town on a Saturday afternoon, when they came in from off the nearby reservation. I could scarcely believe they were Indians. They were parodies of white men, as a scarecrow is a parody of a man. Instead of beaded moccasins they wore broken-down old bluchers that the poorest poor white would long since have thrown away—possibly had. (I noticed the feet first, no doubt, because I hung my head and kept my eyes cast down.) Instead of fringed buckskin hunting shirts, they wore frayed and threadbare imitation-chamois work shirts, and over them wore baggy overalls of railway-engineer's pattern, black-and-white-striped. Instead of war bonnets of eagle feathers, they wore greasy old wool caps with pinched and broken bills or sweaty-banded old black felt hats with uncreased crowns. No bareback pinto ponies did they ride, but came in creaky old swaybacked wagons drawn by swaybacked mules with collar and trace galls and flyblown sores around their scrawny necks and down their slatted sides from pulling a plow. Along the tailgate of the wagon would sit a row of dark, runty children, stiff and impassive as a row of prize dolls in a carnival tent.

When, aged twelve, I accidentally opened our family skeleton cupboard one day and discovered hidden therein the fact that I myself had Indian blood, I at first did not know which to be, overjoyed or infuriated. I felt like the changeling prince in the storybook must have felt on discovering his true birthright, and discovering simultaneously that he had been done out of it, stolen and brought up by peasants as a peasant. I reproached my kin for having kept me in ignorance of this most important fact of my heritage. I begged for further knowledge. They seemed to know little and to care less. She was a Cherokee or a Choctaw, no one was sure which, and the man who had brought her into the family was dismissed as the squaw man. Possibly even she had been a half-breed (they seemed to prefer to think so), and so my share was only about one sixteenth, an amount to which most everybody in Oklahoma would probably have to own. Better just forget it, they said. Family matters, they seemed to be telling me, were best kept in the family. I vowed that when I grew up I would join a tribe and become an Indian.

Well, I grew up, all right, and in the process I lost my desire to become an Indian. Dirty pigs! My God, a white man may be poor, but if he's got any self-respect at all, he keeps himself clean, at least. They haven't got bathtubs? No running water? We never had, either. We toted the water in by the bucketful from the cistern, heated it in kettles and pots on the range, bathed in a number-three washtub on the kitchen floor. But we bathed. Every Saturday night. When we got done, and Mama got done reaming out our ears, and we stepped out, the water in that tub looked like blood, like a hog had been scraped in it, from that red Oklahoma dirt. We might have been poor, but we were always clean.

And poor as we were, we held on to our morals. We got pretty hungry, too; but we never stole, nor let our children thieve right out of the store bins in town. We'd have starved sooner than do that. And sooner than see our daughters and our sisters do what some of those Indian girls did for money, we'd have killed them first.

You can't help people that won't help themselves: that's another thing I learned in growing up. You've got to have ambition. Whenever we got a dollar ahead, we didn't come into town with it and buy a quart of white lightning from some bootlegger in a back alley, get drunk and go crazy and start taking the place apart, wind up in jail with a head caved in from the constable's billy club, no use to ourselves or our families for the next thirty days. Indians just can't hold their liquor? In that case they ought to let it alone. I've heard it said they drink because they're downhearted. Because they've had it rough. Had a raw deal. We've all had it rough. We've all had a raw deal. But did we sit around moping about it forevermore? We bettered ourselves.

And just how rough did they have it when it was really rough all over? Living out there on the reservation all through '31, '32, '3, '4 on a steady government dole? Not much of a dole? Well, it was more than we got—and we paid taxes! They never had to worry that the bank was going to come around one day and say, "Well, Ed, old friend, you've been here a long time, and I hate to have to say it, but looks like you'll have to get off, you and your wife and kids." Best landlord in the world, good old Uncle Sam!

An Indian won't work. And don't give me none of that stuff about not having incentive. The answer to that argument is here: in 1935 a law was passed that the tribes could no longer hold the reservation lands in common (which is socialism) but it had to be divided up and parceled out among the members. The idea was to drag them into the twentieth century. Give them some incentive. Teach them what it means to a man to own his own little plot of ground, and to want to increase it, come up in the world. To weed out the freeloaders and give the real hustlers a chance to rise to the top of the heap. Did those lazy, good-for-nothing Indians work that land any harder when it was their own? They did not.

Now 1935, the year that law was passed, just happened to be the year when oil was first brought in around our section. I am not saying there was any connection; but once each Indian owned his own piece of land he was free to sell it if he had a mind to, not be told by the tribal council that the land didn't belong to him, couldn't be traded. And how do you suppose they spent the money they got for the sale of their land? Well, I got my share. If they didn't have any better sense than to spend it with me, that was their lookout. They wanted what I had to sell, and if I hadn't taken their money, there were plenty more who would have.

I had set up in business for myself in '33. I had the local distributorship for Cadillac. As you can just imagine, a man was not getting rich selling Cadillacs to Oklahoma tenant farmers in 1933 and '4. But all of a sudden the smart alecks who wouldn't let me in on the small family cars just a year or so before were all laughing out of the other sides of their mouths. For when a redneck who has followed a plow all his life lays down the traces and picks up a fortune in oil one day, he don't want him no Ford nor Chevrolet, he wants him a *car*—the longest, fastest, gaudiest thing on wheels. And there was I, with just what he was after. "The car you never thought you'd own"—that was my motto.

I sold them with all accessories already on. Radio and heater, chrome tailpipe, venetian blinds, seats upholstered in leopard, zebra, spotted calf. The only thing that was optional was the steer horns on the radiator grille. I stocked Cadillacs in fire-engine red, oyster white, sky blue; but my hottest number of all was a bile yellow that sharpened your teeth like the smell of a sour pickle. That was the wagon that really got the braves from off the reservation.

Some people—especially those on whose own farmsteads one after another dry hole had been drilled—were complaining in those days that the Indians had been given all the oil-rich land. Others were not just sitting on their hands and howling, they were busy buying the redskins out. Some of those Indians sold out without even waiting for a drilling sample. Show them a few thousand dollars and that was all they needed to see—especially if they were seeing double. Others were told yes, no doubt about it, there was certainly oil lying under their land. But who knew how much? It might turn out to be a million barrels, and then again, it might not. It was a gamble, either way, but a bird in the hand . . . And there was I, or one of my men, before the ink on their X was dry—in line, I might add, with the Packard, the Buick, and the Pierce-Arrow dealers.

And then, a few months later, after they had run out of money to buy gas to put in them, or after they had driven them without any oil in the crankcase, you might see on a country road one of those Packards or Pierce-Arrows or Cadillacs hitched to a team of mules with the brave sitting on the hood on a blanket holding the reins, while inside, with the windows all rolled up regardless of the heat, sat the squaw and the papooses. Drive on a little farther down that same road, and you were apt to pass three or four more big-model automobiles upside down in the ditch or crumpled against telegraph poles.

But for running through cars, the Indian I am going to tell about holds the record.

One day one of my salesmen brought in a prospect known to everybody around town as John. If he had a second name, I had never heard it. John had sold out that very morning. Not being a very convivial sort, even in his cups, John had held out for and had gotten nine thousand dollars—plus a second bottle—out of the men who bought him out. He was a big buck with a face like a stone on the bottom of a creek, flat and featureless, and just as full of smiles. Underneath his arm, the one without the bottle, he carried a bundle wrapped in newspaper and tied with twine, which I knew to recognize. They always insisted on cash, and they wanted it always in ten-dollar bills, possibly because those of larger denomination did not look like money to them, and a ten really did.

Our demonstrator was one of those yellow dogs, and my man had brought John in, at around eighty-five miles per hour, in it. That was what he wanted, and he wanted it now. I had sitting out back some three dozen jalopies and homemade pickups cut down from old passenger sedans and coupés and touring cars—Stars, Moons, and so help me, one Marmon V-16. I had buggies, I had buckboards, I had I don't know how many wagons, I had me about half the mules in that county, for I'd seen booms before and I'd seen busts, too, and I was hedging against the day when they would need those wagons and teams again; I drew the line only at travois. On this deal, though, I wasn't going to have to take any trade-in.

I had on the showroom floor one exactly the same, but no, John here wanted that demonstrator. She had a few thousand miles on the speedometer, and I supposed he wanted that particular car, thinking he would get a little something off on the price. Little was what he would get, all right; but I was prepared to powwow. However, John did not want to bargain. He wanted that car the way he might have wanted a particular woman for a squaw and not her twin sister. He had seen what the one could do. I took his parcel from him (this had to be done cautiously—no sudden movements—like taking a bone from a dog), untied the string, and counted out four hundred and twenty ten-dollar bills. I told him that was what I wanted for my automobile. John studied the stack I had made for a time, then he stacked the rest alongside and studied the two of them. After he had my car he would still have more money than I would have. With a grunt, he pushed the smaller stack towards me. The bottle, too. To close the deal I had to drink with him.

While I was drawing up the bill of transfer, the salesman took the customer out for his driving lesson. This was a little service I offered, free of charge. They were gone about half an hour. When they returned, Doyle—Doyle Gilpin, my star salesman, himself part Kiowa—had a big purple knot over one eye. John X-ed the contract where I showed him to and I turned his ignition key over to him. I counted out to Doyle his commission, locked the money in the strongbox, locked the strongbox in the safe, and went to the show window to watch. The other salesmen, the parts-department man, and the mechanics from back in the shop all came out and joined us. These performances were always a sketch.

To see that Indian come up on that automobile was worth the price of a ticket. He carried the key hidden behind his back, as if it were a halter, and Doyle swore he was talking to that automobile under his breath all the while he sidled up to it, to coax it into standing still. Though he had been behind the wheel for his driving lesson, old habit was strong, and now he did not come at her from the driver's side because, unlike a white man, an Indian mounts a horse from the right. He stood stroking the door panel for a minute, then opened the door, saw he was on the off side, nodded to himself, shut the door, and, holding on to her all the while, made his way around the front end—never go behind them: that's where they can kick you.

"You say he claims to know how to drive?" I asked Doyle.

"Ugh," Doyle quoted.

It didn't look like it. He sat for the next five minutes behind the wheel doing nothing at all. "Hellfire," I said, "he don't even know how to switch it on. Go out there and show—"

But John had known all along what to do; he had been just sitting there enjoying himself, like not wanting to put the match to a new brier pipe for savoring that never-to-be-recaptured moment of unused, fresh, factory-smelling ownership. The car John never thought he'd own for sure was his. They will tell you an Indian never smiles, but I have yet to see the one who doesn't when he switches on the ignition of his own new yellow Cadillac for the first time.

He put his foot on the accelerator and raced the motor up to where it sounded like a power saw, while we inside all winced. That was the one thing that used to bother me; I do hate to see a fine piece of machinery misused by falling into the wrong hands. Then he let out the clutch, or rather jerked his foot off of it, and away he went. He was right about that car: it bucked, it pitched, it snorted, it pawed, it leaped like—and in his hands, it was—a horse—an outlaw, a cayuse.

"Now you know," said Doyle, "how I got this bump on my head."

"Didn't you show him how to ease his foot off the clutch so as to keep that from happening?"

"Yeah, I showed him. He don't want to keep it from happening. That's the part he likes."

Now he rode her to earth. The gears meshed, and with a sound like satin ripping, he was off, discovering the horn in the process. And for the next hour he raced up and down Main Street, chasing pedestrians up onto the sidewalks, running up on them himself, slamming on his brakes, sitting on the horn, and letting the clutch out fast and bucking like a bronco. The town constable, with a little urging from us car dealers, was not opposed to letting the boys enjoy themselves a little with their new cars, so long as nobody got hurt. There had been complaints about it in the beginning, just as the bankers had complained when pressure was put on them not to open accounts for the Indians; but just as the bankers came to realize that it was better for them as well to keep that money in circulation, so people generally came to realize that what was good for trade was good for the town as a whole. By about the time they had run through their complimentary three gallons of gas, the constable would tell them that was enough, and to go do their racing out on the country roads.

John, however, did not wait to be told. After a time he began to want company and tried to pick up a passenger, but nobody would ride with him. He invited Will Tall Corn, but Will just shook his head. Will's boy Henry was one of two friends to whom I had sold identical convertibles just a short while before, who, to settle a dispute the following week, ran them at one another head on from a distance of half a mile; that settled it, all right. Piqued that nobody would ride with him, John gunned out of town, going past my place and raising a cloud like a dust storm.

And that was the last we saw of him for about two hours, when, looking out the show window, I saw a wagon and team drawing up to the gas pumps, and driving them was John. I was showing a couple a car, but before those two made up their mind there would be three changes of model, so I turned them over to one of my assistants and went out.

"John!" I said. "Here, what's this? What have you done with that new car of yours?"

Well, it seemed that John's new car no go no more. John was disgusted with it. He seemed to expect me to give him that other one in replacement, the other yellow one. I said the warranty stopped just a little short of that, but let's have a look at his, chances were we could put it right if there was something the matter with it, get it going for him again. John, though, was really down on that car, never wanted to see it again, didn't even want to talk about it. Only very grudgingly did he consent to come with us in the wrecker and show us where he had left it.

What was keeping his car from going was a great big mean old tree in the way.

Taking notes on the scene were a couple of highway patrolmen, so while we towed in the wreck, John was taken down to the courthouse and charged with drunken driving, recklessness with an automobile, damage to public property (to get at the tree, he'd had to clip off a couple of the highway department's concrete fence posts), speeding, and if there had been such a thing as driver's licenses (there was later, of course, and it all but ruined the automobile business in Oklahoma for a time, especially the literacy test, but I wasn't hurt; on the contrary, I'd seen it coming and gotten out while the getting was good), why, I suppose they would have booked him for driving without any. As for the damage to his car, it looked a lot worse than it was. The front end was all smashed in, fenders and head lamps, bumper, grille, and the hood was sprung; but apart from the radiator and a bent fan and fan shaft, mechanically it was unharmed. For three hundred and fifty dollars—say five hundred—we could have it looking like new, almost.

But I never even got to quote him a figure before John started in again about wanting that other car, the one sitting on the showroom floor. His own, he refused even to come out and look at it. With that car John was finished. I was growing just a trifle impatient with trying to get it through that thick skull of his by sign language that cars weren't guaranteed against trees alongside the road, when John, pointing once again at the car on the floor, took from under his arm his parcel wrapped in newspaper, now considerably lightened, and put it in my hand.

It took me a minute to catch on, and when I did, I still didn't believe it. It's hard to credit foolishness, even when you've seen as much of it as I have. "You want to *buy* it, then?" I said. "Is that what you're saying? You want to *buy* that car?" There stood that savage without socks on his feet, wanting to buy his second Cadillac of the day!

What was more, he was ready to pay cash for it. No trade-in. He never even asked me to make him an offer on his other one. He could hardly wait for me to count the money. "Same," he said. "Same." Meaning it came to as much as he paid for his first car.

"That may be," said I. "But the price ain't the same. This car here costs a little more than your other one. Because this one ain't never been rode by anybody, see?"

I figured he ought to have a good bit more money left than he had paid for his first car. That one had cost him forty-two hundred dollars, which, taken from nine thousand, left forty-eight hundred. Less twenty for wrecker service: forty-seven eighty. However, he had only forty-two hundred and eighty dollars on him. Where the other five hundred had gone didn't take three guesses. Fine or bail bond to those shysters down at the courthouse.

"Not enough," I said. Not caring particularly for the look on his face, I gave Doyle the sign, and he came over and joined us.

"I give you," said John, "my wagon and my team."

Not his other car. I'm slow, as I say, when it comes to taking in foolishness of that depth, but now it dawned on me that as far as John was concerned that other car of his was dead. Having no value to him anymore, it had none that he could imagine for anybody else.

"I got me a wagon," I said. "I got mules."

"Good wagon," said John. "Good mules."

It wasn't a bad-looking team. Underfed, like all Indians' animals, but good stock. Not a bad-looking wagon, either.

"Wagons and teams not fetching much now," I said. "Everybody like you, wants a car. Nobody wants a wagon and team."

He just stood there, looking at me. I wondered what was going through that head. Nothing, it appeared.

Then Doyle spoke up and said, "How much does John need to have enough to buy him that yellow car?"

I said, figuring twenty-five dollars for the wagon and team and the harness, that would leave him still shy one hundred and fifty-two dollars and ninety-seven cents. "Make it a round hundred and fifty," I said.

"You don't suppose," said Doyle, "that we could allow John

that for the wreck, do you? We ought to be able to strip a few spare parts off of it, oughtn't we?"

"Who are you working for," I said, pulling a sour face, "me or John?"

Then, with as good grace as I could, I gave in.

"Come see what our friend John has gone and done with his new car." It could not have been more than an hour later when Doyle Gilpin came in from giving a prospect a ride out in the country in our new demonstrator and said those words to me.

"Don't tell me," I said.

"Just come see," said Doyle.

I got up and followed. Doyle at the wheel, we drove out of town about five miles, being overtaken and passed by a siren car. We pulled up to where a line of cars alongside the road was already pulled up.

It was not a tree this time, it was a curve in the road, and he must have tried to take it at no less than a hundred, for the car had finally come to rest a good fifty yards in the field beyond and must have turned over no fewer than half a dozen complete turns. Alongside the wreck, where the impact had thrown him, lay John —by old General Phil Sheridan's definition, a very good Indian.

There being no hospital in our town, thus no ambulance, the corpse was removed via pickup truck, to be left until called for by family or friends at the local funeral parlor.

The body gone, the crowd left. I stayed studying the wreck until all were gone. I would never have believed you could smash up a car to look like that.

"Nothing to do with that one," said Doyle, "but set a match to it."

It was just what I was thinking myself. No point in leaving an ugly sight like that to disfigure the beauty of the landscape, and to scare away trade.

"You got one on you?" I said.

"One what?" said Doyle.

I gave him a cigar, put one in my own mouth.

"One match," I said, waiting for a light.

And here now is the end of my story.

A little later in the day I was working at my desk when I had the feeling that somebody was watching me and looked up, and there standing in the doorway was this squaw. She was built like a sack of potatoes, and dressed like one, had a face the shape and the color of a deep-red potato. I hadn't heard her come in—you never do, they're as slinky as a cat and don't know that a door is for knocking on—but I felt she had been there for some time already before I noticed her, watching me out of those narrow, shiny black eyes.

"What can we do for you?" I said. For you never knew: tomorrow she might be a customer.

She never said anything.

I said, "It's around to the side there, if that's what's on your mind. Make yourself at home. It's free."

She just stood there, never batting a lash.

"Can't speak a word of English, I bet, can you?" I said. And I tried a couple of words on her which proved she couldn't. Can you just imagine it, a full-grown woman, born and brought up in the United States of America, and too lazy or too dumb or just too plained damned contrary to learn to speak the language? What are you going to do with people like that, I ask you.

Doyle Gilpin came in from the shop.

I said to Doyle, "Minnie Ha Ha here looks like she would like to use the Ladies'. Show her where to find it, will you?"

She and Doyle talked until it commenced to get on my nerves. It don't take much of that grunting and hawking to do it.

"What's all the palaver about?" I said.

"This here," said Doyle, "is Mrs. John. His squaw."

"Well? What does she want?" I said.

"She says, can she have back the wagon and team?"

"Oh, she does, does she? Well, would you please just explain to Mrs. John there that I took that wagon and team in on a trade on an automobile. And you might say that with things as they are I allowed about twice as much for it as it's worth."

More grunting, more hawking. "What's she jabbering about now?" I said.

"Says she needs it to take her man away in."

"Well, hell, lend her a wagon and a damned team. Let her have them two we took in on Monday. They ought to just about make it to the graveyard."

"She says she needs it to move with too. She's got to get off the place tomorrow so they can start drilling for the oil."

"All right! Tell her she can borrow them for that too. Well, now what?"

"She says now that their land is gone, she ain't got no place to bury him in."

That was when I blew the whistle. "What in the infernal hell," I said, "has that got to do with me, I'd just like to know? Am I supposed to include a cemetery plot with every car one of these jokers buys from me?"

A Job of the Plains

I

THERE WAS a man in the land of Oklahoma whose name was Dobbs; and this man was blameless and upright, one who feared God and turned away from evil. And there were born to him three sons and four daughters. His substance also was one lank Jersey cow, a team of spavined mules, one razorback hog, and eight or ten mongrel hound pups. So that this man was about as well off as most everybody else in eastern Pushmataha County.

Now there came a day when the sons of God came to present themselves before the Lord, and Satan also came among them. And the Lord said unto Satan, "Whence comest thou?" Then Satan answered the Lord and said, "From going to and fro in the earth and from walking up and down in it." And the Lord said unto Satan, "Hast thou considered my servant Dobbs, that there is none like him in the earth, a blameless and upright man, one that fears God and escheweth evil?" Then Satan answered the Lord and said, "Does Dobbs fear God for nought? Hast Thou not made an hedge about him, and about his house, and about all that he hath on every side? Thou has blessed the work of his hands, and his substance is increased in the land. But put forth Thy hand now and touch all that he hath, and he will curse Thee to Thy face."

There was actually no hedge but only a single strand of barbwire about all that Chester Dobbs had. The Devil was right, though, in saying that the Lord had blessed the work of Dobbs's hands that year (1929) and his substance had increased in the land. There had been a bumper cotton crop, Dobbs had ginned five bales, and—the reverse of what you could generally count on when the crop was good—the price was staying up. In fact it was rising by the day; so that instead of selling as soon as his was ginned, Dobbs, like everybody else that fall, put his bales in storage and borrowed from the bank to live on in the meantime, and sat back to wait for the best moment. At this rate it looked as if he might at last begin paying something on the principal of the mortgage which his old daddy had left as Dobbs's legacy. And in fifteen or twenty years' time he would own a piece of paper giving him sole and undisputed right, so long as he paid the taxes, to break his back plowing those fifty acres of stiff red clay.

Then the Lord said unto Satan, "Behold, all that he hath is in your power. Only upon himself do not put forth thy hand." So Satan went forth out of the presence of the Lord.

"Well," said Dobbs, when those five fat bales he had ginned stood in the shed running up a storage bill and you couldn't give the damned stuff away that fall, "the Lord gives and the Lord takes away. I might've knowed it was too good to ever come true. I guess I ain't alone in this."

He had known bad years before—had hardly known anything else; and had instinctively protected himself against too great a disappointment by never fully believing in his own high hopes. Like the fellow in the story, he was not going to get what he thought he would for his cotton, but then he never thought he would. So he borrowed some more from the bank, and butchered the hog, and on that, and on his wife's canning, they got through the winter.

But instead of things getting better the next spring they got worse. Times were so bad that a new and longer word was needed: they were in a depression. Cotton, that a man had plowed and sown and chopped and picked and ginned, was going at a price to make your codsack shrink, and the grocer in town from whom Dobbs had had credit for twenty years picked this of all times to announce that he would have to have cash from now on, and would he please settle his bill within thirty days? He hated to ask it, but they were in a depression. "Ain't I in it too?" asked Dobbs. What was the world coming to when cotton wasn't worth nothing to nobody? For when he made his annual spring trip to the loan department of the bank and was told that not only could they not advance him anything more, but that his outstanding note, due in ninety days, would not be renewed, and Dobbs offered as collateral the other two of his bales on which they did not already hold a lien, the bank manager all but laughed in his face and said, "Haven't you folks out in the country heard yet? We're in a depression."

Nevertheless, when the ground was dry enough that you could pull your foot out of it Dobbs plowed and planted more cotton. What else was a man to do? And though through the winter there had been many times when he thanked God for taking Ione's uterus after the birth of Emmagine, now he thanked Him for his big family. There was a range of just six years among them, one brace of twins being included in the number, and all were of an age to be of help around the place. The boys were broken to the plow, and the girls were learning, as plain girls did (might as well face it), to make up in the kitchen and around the house for what they lacked in looks. Levelheaded, affectionate, hard-working girls, the kind to really appreciate a home and make some man a good wife. And while boys went chasing after little dollfaces that couldn't boil water, they were left at home on the shelf. But, that's how it goes. Meanwhile they were a help to their mother. And when cotton-chopping time came they knew how to wield a hoe. And when cotton-picking time came all would pick.

Still, there were nine mouths to feed. Big husky hard-working boys who devoured a pan of biscuits with their eyes alone, and where were they to find work when men with families were standing idle on the street corners in town, and in the gang working on the highway you saw former storekeepers and even young beginning lawyers swinging picks and sledge hammers for a dollar a day and glad to get it? By night around the kitchen table the whole family shelled pecans with raw fingers; the earnings, after coal oil for the lamp, would just about keep you in shoelaces, assuming you had shoes.

On top of this a dry spell set in that seemed like it would never break. In the ground that was like ashes the seed lay unsprouting. Finally enough of a sprinkle fell to bring them up, then the sun swooped down and singed the seedlings like pinfeathers on a fowl. Stock ponds dried up into scabs, wells went dry, folks were hauling drinking water. The boll weevils came. The corn bleached and the leaves hung limp and tattered with worm holes. The next year it was the same all over again only worse.

It got so bad at last a rainmaker was called in. He pitched his tent where the medicine shows were always held, built a big smoky bonfire, set off Roman candles, firecrackers, sent up rubber balloons filled with gas and popped them with a .22 rifle, set out washtubs filled with ice water. Folks came from far and near to watch, stood around all day gawking at the sky and sunburning the roofs of their mouths, went home with a crick in their necks saying, I told you it'd never work. Church attendance picked up and the preachers prayed mightily for rain, but could not compete with the tent revivalist who came to town, pitched his tabernacle where the rainmaker had been, a real tongue-lasher who told them this drought was punishment for all their sins, bunch of whiskey drinkers and fornicators and dancers and picture-show-goers and non-keepers of the Sabbath and takers of the Lord's name in vain, and if they thought they'd seen the worst of it, just to wait, the good Lord had only been warming up on them so far. About this time word spread that on the second Tuesday in August the world was going to come to an end. Some folks pshawed but that Tuesday they took to their storm cellars the same as the rest. Towards milking time they began to poke their noses up, and felt pretty foolish finding the old world still there. The first ones up had a shivaree going around stomping on other folks' cellar doors and ringing cowbells and banging pots and pans. Afterwards when you threw it up to the fellow who'd told you, he said he'd got it from old So-and-so. Whoever started it nobody ever did find out.

One day the following spring an angel fell from heaven in the form of the county agricultural agent and landed at Dobbs's gate with the news that the government was ready to pay him, actually pay him, not to grow anything on twenty-five of his fifty acres.

What was the catch?

No catch. It was a new law, out of Washington. He didn't need to be told that cotton prices were down. Well, to raise them the government was taking this step to lower production. The old law of supply and demand. They would pay him as much not to grow anything on half of his land as he would have made off of the cotton off of it. It sounded too good to be true. Something for nothing? From the government? And if true then there was something about it that sounded, well, a trifle shady, underhanded. Besides, what would he do?

"What would you do?"

"Yes. If I was to leave half of my land standing idle what would I do with myself half the day?"

"Hell, set on your ass half the time. Hire yourself out."

"Hire myself out? Who'll be hiring if they all go cutting back their acreage fifty per cent?"

That was his problem. Now, did he have any spring shoats?

Did he! His old sow had farrowed like you never seen before. Thirteen she had throwed! Hungry as they all were, at hog-killing time this fall the Dobbses would have pigs to sell. And what pigs! Would he like to see them? Cross between Berkshire and razor-back, with the lard of the one and the bacon of the other. Finest-looking litter of pigs you ever—well, see for yourself!

He had asked because the government was out to raise the price of pork, too, and would pay so and so much for every shoat not fattened for market. The government would buy them right now, pay him for them as if they were grown.

"Why? What's the government going to do with all them pigs?"

"Get shut of them. Shoot them."

"What are they doing with all that meat?"

"Getting shut of it. Getting it off the market. That's the idea. So prices can—"

"Just throwing it out, you mean? With people going hungry? Just take and throw it away? Good clean hog meat?"

"Now look a-here. What difference does it make to you what they do with them, as long as you get your money? You won't have the feeding of them, and the ones you have left will be worth more."

"That ain't so good."

"How come it ain't?"

"The ones I have left I'll have to eat—the expensive ones. I won't be able to afford to eat them. Say, are you getting any takers on this offer?"

"Any takers! Why, man, you can't hardly buy a suckling pig these days, people are grabbing them up so, to sell to old Uncle Sam."

"No!"

"I'm telling you. And buying up cheap land on this other deal. Land you couldn't grow a bull nettle on if you tried, then getting paid not to grow nothing on it."

"What is the world coming to! Hmm. I reckon my land and me could both use a little rest. But taking money without working for it? Naw, sir, that sound I hear is my old daddy turning over in his grave. As for them shoats there, well, when the frost is in the air, in November, and I get to thinking of sausage meat and backbone with sweet potatoes and cracklin' bread, why then I can climb into a pen and stick a hog as well as the next fellow. Then it's me or that hog. But when it comes to shooting little suckling pigs, like drownding a litter of kittens, no sir, include me out. And if this is what voting straight Democratic all your life gets you, then next time around I'll go Republican, though God should strike me dead in my tracks at the polling booth!"

The next thing was, the winds began to blow and the dust to rise. Some mornings you didn't know whether to get out of bed or not. It came in through the cracks in the wall and the floor and gritted between your teeth every bite you ate. You'd just better drop the reins and hightail it for home and the storm cellar the minute a breeze sprang up, because within five minutes more it was black as night and even if you could have stood to open your eyes you couldn't see to blow your nose. You tied a bandana over your face but still it felt like you had inhaled on a cigar. Within a month after the storms started you could no longer see out of your windowlights, they were frosted like the glass in a lawyer's office door, that was how hard the wind drove the dirt and the sand. Sometimes you holed up in the house for two or three days —nights, rather: there was no day—at a stretch. And when you had dug your way out, coughing, eyes stinging, and took a look around, you just felt like turning right around and going back in the house again. The corn lay flat, dry roots clutching the air. And the land, with the subsoil showing, looked red and raw as something skinned.

Then Faye, the oldest boy, who had been bringing in a little money finding day work in the countryside roundabout, came home one afternoon and announced he'd signed up to join the Navy. Feeling guilty, he brought it out surlily. And it was a blow. But his father couldn't blame him. Poor boy, he couldn't stand any more, he wanted to get far away from all this, out to sea where there was neither dust nor dung, and where he might be sure of three square meals a day. Trouble always comes in pairs, and one night not long afterwards Faye's little brother, Dwight, too young to volunteer, was taken over in Antlers with a pair of buddies breaking into a diner. He was let off with a suspended sentence, but only after his father had spent an arm and a leg to pay the lawyer his fee.

Then the Dobbses went on relief. Standing on line with your friends, none of you able to look another in the face, to get your handout of cornmeal and a dab of lard, pinto beans, a slab of salt-white sowbelly. And first Ione, because being the mother she scrimped herself at table on the sly, then Chester, and pretty soon all of them commenced to break out on the wrists and the hands and around the ankles and up the arms and shins and around the waist with red spots, sores, the skin cracking open. Pellagra.

A man can take just so much. And squatting on the corner of the square in town on Saturday afternoon, without a nickel for a sack of Durham, without so much as a matchstick of his own to

chew on, Dobbs said to his friends, "What's it all for, will somebody please tell me? What have I done to deserve this? I've
worked hard all my life. I've always paid my bills. I've never diced
nor gambled, never dranked, never chased after the women. I've
always honored my old mama and daddy. I've done the best I
could to provide for my wife and family, and tried to bring my
children up decent and God-fearing. I've went to church regular.
I've kept my nose out of other folkses' affairs and minded my own
business. I've never knowingly done another man dirt. Whenever
the hat was passed around to help out some poor woman left a
widow with orphan children I've give what little I could. And what
have I got to show for it? Look at me. Look at them hands. If I'd
kicked over the traces and misbehaved myself I'd say, all right,
I've had my fling and I've got caught and now I'm going to get
what's coming to me, and I'd take my punishment like a man. But
I ain't never once stepped out of line, not that I know of. So
what's it all for, can any of yawl tell me? I'll be much obliged to
you if you will."

"Well, just hang on awhile longer, Chester. Maybe them fellows will strike oil out there on your land," said Lyman Turley.

"Like they have on yourn," said Cecil Bates. "And mine."

"Lyman, you and me been friends a long time," said Dobbs. "I
never thought you would make fun of me when I was down and
out."

"Hellfire, we're all in the same boat," said Lyman. "What good
does it do to bellyache?"

"None. Only how can you keep from it?" asked Dobbs. "And
we're not all in the same boat. I know men and so do you, right
here in this county, that are driving around in big-model automobiles and sit down every night of their lives to a Kansas City
T-bone steak, and wouldn't give a poor man the time of day. Are
they in the same boat?"

"Their day of reckoning will come," said O. J. Carter. "And on
that same day, if you've been as good as you say you have, you'll
get your reward. Don't you believe that the wicked are punished
and the good rewarded?"

"Search me if I know what I believe anymore. When I look
around me and see little children that don't know right from

wrong going naked and hungry, men ready and willing to do an honest day's work being driven to steal to keep from starving to death while other men get fat off of their misery, then I don't know what I believe anymore."

"Well, you can't take it with you," said Cecil.

"I don't want to take it with me," said Dobbs. "I won't need it in the sweet by-and-by. I'd just like to have a little of it in the mean old here and now."

A breeze had sprung up, hot, like somebody blowing his breath in your face, and to the south the sky was rapidly darkening over.

"Looks like rain," said Cecil.

"Looks like something," said O.J.

"Well, men, yawl can sit here and jaw if you want to, and I hope it does you lots of good," said Lyman. "Me, I'm going to the wagon. I'd like to get home while I can still see to find my way there."

"I reckon that's what we better all of us do," said Dobbs.

The sky closed down like a lid. Smells sharpened, and from off the low ceiling of clouds distant noises, such as the moan of a locomotive on the far horizon, the smoke from its stack bent down, broke startlingly close and clear. The telegraph wires along the road sagged with perching birds. They were in for something worse than just another dust storm.

To the southwest lightning began to flicker and thunder to growl. The breeze quickened and trees appeared to burst aflame as the leaves showed their undersides. Suddenly as the Dobbses came in sight of home the air was all sucked away, a vacuum fell, ears popped, lungs gasped for breath: it was as if they were drowning. Then the wind returned with a roar, and like the drops of a breaking wave, a peppering of hailstones fell, rattling in the wagonbed, bouncing off the mules' heads. A second wave followed, bigger, the size of marbles. Again silence, and the hailstones hissed and steamed on the hot dry soil. In the black cloud to the west a rent appeared, funnel-shaped, white, like smoke from a chimney by night, its point stationary, the cone gently fanning first this way then that way, as though stirred by contrary breezes. Shortly it began to blacken. Then it resembled a great gathering swarm of bees. Out of the sky fell leaves, straws, twigs, great hailstones, huge unnatural raindrops. The team balked, reared, began scrambling backwards.

"Cyclone!" Dobbs shouted. "Run for it, everybody! To the storm cellar!"

The boys helped their mother down the steps, pushed their sisters down, then tumbled in themselves while Dobbs stood holding the flapping door. He started down. As he was pulling the door shut upon his head there came an explosion. He thought at first they had been struck by lightning. Turning, he saw his house fly apart as though blown into splinters by a charge of dynamite. The chimney wobbled for a moment, then righted itself. Then the door was slammed down upon his head and Dobbs was entombed.

Hands helped him to his feet. His head hit the low ceiling. He sat down on the bench beside a shivering body, a trembling cold wet hand clutched his. God's punishment for that wild talk of his, that was what this was. Dobbs reckoned he had it coming to him. He had brought it upon himself. He had also brought it upon his innocent family. Down in the dank and moldy darkness, where he could hear his wife and children panting but could not see their faces, and where overhead through the thick roof of sod he could hear the storm stamping its mighty feet, Dobbs sat alternately wishing he was dead and shivering with dread lest his impious wish be granted and his family left without support. Someone sobbed, one of the girls, and frightened by the sound of her own voice, began to wail.

In a husky voice Dobbs said, "Well now, everybody, here we all are, all together, safe and sound. Let's be thankful for that. Now to keep our spirits up let's sing a song. All together now, loud and clear. Ready?" And with him carrying the lead in his quavering nasal tenor, they sang:

> "Jesus loves me, this I know,
> For the Bible tells me so . . ."

II

And then there is such a thing as foul-weather friends.

While people who had always been rather distant all went out of their way to be polite after oil was struck on Dobbs's land, all his old acquaintances avoided him. They had all come and bemoaned and comforted him over all the evil the Lord had brought on him, every man giving him a piece of money, taking in and housing the children, chipping in with old clothes after Dobbs's house was blown down; but as soon as his luck turned they would all cross over to the other side of the street to keep from meeting him. At home Dobbs grieved aloud over this. Good riddance, his daughters all said, and wondered that he should any longer want to keep up acquaintance with the Turleys and the Maynards and the Tatums, and other poor whites like that.

"The only difference between you and them pore whites is you ain't pore no more," said Dobbs. "Which you always was and very likely will be again. Especially if you talk thataway. Now just remember that, and meanwhile thank the Lord."

The girls clamored to leave the old farmstead and move into town. They wanted to live in the biggest house in town, the old Venable mansion, which along with what was left of the family heirlooms had been on the market for years to settle the estate. You could have pastured a milch cow on the front lawn, the grass so thick you walked on tiptoe for fear of muddying it with your feet. On the lawn stood a life-size cast-iron stag, silver balls on concrete pedestals, a croquet court, a goldfish pond with a water fountain. To tally all the windows in the house would have worn a lead pencil down to a stub. Turrets and towers and cupolas, round, square, and turnip-shaped, rose here, there, and everywhere; it looked like a town. You wanted to go round to the back door with your hat in your hand. Take a while to remember that it was yours.

At the housewarming it turned out that Dobbs and his daughters had invited two separate lists of guests, he by word of mouth, on street corners on Saturday afternoon, in the barber shop, hanging over fence gaps—they by printed invitation. Nobody much from either list showed up. First to arrive were their kin from the country, in pickup trucks and mule-drawn wagons and lurching jitneys alive with kids. The men in suits smelling of mothballs, red in the face from their starched, buttoned, tieless collars, wetted-down hair drying and starting to spring up like horses' manes, all crippled by pointed shoes, licking the cigars which Dobbs passed out up and down before raking matches across the seats of their britches and setting fire to them. The women in dresses printed in jungle flowers, their hair in tight marcelled waves against their skulls. The kids sliding down banisters, tearing through the halls, and skidding across the waxed parquet floors trying to catch and goose one another.

After them came a few of the many old friends and acquaintances Dobbs had invited. Then began to arrive the others, those who knew better than to bring their children, some with colored maids at home to mind them when the folks stepped out, people whom Dobbs had always tipped his hat to, little dreaming he would one day have them to his house, the biggest house in town, some of them the owners of the land on which his kin and the people he had invited sharecropped, so that quicker than cream from milk the two groups separated, he and his finding their way out to the kitchen and the back yard, leaving the girls and theirs to the parlor and the front porch. Then through the mist of pride and pleasure of seeing all those town folks under his roof, Dobbs saw what was going on. All of them laughing up their sleeves at the things they saw, passing remarks about his girls, who would take their part against him if he tried to tell them they were being made fun of by their fine new friends. Poor things, red with pleasure, stretching their long necks like a file of ganders so as to look a little less chinless, their topmost ribs showing like rubboards above the tops of their low-cut dresses. And his wife forgetting about the Negro maid and waiting on the guests herself, passing around the tea cakes and the muffins, then getting a scorching look from one of the girls which she didn't understand but blushing to the roots of her thin hair and sitting down with her big red knobby hands trembling uselessly in her lap. Jumping up to say, "Oh, yawl ain't going already? Why, you just this minute come. Let me get yawl something good to eat. Maybe you'd like to try one of these here olives. Some folks like them. You have to mind out not to bite down on the seed." And through it all his old mama upstairs in her room, dipping snuff and spitting into her coffee can, refusing to budge, saying she didn't want to put him to shame before his highfalutin new friends, only he might send that sassy nigger wench up with a bite for her, just a dry crust of bread, whatever the guests left, not now, later, she didn't want to put nobody out.

Sight-seeing parties were conducted through the house, the country kin making coarse jokes over the eight flush toilets which made his daughters choke red, though it was certainly not the first time they had heard the very same jokes. Others like Mr. Henry Blankenship saying, "What! Two hundred dollars for that rug? Oh, Chester, I'm afraid they saw you coming. Why oh why" —forgetting that until the day before yesterday they had never in their lives exchanged more than good afternoon—"didn't you come to me? I could have jewed them down fifty per cent at least."

The party broke up early, leaving mounds of favors; but not before each and every one of the relatives had gotten his corns stepped on. The townspeople went home sniggering with laughter, or fuming with outrage in the name of the vanished Venables. Both groups found excuses for declining future invitations, and in the evenings the big house on the hill heaved with sighs of boredom.

Dobbs continued as before to awake at four o'clock, and could not get back to sleep. The habit of a lifetime is not easily broken. But he could and did lie there smiling to think that he did not have to get up. No cow was waiting for him to milk her, no mule to be harnessed, no field to be plowed or picked of its cotton. Except that once awake Dobbs saw no point in not getting up. In fact, it bored him to lie in bed doing nothing. What was more, it seemed sinful.

He did not want to waste a moment of his leisure. Each day, all day, was his now, to spend as he pleased, according to his whim. Mere loafing was no pleasure to Dobbs; he had to be doing. The list of pastimes known to him was somewhat short. He went hunting with his fine new gun, went fishing with his bright new tackle, went driving in his big new car. One by one he slunk back to his old single-shot with the tape around the stock, with which he was a much better shot, back to his old cane pole, relieved to be rid of his level-wind reel which was always snarling in a knot and that boxful of artificial baits of which he never seemed to be using the right one. Fishing and hunting were not nearly so much fun when the time was not stolen from work. As he sat alone on the bank of a creek enjoying the blessings of unmixed leisure and telling himself how happy he was, Dobbs's hand would steal involuntarily to the nape of his neck where a welt, a rope burn which made it look like the neck of a hanged man, was, though fading now, still visible. It corresponded to the callus rubbed by the hames on the neck of a mule, and had been bitten there by plowlines, beginning at the age of eight. Dobbs rubbed it with a tenderness akin to nostalgia.

Other men were not to be found on the streets of town on a weekday; they were at work, and a lifetime of doing the same had left Dobbs with the feeling that it was wicked and immoral of him to be there at that hour. Those who were on the streets were those who were there at all hours, who often slept there: the town ne'er-do-wells and drunks.

Like all farmers, Dobbs had always lived for Saturday. That had been the day when he slipped the reins and came into town. It was not the rest he enjoyed, though God knew that was sweet, so much as the company. A man can plow a field and plod along for five days at a stretch with nothing to look at but the hind end of a mule and no company but the cawing crows overhead, but then he has to see faces, hear voices. Now that every day was a Saturday Dobbs found himself looking forward to Saturday with a sense of deliverance. But though they did their best to make him welcome in his old spot, squatting among his cronies on the square and whittling away the afternoon, his company obviously embarrassed them. People he had always known began to call him Mister, and many seemed to believe that Dobbs thought they were no longer good enough for him. People still said, as they had always done on taking leave, "Well, yawl come," and Dobbs said it to them. He meant it more sincerely with each passing day. But nobody came and nobody was going to come. How could they drive up that long raked gravel drive of his in a wagon and team or a homemade pickup truck, traipse in their boots across those pastures of carpet, come calling in overalls and poke bonnets? And how could he draw up before their unhinged gates and their dirt yards in that great long-nosed Pierce-Arrow of his?

Three or four friends Dobbs lost forever by lending them money and expecting them to pay it back. He supposed they felt he would never miss it, but he thought they would despise themselves, as he would have, if they did not repay him. And he lost more by refusing them loans. Some people complained of the way he spent his money, others of the way he hoarded it.

Which last, in fact, he had begun to do. Having done nothing to deserve his sudden wealth, Dobbs feared it might just as suddenly be taken from him. Being a wagon-and-team man himself, he didn't much believe in oil, nor in money which came from it. His bank statements frightened him; he thought not how much he had, but how much it would be to lose! He developed a terror of being poor again. He knew what it was to be poor. So he told his children when they whined at him to buy them this and buy them that. Did they see him throwing money away?

True, he himself lived simply, indeed for a man in his position he lived like a beggar. But though he prided himself on his frugality, the truth was, and he knew it, that after a short while he found he simply did not like (he said he couldn't digest) filet mignon and oven-roasted beef and oysters and other unfamiliar and over-rich foods like those. After thirty years of Duke's Mixture he liked it, preferred it to ready-rolls. And cold greens and black-eyed peas and clabber: these were what he had always called food. Even they tasted less good to him now that he never worked up any appetite, now that they were never sauced with the uncertainty of whether there would be more of them for tomorrow. In fact, he just minced at his food now. Sometimes after dinner, as his girls had begun to call supper, and after everybody was in bed asleep, Dobbs would steal down to the kitchen, about half a mile from his bedroom, and make himself a glass of cornbread crumbled in sweetmilk or have some leftover cold mashed turnips, but he did not enjoy it and would leave it half finished. The Scriptures say, "Thou shalt eat thy bread in the sweat of thy face," and the sad truth is, to a man who always has, bread which does not taste of his own sweat just does not have any taste.

III

In all of Oklahoma no women were found so fair as the daughters of Dobbs; their father gave them equal inheritance among their brothers.

In his days of poverty the problem of marrying off his daughters had weighed on Dobbs's mind like a stone. He had felt beholden to them. For he had only to look in the mirror to see where they got their plainness from. But they were cheerful and uncomplaining, and when boys dressed in their best overalls and carrying bouquets went past their gate on Sunday afternoon as if past a nunnery, they had not seemed to mind. Now the problem was to keep them from marrying the first man who asked them. It was as if all four had come into heat simultaneously, and all day long and all night, too, baying and snapping and snarling at one another, a pack of boys milled about the house and yard. They had given up all hope of ever catching a husband; now sweet words went to their heads like a virgin drink of spirits. "Don't you see that that rascal is just after your money?" Dobbs would say. And they would weep and pout and storm and say, "You mean you're afraid he's after your old money. That's all you ever think about. You don't know Spencer like I do. He loves me! I know he does. He would marry me if I was poor as a church mouse. He told me so. If you send him away you'll break my heart and I'll hate you till the day I die."

Dobbs even had to buy off one of them. One of the suitors, that is. Pay him to stay away, keep him on a regular monthly salary.

So inflamed did poor Denise get that she eloped with a fellow. Dobbs caught them in Tulsa and brought her home fainting and kicking and screaming. Even after it had been proved to her that he was wanted for passing bad checks from Atlanta to Albuquerque, she still sulked and went on pining for her Everett. The twins, who before had always gotten along together like two drops of water, now decided they each wanted the same boy, though Lord knew there were plenty to go around, and they only patched up their quarrel by turning on their father when he said that only over his dead body would either of them marry that no-good fortune-hunting drugstore cowboy.

One by one they beat him down. For Denise another Everett came along and she told her father she meant to have this one. The old refrain: he's only after your money. "I'm free, white, and twenty-one," she said, "and seeing as it's my money, I'll spend it on what I please." Dobbs shook his head and said, "Oh, my poor girl, my poor little girl, you're buying yourself a bushel of heartache." She replied, "Nonsense. If this one don't work out to suit me I'll get shut of him and get me another one." And that in fact was how it did work out, not once but four times.

She had the biggest wedding the town had ever seen. Dobbs spared no expense. At the wedding reception in his own house he was a stranger; he knew no one there. Then the twins were married in a lavish double ceremony. People said you couldn't tell the girls apart; what Dobbs couldn't tell one from the other were their two husbands. Emmagine was not long behind them, and her wedding put theirs in the shade, for she had married a Lubbock of the Oklahoma City Lubbocks. This time there were two wedding receptions, one at Dobbs's, the other at the home of his son-in-law's people. Dobbs attended only the one, though he paid the bills for both. In fact, the day after the ceremony he began to receive unpaid bills from his son-in-law's creditors, some dated as far back as ten years.

Then Ernest, the middle boy, brought home a bride. Mickey her name was. She had hair like cotton candy, wore fishnet stockings, bathed in perfume. Thinking she might have caught cold from going around so lightly dressed, Mrs. Dobbs recommended a cure for her quinsy. But there was nothing the matter with her throat; that was her natural speaking voice. She and her sisters-in-law backed off at each other like cats. The family seldom saw Ernest after he left home. The checks his father sent him came back cashed by banks in faraway places. He wrote that he was interested in many schemes; he was always on the verge of a really big deal. To swing it he needed just this amount of cash. When he returned once every year to discuss finances with his father he came alone. His mother hinted that she would have liked to see her daughter-in-law and her grandson; as luck would have it, one or the other was always not feeling up to the trip. Once the boy was sent alone to spend a month with his grandparents. Instead of one month he was left for four. To his shame Dobbs was glad to see the boy go. When Ernest came to fetch him home he took the occasion to ask for an increase in his allowance. He and his brother quarreled; thereafter he stayed away from home for even longer stretches.

Back from his hitch in the Navy, and back from his last cruise parched with thirst and rutting like a goat, came Faye. Feeling beholden to the boy for the hard life he had had on the farm and on shipboard, Dobbs lavished money on him. When he was brought home drunk and unconscious, battered and bruised from some barroom brawl, Dobbs held his tongue. To hints that he think of his future he turned deaf. The contempt he felt for work was shown in the foul nicknames he had for men who practiced each and every trade and profession. Once to Dobbs's house came a poor young girl, obviously pregnant. She claimed the child was Faye's. He hardly bothered to deny it. When his father asked if he meant to marry the girl he snorted with laughter. He suggested that she would be happy to be bought off. Shrinking with shame, Dobbs offered her money; when she took it he felt ashamed of the whole human race. He told his son that he was breaking his mother's heart. He said there would always be money to support him but that it was time he settled down and took a wife. The one he got persuaded him that while he was away in the Navy his sisters and brothers had connived to cheat him of his share of the money. He had been cheated of something, he somehow felt; maybe that was it. To have a little peace of mind, his father gave him more; whatever the amount, Faye always felt sure it was less than he had coming to him. He quarreled with his sisters. Family reunions, rare at best, grew more and more infrequent because of the bad feelings between the children.

It was Dwight, his youngest son and always his favorite child, on whom his father placed his hopes. Totally reformed after that one scrape with the law, he never drank, never even smoked, never went near a poolhall nor a honky-tonk. Most important of all, girls did not interest him in the least. He was in love with the internal combustion engine. His time was spent hanging around garages, stock-car racetracks, out at the local cowpasture with the wind sock and the disused haybarn which was hopefully spoken of as the hangar. He worshiped indiscriminately automobiles, motorcycles, airplanes, whatever was driven by gasoline. The smell of hot lubricating oil intoxicated him. Exhaust fumes were his native air. Silence and sitting still drove him distracted. He loved having to shout above the roar of motors. He spoke a language which his father could only marvel at, as if he had raised a child who had mastered a foreign tongue, speaking of valve compression ratio, torque, drop-head suspension, and of little else.

Dwight had known the ache, the hopeless adoration worlds removed from envy, too humble even to be called longing, of the plowboy for cars that pass the field, stopping the mule at the sound of the approaching motor and gazing trancelike long after it has disappeared in a swirl of dust, then awakening and resettling the reins about his neck and pointing the plowshare down again and saying to the mule, "Come up, mule." Now he saw no reason why he shouldn't have one of his own. He was sixteen years old and his old man had money to burn. Car or motorcycle, he would have settled for either; the mere mention of a motorcycle scared his father into buying him a car. He was not going to kill himself on one of them damned motorsickles, Dobbs said, words which just two months later came back to haunt him for the rest of his life.

It was a Ford, one of the new V-8's. No sooner was it bought than it disappeared from sight. He was working on it, said Dwight. Working on it? A brand-new car? If something was the matter with it why not take it back? All that was the matter with it was that it was a Detroit car, off the assembly line. He was improving it.

"You call that improving it!" said Dobbs on seeing it rolled out of the old Venable coach house a week later. It looked as if it had been wrecked. The body all stripped down. The entrails hanging out of the hood. Paint job spoilt, flames painted sweeping back from the nose and along the side panels in tongues of red, orange, and yellow. Dwight said he had added a supercharger, a second carburetor, advanced the timer, stripped the rear end. Well, just drive careful, that's all. Two months later the boy was brought home dead. Coming home from the funeral Dobbs's wife said, "This would never happened if we had stayed down on the farm where we belonged. Sometimes I wish we had never struck oil."

The same thought had crossed Dobbs's mind, frightening him with its ingratitude. "Ssh!" he said. "Don't talk like that."

With the death of Dwight, Dobbs and his wife were left alone in the big house with only Dobbs's old mother for company. She threatened to leave with every breath. She could see well enough where she wasn't wanted. She would not be a burden. If she wasn't good enough for her own flesh and blood just say so and she would pack her bag. The visits home of Faye and Ernest all but ceased. As for the girls, they were never mentioned. Both Dobbs and his wife knew that they were ashamed of their parents.

And so the Lord blessed the latter end of Dobbs more than his beginning. For in addition to his oil wells, he had (he never did come to trust oil, and old country boy that he was, converted much of it into livestock) fourteen thousand head of whiteface cattle and five thousand Poland China hogs.

He also had two sons and four daughters. And he gave them equal inheritance, though there was not one who didn't believe that the rest had all been favored over him.

After this lived Dobbs not very long. Just long enough to see his sons' sons, and despair.

So Dobbs died, being old before his time, and having had his fill of days.

Mouth of Brass

I

"MOLLY OT! Hot tamales!"

Down from the top of our street each weekday afternoon that cry, in a voice deeper than any I have ever heard in all the years since, used to come rumbling like thunder.

"Finus! Here comes Finus!" I would run shouting to my mother.

Shaking her head, my mother would declare, "Boy, you're going to ruin your digestion eating those things. Going to just burn the lining of your insides right out. Wait and see." However, she always ended by saying, "All right. Go find me my purse." For it was true, hot spices kept a child purged of worms. And often instead of a nickel my mother would give me a dime, saying, "Might as well get me a couple too while you're at it." They were so delicious the way Finus made them that afterwards we used to suck dry the cornshucks they came wrapped in.

Meanwhile his cry, nearer now, would roll out again, sonorous as a chord drawn from the deepest pipes of a church organ. And if outside our house he should loose another, the chimes of our doorbell shuddered softly and teacups rattled on their saucers.

No matter what Finus said it came out sounding proud and mighty; so he said as little as he could without risk of seeming impolite. In another place, or at some later period perhaps, his voice might have made Finus's fortune; but in Blossom Prairie, in east Texas, in 1930, to be answered by a Negro in that powerful bass brought the blood to some men's cheeks quick as a slap. His size alone was a standing challenge, the silence in which he took refuge easily misinterpreted as surliness; add to these provocations the sound that came out of him whenever he did speak, and Finus was often in trouble of the kind I myself had witnessed one Saturday afternoon on the town square when a sailor knocked him down, saying, "I'll teach you to talk back to a white man in that tone of voice." From where he lay amid the cornshucks from his tamales strewn on the pavement Finus said, and the weariness of his tone deepened it further still, "I speak to everybody in the voice God give me." He was born loud as surely as he was born black: his name will tell us so. For although he was called, and called himself, Finus, to rhyme with minus, this is doubtless a corruption of Phineas, and that, as someone knew who heard the infant utter his first wail, means in Hebrew "mouth of brass."

II

His last name was Watson, though there were probably not a dozen people in Blossom Prairie who ever knew it, despite the fact that he had been there long enough to have become a fixture of the place. To sell his hot tamales "Finus" sufficed him. He made his daily rounds and cried his wares; otherwise, being black, he passed unnoticed, except from time to time when somebody, most often a man from out in the country, unused to our stentorian Negro, took exception to his attitude—mistaking his voice for his attitude.

He lived all alone in a shanty down behind the Catholic church, across town from the section along the creek north of the jailhouse where the other Negroes all lived. There in a series of old packing crates Finus raised the chickens that went into his hot tamales, and on a small plot of ground grew the red peppers and the herbs with which they were seasoned. He was said to have

Mexican blood, and in a certain light could be seen a dark gleam on his high cheekbones as of copper beneath a coat of soot. To this drop of Mexican in him was attributed his independence—his "impudence," some called it—the reserve with which he held himself aloof from the other Negroes of the place, and the flavor of his tamales, the inimitable tang of his barbecue sauce. This last he produced at Fourth of July celebrations, for which he was always in demand as cook, and on Juneteenth—June the nineteenth, observed by our Negroes as the day in 1863 when, six months late, news of the Emancipation Proclamation reached Texas. At the time I first knew him Finus was in his late forties or early fifties—long a familiar figure in my home town. Into every quarter of it his fixed round brought him daily, Saturdays and Sundays excepted; and it was said that so punctual was his appearance in each of the streets along his route the people there all set their clocks by the sound of his booming voice.

Our street, which he reached just at four, lay towards the end of Finus's route. After he and I became friends I used to meet him at the top of our street every afternoon and he would give me a ride down to my house on the lid of his box, which hung by a strap from his shoulder. This box was a marvel of Finus's own making. Sitting on it one felt no heat at all, but when it was opened heat burst from it as from an oven. An oven, in fact, it was: inside it burnt a smokeless charcoal fire, and on cold days when Finus raised the lid he would be momentarily enveloped in a cloud of spicy steam.

When Finus knelt and opened his box to sell me my tamales I could see that it was nearly empty. Yes, he said, he was heading for home now. But in the morning when he set out, his box was full to the top—too heavy for him to give a boy a ride on it. I questioned him about his route, and when he told me he went as far as the ice house and the railway depot, the cotton compress and the courthouse, that he crossed the public square not once but four times every day, I listened in wonder and longing, as one who has never left home listens to the tales of a traveler. I had myself seen those same sights, to be sure; but usually from a back window of the car, and even so, not very many times.

"How would you like to come with me one day?" asked Finus.

I knew that "one day." It meant when you are big. It meant never.

But not when Finus said it. "All right, you ask your mama," he said. "If she says you can go, then you pick the day and I'll take you with me."

I started to ask my mother at once, as soon as Finus had set me down at our door. But I checked myself. I feared that should she say no Finus might take it as a rebuff. Instead I waited until I heard his voice come up from below as, turning the corner, he proclaimed his advent in the next street.

"Well, wasn't that nice of Finus," said my mother. But before saying whether or not I could accept his invitation she would first have to talk it over with my father. I coaxed from her a promise to speak to him that evening. In bed that night I awaited his decision anxiously. I sensed in my father a reservation about my friendship with Finus. It was not that he frowned at it exactly; he seemed rather to smile at it somehow. When my mother came to kiss me goodnight she said I could go. When I told Finus the following afternoon he proposed that we make it the very next day. What was more, I was to come early to his place and help him make his tamales.

III

If I should tire out and become a burden on him he was to leave me off at my father's shop on one of our trips through the square: with this parting instruction to Finus my mother left me in his care and drove away. I experienced a moment's homesickness then and wished I had not come.

I had never been inside a Negro's house before, and through the dark opening of Finus's doorway I passed as through a wall. The house consisted of just one room, most of it devoted to the manufacture of hot tamales. A big black cast-iron wood range, heavily scrolled and garlanded, squatted on its paws against one wall. In the center of the room stood a long wooden table, its top as scarred as a butcher's block and bleached colorless from scrubbing, on which was heaped a mound of finely shredded cooked chicken meat. From nails on the walls hung clusters of dried and shriveled red peppers and bunches of dried herbs. In one corner stood Finus's cot. Beside it stood a washstand on which sat a basin and ewer. The bare simplicity of Finus's way of living made it seem to me like play, and this combined with my sense of strangeness at being inside a Negro's house to remind me of the time I had timidly knocked at the door of a clubhouse built of scrap lumber and belonging to a gang of older boys and had snatched one tantalizing glimpse of the snug interior before being told that members only were allowed inside, scram! Finus's house was like but better than that clubhouse, and I had been invited in.

The chickens for his hot tamales, Finus explained, were always killed and partly cooked the night before. Now into one of the two huge caldrons steaming on the range he emptied a sack of cornmeal. In with the meal then went the meat, stirred in with an ax handle which from long usage had been boiled white as a bone. Into the other caldron went an armload of dry cornshucks. For poking these down so that more could be added as they softened in the hot water Finus had another ax handle, like the first whitened by boiling. After the meat and the mush had cooked together for a while Finus opened a large jar filled with a red powder and poured in about half the contents, and the air of the room sharpened suddenly with the odor of hot chili peppers.

Then the limp wet shucks were spread out in rows on the tabletop like a game of solitaire and the pot of mush brought steaming to the table. A spoonful of it on a shuck, a lengthwise roll, a fold at each end: and there you were. Between us we made two hundred hot tamales. I made three and Finus made the other hundred and ninety-seven. Next to his mine looked like roll-your-own cigarettes next to ready-rolls. I was promised my three for my dinner. Two hundred hot tamales on weekdays, twice as many on Saturdays . . . somebody had once worked it out for him, and it came to nearly two million tamales that Finus had made in his time. And while chicken feed had gone up to two dollars a sack and cornmeal to four dollars a barrel, he still charged the same as always: "Two for a nickel, two bits a dozen!"

IV

Actually to be making his rounds with him when Finus rumbled "Molly ot! Hot tamales!" filled me with such pride that my face ached from grinning.

"Got yourself a helper today, I see, Finus," said housewives who came out to buy from us.

"Yes, ma'am, that's right, I've taken me on a partner here," Finus solemnly replied; and I observed that even when Finus meant to agree, and repeated what had been said to him, his voice made it sound rather as though he were correcting the person.

When children came to buy and Finus let me fill their orders from out of his box and collect their nickels I swelled so with self-importance I could scarcely contain myself. And the best was yet to come. Before we had gone far, just as we were entering a new street, Finus said, "You want to holler 'Hot tamales'? Go ahead." I nearly tore my lungs loose trying to make it sound loud and grand like Finus's cry. Thereafter, for as long as my voice held out, sometimes I hollered, sometimes Finus, sometimes we hollered both together. It must have sounded like a tuba accompanied by a piccolo.

Certain streets down which we went I knew, or I recognized as those on which lived playmates of mine to whose houses I had been brought to spend an afternoon. Other streets were entirely new to me, and leading off these were dozens more. I wondered how people could speak of our town as a small town. Finus, who knew it better than anyone else, who traversed its length and breadth daily, estimated it to be five miles long east to west, only a little less north to south. That was plenty big enough, we agreed. It was the county seat, with a population of three thousand. A person could live there and believe just about anything and find somebody to agree with him—and a lot more to disagree with him: there were (Finus had counted them) nineteen churches, white and colored, scattered around town. The dog population Finus put at eight hundred and seventy, most of them known to him personally by name.

We crossed the square for the first time and went out by the street running behind the post office. This brought us to the cotton compress and the cottonseed mill, which always smelled so good. There we turned and went skirting along the railroad tracks until we came to the depot. We came back down Depot Street, then turned into Negrotown, where the paved streets gave out and became dirt streets. Clotis, who did our wash, came out and bought half a dozen tamales from me. We came out between the courthouse and the jail, crossed Market Square, and passed through the public square for the second time. Finus asked was I tired and would I like to stop and stay with my father. I spurned the suggestion and we continued on.

It pleased Finus to stop and ask, "Know where you're at now?" I would have to say no. Shortly I began, so great was my pleasure in this game, so confident was I of the next turn it would take, almost to shout with glee, "No! Where, Finus?" For when he had turned me around and around and had me completely lost, precisely then would Finus take my hand in his, lead me around a corner, and there we were before some dear familiar landmark of the town: the courthouse tower, the steeple of one of the churches, one of the bridges over the creek, or most frequently, and always with the greatest surprise, the keenest joy, the bright, busy square, heart and center of my world, scene of my Saturdays.

I began that day to acquire a sense of the relation of these places one to another, of the overall plan of my town. As in those puzzles in which one draws lines between dots until suddenly a recognizable creature or object emerges, I was drawing lines between what before had been disconnected dots forming no pattern or design. It was doubly delightful because it was both new and familiar.

Nor could I, in getting to know my fellow townsmen, have found a better guide than my friend Finus, the hot-tamale vendor. Cliff Allen, the livery-stable owner; Mr. Kirkup, the blacksmith; Mr. Green, the garage mechanic; the firemen at the firehouse: all the most interesting people liked hot tamales. Even among the housewives the ones who came to their doors in answer to Finus's cry were those unsoured by dyspepsia, the jolly young spice-loving ones. In Market Square the farmers at their wagons bought from us, and the prisoners in the jailhouse, hearing our cry, called down from their barred windows and sent the deputy sheriff, a handsome, stern-looking man with a stag-handled pistol in a holster on his hip, out to buy theirs for them.

When Finus, having ridden me down on the lid of his box from the top of our street, as usual, set me down at my door that afternoon, exhausted, hoarse from yelling, and deliciously happy, I was a different boy from the one who had left home only that morning. The world had been revealed to me much bigger and much more exciting than I had dreamed. With much of it I was now acquainted, much of it I had yet to explore. For both this knowledge and this promise I had Finus to thank, and as I heard his voice swell up from the bottom of the street my heart swelled with gratitude and affection for my friend, my guide.

V

On Saturdays, as I have said, Finus did not make his rounds; instead he stood with his box, or rather two boxes, on the northwest corner of the square, lifting his cry from time to time above the din. For in Blossom Prairie nobody stayed at home on Saturday unless forced to; all who could possibly get there spent the day downtown. The population doubled—in ginning season tripled—as country folks poured in by the car, the truck, and the wagonload. The square was a carnival. The storefronts were decked with streamers offering prizes and free toys. From the open window of its projection room, above the whirr of the machine, the picture-show discharged the thump of the overture to *William Tell* and "The Flight of the Bumblebee," and laid down along the sidewalk beneath the marquee the odors of hot buttered popcorn and heated celluloid. Children out of school with their allowances burning their hands and grown-ups with their weekly paychecks in their pockets thronged the walks, windowgazing. All the air was spiced with the odors of holiday foods from the busy cafés, the confectionery, the street vendors, like my friend Finus, of hot tamales and hotdogs, parched peanuts, doughnuts, watermelon. Town folks met their country kin on the square that day, and country folks met their friends from other parts of the county. In the evening after work and after an early supper families drove down and parked their cars against the curbs and watched the promenaders stroll past, took a few turns themselves; then the men gathered for talk on the corners, the children played games around the Confederate monument in the center plaza, and the women exchanged visits with one another in the cars.

From the time I was born I was taken regularly each week to join that festive crowd; but not until after my tour of the town with Finus, and then not at once but only after much wheedling, did my mother consent to let me go down on the square "all by myself." When she did I felt I could begin to think of myself as a big boy, though still a dozen *dont's*—enough to make a person wonder whether the world was a safe place to live in—were repeated to me each time I set off from home, the one above all being not to go into any of the alleyways that enclosed the square like a moat on four sides. It was in their shadowy depths, at the back doors of the domino parlors and the poolhalls and the cafés, that the bootleg whiskey flowed on Saturdays, the dice games were played, the fistfights fought. But I am getting ahead of myself. Of that side of life in my home town I knew nothing until one day in my tenth year. After that nothing was ever the same for me again.

Say that the first scene I saw was at four o'clock in the afternoon, then the drama began at three fifty-five when from out of one of those back alleys where he had drunk too much whiskey and gambled away too much money this Jewel Purdom returned to his car parked against the south-side curb to find his young though already large brood quarrelsome and hungry and sent one of them, his boy Gilbert, across the square to buy a dozen of Finus's hot tamales.

Afterwards nobody could be found who had seen the boy make his purchase. Nobody could be found who had seen anything of all that happened, despite the fact that it was a Saturday in early fall when crops were in and farmers idle and with money for their wives to spend and on all four corners of the square the crowds stood elbow to elbow. I was playing around the monument in the plaza at the time; however, I can relate how it went as surely as if I had been present on the spot, for Finus had a little routine with children: I have seen it many times and it never varied.

"Put your hands together and hold them like this," he always said, kneeling and putting his hands together, the polished yellow palms opened upwards. Upon the child's hands he laid a pad of three or four sheets of newspaper. He then raised the lid of his box, releasing that mouth-watering aroma. When the child was one the age of Gilbert Purdom, Finus gave him a lesson in how to count, speaking the numbers slowly and enunciating with ponderous care in that deep voice of his and encouraging the child to repeat after him as with his tongs he stacked the tamales on the paper. "And twelve makes a dozen," he concluded. Then he added one more.

Gilbert Purdom thought when he was given that extra hot tamale that he was getting preferential treatment. He did not know that Finus always gave thirteen to the dozen. He reasoned that his father and mother and his brothers and sisters were not expecting an extra free tamale either. So as soon as he had gotten among the crowd Gilbert popped that tamale in his mouth. It went down so quick that before he knew it he had eaten another. Gilbert may have been surprised then but he was not alarmed. He had that one coming to him. The first one nobody would know to miss, the second one was his share. What did it matter when he chose to eat it, now or together with the family? Still, Gilbert quickened his pace so as to put temptation behind him. But in front of him, right under his nose, Gilbert had eleven spicy hot tamales—or rather, ten. And now as he dodged among the crowd Gilbert's short thin legs were pumping as fast as he could urge them and he was panting, not so much from exertion as from fear —fear of the devil that had gotten into him.

Gilbert was across the square and back at the car within two minutes after leaving Finus. Yet all he got back with were eight tamales. And already Gilbert was beginning to wish he had not done what he had done for more reasons than one.

Gilbert had not thought up any trick to save himself from the resentment of his brothers and sisters and the anger of his father. He had not had time to think. Besides, his crime was so gross that he despaired of escaping punishment. He had given himself up for lost with the eating of that third tamale. So as not to add insult to injury he had wiped the grease off his mouth, but he did not even attempt an alibi, just held out the package with a blank look on his face that passed for innocence. Gilbert would have lied, though he knew the truth was bound to come out sooner or later, for by then he was as heedless of the consequences of being caught in a lie as he was of being caught stealing when that fourth tamale, now beginning to cause him such different sensations, was just melting in his mouth; only he could not think of any lie. What saved Gilbert was not native cunning or sudden inspiration, it was sheer luck. It was his father's saying, "Is these here all that nigger give you for your money?"

I was to see the Purdoms father and son on the square on Saturday afternoon many times in after years—I would once even see Jewel Purdom lounging against the wall of the bank in the very spot that had once been Finus's old spot; but I heard the name and saw them both for the first time to my knowledge that day; saw them twice. The first time was when, sitting on the curb of the plaza resting from my game of tag, I saw this man stalk past carrying a package wrapped in greasy newspaper and dragging this little boy by the hand. The looks on their faces made me say to myself, "Uh-oh. There's a boy who's fixing to get a whipping." Not that I felt very sorry for that boy, even so.

The second time I saw the Purdoms was less than five minutes later. I was still catching my breath, still sitting in the same spot, when they came back, the man still dragging the boy and the boy now looking as if he had been beaten almost senseless. Then I did feel sorry for him. He was stumbling blindly along at his father's heels hardly able to lift his feet. Not far from where I sat he suddenly went limp. Feeling him falter, his father lifted him off his feet; otherwise he would surely have pitched to the pavement. As he dangled there by one wrist there passed over his face an expression of dismay followed instantly by no expression whatever, a pallor that almost obliterated his features, weak at best, and then he vomited copiously and at length.

"That boy," I observed to myself, "has been eating too many hot tamales."

He was still retching when his father gave him a shake, set him on his unsteady legs, and viciously kicked him.

"Get to the car!" I heard the man hiss. "Don't even look behind you."

Then my attention was diverted from them. They were going in the opposite direction from the one that other people were going, at a run, all over the square.

On the edge of the crowd, which was impenetrable, I listened to a man tell how Jewel Purdom had first ordered Finus to say how many tamales there were in the package he held out to him, and how Finus, after blinking at him a time or two, had turned his head and looked down at the little boy, staring at him with wonder and consternation. For there had scarcely been time for him to have swallowed, much less chewed, as many hot tamales as were missing now from the baker's dozen he had been given. Finus frowned and shook his head at the boy in remonstrance, perhaps intending also to convey a warning that he was in for an upset stomach, but he failed to effect any change in the increasingly self-preoccupied vacancy of Gilbert's expression.

All of which was taking too long to answer than suited Jewel Purdom in his present mood. "Didn't you hear me?" he asked. "I said, how many hot tamales is this?"

"I heard you," said Finus, not looking at him. "It's eight."

"Then you *can* count," said Jewel Purdom, his voice rising with his rising anger. "You just figured that little boy couldn't. Or is eight as high as you can go?"

Still Finus did not look up but stared on at the little boy, until at last Gilbert, by then feeling very unwell, said to the author of his discomfort, "Old nigger, you."

Into Finus's face came a look of wild terror. He cried, not to the man menacing him, but to the crowd at large, "Still two for a nickel! Still just two bits a dozen!" No one came to his aid. Falling back against the wall, he began frantically to tear open his shirt, as if his breathing were obstructed, popping off the buttons in his haste. There never was agreement afterwards on what made Finus do that. Some said he wished to show that he was unarmed, the Negro notion of a weapon being a straight razor worn beneath the shirt on a string around the neck. To others he seemed to be baring his chest in defiance, daring the man to do his worst. Still others saw in it a gesture of despair and resignation to his fate.

In any case, the unexpectedness of it stayed Jewel Purdom's advance. At this somebody from the crowd intervened, although the man telling about it was prevented by a cough from identifying the person, somebody who knew Jewel and drew him aside, talking to him all the while, and who might have succeeded in cooling him off and getting him away and nothing more have come of the affair if only Finus had kept his big mouth shut. Instead he had chosen the moment to release his cry, "Molly ot! Hot tamales!" louder even than his usual, and sounding, whether he meant it to or not, taunting, derisive, exultant. It may be that in the pasty face of seven-year-old Gilbert Purdom Finus thought he had recognized at last the doom that had stalked him down the years, and now was giving vent to his fear and his relief. He may just have been trying to clear the atmosphere, break the tension, restore things to normal, and get back to his business of selling hot tamales. Whatever his intentions, his cry had not ceased reverberating when Jewel Purdom sprang, knife in hand.

As I turned away I heard the speaker say, "No, Otis, I didn't. Not a thing, although I was standing not ten feet away right through it all. I was engaged in conversation with a friend of mine and looking the other way. Never knew anything had happened till people came running up. That's all right. Just sorry I can't be of any help to you."

Otis was Otis Langford, the town constable.

Without their fathers to set them on their shoulders small boys like I was then got to see sights only after their elders had looked their fill. By the time I got near enough to see it the wide pool of blood on the pavement where Finus had fallen was, though still wet, beginning to congeal. An iridescence playing over its surface in waves and slow swirls made it appear to shrink from exposure to the air like a living, that is a dying, thing. The way a fish fresh out of water grows more vivid and lustrous as it struggles and gasps, then fades as it dies, so Finus's blood brightened and shone as I watched, then darkened and lay still beneath a spreading dull film. Just before that final stage, however, came another.

Struck by the glare of the sun, the pool of blood became a mirror, and in it I saw reflected—and can see still, though this was long ago and Blossom Prairie now far away—the buildings of the square in sharp perspective, the courthouse tower, the Confederate soldier mounted high on his marble shaft, the steeple of the Methodist church that sat a block away on a hill overlooking the creek.

VI

Our house all day Sunday was as still as a house in mourning. Worried looks passing between my parents hung heavily over my head. Whenever I glanced up they put away their thoughts, but I could see them still, as I could see the tops showing of bottles put on shelves out of my reach.

That afternoon when I was supposed to be napping I heard my mother say to my father, "What do you reckon they will do to the man that did it?"

My father's newspaper rustled. "You are referring, I suppose," said he, "to yesterday's ruckus on the square, and to the man who—?"

"Well, what on earth else would I be talking about?" my mother cried. Then remembering me: "Ssh!"

"There are other things on earth you might be talking about," returned my father testily, "and I wish you would. However, to answer your question. What will they do to Jewel Purdom, of that ilk, for knifing on dire provocation a lone, unsurvived darky with a reputation for independence and a voice such that even a white man would have to be careful what he said with it? Well, there were, let's say, three dozen witnesses to the event. If the matter ever comes to a trial one dozen of these will testify that they happened to be looking the other way at the time and never saw a thing until it was all over. Another dozen will produce friends and relations to prove they were somewhere else twenty miles away all day long. And the remaining two dozen—"

"You only had three dozen to start with."

"That's right. And the remaining two dozen will swear on their Bible oath that the defendant acted in self-defense. Afterwards in

Market Square as the jug is passed around the acquitted and the members of the jury— Why do you ask me foolish questions? You've lived here all your life the same as I have."

"But there were some there who can't be got to say that. Who saw what happened. Yes, I have lived here all my life, and I know there must have been some there who would come forward and—"

"Would you?"

"Me? Why, I wasn't . . ."

"Well?"

"Well yourself! Would you?"

"No, I wouldn't, if it makes you feel any better."

"It doesn't make me feel any better."

"Me neither."

Later that evening my father came in and sat down on the edge of my bed. Before he could speak I said, "Daddy, I don't want to live here anymore. Let's move away. Let's go somewhere far—"

My father scowled. "Are you still at it?" he snapped. Hearing himself made his voice turn shrill. "Isn't that about enough of this now? How much longer are you going to mope over that damned nigger?"

I started back, drawing my bedcovers up, and stared at my father aghast, frightened at the violence of his outburst. Under my gaze my father reddened. In his eyes I saw a troubled plea for my forgiveness. My father was not angry at me but at the world which was all he could give me and which he was as helpless to cope with as I.

Monday came.

By afternoon my mother had given up trying to occupy or divert me. I sat at the window watching the empty street. The time drew near when down from above had always sounded Finus's cry. In heavy silence the clock on the mantel tolled four. I felt my chin pucker and tremble, my bruised heart swell with pain. My mother cleared her throat to speak but checked herself, fetching a deep breath instead. Then releasing her breath she said, "Oh, honey, don't try any more to hold it all in. Come to Mama and let yourself go and cry."

For a second I felt myself waver. But I knew the moment was a crucial one for me. It would be a long time before this hour of a weekday afternoon could come without my hearing, wherever I might find myself, the friendly thunder of Finus's voice rolling down from the top of our street; but the time would come. For a while afterwards I would see in the gutter at the curbstone or blown into a corner against a storefront a cornshuck as colorless as if it had been boiled, chewed, sucked dry; but after a time I would not see them anymore. It would take many Saturdays before I could pass that spot on the square where Finus's blood had lain on the sidewalk; but I could not live in my town without passing that spot, so that time too would come.

"What!" I cried, tears for Finus, for myself, for my father, for all the world gushing from my eyes, "me cry over an old nigger?"

"Ssh!" said my mother, drawing me to her own heaving breast. "You mustn't say that, hon. Nice people don't use that word."

A Home
Away from Home

"THINK of it!" said Elgin Floyd to Sybil, his wife. "Just think of it! If they should strike oil we could be millionaires."

"Mmm," said Sybil.

"Millionaires!"

"Mmm. Yes, well, don't go spending it all for a while," said Sybil. "They haven't struck any yet."

"No, but they struck it on Alvah Clayton's place, just eight miles from here. If they can strike oil on that damn fool's land, why not on mine?"

"Why not? You're as big a damn fool as him any day of the week, ain't you? Now what I want to know is this: how far down do they go without hitting anything before they decide to give up?"

"How's that again?"

"I say, how long do they go on boring before they either strike oil or quit?"

"Oh. Why, it all depends. Where they've got good reason to believe there is oil, why, they'll drill down as much as a mile. Maybe even further."

"How long does that take them? A mile, I mean."

"Depends on what they run into. Where there's lots of rock, for instance, that slows things down."

"In that case I expect they'll be a good while on this one of ours."

"Now on that well of Alvah's—*Mister* Clayton, I mean to say— they were drilling all spring long. Went down fifty-seven hundred feet. Good thing for the Claytons they did strike oil, too; for Alvah never done a lick of work all spring, out there hanging around that derrick from morn till night and getting in the men's way when he ought to been plowing and plant—"

"How big a crew do you suppose they aim to send out here to drill this one of ours?"

"Eh? Crew? Why, on that one of Alvah's they had about a dozen men, sometimes more. Why?"

"And how do you suppose they aim to feed and house all that many men for maybe as long as three or four months?"

"Don't ask me. That's their problem."

"It's a problem, all right, out here in the middle of nowhere. And I think I may have the answer to it. Now where do you suppose a person might round up a dozen bedsteads and springs and mattresses in a hurry, hmm?"

"Why, what would a person want with a doz—?"

"Now then, Elgin, up! I want you to stop daydreaming about being J. P. Rockefeller for a minute and get out of that easy chair and go down to the garden with a spading fork. I want to see a dozen rows of fresh ground turned by nightfall, hear? Where's Geraldine? Geraldine!"

"Yes'm? Directly."

"No, you come here right this minute. Now, Geraldine, how many times do I have to tell you not to go around barefoot? You're going to have feet on you like a pair of flatirons, if it's not too late already. Slip on some shoes now, you're coming with me. I'll let you out at the store, you can walk back. Elgin, give Geraldine a dollar bill. Geraldine, I want you to buy a flat of tomato plants, four packages of string-bean seeds, two of—"

"Mama, what in the world do you want with all that many seeds and plants? We've already got more stuff growing in that garden than we can put up, much less eat."

"I'm not intending to put them up. I'm expecting company."

"You are! Oh, goodie! Who, if I may ask?"

"Just do as you're told and you'll see. Elgin, give me the key to the truck. I've got lots of running around to do. That tourist camp that just went broke out east of town: there's where I bet you can pick up some beds and things at a bargain."

"Now just a minute," said Elgin. "Just whoa right where you're at, Mrs. Floyd. I see now what you're up to. Well, you can just stop before you go a step further. No, sir, I ain't taking in no boarders."

"Oh, Papa, hush," said Geraldine.

"Take in boarders? People like us, that may be millionaires any day now? No, sir. Not if I know anything about it. You hear me, Sybil? Here's where I set my foot down."

"Careful you don't set it where it's liable to get stepped on, hon. Now when you get back from the store, Geraldine, take and start in on them attic rooms with the broom and the dust mop. When you get done up there—"

"What!" Elgin snorted. "You think anybody will pay to sleep up there in that dusty, hot old attic?"

"No. I think they'll pay to sleep in our rooms while we sleep in that dusty, hot old attic."

With half the family's savings Sybil Floyd bought, in addition to the beds and bedclothes, a second cow to add to the one she already milked, a secondhand cream separator, a bigger churn. To her flock of layers she added another four dozen. She bought pullets to raise for fryers. She laid in stores of staple goods. When Elgin saw all the things she had bought he cried, "You talk about me spending money before we've seen it!"

But the geologists and engineers, suntanned men in whipcord riding breeches, lace boots, and suede-leather jackets, who came out in a big dusty misused expensive passenger car to survey the Floyd place, had sampled Sybil's cooking and their praises gave her confidence in herself. "When they strike oil, Elgin, honey," said she, "I want you to spend the money just as fast as you can lay your hands on it. All this is just in case they don't. Now on your feet! I've got another job for you. Get your hammer and saw and follow me. You'll need your pick and shovel, too. A one-holer ain't going to do when there are fifteen of us staying in this house."

Roughnecks, they were called—they gloried in the name. And they looked the part: hard-working, hard-living, coarse, rowdy men. Seeing Geraldine in their midst—a dozen men who had knocked about the world, many of them unmarried, others used to living apart from their wives—Sybil wondered what she had done. Suddenly Sybil's little girl was a big girl. She grew three inches overnight, rounded out as though she had just freshened with milk. The added height was owing to the high-heeled shoes which she would not change for more comfortable ones even when waiting on table. As yet the crewmen were too interested in their food to notice the girl whom their coming had made a woman of. Observing this, Sybil hoped to keep them well behaved by keeping them well fed.

Fine specimens of men they were—muscular, real men—big men for a big job of work. Dirty! They would come clomping in to dinner at noon looking as if they had struck oil already, only a circle of white around their eyes, black with grime, machine oil, axle grease. To wash themselves up before supper they required a hundred gallons of water boiled in drums in the back yard, blackened two dozen towels daily. And how they did eat! Geraldine was kept going at a steady run from the kitchen to the table and back. Platters of fried steaks, pans of biscuits, stacks of hoecakes vanished in a trice. For Sybil, even without other reason, it was hard to remember to be cautious as she heaped up those platters of food. Keeping a boardinghouse was new to her; in her older and more congenial role as housewife and occasional hostess it flattered her vanity to see men relish her cooking so.

Her boarders spoke of the countless boardinghouses which in the course of their footloose lives they had known, heaping scorn upon the grasping and cheating tribe of professional boardinghouse keepers. Not only to Sybil's face but among themselves at table they declared loudly that none could compare with her. Hearing this out in the kitchen, Sybil felt ashamed of her impulse to stint them, and taking from the pantry the cutlets or the chops intended for tomorrow's supper, and rousing the fire with a shake of the ash hopper, she refilled the four big skillets just beginning to cease to sputter on the range.

For the drilling crew the day's work began at seven, for Sybil at five. First she split kindling, brought in stovewood, and started the fire. Then she milked the cows, separated the cream and churned butter, collected the eggs. She kneaded dough and stamped out biscuits and when the range was roaring and hopping on its feet and the heat in the kitchen enough to singe your brows, she made breakfast. For each man four fried eggs. Bacon and sausage and fried ham, grits and red gravy, fried potatoes, coffee by the gallon. Breakfast finished, the table cleared, the dishes washed and dried and the table reset, it was time to begin making dinner. There were peas by the bushel to shell and potatoes by the bushel to peel, roasting ears to shuck in stacks like cordwood. There were chickens to kill and pluck and draw, fish to scale, meat to grind. After dinner a dash in the truck into town to shop for the next day while at home Geraldine made the beds and swept, then back in time to scrub and wring and hang out the bedsheets and the towels and iron and start the pies and cakes baking for supper and slice the peaches or the strawberries for ice cream and set Elgin to cranking the freezer. By bedtime Sybil's face was bright red from standing over the range and peering into the oven door, the skin drawn taut, her eyes glazed; and lying beneath the eaves in the attic where the heat made the kitchen seem cool, she passed out murmuring her assent to Elgin's latest plan for where they would go and what they would buy when the money started pouring in.

Elgin could do nothing for hanging around the works all day. All that activity was just too engrossing for a man to tear himself away. To go alone down to the field while all that was going on, to follow behind the mule breaking the stubborn soil beneath a broiling sun while visions of ease filled his mind—Sybil hadn't the heart to nag him. To the tapping of the carpenters' hammers the derrick rose skywards in diminishing X's. The heavy gear was brought in, unloaded from the great tractor trailers, and maneuvered into place. The generator hummed to life, the drilling rig clattered and clanked, the earth shuddered. At night there was a report of their progress: a hundred feet, five hundred feet, a thousand. A thousand feet! As far as out to the chicken house and back down through that stiff red earth which to have to open one foot of with a plow strained a man's back. Elgin's vocabulary blossomed. He spoke of faults, of lignite, of casings, and when they began to break, of diamond-head drilling bits.

Encouraged by their loud and constant praise, Sybil regaled her boarders with more and more tasty and elaborate dishes. The competent-looking and noisy bustle going on outside, the table talk, rich in the jargon of oil, which reached her out in the kitchen, Elgin's enthusiasm, all combined to lull her prudence asleep. The profit she might expect to make from her enterprise came to seem trifling when compared with the fortune she soon might have. To wish to profit from those who were working so hard on her behalf seemed mean. Sybil ceased to consider the crew as paying boarders and began to consider them her guests. Before long in her off moments she was darning their socks, patching their pants, mending and sewing buttons on their shirts: making for the boys a home away from home. To save, she scrimped the family. She and Elgin and Geraldine ate in the kitchen after the men had finished and were sitting around the parlor listening to the battery-set radio which Sybil had provided for their evening entertainment.

By the end of the first month they were down to fifteen hundred feet and the string, as they called it, was drawn out for a test sample. This indicated the kind of soil associated with oil. Elgin was elated and Sybil also was cheered. She had been sobered to learn when the bills from the butcher and the grocer came in that her expenses exceeded her income and that to make up the difference she would have to make a further withdrawal from the family savings account.

They were down to twenty-one hundred feet when one evening just as the men were starting in on second helpings at the table the world exploded and caught fire. The noise was as though the earth were a balloon and a pin had been stuck in it. On the site of the derrick a column of fire too bright to be looked at shot from the ground up to heaven.

"We've struck gas!" groaned the foreman.

"We've struck," said Elgin in tones of awe, "Hell."

A telegram was sent off to the company's head office. Next day a black motorcycle, its noise silenced by the roar of the fire, stopped at the gate in a puff of dust and the driver dismounted.

He looked like a man-sized bug, shiny black, with big yellow bug's eyes sticking out beyond the sides of his head. He wore an aviator's black leather helmet strapped underneath the chin, the immense wraparound goggles, seated on sponge-rubber padding, made of amber glass, reflecting the light like the multicellular eyes of a fly seen under a microscope. He wore a black leather bow tie and a leather jacket with, counting those on the elbows, a dozen zipper pockets, fringed leather gauntlets, black pants as tight as a coat of lacquer, and knee-high black puttees with chrome buckles. Dividing his thorax from his abdomen was a waist no bigger around than a dirt dauber's enclosed in a black kidney belt studded with cat's-eyes in hearts, diamonds, clubs, and spades.

He removed the helmet, disclosing a head as hairless as a hard-boiled egg and of the same whiteness. He had neither eyebrows nor lashes nor trace of beard: all had been burnt away. His features were fixed, rigid, expressionless; only the eyes, beneath their lashless lids, moved. A weathered china doll decorating the grave of a long-dead child was what he reminded Geraldine of.

Judging from appearances he was ageless, but according to the crewmen he was no more than twenty-five. And it would surprise them all if he ever lived to see thirty. In that boy's trade few grew old. If he didn't kill himself on that motorcycle first he would either be burnt up or blown up one day.

What on earth would anybody do it for then? Sybil asked.

Some for the money, others because they were too dumb to know any better, Speed here because he was drawn to flame like a moth and because he loved explosives. For what he was about to do, which in actual work time would amount to maybe half a day, he would be paid two hundred dollars at the least. He, however, though at twenty-five his burns had left him hardly any original skin of his own for further grafts, and though he had one elbow stiffened in a permanent half-bend, was missing a finger on one hand and the thumb on the other, and wore a silver plate in his skull the size of a tea saucer—he would probably have done it without pay. He was an artist—and every bit as temperamental; not with a brush nor with mallet and chisel: an artist in dynamite.

"Well, I just hope he don't blow hisself up here," said Sybil.

"I hope not too," said Geraldine.

"I'd sooner not have the oil than for anything like that to happen," said Sybil.

"Poor little old burnt bashed-up thing!" said Geraldine.

He refused Sybil's offer to fix him a bite to eat. Unfortunately she did not have in the house any RC Cola and Tom's Toasted Peanuts, which according to the crewmen was what he lived on. If she had known he was coming she would have gotten some.

In his fire-fighting suit, a padded and quilted asbestos coverall as white as his road costume was black, as bulky as the other was sleek, Speed looked more than ever like a bug, this time one wrapped in its cocoon. Again great goggles, these of brown isinglass like the windowpane of a stove, covered his eyes. In this outfit, it soaked with water, he was going to approach the fire carrying a charge of dynamite fused to go off within seconds and drop it down the hole. When told this, and that it was the only way to put out the fire, Sybil said, "Then let it burn." Elgin seconded her. He had decided, he said, that he didn't care any more whether he struck oil.

"You may not," the foreman said, "but we got money down that hole."

From the parlor window Sybil and Geraldine watched up to the point where, carrying his bundle of sticks of dynamite with its sputtering short fuse, Speed got near enough to the blaze to be forced to crawl on his hands and knees. One, two, mother and daughter both passed out. When they came to the fire was out. The gas capped, the crewmen were piping it to the adjacent field. From the escape pipe, ten feet high, it issued with the hiss of five hundred blowtorches. Such was its force that when it was ignited the base of the flame was twenty feet above the opening of the pipe. The flame itself stood six stories tall, pointed and shaped like a blade. The even pressure kept it ever the same. Not even the wind off those Oklahoma plains could sway it.

"How long you reckon it will take to burn itself out?" asked Elgin.

"Got 'em down south Texas been going like that forty years," said the foreman.

Speed reappeared in his road costume. The women went out to bid him good-by, Sybil offering up to the time he stomped the starter pedal to fix him a bite to eat, a sandwich for the road, he again with that look of slight nausea in his eyes which the mention of food brought on. He disappeared behind his goggles. He stomped the starter pedal and the cycle roared to life. He lifted his gauntleted hand in a brief farewell.

"Wait! I'm coming with you!" Geraldine yelled. "Can I?"

His reply exceeded in length everything else he had said since his arrival put together. "Hold on you can. Ast for no sidecar. One em thangs on go no fastern a kiddycar."

"Geraldine!" Sybil shrieked. "Get down off of that thing this minute!"

"Mama, you'll have to just manage the best you can without me," said Geraldine, straddling the saddle seat, her skirt three quarters of the way up her thighs, her arms hugging that narrow waist encased in its jeweled kidney belt. "Good-by. Tell Papa good-by. I'll write when I get a chance."

Speed twisted the handlebar grip. The engine responded impatiently.

"I hope," Geraldine shouted back, "yawl hit oil."

But although a new derrick was erected and a new string brought in and sent down fifty-one hundred feet, six weeks later the foreman was saying, "Well, Floyd, that's how the dice roll. Sometimes you strike it lucky, sometimes you don't. Right?"

"Yeah," said Elgin. "Yeah, that's right. Sometimes you strike it lucky, sometimes—"

"It's all in the game," said the foreman. "Right?"

"Yeah," said Elgin. "Yeah, that's—"

"Can't bring them all in," said the foreman. "Right?"

"No," said Elgin. "No, you can't bring them all in."

They were dismantling the derrick from the top, throwing down the pieces and stacking them in a trailer. Others meanwhile took apart the toolshed. When they were finished all that was left was the enlarged outhouse which looked now like a boxcar forgotten on a railroad siding, a hole in the ground seven eighths of a mile deep, and an eternal flame. When all the equipment was stowed they drove away. In one truck rode the crew, waving back as they went, beginning already on the box lunches Sybil had packed for them. The Floyds waved until they were out of sight, sighed, and turned back towards the house. Over everything a stillness settled, made more intense by the hiss of the flare.

With only the two of them to cook and keep house for Sybil did not know what to do with herself. She sat in the kitchen or out in the yard peeling potatoes or shelling peas in piddling amounts, rousing herself with a jerk now and again from out of a study, dashing a tear from her eyes from time to time at the memory of Geraldine. Elgin poked about the spot where the derrick had stood, kicking clods. It was too late in the year to think of planting a crop, though how they were to get by without one was hard to figure, Sybil having told him that rather than making a profit on her boardinghouse venture she had used up their savings and owed the butcher and the grocer the bills for the last three weeks. They tried to occupy themselves but they both just moped. Their lives had gone flat. The gas flare made it impossible to do anything. Its light kept them awake, its noise deafened them, its heat scorched them. Too bright to be looked at even in the glare of noon, it illuminated the midnight: a flaming sword, like the one set to guard the east gate of Eden.

"Well, Elgin, never mind, hon," said Sybil. "We've still got our health and we've still got each other. So don't go breaking your heart over that million dollars."

"Aw, for pity's sake, Sybil," said Elgin, "what kind of a fool do you take me for? Do you think I ever really believed we were going to strike oil? Me?"

The Rainmaker

I

THE HUNDRED-MILE stretch of the Red River from the Arkansas-Oklahoma line west to Hugo (or if you were on the other side, from Texarkana west to Paris, Texas) was, in 1936, served by a single ferry: the one on the Clarksville-Idabel road. You were, in either case, always on the other side from the side the ferryboat was on when you drew up at the landing; and as it had no schedule, not even one to fall behind in, you could sit there honking till the cows came home, the ferryboat would cross over for you whenever its owner felt like it and not before. Maybe not then. For if, in running his trotline as he came across (he hauled in sometimes as much as twenty pounds of channel catfish), the ferryman should sight an alligator gar, he would drop his tiller and cut loose with his .30-30—the bullets whining off the water and over the heads of any waiting passengers—and he might on such rudderless occasions fetch up a mile or more downstream from the landing; for the current is deep-running and strong, though on the surface it does not look as if there is any current; indeed, it does not look like a liquid, but rather like a bed of red clay, of the consistency of what potters call "slip," and looks as if it would not only be unsuited to any of the uses to which water is generally put, but that getting it to pour would be like starting a new bottle of ketchup.

The ferryboat (raft, really) took but one car at a time. If there should happen to be more than one they just had to wait while the boat went across and came back—an inconvenience which the driver of the lead machine in the field of fourteen bearing down upon the Oklahoma landing one July day in 1936 was counting heavily upon. He was a stranger to those parts, but no stranger to back-road ferries. Neither, however, was he a stranger to the tricks of fate; and should the boat happen to be on the other side, well, he thought, with a glance of his strained and bleary eyes into the rearview mirror, he might just as well drive right into the river. And with a glance at the speedometer and a thought for his brake-drum linings, or lack thereof, he might not be able to keep from it if he tried.

By chance the ferry was on the Oklahoma side that day, having been trapped there the previous noon when the wind began to rise and the sky to blacken over. Now the wind had died but the darkness lingered. It was not evening or even very late afternoon, but over everything lay, lower than any cloud, denser than fog or smoke, and of a color like snuff, and almost as acrid, a uniform suspension of fine red dust, so that the air was to air what the river water was to water. And so the ferryman could hear the cars coming long before he could see them, could hear the horns honking steadily as a flight of southering geese and growing louder, nearer, in numbers such as had never before demanded his services at any one time, hardly in any two weeks' period, sounding like a wedding cortege or like a high school celebrating a victory of its football team. So he was ready and waiting for them, with his engine started and idling, the gate chain lowered, his two running lights lit, the hawser poised to cast off, and his other hand out for his half dollar. He coughed and spat, thinly and of the color of tobacco juice, though at the moment he was not chewing. This dust was not something raised by the approaching cars; it was the prevailing atmosphere in Oklahoma that spring and summer, and the one before, and the one before that, when with dust storms following one another often not two days apart, dark as night piled on night, it had come to seem almost the native air. This had been one of the worst.

Then the ferryman saw them, the headlights filtering blood-shot and diffuse through the red pall, then saw the line of cars, with one, a truck or a van or a bus, away out in front, the ones in the rear all closely strung together and undulating in waves over the rutty road like the segments of a caterpillar, the horns whooping now like a pack of hounds, and all of them coming at considerable speed—considering, that is, the visibility, the state of the road, and the fact that the combined age of the fourteen cars and pickups running the race was in the neighborhood of two hundred and fifty years.

The river level during the past three rainless years had dropped steadily; now there was a long sandy incline down to the ferry landing. When it reached the top of this bank the winning car was a good hundred yards in the lead. If the driver even paused to see whether the boat was there, it was not apparent to the ferryman. The car came down the bank lurching and swaying from side to side, rattling, the radiator boiling, out of control or with a flat tire or, as was entirely possible from the look of it, with no brakes, picking up momentum as it came and headed for the boat as if with deliberate intent to sink it. The ferryman had no time to shout and barely time to jump. He jumped onto the boat rather than aside on the bank; had he not he would surely have been left ashore, for with the propulsion imparted by the car the boat shot twenty feet out into the water at one bound. It slapped down, scattering spray, bounced again and then again, skipping like a flat skimming stone, the front end leaping so high that whereas in the first moments it had seemed certain the car would plunge over the wheel chocks and through the forward chain, it seemed certain the next moment to roll into the river off the stern. Each time the bow slapped down it lunged forward, then as the bow rose it scurried backwards, and now with the deck awash it began skidding sideways. All this while the ferryman was down on his knees looking as if a mule had kicked him and slipped the knot in that hawser in his hand. The truck heaved a final burp from the radiator, sputtered, and died. The ferryman staggered to his feet, fetched breath, and commenced cursing. Clenching his fists, he started forward. From behind him on the shore came a chorus of derisive honks and laughter and shouts.

"You sorry, low-down, no-good, smart-alecking, son of a—" he said.

By then he was alongside the cab. And what so suddenly silenced him was not the bandit's mask, a spotted red bandana, covering from the eyes down the face of his passenger; that was a sight to which the ferryman had grown so accustomed that he hardly noticed it anymore during this and the last two dusty summers, when often the entire population of both sides of the river would appear, when issue out of doors at last they must, gotten up as desperadoes, male and female, large and small; and only by oversight—for this had been a bandana day if ever there was one—was he not wearing one himself. No, what stopped the ferryman's tongue while opening still wider his mouth was that between the two fingers sticking out of the window of the cab was something that looked like a ten-dollar bill, and unless his ears deceived him the voice from behind the bandana had just said to keep the change. At that price he was welcome to take another shot at sinking the boat! Meanwhile there came no shooting from the shore, no *Halt! in the name of the law.* Evidently his passenger was not a fugitive.

What he was, what the whole gang was, the ferryman concluded after a quick appraisal of the vehicle, coupled with the continuing whoops and catcalls from the shore, was a road show of some kind, a small-time carnival, a tent show or a medicine show. The truck—truck or van, bus, whatever the hell it was—was really a house on wheels, with a curtained window in the body just above the cab, and sticking out of the roof a stovepipe out of kilter, and hanging off the rear a rickety flight of steps leading to a door. Along the side was painted a picture (the other side, he would find as he passed it later coming forward to dock in Texas, was, or was as nearly as an amateur hand could make it, a duplicate) in colors whose kindergarten brightness not even the thick coat of dust nor the prevailing duskiness could dim. Hard to say just what the moment intended to be depicted was—the coming of a storm or the passing of one. The sun, of a fiery orange and spoked with beams, was either just emerging from or just going behind a huge inky cloud rent by a jagged bolt of lightning the shape of a flight of stairs in profile, sharpened at the point, rendered in aluminum. Out of the cloud a shower of raindrops was falling, a direct hit from any one of which was apt to prove fatal to the people living in the farmhouse down below or to the two-legged animal (one hind, one front) in the barn lot. Above and below the depicted scene, in a mixture of print and script, small letters and capitals, all staggering and wavy and falling steadily downhill and all bunched together at the end, was a hand-lettered sign.

"Say," said the ferryman, "you fellers a tent show or something?"

"Say," said his passenger, "don't it seem to you like we're kind of drifting?"

The ferryman scooted back to his tiller and nosed back upstream. He shifted gears on his engine. Now he could see the lights from the cars on the Oklahoma shore only dimly, but he could still hear, though unable to make out the words, shouts and laughter. Bunch of cut-ups, he said to himself, who had had a bet among themselves which would get across the river first, not caring a damn how many lives they endangered along the road and obviously not whether they sank his boat and him along with it. Drinking probably. Road-show people. He had ferried their kind across before. Free spenders always. Easy come easy go. He would really rake in the money tonight!

The old engine was in high gear, and presently the ferryman discerned, down at the bottom of his vision, like the sediment at the bottom of a glass of the river water, a darkening, a shoreline: Texas. Then for the first time his passenger poked his head out. He inched it out cautiously as a turtle and looked back towards Oklahoma. There was nothing to be seen, yet in the light of the running lamp on its pole, above the mask, the eyes smiled. As Moses must have smiled on reaching the far shore of another body of red water and looking back.

"Say," said the ferryman, stopping on his way forward to dock, "tell me, what does it say here on the side of your truck? I seem to have mislaid my specs." (The letters were a foot high.) He could hardly see the man, not only because it was dark and so little of him was unmasked, but also because of the height of the cab.

"Lost your glasses, eh? Your reading glasses, was they?"

The ferryman said nothing, only gritted his teeth.

"Well, I'll tell you. See that picture? That thundercloud? That bolt of lightning? Them raindrops? What the words spell is, 'Lightning rods for sale.' "

"Can't read a word without my specs," said the ferryman, squinting. "But now that you say so, I can make it out for myself. Lightning rods for sale." Thinking of that ten-dollar bill, and of the weather for the past several years, he said, "Hmm. I wouldn't have thought your business had been so good here lately."

They bumped the dock. The driver started his motor. He revved it. The ferryman threw his hawser and dropped the chain with a clatter. As the driver went past, the ferryman said, "Pull over to the side of the road there if you like and . . ." The rest was finished on a falling cadence—the spoken equivalent of that line of lettering along the side of the truck—as, with a low-gear growl, taillight wigwagging over the bumps, the truck shot up the hill. ". . . and come back with me to . . ." The taillight disappeared. ". . . pickyourbuddiesup."

II

When it had gone about a mile down the road the truck turned right down a side road running parallel to the river. Over this it jounced and swayed for about a mile until it turned down an even rougher road—"gully" would be a better word—an old logging trail hacked through the tall pines which led back to the river. He was not driving fast now, not only because the road was rough and the dust in the air such that he could not, but because he was safe now. He knew what the ferryman did not know, that he would find no customers waiting for him when he got back to Oklahoma.

He came out of the trees and into a clearing at the river's edge. He drove down as near to the water as he could. Leaving the headlights burning, he got out. Had anybody been there (in which case he would not have gotten out) that person would have seen that the mask and a pair of ankle-top shoes, socks, and supporters was every stitch the man had on. Not that he was exactly nude, but there are no seams in a suit of feathers and tar.

Basically he was white Leghorn, but there was an inter-sprinkling of barred rock, Rhode Island red, some gray goose, some guinea hen, and even some bright bantam rooster, all fluffy and fine, being pinfeathers and eiderdown of the kind and assort-ment to be expected from the stuffing of a featherbed, saved over the years by some farmwoman from all the poultry killed and plucked for many a Thanksgiving and Christmas and family-re-union dinner. The man's long, red, wrinkled, leathery neck, notched with bones, his crawlike Adam's apple, the wattles un-derneath his chin and his beak of a nose enforced his resem-blance to a chicken—one in molt. His eyes, probably blue, were so bloodshot they were purple. He was bald on the crown, though his straggling reddish-gray hair was long enough to drape over the bare spot ordinarily. But upon his pate someone had recently wiped a paintbrush well charged with creosote and there a solitary pinfeather now stuck up like a cowlick. He was around forty-five years old, a stringy man of medium height who looked taller because of the stoop in his shoulders, the unmistakable stoop of one who from boyhood has followed the plow. He had long stringy arms on the lower parts of which where the feather-ing was sparse the veins stood out in permanent high relief like the grain in old weathered wood, say the side of an abandoned and never-painted haybarn. He was in a state far past mere weari-ness, bordering on collapse, and he was swearing steadily, possi-bly unconsciously, a sort of unedited imprecation almost as if he were humming to himself without any tune.

He went now around to the back of the van and hauled himself up the steps, opened the door with his shoulder, and fell inside. A crash sounded and a yelp of pain as he stumbled over something. He was out again shortly with a battered pail and a three-foot length of frayed-ended garden hose. He removed the Irish potato that served as a cap to the gas tank, poked the hose down the hole, put the end in his mouth, sucked, spat, and directed the flow into the pail, all with a polish which showed a good deal more practice than could have been gained on a single gas tank. He stepped into the light of the headlamps and, raising the pail shoulder high, poured half the contents over himself. He commenced plucking. In time a pile of sodden feathers lay at his feet; it looked as if half a dozen fryers had been scalded and plucked on the spot. He went back inside the van, returning this time with a thin cake of soap and a napless threadbare towel.

He eased himself into the tepid, opaque water, his head sticking up like a turtle's on that long seamy neck. Taking a deep breath, he ducked under. He came up spitting. He lathered his head and his underarms and his chest and ducked under again and came up spitting once more. He climbed out on the bank and rubbed himself down. When dry, the reddish-gray mat of hair on his chest looked like rusty steel wool. The smell of tar and gasoline had by no means been washed away.

He returned to the van and went inside and lighted a lamp, revealing some kind of broken machine in a heap in the middle of the floor, a huge round one-legged claw-footed dining table, a high-backed hickory-splint rocking chair, an oval dirt-colored rag rug, an immense chifforobe of black wood, three cylinders of cooking gas, a small potbellied stove, a woodbox (empty), a two-burner Coleman range on a shelf and on the floor beneath the shelf a coal-oil can with a sodden corncob stopper, an unmade daybed. A shelf ran high along one wall, and he began searching among the stuff on it. While his back was turned a small tarred and feathered dog, possibly of the rat-terrier breed, divided about equally between dog and long feathered tail, recently very wet and still very moist, slunk up the steps with its tongue lolling and into the room, and trying to make itself still smaller than it was, stole unnoticed underneath the bed.

The assortment of paraphernalia on the shelf included some half-dozen road flares of the kind left by night alongside detour signs, three or four old automobile batteries, two wooden boxes, one opened, the other unopened, labeled EXPLOSIVES, HANDLE WITH CARE, and a collection of apparatus vaguely electrical-looking, including coils and switches and fuse boxes and a hand-cranked generator with a much-worn armature rather resembling a large old-fashioned coffee mill. Behind all this he found what he was looking for (though success in his search brought no pause in that steady mumbled cursing) and began taking them down: quart cans of paint. He pried the lids off. There, scummed over, was the orange of that sun on the side of the van, and there the blackish blue of the cloud and there the red of the barn, the white of the raindrops—when all was dumped together into a pail and stirred, it was the color of mud.

As he stirred, the man regarded two other cans on the shelf above the cookstove. These were cans of tomatoes, with labels like miniatures of the sun painted on the panel of the van. He stopped stirring, rose, and went towards them, his eyes glazed, entranced. Then he caught himself and returned to the paint bucket.

Still naked, he went outside carrying the bucket and a brush, a worn-out broom, and a rickety stepladder. He swept down the side of the truck, coughing at the dust he raised. He stood the ladder beside the truck and climbed it to the top carrying the bucket. The paint was thick; one coat was going to have to do. He started in on top, first turning up the volume of that constant maledictory static he was making, and with three broad strokes of the brush, one of which he had to stretch so far to complete that he almost toppled off the ladder, he slashed through the words:

THe 1 & OnLY ProF. ORViLLe SiMMs

He coughed, stepped down a rung, and painted out the ascending sunrays. Stepping down another rung, he painted out the cloud, the base of the lightning bolt, the face of the sun. He rested a moment, coughing, rubbing his eyes, swearing, then stepped down and painted out the tip of the bolt of lightning, the remainder of the cloud. Then he had to come down off the ladder and rest. He had not slept in thirty-six hours. Not slept? He had not drawn one unterrified breath in all that while! His eyes felt as if all the dust in the world, or at least in Oklahoma, was underneath the lids. He climbed the ladder again and blotted out forevermore the falling raindrops. Stepping down, he painted out the farmhouse and barn and that one sui-generic head of livestock. Then dipping his brush in the paint and not even wiping it on the lip of the pail, with a curse (he would have all this to do again around on the other side), a vicious swipe and a spattering of mud-colored drops, he painted out the large bottom word:

RAiNMAKeR

III

Just plain unemployed Orville Simms, dressed now in khaki pants and shirt, drove that night until he could drive no farther, until his eyelids began to anneal, his hands to palsy on the wheel, until he began to have waking nightmares of windmill derricks, whole forests of them alongside the road and stretching away into the night, going south now through Red River County and into true night, the vast Texas night, with stars overhead, not the daytime night of dust; and then, after he had awakened barely in time to keep from going off into the ditch for the third time, he pulled off into somebody's cowpasture, started to get out of the cab and go back to his bed, and passed out at the wheel. His sleep was sound—too sound—comatose. He moaned, he whimpered, he twitched. Throughout the night frequent shudders shook him, jerking him almost awake, as in his dreams he felt himself falling from a height. . . .

Two days earlier, in Oklahoma, Prof. Simms was driving down a country road when his radiator came to a boil. The truck was an old enough model to have for a radiator cap one of those round glass gauges with a mercury column inside. It was older than that: not only Prof. Simms but numerous previous owners, though occasions had not been wanting, had come too late ever to see that thermometer rise. What it had long done instead was steam up inside the glass, and in another moment any mercury column would have been invisible anyhow—the whole cap was, the whole front end.

It never occurred to him to look for any standing water in the roadside ditches, where now not even weeds could any longer get a hold, and stockponds that he passed, or what had been stockponds, were dry white scabs covered over with a cracked layer of thin curling crust and invariably with an old car-casing, sometimes an old car, standing half-buried in the middle. Besides, the last three farms he had passed had shown evidence of habitation—that is, at each one dogs had come out to bark at him as he went past. This boiling of the radiator was a frequent occurrence, and what with that sign along the side of the truck, Prof. Simms had grown timid about stopping to ask for water, even a dipperful to drink. Especially he sought to avoid cross-roads stores with their one gas pump and garden watering can meant for radiators, but with also along their porch the usual group of whittlers and spitters. To pull up with that radiator going like a factory whistle at noon and shooting up like Old Faithful when the cap was loosened, and beneath that collective gaze to go and get the watering can was more then the 1 & OnLY ProF. ORViLLe SiMMs, RAiNMAKeR, could take. At such times he especially regretted that self-conferred title of Professor.

Meanwhile the sight of that steaming radiator was a joy to Prof. Simms, and the farther he drove without finding a drop to pour down it, or down his own long dusty gullet, the more joyfully he licked his parched lips with his dry tongue. For fifteen miles he had been driving alongside fields where the cornstalks slanted earthwards and the brown leaves hung tattered and limp and where cotton in scraggly rows stood with bolls which ought long since to have burst white and were instead whole and hard, the shape and the color of and not much bigger than bottled olives. Once he stopped and got out to look closer, and found the earth pimpled and pocked from the last light shower, each pebble perched upon a column of dirt half an inch high and conforming exactly to its outline: a sort of microscopic badlands. Not God's country, perhaps, but the 1 & OnLY ProF. ORViLLe SiMMs's country for sure. If not too far gone even for him.

Just how far gone he learned when he stopped at an abandoned farmhouse for water. He learned then, too, that the countryside was blessed with the only other thing it needed to make it ideal for his purposes: a long mental drought. He pulled up at the sagging gate and got out and went around back of the house to the well, from the rusty pulley of which hung a bucket that even folks giving up and leaving would not bother to take along. He let it drop, and listened, and heard a sound which, though it augured well for his business, could not but strike an old farmboy as sickening: not the expected sideways slap of an empty bucket striking water, but the dull dry *kachunk* of the bottom of the bucket upon hard dirt. Then behind him he heard a snort of dry, unamused laughter.

"Wasting your time there, Mister," the man said. "Been bone dry since last fall a year. If you're thirsty, step into the house here."

"Thank you just the same. If your well's dry then I don't expect you've got much water to spare."

"Enough to give a thirsty man to drink. When we ain't got that no more then I'll pull out."

"Thank you kindly. But . . . well, I hate to ask it, but what I need is more than just a drink. My radiator's dry. If you're having to haul water, why I'll be glad to buy a bucketful from you."

This suggestion the farmer did not even bother to spurn. Out of the drum he hauled it in he dippered a bucketful of water and, to Prof. Simms's embarrassment, himself toted it out and opened the explosive radiator and poured it in. Poured it in, that is, after letting the radiator cool down, and while waiting he came round and silently studied the picture and text on the side of the truck. After a while he spoke. He did not ask why a man who presumably could call it down from the skies whenever he felt like it had had to stop and beg a bucketful of water from a man who had to haul it in an oil drum from eight miles off, but, apparently unconscious that his illiteracy was a handicap, and certainly not conscious that any stigma attached to it, but rather as if a man who could read and write was something of a curio, if not indeed a freak, asked to know what the words meant. Prof. Simms told him.

"Is that a fact! Well, Mister, I mean Professor, we can sure use you around here! You have sure come to the right place!"

He believed he had. He believed he had. It was almost too good to be true.

"Yes, sir, we been just waiting for you to come along. We been trying to drum us up a rainmaker."

"Is that a fact?"

"Yes, sir. Preachers done all prayed theirselves hoarse. Methodist. Baptist. Campbellite. Adventist. None of them done any good. Last week a gang of us men even went out to the reservation to ask the chief out there if he would have a try. The Indians, you know, they always pray for rain. Not to God, to the Great Spirit. But hellfire, we wasn't particular who sent it, as long as it come. So the men in town they thought it just might do some good and surely do no harm to ask him to see what he could do."

"Yes? What happened?"

"Why, be derned if that old buck didn't turn out to be a deacon in the Presbyterian church! Called us a pack of heathens and run us off his place. As we was piling into the truck to leave another one come up, claimed he was the medicine man and could make it rain pitchforks and nigger babies, but he never looked like he could even make water. The only spirits it looked like he had been in touch with was liquid all right but not water. So it sure looks like you have come to the right place all right, Professor."

"Just when was the last time you folks had rain around here?" Prof. Simms asked.

"Last is right. Last it's ever going to, I was beginning to think. Before you came along, that is."

So he never even had to go to them. All he had to do was drive into town (it was called Arrowhead—he hardly noticed the name, though he was never to forget it) and leave the truck sitting in front of the feed and grain store, and when he came back from the diner picking his teeth half an hour later they were there waiting for him, some two dozen of them.

At first he gave them a flat no. Said he was just passing through their town on his way to another one where his services had been contracted for. He had to agree when one of them said they couldn't need rain over there any worse than they did right here. And furthermore, he said, he never guaranteed a thing. He had his methods, and his methods had been known to work. To work where prayer and witchcraft had failed. Because his were scientific methods. But they ought to know that rain did not come down just whenever you stood up and snapped your fingers. He knew a few more things to do than just snap his fingers. Still, he never guaranteed a thing. He had been known to fail.

Because that was the way to do it: rush right in instead of waiting for some skeptic in the crowd to sneer. This he had learned, as he learned everything, the hard way. At first, when he was just starting out, he had tried to sell himself to the doubters. A big mistake. Once you had done that you had painted yourself into a corner. Then the only way out was to produce. The thing to do was, act as if nobody knew better than you what the odds were against your succeeding. Laugh at them if they even hinted that you set yourself up as infallible. Make them look like fools. Rain? Hardest thing in the world to produce on demand. Yes, that *was* his business. It was a doctor's business to get you well, too, wasn't it? But sometimes you died, didn't you? And when they said they had not had rain in six months, or twelve, and had begun to think it was never going to rain again and didn't see how he or anybody else could hope to make it, say, that's what I think myself. If you folks haven't had rain in all that long a time it looks to me like you ain't never going to get no more, and make as if to leave. Then it was they trying to convince him that he could if he just would, saying, yes, they understood how hard it was, the odds were all against it, they didn't expect the impossible, they would have no kick coming if he failed, only just take their money and do his best for God's sake, try.

But this was the driest, dustiest, thirstiest-looking crew he had ever struck across yet! And the trustingest. They gawked at him as if to say, yes, we understand you don't want to brag. We appreciate it. But you've made your point and shown your manners and so would you please just take our money and say the charm and start the rain, we've been waiting a right long spell. No doubters here. He doubled his usual fee. They swallowed hard all around and looked at one another and licked their lips, and promised to have it for him in the morning—in advance, that is to say, of his performance. A site was fixed upon, one answering to his specification for a windmill or a silo, or some similar elevation. In parting he reminded them again that he didn't promise a thing. As a matter of fact, having consulted *Miles' Almanac* he knew that light showers were forecast for the morrow. He hoped *Miles'* was righter for once than it generally was. He pitied these folks, and his pity was heightened by the thought of what he himself was doing to them. He knew what it was like. He had been a farmer once himself. And he knew what it was to be taken in. His old farm had sat just far enough inside the Arkansas-Oklahoma line to justify the sign that hung on the gap-toothed paling fence, which, once the s's and the e's and the n's and the y's had been unreversed, read:

TRy yOUR LUCk
HUNt fOR OZARk DiMoNds
Big 1s HAVe BeNN FOUNd
1$ peR. HR.

For which in all the years it hung there the only taker he ever got, and this was after he had scratched out the 1$ and made it 50¢, was one wiseacre in a car with a Missouri license tag who stopped one day, and then said on second thoughts he believed he wouldn't after all, because he could tell just by looking that he, Simms, had done already found all the real big ones. Nor had he ever had any much better luck with his other attraction, the cave. Because nobody could stand to set foot inside it and he always had to refund their dime. Even before you stuck your head in, even from fifty feet away, the smell was enough to knock you down. It was the smell of guano, though he learned to call it that only after he had sold out and was packing to leave. The first to call it guano was the man who had bought the place from him, a stranger whom he had taken to be the second diamond prospector, and the first one to think he could tell by looking that he, Simms, had not already found all the big ones, until the man said (this after he, Simms, had tried everything, including drilling another dry hole every time a fresh breeze blew up from Texas with a whiff of petroleum on it, including even farming the damned place), "Diamonds? You trying to be funny? I'm going after that guano. There must be half a million tons of it in there."

"That what?" said Simms.

"Bat shit to you. Most valuable fertilizer in the world. My God, you have got a gold mine in that cave. I mean, I have got a gold mine in it."

And so, feeling sorry for these Arrowhead folks, he determined to give them a good show for their money. The rainmaker's art, as Prof. Simms had been quick to learn, consisted entirely in this: to make the audience forget what they had come to see, then get away before they recollected. Providentially it worked out that the people most willing to pay for rain were those who were the easiest to beguile, being the ones to whom amusements and spectacles were the greatest rarity.

The production, or as Prof. Simms preferred to style it, in order to stress its experimental nature, "the trial," was set to take place on a farm known as the old Maddox place, chosen because it answered to the Professor's stipulation for a windmill, and because it stood on what passed in those parts for a hill and thus served as a signal beacon and center for community gatherings. From his overnight campsite on the edge of town Prof. Simms set off the next morning bright and early—and a very bright morning it was, with the sky glowing behind the sun like the reflector of a heater—to find the place. He did not have to ask the way. He had only to fall in with the traffic already clogging the road. The line included passenger cars and pickups, motorcycles with sidecars, buggies and wagons, more than one of them its bed loaded with empty barrels, oil drums, washtubs, to catch the rain and carry it back home in. This testimony of simple faith in his powers touched Prof. Simms. Seeing his van, the drivers of the vehicles pulled off into the ditch, the people on foot stood aside to let him pass. Kids sitting along the tailgates of the wagons dangling their rusty bare feet gaped at him as he went by, the women ducked their chins in a quick shy curtsey, the men bared their heads. They were certainly a dry-looking bunch! Their lips chapped and cracked from constant licking, mouths hanging open, their expressions fixed, baked on, they looked like those characters in the moving pictures shown stumbling across Death Valley towards some mirage of an oasis. Near the head of the procession he passed two wagonloads of people dressed all in white nightgowns. In his or her hands each of them clasped a small black book. Even more like wanderers in the desert, their eyes trained on a vision, these folks in their nightgowns looked. Converts, believers in total immersion, they had been a long time waiting for baptism; now beatific smiles wreathed their parched and peeling lips. Prof. Simms was moved, and he renewed his vow to put on a good show for these folks, take their minds off their troubles for one day, at least.

Waiting on the site already were still more. Some looked as if they had spent the night there. Prof. Simms had barely arrived when, passing among the crowd on his inspection of the grounds, he overheard the following exchange:

"When is the rain going to start, Papa?"

"In a minute, son. Give the man time."

"Brung along the family, have you, Dunc?"

"Just this'n here. He ain't never seen rain. Not that he remembers."

Looking down, Prof. Simms saw a boy of four, going on five. He was dressed for the outing in a new yellow oilskin slicker, with a matching sou'wester, and a pair of rubber boots. The slicker having been bought three or four sizes too big, so that he might grow into it, the little boy rattled around inside it like the clapper inside a bell.

By eight o'clock it looked as if everybody had come who was going to come. Gathered on the field were five to six hundred people, young and old, white, black, and red. From the top step of his van Prof. Simms, his fee in his pocket, addressed the crowd in these words:

"Folks, if we're all here I will ask you now to give me your attention, please, while I explain just what we are going to do."

From the audience arose a silence so profound that he could hear the regular breathlike swish of the palm-leaf fans with which the ladies fanned their faces. Before him were ranged five hundred open mouths, as though awaiting the consecrated host.

"I will tell you everything," he continued. "I mean to keep nothing from you. There is no mystery, no magic, to making rain. It is a science, and science has no secrets. I am not here to mystify you good people with a lot of hocus-pocus. I am not going to lead you all in prayer. I am not going to daub myself with paint and dance around in a ring rattling a gourd. All that is known of the science of rainmaking I mean to put to use here today for the benefit of you folks; any man who claims to know more is either fooling you or fooling himself."

Prof. Simms paused to wipe his forehead with his bandana. Lord, it was a scorcher of a day! Imagine anybody simple enough to believe that anybody else could make rain fall from a sky like that!

Rain, the Professor mused; what was rain? Not being scientists, they perhaps thought that rain was water. Well, they were only partly right. There was something else in rain besides water, as anybody could testify who had ever let a bucketful of rainwater settle for a while: dirt. And he proceeded to explain how, according to the findings of science, every drop of rain contained, was formed around, a single grain of dust. So the first thing they were going to do this morning was to raise a little dust.

He turned and disappeared into the recesses of his van. When he came forth again some moments later he was carrying a crate on which in large red letters was stenciled DYNAMITE, and on top of the crate a detonator and several coils of wire.

Prof. Simms directed the digging by volunteers of four holes, one at each corner of the field, and the placing therein of half a stick of dynamite each. Wires were then laid from these to the detonator. Even as he went about this first number on his program, Prof. Simms was mindful to raise an occasional glance to the bright, blank heavens, and to follow this with a slow, slight shake of his head. This show of doubt cost you nothing of your expert standing; it lent you a human touch, meanwhile it opened, by a crack, the door out by which you were going to have to excuse yourself later on.

When the charges had been laid, capped, and fused, the crowd was advised to draw close together and to sit down on the ground. Children were gathered to their mothers. An expectant hush settled over them. Prof. Simms pushed the plunger. Four simultaneous muffled booms went up, raising four geysers of red dust. Gravel rained down upon the people's heads. Pebbles rattled on the hard ground. As the dust cleared Prof. Simms studied the faces of his audience. Usually the dynamite blasts could be counted on to loosen a crowd up, enliven them, begin to distract their minds. This bunch just lifted their dust-powdered heads and gaped at him, waiting to see what was coming next. Among five hundred faces scarcely half a dozen smiles were to be counted. Even the kids were a solemn lot. It was a very single-minded crowd.

Having astonished his audience with the information that rain was something more than water, Prof. Simms next informed them that water was really a gas, in liquid form. Rather, two gases: hydrogen and oxygen. H_2O. To make this go down he employed another homely illustration. When you boiled water on the range, what happened? It went off into the air in the form of a gas, steam. And when you put a lid on the pot it condensed back into a liquid. Now they had the dust that was needed for the drops to form around up there in the atmosphere; the next thing was . . .

Again he went inside the van, emerging this time with three cylinders of cooking gas on a hand truck, two of them labeled HYDROGEN, the third OXYGEN. He went inside once more and came back with a carton of rubber balloons. For the next three quarters of an hour Prof. Simms was kept busy inflating balloons and tying their necks and passing them to the kids who had volunteered to hold them. When all the balloons were blown up he again went inside his van, returning this time with an automatic .22 rifle. He called for a volunteer from the audience who was a crack shot. Nominations closed upon a single name, and after some coaxing a cross-eyed youth of twenty came forward dragging one foot and grinning bashfully. Prof. Simms gave him the rifle and a box of cartridges.

The balloon holders were divided into teams, like contestants in an unequal spelling bee, Oxygens on one side, Hydrogens, two to one, on the other.

"Now then, when I say 'Go!' " said Prof. Simms, "the first of you Oxygens and the first two of you Hydrogens let go of your balloons, and you"—turning to the rifleman—"hold your fire until I tell you, then as quick as you can, bust all three balloons. Don't miss any or we'll get the wrong proportions. Go!"

Three balloons, a blue one, a red one, and a yellow one, soared aloft. The cross-eyed youth raised the rifle to his shoulder, blinking at the glare, wetting his lips. Up, up, the balloons soared, smaller and smaller. The rifleman licked his lips more rapidly. At last:

"Fire!" said the Professor.

Three cracks: three clean hits. The balloons disappeared. Tatters of colored rubber fluttered to earth. *Go! Fire! Go! Fire!* So for the next half hour. The kids were diverted, but as for their parents and grandparents, they turned their faces up, observed the bursts high overhead, then looked down, looked at him to see what was coming next. There was not a smile among them, not even a kindling of interest, just patience, stolid, dumb, unimaginative patience. Not that they were skeptical. On the contrary, with these people a problem different from the one he was used to coping with began to disclose itself to Prof. Simms. Folks generally had to be convinced that he could make it rain; these were going to have to be convinced that he couldn't. Prof. Simms felt a moment's panic. He had put down his toe and found that he was swimming in depths of gullibility over his head.

Prof. Simms next brought out his rockets. The first of these was launched at half past ten. It burst with a satisfying bang, placing a puff of white smoke high above, the only thing visible in the vast, empty sky. He sent up, at a dollar and thirty cents apiece, two dozen of them. As each went off he studied the upturned faces. Ordinarily a fireworks display tickled them so they forgot everything else; when they remembered, and realized that in fact no rain had fallen (by which time he was in the neighboring county), they said, well, he had put on a dern good show, that alone was worth the price. But though fireworks must have been a rarer event in their lives than in most, this crowd could think of just one thing. Dynamite, balloons, rockets: all this excitement they had had, and still they stood there solemn as a convention of cigar-store Indians, waiting for rain. He had, however, one trick left: a performance on Old Magnet. If that didn't get them, nothing would.

Magnet, the *pièce de résistance* of his act, was an invention, rather a collage, of Prof. Simms's own. Ordinarily Old Magnet had merely to make her appearance for somebody in the crowd to declare, " 'Fore God!" or words to that effect, "Would you just look a-here what's coming now! I George, Sam, if that contraption can't make it rain, be about the only thing it can't do, won't it? Sounds," the speaker was apt to observe, as soon as Prof. Simms began fiddling with the dials, "like she's clearing her throat to get ready to say something." Which in fact she once did. Suddenly remembering her long-dormant, not to say dead, function, she brought in station KRLD, Dallas, and gave out five whole minutes of Chicago cotton and grain futures before she could be tuned out. However, an early-model battery-set radio was merely a part of Old Magnet. Above a bank of switches like the manual of an organ were arrayed needle gauges, fuses, the works from a telephone box, the exposed coil from a Model-T Ford, more vacuum tubes, an electrical rheumatism cure, and a great deal more junk the origin of which Prof. Simms himself did not know. Leading off all this was a long coil of wire attached to a large horseshoe magnet.

For, as Prof. Simms explained—unless there was somebody in the audience to do it for him, and generally there was: some know-it-all who would save him the necessity of a further lecture, and to whom the Professor would listen with a quizzical brow and a half smile, although if there were not, as here, he employed the same explanation himself—it was your magnetism that drew all your other elements together. That charged your dust particles and made them draw your atoms of oxygen and hydrogen and form your drops which your clouds then soaked up. For a cloud was nothing more nor less than a sort of sponge, as you might say, a dry sponge looking for some water. There were your clouds (they still hung there, unmoving, not a breath of wind to stir them, hardly a breath of breath); your dust and your oxygen and your hydrogen were there. Now the thing was, to send up some magnetism. If that didn't do it . . .

Well, if that didn't do it, then the only thing to say was, there were times and places when all the advancements of science were to no avail. Time to begin to take the moral approach, or rather *re*proach. Half jokingly now, to be borne down on harder a little later on. But as of now to say, "Well, if what we're about to do next don't turn the trick, then it's for you folks to say why, not me. I don't know what you all have been up to, but if the Good Lord is displeased with you—and that's about the only thing I can think of to explain a sky like that after all we've done—why then you realize, of course, that Albert Einstein himself if he was here couldn't make it rain. It's for you all to say why He is down on you; but till you folks make it right with the Lord, why, I'm just wasting my time and talents. When all's said and done, He's the one that's got His hand on the hydrant, you know."

To this, as to everything else, they listened without so much as nodding their heads—never even scratched them. Even that little boy in the slicker, following at his heels as he played the wire off the coil to the base of the windmill, just gaped solemnly at him.

An assistant from the audience was instructed in what order to throw the switches once Prof. Simms was on top of the windmill. He stood at the base of it, the horseshoe tucked into his belt, the wire trailing from him, looking up at the fan. Prof. Simms disliked heights, and he never failed at this point to think, surely there must be a better way than this to make a living. Taking a deep breath, he commenced hauling himself up the rungs of the tall, narrow ladder.

Just beneath the fan blades a narrow platform ran around the derrick. Standing on this platform the Professor signaled to his assistant down on the ground. Grasping the derrick with one hand, with the other he pointed the magnet out into space. Hardly was the last switch thrown when over the horizon appeared a huge black cloud.

"Great God!" gasped Prof. Simms.

Recovering himself at once, he said, "Don't be a fool, like those down on the ground, Orville."

But even as he said this the cloud doubled in size. "If you didn't know better," said Prof. Simms, "blessed if you wouldn't almost believe there was something in it." And despite himself a small shudder of fear, of awe ran through him—fear of, awe of himself.

Meanwhile the people down on the ground had not yet seen his cloud. He leaned as far out from the derrick as he safely could, holding out his magnet. Slowly he drew it back to his chest. Be damned if the cloud didn't leap to follow it! He repeated the gesture: again the cloud raced nearer as if in response. "Well! If this don't beat anything I ever saw!" said Prof. Simms.

Now the people down below saw it. Heads snapped around in that direction and fingers pointed and even up on his perch Prof. Simms heard the universal intake of breath. Three or four times more he repeated his gesture of drawing the cloud on with his magnet, and each time it leaped obediently to follow. The whole sky in that direction, from the ground up to the dome, was now solid black.

A gust of wind whipped his face, followed by another which shook the derrick and turned the fan blades over a couple of revolutions. Prof. Simms looked down. "There! That ought to satisfy you!" he said. He laughed to see them scurrying for shelter down below, drawing their jackets over their heads, whipping up the teams of their wagons, some diving underneath the wagonbeds. He had not long to gloat, however; a blast of wind shivered the derrick, very nearly plucking him off. The fan blades spun. He decided to climb down. He put his foot on the first rung of the ladder, looked down, and saw nothing. People, wagons, his own van, the base of the windmill, everything had disappeared. At that moment he got an eyeful of dust. In another moment all thought of getting down was put out of his mind by the blast.

And there, like a possum up a persimmon tree, clinging for dear life, while the derrick shook and shuddered and the dust came at him like a sandblast and the fan blades whirred like an airplane propeller, his eyes squeezed shut, the 1 & OnLY ProF. ORViLLe SiMMs spent the next twenty-four hours.

At the end of that time, when the wind had died and over everything had settled a Pompeian silence, Prof. Simms ventured down to reconnoiter. Halfway down he still could not see the ground. At that point he paused to listen. It was then that he noticed for the first time the smell, like a freshly surfaced asphalt road; but hearing no sound, he figured they were all still indoors or in the storm cellar, unaware that the storm had stopped, and that this was the moment to make his break. So he went down farther. Then he saw them. They were squatting around the base of the derrick waiting for him like a party of hunters waiting for a treed coon to come down. Like himself, they wore bandanas over their faces, only to them it lent the sinister look of a band of vigilantes. Halting in his descent, he called down, "Well, I told you all I never guaranteed anything, didn't I?"

No one responded. They didn't even look up. In the silence he heard the familiar whimper of a dog. That smell he had noticed earlier rose more sharply on the still air. Like asphalt, or like a new telephone pole, freshly creosoted. He saw a fire; on it an oil drum steamed. The society below, he now noticed, was exclusively male. He scampered hastily back up the ladder four or five rungs. "Dern it!" he cried. "Whose idea was this anyhow, yawl's or mine?" He clambered back up into the protective gloom and to that rung of the ladder he clung for another hour, calling down from time to time, "Maybe yawl would like a refund? Hey? What do you say to that? Maybe yawl would like a refund, hey?"

IV

When Simms woke up in Texas he thought at first that he was still asleep and having nightmares. All around him for as far as the eye could stretch stood windmills thick as trees. He closed his eyes with a shudder, opened them and looked again. They were still there, but now he noticed that they lacked fans. Not windmills, then: oil-well derricks.

After breakfast, at which he was reunited with Samson, his dog, and after plucking Samson of his feathers, Simms drove down the road to the first gas station and general store he came to. Along the porch sat half a dozen men. Simms thought he had seen ignorant, backwoods, gate-mouthed, dull-eyed faces in Oklahoma, and before that in Arkansas, but here . . . Well, he was about ready to restore the sign on his truck. Memories of Arrowhead braked that thought. But before he knew it he had asked, "Been this dry hereabouts for a good spell, has it?"

"Dry? Mister, 'dry' don't cover it. They haven't invented the word yet for the weather we been having."

"Crops all burnt up, are they?" asked Simms, trying to look sympathetic and not grin.

"Ain't much left in the way of crops around here."

"Folks having to haul water, are they?"

"If they are I just wish you'd tell me where they're finding it."

"Ain't nobody much trying to raise crops around here no more. Folks in this section have done all give up farming just about."

"How much rainfall you folks had this year?"

"Oh, Lord, Mister, we done all just about forgot what rain

looks like, ain't that right, O.B.? When do you reckon was the last time we seen rain?"

"Well, let's see. I remember it was raining when my wife was fixing to have our last boy. The last boy, that is, not the girl. And only yesterday she had to warsh his mouth out with soap for using dirty talk. He's precocious, still that'll give you some idea."

"What did she use for water?" asked one of the others.

"Wellsir," said a third, "I have paid up to six bits a pint for it right on the streets of Delco. R. D. Blair, that's got that deep artesian well, why my godamighty he's made more money off of that thing than most men has off of oil wells. I've seen bottled water go for twenty-five cents one of them little bitty old Dixie cups full. It's got so around here we dilute our water with whiskey, stranger. Costs too derned much to drink it straight."

"Is it water you're talking about? Selling drinking water on the streets? In bottles? In paper cups? Like soda pop?"

"Naw, sir, not like soda pop. Soda pop don't cost but two bits a bottle. And if you take my advice you'll keep away from it. Won't nothing raise a thirst like a bottle of that damn pop. Worse than salted peanuts."

"Well! I thought I'd seen dry sections of the country before, but this sure beats them all."

"Yes, Lord, I reckon the man that comes up with a way to turn crude oil into drinking water will make him a killing here in Texas."

"I hear they're fixing to bring it out in powdered form soon now."

"Fixing to bring what out in powder form, Gus?"

"Water. Powdered water. Dehydrated. When you're ready to use it you take and mix it with a little water. They say it makes a pretty fair substitute. Tastes a little flat, they say, but does all right for mixing."

"Lord, what won't they think of next, eh?"

It was true what those men said, people thereabouts had all given up farming; but drought was not their reason. They did not need to farm, not with oil wells pumping away in front and back yards and stretching away over former cotton fields for as far as a man could see. If they needed water it was not for the sake of their crops. They could use some to float those cabin cruisers in the one-time lakes that Simms passed. A bit for an occasional bath, maybe, and to water their flowerbeds. Mainly to wash those big Cadillacs and Packards and Pierce-Arrows that stood, sometimes double-parked, outside their cabin doors. They could pay for it, too, as no dirt farmer worried about his crops and his thirsty livestock could ever afford to pay. So in the hardware store in Delco, Simms said to the clerk, "Housepaint. Want some housepaint. Gimme a gallon of the white, quart of red, quart of yellow, quart of blue, and a pint-size can of aluminum. Don't bother to wrap them."

V

The day fixed upon for his performance was just the worst sort of day. With no assistance from Prof. Simms, the sky had clouded over and now thunder commenced to rumble. It was going to rain. You could smell it, could read the signs: birds bunched together along electric wires, leaves of trees showing their undersides, smells sharpening, sounds deepening. After three unbroken years of drought, today it was going to rain, and before he could lay claim to it. He pitched in frantically, trying to get set up and going before it actually started coming down, make it look as if he had a little something to do with it; but even as he tore around, the first drops fell, fat warm drops that struck the hard, unabsorbent earth with a *spat* and scattered in droplets like quicksilver. Prof. Simms only hoped there were others in the audience like the one he overheard say, "Well, if this feller ain't a cutter! He don't even hardly have to do nothing to make it rain, does he?"

The elevation this time was the tower of the county courthouse, seven stories tall. The crowd, biggest he had ever drawn, was gathered on the courthouse grounds. It was to have been the grandest production Prof. Simms had ever staged: a Texas-sized production—was he not being paid a Texas-sized fee? What a stupendous plan he had devised for the dynamite blasts! What a store of skyrockets he had provided! Magnet, inconsiderately tossed inside the van by the mob at Arrowhead, had been refurbished, improved by the addition of a spark-plug tester and something else found on the town dump which Prof. Simms judged to be part of the works of an X-ray machine, and which, when a current was sent through it, reacted with a most impressive crackle. He had been looking forward to the show himself. Was anything on earth as undependable as the weather?

There was no postponing it: no rainchecks on a rainmaking. The timing was set. Ready or not, rain or shine, on the stroke of ten from the courthouse clock things would get under way with a bang. Four bangs, to be exact.

Observing that the signs looked promising, Prof. Simms, face dripping, soaked to the skin, began his address to the crowd. He disavowed magic and mystery. His was a science, he said, and science—here he had to raise his voice to make himself heard above the patter—had no secrets. It was coming down harder every moment as he explained the origin and composition of raindrops, the need to raise some dust. The clock overhead wound itself up to strike. Prof. Simms brought down his upraised hand and the earth shook as sixty sticks of dynamite, fifteen to each of four charges, went off outside the city limits. But instead of the cloud of dust that was to have arisen, down fell a torrent of rain.

Just my luck, thought Prof. Simms, looking down from the top of the courthouse steps upon the umbrellas popping up like mushrooms all over the grounds. Maddening to think that those umbrellas, faded from disuse, dotted with holes, had been brought there out of faith in his powers. His hand stole to his pocket and fondled regretfully the fat roll of bills nestled there. For a moment he toyed with the thought of absconding with it. For only a moment, though; then he remembered the tales he had always heard about Texans, how mean they were, how dangerous it was to trifle with one of them. In tones forlorn he silently chanted, "Rain, rain, go away, come again another day, little Orville wants to play."

"Will wonders never cease!" Prof. Simms exclaimed to himself when the rain promptly complied with his request. The sky brightened by several shades. It was probably as well, however, that precipitation did not cease entirely, just slackened off to a steady drizzle; for Prof. Simms was not there to prevent rain, after all, as to some credulous minds he might appear to have done. Moreover, this was only a lull in the storm; from the west fresh battalions of clouds were moving up, dark as the one in the sign on his van. Could he—perhaps by dropping one act, say the skyrockets, from his program—be ready for it when it got there? Nothing ventured, nothing gained.

In his race against the advancing storm clouds, Prof. Simms explained the molecular structure of water while at the same time inflating his balloons. For the occasion three instead of the usual one marksman were recruited and armed with rifles. The first release of balloons numbered nine, in proportions proper to the valence of the elements. But before a shot could be fired, even as the word "Fire!" was already in Prof. Simms's mouth, such a cloudburst poured down it was enough to make a person wonder whether God had broken the promise He made to Noah of old.

This was no passing shower, this was the real thing, good for all day and into the night, if Prof. Simms was any judge. "Well, old hoss," he consoled himself, "you did your best. The elements were against you. Better luck next time." Giving the bankroll one last feel, peering through the gaps in the curtain of rain, he searched the crowd for the faces of the men with whom he had contracted for today's performance, intending to refund their money. He could not discover them. What Prof. Simms discovered instead was one of those insights that can change the lives of men and alter the shape of history. He saw all those faces looking up at him, streaming wet, waiting patiently to see what he was going to do next, cupping their ears to hear him, hushing up their children whining to be taken in out of the wet, their heads still nodding in conviction, comprehension of his last-spoken words. Modesty, and a lifelong inclination to think too well of people, almost made Prof. Simms deny the moment of his greatness. Nobody could be that stup— Through a momentary parting in the curtain, he looked again. You could have heard a pin drop in the silence of Prof. Simms's mind.

"*Orville, my friend,*" he said to himself in an awestruck whisper, *"if you had just half the belief in yourself these folks have in you, you could be governor of this state."*

By seven o'clock in the evening the county records had been twice removed: first from the flooded basement to the ground floor, thence to the second floor of the courthouse. Since half past four the building had been without electricity, at six telephone service was disrupted. To have stepped outdoors would have been to commit suicide by drowning; therefore those who had taken shelter and were now trapped inside were resigned to going supperless and to spending the night sleeping on the floors, the women and children in the offices, the courtrooms, and the judges' chambers, the men in the corridors.

By that hour Prof. Simms had for some while felt himself to be the target of resentful looks and the subject of discontented mutterings. So when the committee of three men who had contracted with him for his services came seeking him out, he was expecting them. One look at their faces and Prof. Simms thought he detected the odor of warm tar, and he felt himself break out all over in goose feathers.

"Well, Professor!" said the first man, and stood waiting for an answer. He was a burly six-footer whose bone-crushing grip Prof. Simms remembered from the handshake with which they had sealed their agreement.

"Kind of let things get out of hand, ain't you, Professor?" said the second.

"Rain, we said," said the third. "But this—!"

All were silent, Prof. Simms in expectation of violence, they awaiting some practical proposal from him. This was revealed when, none forthcoming, they made their own. Speaking one after the other, the three said:

"So without further ado, maybe you better climb back up the tower—"

"—and put that machine of yours into rearverse gear—"

"—and de-magnetize things, 'fore you drownd us all."

He had learned his lesson, and in commending himself to his Maker, here is what Prof. Simms said:

"Dear Lord, listen to a con man's prayer. Looking to the future

—if I am allowed to have any—please show me the way to some other part of Your creation where You distributed a little bit more sense. Some place where—how does it go?—where you can fool some of the people all of the time and all of the people some of the time, but deliver me, Lord, from a place where you can fool all of the people all of the time. Amen."

VI

The river, after three days and nights, had returned to its banks and on both sides the roads to the ferry landing were now passable. But anybody who thought he was going to buck that current for fifty cents or for that matter fifty dollars had another think coming to him. They could sit there honking till their arms dropped off.

A ferryman's life was just one blamed thing after another. A week ago you couldn't see to blow your nose for the dust; now this. Not a drop of rain for three blessed years, then all of a sudden floods. It was like God had been out of the office all that while and returned to find all those prayers for rain piled up on His desk. It did seem like He might have used a little better judgment than to answer them all at once.

What a time it had been! Rain rain rain—you couldn't see to blow your nose for the rain. River rising and the banks crumbling in, levees washing out. Cabins coming floating down, some with families sitting on the rooftops, black and white, men, women, children, babies at the breast, old grandfolks. One with a nanny goat astraddle of the peak. Later, town shanties with street numbers on the doors. Trees. Wagonbeds. Chicken coops. Barrels. Cows. Hogs. Mules. And there were people who expected him to ferry them across this! Like the one idiot this morning who came dashing up, said he just had to get over to Texas, and asked how much it would cost. "Two hundred dollars," he had replied. "Then you'll own the boat and can ferry your own self across." Like that one in the truck over there right now—truck or van, bus, whatever the hell it was, with a sign painted on its side—honking as if his life depended on it.

The Pump

FOR WEEKS Jordan Terry had been down on his knees promising God to drink the first barrelful if only they would go on drilling and not give up; but they were about ready to haul out the rig and call it another dry hole, when at fifty-nine hundred feet they brought in a gusher. Jordan was digging turnips in a field that he was being paid by the government not to grow anything on when he got the news, and though he went out and drank a barrelful all right, it wasn't oil.

A day or so later old Jordan was rocking on his front porch and smoking a White Owl when he saw a couple of men of the drilling crew up on top of his derrick with hammers and crowbars taking it apart. Barefoot as he was he jumped out of his rocker and tore down to see what the hell was going on. They told him they were fixing to cap his well.

"Cap it?" cried Jordan with a white face. "Put ere a cap on it? Why? For God's sake, Misters, let her come! Don't go a-putting ere a cap on it!"

They explained that the derrick was just for the drilling. Like a pile driver. There was no further need of it now. They were fixing to install a pump.

"Pump? What do we need ere a pump for?" asked Jordan, remembering how it had shot up in the air, like Old Faithful. "The way it spurted out?"

"It's like opening a bottle of beer, ol' hoss," said the chief engineer. "That first little bit that foams over comes by itself. The rest you have to work for."

Work! Hah! Set on your ass in a rocking chair and knock down two bits on every barrelful! That kind of work suited old Jordan to a tee.

So the derrick was dismantled and taken away and in its stead the pump was set up. It was like an off-balance seesaw, a beam the size of a crosstie set off-center in the notch of an upright post. To either end of the beam was attached a rod which disappeared into the ground. Up and down it went, up and down, bowing in frenzied, untiring obeisance. Yes, sir, it said to Jordan, you're the boss! Yes, sir, you're the boss! Yes, sir! Listening with your ear to the ground you could hear, or could fancy that you did, a sound like a seashell makes, of endless vast waves lapping the shores of a vast underground sea. And in the pipe you could hear the mighty surge, like the pulse of a great artery drawing up a steady stream of rich, black blood. Day and night the pump went, night and day, working for him: rocket-a-bump, rocket-a-bump, rocket-a-bump. . . . In the daytime it went at about the same trot that Jordan went at in his rocking chair, at night as he lay awake grinning in the dark each stroke of the cycle matched a beat of his heart: rocket-a-bump, rocket-a-bump, rocket-a-bump. . . .

"How much you reckon she draws every time she goes up and down?" he asked the engineers.

They told him how many barrels it pumped per day. Jordan worked it out from there. He wanted to know just how much he was worth by the minute, how much richer he had grown with each rock of his rocker, each beat of his heart. He got twenty-five cents a barrel. A barrel held fifty-five gallons. It averaged twenty-five strokes a minute. Call it half a cent a stroke. Rocket-a-bump: half a cent. Rocket-a-bump: that makes a penny. Rocket-a-bump, rocket-a-bump—the last thing he heard at night, the first thing he heard in the morning. Sixty times twenty-five was fifteen hundred. Twenty-four times fifteen hundred times three hundred and sixty-five . . .

Jordan—though he was far from being its first owner—had for some years been driving a 1921 Durant. Driving it, that is to say, whenever it felt like going. And only now did he possess somewhere about the amount of oil it demanded. Naturally a man in his position couldn't be seen around in that old flivver anymore. As even the hungriest car dealer was not going to allow him anything for it on a trade-in, it occurred to Jordan that he would be doing a mighty fine deed by making a present of it to his next-door neighbor, Clarence Bywaters. Poor son of a bitch. It must be hard on a man to have oil struck right next door to you. Like a canary bird in a cage hung out of a window, and having to watch a fat sassy old blue jay hopping about in the trees and plucking juicy worms out of the ground. They had begun drilling on poor old Clarence's land even before Jordan's, and they were still at it, but only because they had poured so much money down that dry hole that they just hated to call it quits. They were talking about pulling out any day now. Jordan remembered what he had gone through. He didn't think Bywaters would take exception to his offer. Poor son of a bitch, with all that raft of kids he wasn't in any position to despise a little charity.

Delivery on a new Duesenberg, especially one with as many custom accessories as Jordan had put in for, took some time. Meanwhile he still went about in the old Durant. He hadn't gotten around to giving it to Clarence Bywaters when the news broke one morning that they had brought in a gusher on his neighbor's holdings.

Jordan Terry was not the sort to begrudge another his good fortune. Christ, he had his! He went over and took Clarence Bywaters by the hand and congratulated him. He could not help mentioning his intention to have given him the Durant; but, rather to his irritation, Bywaters thought it was an even better joke than he did. He got fifty dollars' allowance on it (not that he needed the damned fifty dollars, but them that had it never got it by throwing any away) by threatening to cancel the order on his new Duesenberg.

It looked like a Pullman car. And it turned out to use a bit more gas and oil than the Durant. But what the hell! If there was one thing he had plenty of that was it. While he was out burning it up in those twelve big-bore cylinders, back home that little old pump, going steady as the heart in his breast, was bringing up more. And at night while the car rested, and after he himself had been lulled to sleep by that sweet cradlelike rhythm, the pump worked on, rocket-a-bump, rocket-a-bump, rocket-a-bump. . . .

One day the man who maintained the pump, on one of his periodical visits, happened to let drop something which suggested that both Jordan's and his neighbor's wells were drawing upon the same subterranean pool.

"You mean," cried Jordan with a white face, "you mean that son of a bitch is tapping onto my oil?"

What could he do about it? Nothing! Couldn't he go to law? He had got there first. Didn't a man have no rights? Couldn't they do something? Install a second pump? Replace this one with a bigger, stronger, faster one? Sink a thicker pipe? Christ, wasn't there nothing could be done to stop him, keep ahead of him, get it before he took it all?

But they didn't care, the oilmen. The same company (a Yankee outfit) had drilled both wells, his and his neighbor's. They were getting theirs on both sides of the fence, the sons of bitches. What the hell did they care which of them got more on his royalty check? It was all one and the same to them.

Jordan tried to visualize the lake of oil deep underground. It seemed to have shrunk. It had seemed bigger before, when he had thought of it as lying just under his own thirty acres, than it did now that he must think of it as extending also under his neighbor's forty-odd. Twelve acres more of it that damned Bywaters had than he had! To think there was a time when he could have bought him out at fifteen dollars an acre! A piddling six hundred dollars! Christalmighty, he spent more than that a week now. To be sure, at the time he didn't have six dollars cash money, much less six hundred, and wouldn't have spent it on Clarence Bywaters's forty acres of dust and erosion if he had had. It was enough to bring on heart failure when Jordan recalled that he had countered Bywaters's price by offering to sell out to him at ten an acre.

They had had to drill deeper on his neighbor's land. Did that mean that it was shallower on his side, that his oil was draining downhill into Bywaters's deeper pool? Was he just on the edge of it and Bywaters sitting in the middle? Since they had had to drill deeper that meant that his neighbor had a longer pipe. Jordan pictured the two of them underground, both sucking away, and the level of the pool dropping lower and lower, and suddenly his pipe made a sound like a soda straw makes at the bottom of the glass when the ice-cream soda is all gone. But his neighbor's pipe went on sucking greedily away.

The sound of his neighbor's pump, now that he knew it was pumping *his* oil, was like the steady drip of a leaky faucet: Jordan couldn't not hear it. Rocket-a-bump, rocket-a-bump, rocket-a-bump, all day long and into the night, growing louder and louder, drowning out nearer sounds, including that of his own pump.

Once Jordan's pump stopped. He was lying in bed one night, sweating, tossing, the pounding of his neighbor's pump like a migraine headache, hating his wife for her deep untroubled sleep at his side, when suddenly his pump stopped. That was his own damned heart he heard, his pump had stopped. He leaped out of bed, ignoring his wife's sleepy, questioning whine, and dashed outdoors in his BVD's. It was going. Thank God, it was going. The relief was almost more than Jordan could stand. But wasn't it going slower, weaker? It seemed to be going slower. Had it reached the bottom and was it having to strain to draw up the last little bit? Or was it only that his heart was beating so fast?

From that time on the rocket-a-bump, rocket-a-bump, instead of lulling Jordan to sleep at night, kept him awake, listening, afraid it was going to stop, uncertain whether it was his own he was hearing or his neighbor's. He had to give up rocking in his rocking chair: the noise it made interfered with his listening. He sat very still, listening. He was afraid to go off for a ride in his car for fear his pump might stop while he was gone. Sometimes at night, when at last out of exhaustion he dropped off and momentarily ceased to hear the fevered rhythm of his own pulse drum-

ming in his ear against his twisted and sweaty pillow, he awoke
with a jerk, sure that his pump had stopped, that it was the other
that he heard, and at such times as he bolted up in the darkness
his heart gasped and gurgled as if it had drawn up the very last
drop.

The bills for his new style of living began pouring in, bills of a
size to take your breath away, in numbers like germs. Debts
Jordan had always had, money to pay them with never before.
The one was real, the other just paper, something in a bank. He
lectured his wife and daughters on their extravagance. He reminded them how well they had always got by before without
jewels and permanent waves. How much money a rich man
needed!

Meanwhile that s.o.b. next door was really living high. Burning
up the road in a Graham roadster. A blowout every weekend.
Delivery vans from Ardmore and Oklahoma City pulling up to
the door all day long. And his womenfolks going around bundled
up in furs when it was a hundred and ten degrees in the shade,
looking like an escaped zoo. He was not economizing. Whenever
they met, Bywaters gave him such a glad hand and such a big fat
possum-eating grin that the conviction grew on Jordan's mind
that his neighbor was laughing at him. If Bywaters knew—and
how could he not know?—that they were both pumping out of the
same pool, it never fazed him. Which could only mean that he
somehow knew he was getting the lion's share.

Jordan was not the only one to notice those fur coats, those
delivery vans. Complaining that they were tackier now than when
they were poor, his wife and daughters whined at him from morn
till night. Clarence Bywaters now, his wife and daughters were
dressed as women in their position ought to be. Were the Bywaters any better off than they were? And they would catalog the
finery which Mrs. Bywaters and each of the Bywaters girls had
worn to church that morning. As if Jordan hadn't seen! As if it
wasn't him who was paying for every stitch of all those gladrags!
How could he afford to deck out his own women when it was him
who was outfitting Bywaters's like four grand duchesses?

Often poor Jordan chewed the bitter cud of that moment when
his neighbor had offered to sell out to him. The scene was vivid in

his mind. He saw Bywaters's furrowed brow, saw him stroke his stubbly chin, saw his head shake, heard him say, "It's a dog's life. Crops burning up. Soil all blown away. Cotton selling for nothing. If I could just raise the money I'd leave tomorrow. You know anybody that'll give me fifteen an acre?" Jordan had laughed. Oh, how he wished he had it to do over again! Surely he could have raised six hundred dollars if he had only tried. He could have borrowed that on his own place. It already had a first lien on it, but he could have got a second. Oh, why had he let that golden opportunity slip? Then all seventy-two acres of that lake of oil would have been his, both those pumps his alone. These days to lay his hands on six hundred dollars all he had to do was reach in his pocket. He saw himself doing so. He saw Bywaters's face break into a grateful smile, felt the grateful pressure of his hand. His heart melted with pity for his neighbor, poor son of a bitch, and with the warmth of its own generosity. "California, here I come!" said Bywaters, hope shining like a rainbow through the tears brimming in his eyes. "Best of luck, ol' hoss," Jordan said. "I'll miss you." From this dream he was awakened by the throb of his neighbor's pump.

To wash the bitter taste from his mouth Jordan would take a pull at the bottle, drinking red whiskey now instead of white, his sole extravagance. Presently, despite himself, he would slip into another reverie. Rocking faster and faster as the figures mounted, he would calculate how much ahead he would be if his neighbor's pump was to break down, be out of commission for a week, ten days, two weeks. A month. Two months! Three! By then he was rocking so fast that when he caught himself and slowed down he was out of breath and panting, in a sweat. All he had succeeded in doing was in figuring how much his neighbor was making every minute. Then he would feel the hairs on the nape of his neck rise up and tingle as though someone was watching him.

Then Jordan knew he was in for it, and his heart seized with dread. For any misfortune wished upon another is a boomerang, it circles back and hits you. A man can't think one mean thought, not even in a whisper, not even alone in a dark room at night or down in a cave deep in the earth, without Him hearing it and visiting it right back on you. Once a thought has been thought there is no calling it back. It goes out on the air like the radio waves, with the thinker's name all over it. He gets a whiff and says, "Who made that bad smell?" He looks down, right at you, and grabs you by the scruff of the neck and rubs your nose in your own mess.

So it was bound to happen. Try as he might to unwish the wish that his neighbor's pump might fail, Jordan went right on wishing it. So it was only a matter of time until his own broke down. Really. Not just a false alarm. And who knew for how long? Two weeks? Not likely! He had wished three months against Bywaters.

As is so often the case in such matters, for all his anxiety, Jordan was unaware of it when it befell. He had lain awake that night listening so intently to the hateful sound of his neighbor's pump that he didn't not hear his. Or maybe he fondly imagined that it was Bywaters's which had stopped, permitting him to fall asleep at last. The silence awoke him early next morning: steady, throbbing silence, and, in the background, Bywaters's pump going double time. He went out on the porch and looked. The beam hung down as if it had been pole-axed.

Jordan called the Company, his wife called the doctor. Keep him in bed and away from drink, the doctor advised; but he was no sooner gone than Jordan was out on the front porch rocking nervously and drinking steadily as he awaited the repairmen. It was midmorning before they showed up, nearly noon before the one sent for the replacement part got back.

"Have her going for you again in no time now, Colonel," they said.

But they fiddled and laid down their tools to talk and roll and smoke cigarettes and dawdled in the shade over their lunch and started looking at their watches half an hour before quitting time, and by then Bywaters's pump was going in jig time. So was Jordan in his rocker, until all of a sudden he came to a dead stop. He was still warm when they got to him but it was as if rigor mortis had set in while he was still alive. They had to pry him loose from that chair, and getting him into his coffin was like straightening a bent nail.

There is nothing on earth as dry as a handful of red Oklahoma dirt, though deeper down may lie an ocean of black gold. They crumbled their handfuls over Jordan Terry and shook their heads. A crying shame, said Jordan's lifelong friend and neighbor Clarence Bywaters as they were leaving the graveyard, a crying shame the poor son of a bitch had only lived to enjoy his wealth such a little while.

A Voice from the Woods

"Ssh! Listen," says my wife. "You hear? Listen."

"What?" says my mother.

"Hear what?" say I.

"Ssh! There. Hear it? An owl. Hooting in the daytime."

Then I do hear: a soft hollow note, like someone blowing across the lip of a jug: *hoo-oo, hoo-hoo-hoo; hoo-oo, hoo-hoo-hoo* . . .

A ghostly sound, defying location, seeming in successive calls to come out of the woods from all points of the compass. Near at hand one moment, far away and faint the next, barely audible, the echo of an echo. It is not an owl. Yet it cannot be what it is. Not here. So far from home. It comes again, this time seeming to sound not outside me but inside myself, like my own name uttered in a once-familiar, long-dead voice, and my mother says, "Owl? That's no owl. Why, it's a—"

"A mourning dove!" say I.

It is the sound, the solitary sound, save for the occasional buzz, like an unheeded alarm clock, of a locust, of the long hot somnolent summer afternoons of my Texas boyhood, when the cotton fields shimmered white-hot and in the black shade of the pecan trees bordering the fields the Negro pickers lay napping on their sacks and I alone of all the world was astir, out with my air rifle hunting doves I never killed, gray elusive ghosts I never could locate. I would mark one down as it settled in a tree (I remember the finicking way they had of alighting, as if afraid of soiling their feet), and would sneak there and stand listening, looking up into the branches until I grew dizzy and confused. I would give up and move on, and at my back the bird would come crashing out of the branches sounding its other note, a pained squeak, and wobble away in drunken flight and alight in another tree and resume its plaint. They favored cedars, at least in my memory, and cedars in turn favored burial grounds, so that I think of the dove's whispered dirge as the voice of that funereal tree. It would be one of those breathless afternoons when the sun cooked the resin from the trunks of pines and sweet-gums and the air was heavy, almost soporific with the scent. Heat waves throbbed behind the eyes. The fields were empty, desolate. High overhead a buzzard wheeled. The world seemed to have died, and in the silence the dove crooned its ceaseless inconsolable lament: *hoo-oo, hoo-hoo-hoo; hoo-oo, hoo-hoo-hoo* . . .

"A what? Mourning dove?" my wife says. "I never knew we had them here." *Here* being among the budding sugar maples and the prim starched white paper birches in the bustle and thaw of a crisp New England spring.

"I never knew you did either," says my mother. "What is a mourning dove doing way off up here?"

"What are you doing way off up here?" I say.

For my mother, too, has left Texas, lives out in Indianapolis. Now she has come on her annual visit to us. We sit on the sun porch, rushing the season a bit. As always, we two have fallen to reminiscing of Blossom Prairie and our life there before my father's death, telling stories by the hour which both of us have heard and told so often now that it is the rhythm which stirs us more than the words, our tongues thickening steadily until the accent is barely intelligible to my Yankee wife, who listens amused, amazed, bewildered, bored, and sometimes appalled.

"Son, do you remember," my mother says, "the time the bank was held up?"

I am still listening to the dove, and I have to ask her what she said. But now she is listening to the dove and does not hear me.

"The time the bank was held up? No, I don't remember that. First time I ever heard of it."

"Hmm? What did you say? First time you ever heard of what?"

"Of the bank being held up. The bank in Blossom Prairie?"

"Really? Oh, you remember such funny things! Old Finus, that used to come around to the house every afternoon selling hot tamales. Why anybody should clutter up their memory with him, I don't know! Lord, I would never have given him another thought this side of the grave. And not remember the great bank robbery! You were old enough. You remember lots of things that happened long before that. I took you with me, and we saw the dead men lying on the sidewalk on the square. You've forgotten that?"

"Dead men? Lying on the sidewalk? On the square? What dead men?"

"The bank robbers. All shot dead as they came out of the bank. You don't remember?"

"What!" says my wife. "You took a child to see a sight like—"

"That's the kind of thing I remember! Not an old boy who used to come around crying, 'Hot tamales!' Why, that was just about the biggest thing that ever happened in Blossom Prairie, I should think."

I open more cans of beer, and she drinks and sets down the can and wipes her lips and says, "Well, it was back in the bad old days. When lots of men were out of work and some of the young ones, who had all cut their teeth on a gun, took to living by it. The age of the great outlaws, when we had Public Enemy Number One, Two, Three. In our parts Pretty Boy Floyd was carrying on. And Clyde Barrow and Bonnie Parker."

"Did Clyde and Bonnie stick up the bank in Blossom Prairie?"

"No, no, it wasn't them. But it was in those days and times. No, the ones that stuck up the bank in Blossom Prairie—"

"Wait. Who was Pretty Boy Floyd?" asks my wife. "Who were Clyde Barrow and Bonnie Parker?"

"You never heard of them?" asks my mother, wiping away her mustache of suds.

"Now we will never get the story of the Blossom Prairie bank robbery," say I.

"Never heard of Clyde Barrow and Bonnie Parker? Never even heard of Pretty Boy Floyd?"

"Pretty Boy!" my wife laughs. "Pretty Boy!"

"Clyde Barrow," I say, "was a notorious outlaw, and Bonnie Parker his gun moll. They came out of West Dallas, the real low-down tough section of the town. They tore around sticking up banks and filling stations and honky-tonks, and between them shot and killed any number of bank tellers and gas-pump operators and law officers in Texas in the early thirties. We used to follow the exploits of Clyde and Bonnie in the newspapers every day, like keeping up with the baseball scores. We really cannot claim Pretty Boy Floyd. He was an Oklahoma hero."

"You're making fun," says my mother. "Well, no doubt they did a lot of bad things, but let me tell you, hon"—this to her daughter-in-law—"you can go back down there and out in the country and to this day you'll find a many an old farmer will tell you he was proud to give Pretty Boy Floyd a night's lodging when the law was hounding him down like a poor hunted animal, and more than likely they found a twenty-dollar bill under his breakfast plate after he had left the next morning. And he never got that nickname for nothing. Oh, he was a good-looking boy!"

"Well, what about the ones that held up the bank in Blossom Prairie?"

"He was a good-looking boy, too. All three of them were."

"She just never could resist an outlaw," I say.

The dove calls again, and my wife says, "What a sad, lonesome sound. I hope she doesn't come to nest around here. I wouldn't like to listen to that all day."

"As a matter of fact," says my mother, "as a matter of fact, I knew one of them. Travis Winfield, his name was. He was the leader of the gang. You wouldn't remember the Winfields, I don't suppose? Lived in that big old yellow frame house beyond the bridge out on the old McCoy road? A wild bunch, all of those Winfields, the girls as well as the boys, but good-looking, all of them, and Travis was the best-looking, and the wildest, of the lot. Well, anyway. One day when you were—oh, let's see, you must have been six or seven, which would make it—how old are you now, hon, thirty-eight?"

"Seven."

"Thirty-seven?"

"Yes'm."

"Are you sure?"

"I *was.* Aren't you?"

"Oh, you! Well, anyway, it was during the summer that you had your tonsils and adenoids out. Remember? We were living at the time in Mr. Early Ellender's little cottage out on College Avenue. I had that little old Model-A Ford coupé that your daddy had bought me."

"Was there a college in Blossom Prairie?" my wife asks.

"No!"

"Well, you were just getting over that operation, and that's how you happened to be at home at the time and not off somewhere or other out of call. I remember I was fixing dinner when the telephone rang. . . . No, honey, there wasn't any college in Blossom Prairie. It was just a little bitty old place—though it was the county seat, and we all thought we were really coming up in the world when we left the farm and moved into town. It was so little that his daddy used to come home for his dinner every day. What you call lunch. . . . Well, the telephone rang and it was Phil. 'Hop in your car and come right down!' he said. 'They've just shot and killed three men robbing the bank!' "

"Then why was it called College Avenue? That doesn't make much sense."

"Don't ask me. I just grew up there."

"Well, but didn't it ever occur to you to wonder why they would call it that when there wasn't any—"

"Now, here is what had happened. These four men—"

"Three, you just a minute ago said."

"I said three were killed. These four men had been camping out down in Red River Bottom and— However, I better start with the woman. There was this woman, see. She had come into town about a month before. A stranger. She took a house, and she gave herself out to be a widow woman interested in maybe settling in the town and opening some kind of business with the money her husband had left her. And she had had a husband, all right, but she was no widow, nor even a grass widow. That came out at the trial. In fact, her husband showed up at the trial. When the judge sentenced her to eighteen years in the penitentiary this man stood up in the courtroom and said, 'Mildred! I'll still be waiting for you!' And she said, 'You'll wait a lot longer than any eighteen years!' And as they were taking her away he yelled, 'Mildred! Darling! I forgive you!' Meaning he forgave her for leaving him and running off with Travis. And that she-devil turned and told him I-can't-tell-you-what that he could do with his such-and-such forgiveness, right there in front of the judge and jury and the whole town and county. And still the poor fool did not give up but went round to the jailhouse and yelled up at the window of her cell until finally she came to the bars. And do you know what she told him was the one thing he could do that might win her back?—and this, you understand, would be after waiting for her to come out of the penitentiary for eighteen years. To get a gun and go shoot the one that had told on them to the law and had got the lover that she had run off with killed. However, it was not him that did it."

"That did what? Wait. I don't—"

"She was a cutter! Well, shortly after coming to town she went to the bank one day and opened an account. The very next day she was back and said she had changed her mind and wanted to draw her money out. They asked her why, and she said she had had her money in a bank once that had been held up, and she seemed to imply that that bank had looked a lot stronger than what she saw of ours. This piqued the manager, and he took her on a tour of the place to convince her that her money was safe with them, showing her all the strong vaults and the time locks and the burglar-alarm system and how it worked and whatnot. Besides, he said, there had never been any bank robberies in Blossom Prairie. So he convinced her, and she said she would let her money stay. After that she would come in every so often and make a deposit or a withdrawal, and she got to know the layout of the bank. She was making a map of it at home, and after each trip she would go and fill it in some more and correct any mistakes she had made in it. That way, too, she came to know when the big deposits were made by the business firms and the big-scale farmers and when there was always the most cash on hand in the bank.

"Meanwhile, she wasn't spending much time in that house in town. She told her neighbors—and of course they told everybody and his dog—that she still hadn't made up her mind to settle in Blossom Prairie and was looking over other spots around the county before deciding. She was seen on the road a lot, and she was a demon at the wheel. I was a pretty hot driver my own self, but—"

"Was! You still are. You scare me half to death."

"Well, that redheaded woman handled a car like no other woman and few men that I ever saw. In town she would spread her shopping over all the grocery stores so it wouldn't look like she was buying more food than a lone woman could eat, and she bought a good deal of bootleg liquor too, it came out later, and she would fill up the car and slip off down to Red River Bottom where Travis and his gang were camped out, though of course nobody knew that at the time. Whenever any squirrel hunter would happen to come up on them Travis kept out of sight, as he was the only local boy among them, and the other three made out that they were a hunting party too.

"Travis had been gone from home for some years, and everybody had pretty well forgotten him, except for maybe a couple of dozen girls who would have liked to but couldn't. Word would get back every now and again of some trouble he had gotten into and gotten himself out of. Now he had rounded up this gang and come back to rob the bank in his old home town. But though he had grown up there, he had to have that woman, or somebody, to draw him a map of the bank, for I don't suppose poor Travis had ever set foot in it in his life.

"All the while that he was holing up down there in the woods laying his plans Travis had living with him in that tent, and eating and drinking with him, one man who was in constant touch with the sheriff. He had told him all about that woman and about that map she was drawing of the bank and every little detail and switch in their plans. Imagine it? Living with three men for a whole month and letting on to be their friend, listening to them plan how they'll do this and do that to get the money and make their getaway, and knowing all the while that they were walking into a death trap that he himself had set, for pay, and that they were doomed to die as surely as if he himself had pulled the trigger on them? I'm not saying that what they were meaning to do was right, you understand. But can you just feature a skunk like that?

"I and Phil must have been just about the only people in town that didn't know the bank was set to be robbed that Monday morning. The sheriff had gone out and hired eight extra deputies, old country boys, good shots, squirrel hunters, and had them waiting, each with a thirty-thirty rifle, on the roofs of the buildings on each corner across the street from the bank, the old Ben Milam Hotel and the other, well, office buildings, stores downstairs on the street and doctors' and lawyers' offices upstairs, four stories high. The tellers in the bank had all been told not to put up any resistance but to give them what they asked for, to fill up their sacks for them, they'd have it all right back. The tip-off man was to wear something special. I seem to recall he wore a sailor straw hat, so they would recognize him and not shoot him.

"You remember, the bank in Blossom Prairie sits on the northwest corner of the square. The street that goes out to the north, Depot Street, goes past the cotton compress and over the tracks and past the ice house and towards the river. That would be the street they would come in on. The one going out to the west went past your daddy's shop and over the creek and on out of town in the direction of Paris. Down this street that morning, headed towards the square, came a wagon loaded high with baled hay. On the wagon seat, dressed up in overalls and a twenty-five-cent hardware-store straw hat, sat Sheriff Ross Shirley, and under the seat lay a sawed-off pump shotgun. At twenty minutes to eleven he set his team in motion with a flick of the reins. A moment later a car came round the corner and pulled up alongside the curb, and four men got out and ducked into the bank. As soon as they were inside, the sheriff says 'Come up' to his team, and up on the rooftops the rifle barrels poke over the walls and point down, followed by the heads of those eight deputies. The woman was driving, and she stayed in the car, keeping the engine idling. The wagon came down the street towards her, rattling over those old *bois-d'arc* paving bricks, until it got to just a little ways in front of the car. There suddenly the left rear wheel flew off the axle, the load of hay came tumbling down, scattering clear across the street, bales bouncing and breaking apart, the street completely blocked. The woman in the car made a sudden change in plans. She threw into reverse and backed around the corner into Depot Street, thinking that now, instead of going out by the Paris road, they would have to cross the square and go out by the southwest. Then she sees ahead of her a man fixing a flat tire on a big delivery van out in the middle of the street halfway down the block. This meant, she thought, that she would have to cut diagonally across the square, through the traffic and around the plaza and out by the southeast corner. She didn't know it, but they had her cut off there, too. In another minute or so the men burst out of the bank carrying the sacks.

"The moment they stepped out the door it began to rain bullets on them. Those that were on the square at the time said it sounded like a thunderclap had broken overhead. You couldn't count the separate shots, they said. The bullets chewed holes in the cement sidewalk. The men must have all died in the first volley, but the deputies poured another round and then another into them as they went down. The fourth man had fallen a step behind, deciding not to trust everything to that sailor straw hat, maybe thinking they would just as soon not pay that reward, and when the noise broke he dove back into the bank. He had cast a quick look up above as he came out, and that woman in the car must have seen it. In any case, when he didn't come out with the rest a thousand things that she must have noticed at the time and shaken off suddenly added up like a column of figures in her mind. She didn't even try to run. She jumped out of the car and up onto the curb, swooped down and pried the pistol from the still-clutching hand of one of the bandits, and stepped over the body into the bank. By then the sheriff was one step behind her. He grabbed her and took the gun away from her and held her until help came. She was more than he could manage alone. They said it was all four big strong men could do to keep her from getting at that one and clawing his eyes out, and then when they dragged her outside she broke away and threw herself on the body in the doorway, crying, 'Travis! Travis! Speak to me,

Travis!' They had taken her away, and taken away the informer too and locked him up for his own protection by the time we got there, but the bodies were still lying on the sidewalk where they had fallen.''

"Taking a little six-year-old child to see a sight like that!" my wife says, shaking her head.

"It was a terrible sight to see. Three strong young men cut off in the very Maytime of life, shot down like mad dogs before they even knew what was happening to them. I was sorry I had come. I wasn't going to look any closer. I tried to back out of the crowd. Then Phil said, 'My Lord! Why, ain't that one there that Winfield boy, Travis?' Oh, what a funny feeling came over me when I heard Phil say that!''

"Why, had you known him pretty well?"

"Yes. In fact—well, in fact, I had gone with Travis Winfield for a time, before I married your daddy.''

"You had!"

"In fact, Travis Winfield had once asked me to marry him. He was not a bad boy then. Wild, yes, but not mean, not any gangster. I—I thought about it awhile before I turned him down. That stung him, and he didn't ask me a second time. I was just as glad. Oh, he was a good-looking boy! I don't know what I might have said a second time. Well, he had quickly forgotten about me and I had gone out with other boys and in time had met and married Phil, your daddy, and wasn't ever sorry that I had. But I want you to know I felt mighty queer standing there looking down at poor Travis—he was still handsome, even there in the dirt and all bloodied—lying on the common sidewalk with people staring at him, and thinking of that wild woman who had loved him so and had shared his wild life and now been dragged off to prison, and I was glad to have you there to hold on to. It was a comfort to me then to have my own child to hold on to his hand.''

Silence falls, and in it the dove utters again its dolorous refrain.

"My daddy and my brothers disapproved of Travis Winfield. I think—apart from the fact that I was infatuated with his reputation for wildness, and his good looks—I think I probably went with him mainly just to devil my brothers a bit, let them all worry over me a little maybe, at least give them some reason for all that concern over my reputation. I don't believe I was ever really serious about him, and I never thought he was serious about me, partly because there were already lots of stories of other girls he hadn't been serious over. So I was taken by surprise when he asked me that day to marry him. I told him I would give him my answer next week. I knew then what it would be, but I suppose I wanted a week of thinking of accepting what I knew I was going to turn down.

"You remember, honey, out back of my old home that little family graveyard where all my folks are buried? It was there that Travis Winfield proposed to me. I said to meet me there again next Sunday and I would give him my answer. I remember waiting for him to come. You know how still it can be on a farm on a Sunday afternoon. The only sound for miles around as I sat there waiting for him was the cooing of a dove. I sat there thinking, I'm going to turn him down, of course, but what if I was not to? What if I was to say yes? What would my life be like?

"There are people just born for trouble, you know; Travis Winfield was one of them. It was written all over him in letters like headlines. Wild. Stubborn. Headstrong. Full of resentment against those who had all the things he didn't have. Proud. Vain. Believing the world owed him a living for the sake of his pretty face. No one woman could ever hope to hold him for long. After a while she wouldn't even want to keep on trying, unless she was an utter fool. But certainly life with Travis wouldn't be dull. It would be different from life on the farm, or in Blossom Prairie in a bungalow that had to be swept out and dusted every day.

"But I knew what I was going to say, and I said it. And maybe Travis wasn't sorry to hear it. Maybe during the week he had begun to wish he hadn't asked me. Most likely it was just his pride. He wasn't used to having a girl say no to anything he wanted. In any case, he didn't ask me again, and I was glad he didn't. He just gave me a hot look and turned and left. After he was gone I sat there a long time listening to the mourning dove. I never saw him again until that day on the square. It's years now since I even thought of Travis Winfield. It was hearing that mourning dove that brought it all back to my mind."

We sit listening for some time to its call. Then something

alarms it, and though we do not see it, we hear the thrashing of its wings among the branches and its departing cry.

"Who did shoot the one who told?" I ask.

"Oh, yes, him. The trustees of the bank voted him a big reward, but he never got to spend it. They found him a week later floating in the river, though it was a wonder, with all the lead he had in him. It was generally known to be the work of that Winfield tribe, but they could never prove it. Never tried any too hard, I don't suppose."

I make a move to rise, but seeing her face I sit down again. Brushing back a strand of her cotton-white hair, my mother says, "Aren't people funny? There in his blood lay Travis, whom I had forgotten, dead, and deservedly so, I suppose, if any man deserves it. There was I, happy, with a good, loving husband and a decent home and a smooth, even life ahead of me and my own child's hand in mine. And yet, thinking of that redheaded woman —even then on her way to prison—I felt, well, I don't know what else to call it if not jealousy. Isn't that crazy? What did she have? Nothing, less than nothing, and I had everything. It only lasted a moment, you understand, yet it comes back to me even now, and if it wasn't jealousy, then I don't know what else to call it."

The Human Fly

In LATE August 1935 this advertisement appeared in our local weekly, the New Jerusalem, Texas, *Lariat and Northern Bee:*

GRIPPO
The Human Fly
He Defies the Law of Gravity
! ! ! ! ! !
On Saturday, October 5
The Great
GRIPPO
Relying Entirely Upon the Strength of His Own Two Hands
Unassisted and Unprotected by
Ropes, Belts, Spurs, Nets, or
Any Safety Devices
Whatsoever
Will Attempt to Scale the Walls and Tower of the
CANAAN COUNTY COURTHOUSE
(Eight Stories Tall)
! ! ! ! ! !
See Grippo Risk Life and Limb in His

DEATH-DEFYING ASCENT
! ! ! ! ! !
Can He Do It
? ? ? ?
Grippo Boasts
"The Building I Can't Climb Has Not Been Built!"
! ! ! ! ! !
Be On Hand for Whatever *May Be Fall*
! ! ! ! ! !
WARNING
Persons who have been Advised by Doctor
or Physician to Avoid Excitement are
Hereby Cautioned that they Attend at
THEIR OWN RISK
! ! ! ! ! !
This ad is your ticket of admission

My over-forty readers will surely remember the human flies. Younger ones, your parents will tell you that the human fly was a craze, like flagpole sitting, marathon dancing, of that desperate period the Great Depression.

Things were as desperate with us in New Jerusalem, Texas, as with others elsewhere in those times, and maybe a little more so; but we had no marathon dancing, no flagpole sitters. And although we had, in our courthouse, the building for it, we never expected to attract to us anything so exciting as a human fly.

New Jerusalem, it must be admitted, was and is rather off the beaten track. The town was not as big in 1935 as it had been in 1905, before Egyptian cotton cut so disastrously into the market for our one crop. An Egyptian will pick cotton for less pay even than a Negro. New Jerusalem had not grown as our grandfathers, the builders of our courthouse, so confidently envisaged it would.

So when in 1935, in the very depths of the Depression, our local Chamber of Commerce received a letter from this Grippo offering, upon a certain guarantee, to come to New Jerusalem and scale our courthouse, it seemed a blessing fallen from heaven. That year we seemed to have hit rock bottom. What the national Depression had left us, our regional dust storms had

taken from us. Trade was at a standstill, with merchants leaning in
their doorways or staring out their windows over the piles of
unsold goods, men long out of work beginning to mutter their
resentment, dangerously in need of some distraction. Our courthouse was just made for a human fly. People would flock to see
him. The day he came to town would see much money change
hands. To a man the C of C voted to accept his offer, assessed
themselves, and raised for Grippo his minimum purse. This was
rumored to be as much as one thousand dollars, which was a lot
more money in those days than it is now, and in New Jerusalem
still is. In return, as a matter of form, Grippo, or his heirs, agreed
to waive any claim upon the town in the event that he should,
while performing on municipal property, suffer any mishap.

During the five weeks that ticket-ad ran, the *Lariat and Northern
Bee*, as I, its owner, editor, and publisher, can avouch, sold more
copies than at any period in its previous, or subsequent, history.
"California" Stan Reynolds might say he wasn't going, but he was
the only person in New Jerusalem, or in all of Canaan County,
who wasn't. Which was right where Stan always stood vis-à-vis his
home town on everything: out in left field all by himself. Stan's
cantankerousness and lack of any civic sense—which is putting it
mildly—was what had earned him his nickname, "California."
That was meant to be derisive. Stan had been telling us for years
how he couldn't wait to shake the dust of New Jerusalem off his
heels; at last one day he announced his imminent departure for
California, the land of his dreams. In a small community it is a
great mistake to say a thing like that and then not do it. Especially
if like Stan, in making the announcement, you burn all your
bridges behind you by telling everybody exactly what you've
always thought of them. Stan got as far as Paris, forty-seven miles
west of here, on that and a couple of subsequent flights, and that
was as close as Stan ever got to California, or ever would now
that, as he himself publicly phrased it, he had saddled himself
with a wife, now that there were two kids with another on its way,
now that he was pushing thirty, and now that hard times were
upon us, it looked like, to stay. So we called him, in mockery of his
blighted dreams, "California," and he called us—whatever he
could lay tongue to. He was the town crab and killjoy, and when

he said he wasn't going he meant it. But if he thought he would be missed he was much mistaken. Everybody was tickled to hear that he would not be on hand to spoil the fun with his sour remarks the day Grippo came to town.

During the five weeks of mounting excitement from the time of the announcement to the great day itself the town took a fresh look at its courthouse. In the speculation that then went on about which face of the building Grippo would choose for his assault, the curbstone attorneys who occupied the benches around the courthouse lawn split into four parties each of which thought the other three were all plain lunatics, although the building was and is exactly the same on all four sides. During that period, as a contribution to the general interest aroused by the forthcoming event, the paper, drawing for material upon the files of the *Northern Bee* (which preceded the *Lariat*), ran a series of articles on the construction, architecture, and history of the courthouse. While doing research for an obituary this past week, we have had the occasion to reread that series. Briefly, what we said at the time was this.

The culture of small Southern towns like ours, we said, had been aptly called a Courthouse Culture. Certainly our courthouse, with its majestic steeple, visible on a clear day for forty miles in any direction, dominated New Jerusalem, despite the fact that it did not, as in many, if not most, Southern towns, occupy the center of the public square, but sat instead a block north of there in a spacious square of its own planted in leafy oaks and tall pecan trees. Constructed throughout of native Texas limestone, pitted like a Swiss cheese with impressions of marine fossils from the Jurassic and Pleistocene epochs, originally white, now mellowed to a pleasing soft cream color, the building had been begun in 1859 with the laying of the cornerstone. Interrupted by the War and the Reconstruction period, construction was resumed in 1878, completed, and the building formally dedicated with appropriate ceremonies still remembered by some of our senior citizens, in 1882.

The style of architecture we labeled Colonial Gothic, a characterization which the passage of years has brought no need to revise.

Originally the basement floor, now the county free schoolbook depository, had housed the prisoners awaiting trial in the court-rooms overhead. By 1885, however, the county crime rate having exceeded expectations, need was felt for more spacious quarters, and the present four-story jailhouse was erected on its site a block to the west. The ground floor, raised some ten feet off the ground, and reached by broad flights of stone steps on all four sides, each leading to arched double doors eighteen feet in height, was square in plan, buttressed at the corners. The second floor duplicated, on a one-quarter-reduced scale, the first. From the second floor the windowless tower rose one hundred and sixteen feet, exclusive of the weathervane, for an overall height of one hundred and sixty-eight feet. On each of the tower's four sides was a round white clock face three feet in diameter. Above the clock was an open lookout. Above the lookout the tower terminated in a tapered cupola which housed the clock bell.

The clock bell, which on still days could be heard and the strokes counted up to ten miles away, with its bass, even some-what solemn, but distinctly musical note, tolled every quarter hour beginning at 6 A.M. and going on until midnight, chiming four times for the quarter past, eight for the half, twelve for the three quarters, sixteen before the hour, and then the hour. This, the *Lariat and Northern Bee* informed its readers, added up to a total 877 chimes per day, 6,139 per week, 26,310 per month—taking thirty days as the average month—and finally, the stagger-ing figure of 320,105 chimes per year!

We omitted in our series to count the number of steps of the stairway inside the tower mounting to the lookout above the clock—and not being as young and spry now as we were then, we must beg to be excused from supplying the omission! But we did remind our readers that the stairway was there, open to the public admission-free, whereupon all of Canaan County, always excep-ting "California" Stan Reynolds, of course, made the climb, many of them, although native-born, for the first time. From the look-out the view over the flat, bare prairies which surround us is extensive in all directions on a clear day. All who made the ascent and looked to earth from that dizzying height roundly declared that nothing, not even a thousand dollars, could induce them to attempt to scale it with nothing but their own two hands. There were some then who opposed permitting even the Great Grippo to make the trial.

To arrive at the courthouse grounds by the hour they did on that Saturday morning, the fifth of October, some of the country people must have been traveling in their horse-drawn wagons since late the previous afternoon. They had begun to gather there by the light of the moon. By the time the clock sounded its first note of the day the lawn was already thronged. Cars with license tags from four surrounding counties were to be seen. Market Square as well as the public square being by then full, those arriving after six were obliged to take parking space wherever they could find it, some in residential streets as far distant as a mile's walk. In the public square bargain sales were announced in loud paint on the show windows of every store. Needless to say, these would open their doors for business only after Grippo's performance, as until then nobody would be doing any shopping, and the storekeepers and their employees were as eager as everybody else to see the show. By the time the clock struck seven the town, except for the courthouse lawn, was everywhere deserted and still. A thief could have walked off with the whole place unopposed, if he could have resisted the desire to see the human fly himself.

All eyes that day were turned steadily skywards. Indeed, for some time afterwards New Jerusalem and Canaan County, being accustomed in the pursuit of its ordinary daily occupations, such as plowing, cottonpicking, sweeping house, scrubbing clothes, et cetera, to an earthwards-inclined posture, was to suffer cricks in the neck in the proportions of an epidemic.

Shortly before eight o'clock a man wearing an aviator's leather helmet strapped underneath his chin and large dark-tinted goggles so that his face was almost entirely hidden appeared at the edge of the crowd and commenced working his way through it.

"Mister," one small boy mustered the courage to ask, "are you Grippo, the human fly?"

"The Great Grippo," replied the man in a husky voice, and to the *ah-hah*s of the one party and the *ugh*s of the other three,

strode to the east face of our courthouse, which was the first one
he came to, and without wasting a second in studying the building but as if he had been born and raised in its shadow, proceeded to climb it. Those who had been waiting for him on the
other sides hastened around to the chosen one, and the crowd
thereupon became so dense that people standing close to one
another had to take turns drawing breath. Small children and
many not so small were hoisted to their fathers' and even to their
mothers' shoulders.

"No! No!" a woman screamed. "I don't want to see it! Take me
home!" A large woman she was, and when she fainted five men
were needed to carry her off.

Grippo began by leaping from the ground and grasping a
window ledge and hauling himself up to it. From there he
stretched across to the next window and the next, going towards
the door. He let himself down onto the porch and opened one
half of the door back to the porch rail. He climbed the rail and
straddled the door and shinnied up its edge like a monkey up a
pole to the top of it. From there with the greatest of ease he
hoisted himself to the roof.

Pausing only to fetch his breath, Grippo assaulted the second
story. This he elected to scale by way of the drainpipe affixed to
its southeast corner. It took him just five minutes by the clock
overhead, but it seemed to all below much longer. Twice he lost
his grasp and slipped downwards. This was no doubt a part of his
act, but the crowd let out a gasp and on both occasions another
woman passed out and had to be removed. The scariest moment
came when, hauling himself over the edge of the roof, he slipped
and hung dangling from the gutter in midair, the snap of his chin
strap popping open and the flaps hanging loose. Then in a pierc-
ing voice a woman screeched, "Get that man down from there!
Get him down, I say, before he falls and kills hisself before our
very eyes!"

When Grippo had gained the second-story roof he stood up
and gave himself a shake and rested for some moments to catch
his breath, panting deeply. Among the crowd down on the
ground, meanwhile, breathing went suspended. Their gaze now
elevated several notches, they studied the lofty tower, all asking

themselves how Grippo meant to meet its daunting challenge. Now came the day's real trial. The building he could not climb might not have been built, but how did Grippo mean to scale those nearly one hundred feet of perpendicularity, its blank surface unbroken but for the courses of gargoyles spaced at intervals of some twelve or fifteen feet?

Grippo took off his shoes and socks and rolled up his trousers and began walking up the wall like a fly. A gasp of amazement ran through the crowd.

"It's not true!" a woman shouted. "I don't believe it! I'm going home!"

How? How was Grippo doing it? He was doing it, the realization dawned, relying on those Swiss-cheese-like fossil holes in the stone for finger- and toeholds!

"Yawl can stay and watch if you want to but I'm going home!" the same woman as before shouted.

Grippo did not go straight up. Searching ahead for holes big enough to hook a finger or a toe in, he was often forced to veer from his path to one side or the other, even to descend and strike out on a fresh route, so that he crisscrossed the entire face of the structure—very much the way a fly climbs. Thus he was twenty minutes in gaining the relative safety of the first gargoyle, upon whose neck he sat for a well-earned five-minute rest. Then could be seen the toll his climb was taking. The knees of his trousers were torn open and his knees scraped raw and red. Hanging as he did sometimes by a mere two fingertips in those jagged and sharp-edged holes, the punishment to them could be imagined.

"I can't stand it anymore! I'm going home where I belong!" that same woman yelled.

After his rest Grippo's rate of climb was slower, and by the time he reached his second gargoyle it was almost nine by the clock. His rest at that station was a long one. It was a stone goat upon whose neck he sat this time, and it seemed to be bucking and trying to throw him off, so deep was his breathing. To the watchers on the ground the tower appeared to have grown in height and people were saying now that Grippo would never make it to the top.

At last he rose and faced the wall again and resumed his climb.

One foot higher he lost his grip and fell. The crowd's cry died away on a vast sigh of relief as he caught the gargoyle in his descent. The jolt of his fall and its sudden arrest popped his helmet off and with it his goggles and sent them flying through the air. It was then in the general hush, broken only by the hysterical sobs of various women, that Mrs. Ernestine Reynolds, pear-shaped with her third child, cried out, "My Lord it's Stan!"

And my Lord she was right. It was. The Great Grippo was none other than our own "California" Stan Reynolds, in his desperation to escape from the home town he hated trying to climb his way out up the courthouse tower. The plump of two thousand hearts high in hopes sinking in sudden disappointment could almost be heard.

"Grippo my foot! Don't Grippo me!" Ernestine was shouting at her neighbors trying to persuade her and themselves that she must be mistaken. "I reckon I know my own husband when I see him—the crazy fool! Stan! Stanley Reynolds! What do you think you're doing? Come down from there! You hear me, Stan? Get down from there before you fall and break your neck! A fine fix that would leave me in, wouldn't it! Children, hush your crying! Stan! You— Oh! Watch out!" And she went green around the gills.

For in struggling to haul himself onto the gargoyle Stan's hold had slipped and he now hung only by his hands with his feet kicking free in space.

"Run get a rope, somebody!" a man yelled.

"A rope! A rope! Run get a rope!" cried several all at once. Mr. McKinney, of McKinney's Hardware, waved his store keys above his head, croaking to get himself noticed. The keys were passed to the rear of the crowd and someone set off running for the square. By the time the man got back with the coil of rope Stan had succeeded in pulling himself up and was once again sitting astraddle of the stone goat. Now that he was about to be rescued, having spoiled the day for all, mutters were heard that it would serve Stan right if he fell and broke his neck. A party of five volunteers ran into the courthouse carrying the rope. In the empty, high-ceilinged hallways their heavy footsteps could be heard, then could be heard no more as they started up the tower.

Stan must have heard them on the stairs inside going past the point where he sat perched. Whereupon he stood up and began again more determinedly than ever crawling up the wall. Shouts from the crowd went up of, "Sit still! Stay where you're at! Wait a second! They're coming with a rope!" and from Ernestine the cry, "Oh! Just wait till I get you home!" But Stan had climbed that high and could see above him the attainment of all his dreams. He was determined to go the whole way and claim his prize—which was to spit in the faces of all those below him and then never see them again. When the men of the rescue party appeared in the lookout and dropped their rope, Stan continued on his way, climbing up alongside it.

That was around half past nine. By ten Stan had gained two more gargoyles and was a little less than halfway to the top. It was an exhibition of frantic determination and mad bravery, and throughout it the crowd's mood had changed. At first, its hopes for a good time dashed, disgusted with being duped and boiling with indignation—a mob rather than a crowd—it was bent on having its own out of "California" Stan as soon as he was let back down to earth. But as Stan inched his way upwards, clinging for life by his fingertips, slipping and nearly falling and bringing every heart into every mouth at every moment, it began to dawn upon them that they were in fact seeing what they had come to see: a man scale the courthouse; and that if it was excitement they wanted they were getting not less but more out of watching an amateur, someone like themselves, do it, than they could have gotten out of watching a professional human fly. Nobody cheered: Stan had made himself too unpopular for that, and it could not be overlooked that that stubborn perseverance was the measure of his hatred of them all. Still it had to be admitted that what he was doing took nerve.

By eleven o'clock nerve was all the man was going on, and when finally he struggled to yet another of those stone billygoats it was plain to all that he had gone as high as he was going to go. Still he would not come down. Even after it must have been clear to Stan that he could go no higher but must give up and come down, he clung to his hard-won height, stubbornly ignoring the rope that dangled by his side, his wife who pled with him, threatened him, cursed him, and cried. Goaded by that hard-dying dream of his, or by the prospect of defeat, descent, he tried again, dragged himself up the wall another foot, then clung to it, unable to go up, unwilling to come down.

The rescue party in the lookout could be heard pleading with him. "Aw, come on, Stan, grab the rope. Please, Stan! Grab the rope, won't you, Stan?" Down on the ground women wailed and shrieked while men called up, "We're not mad at you, Stan, hear? Nobody's going to hurt you when you get down. Just grab the rope. Please!"

The clock struck twelve. Sixteen solemn chimes and then the long slow counting of the hour. The final stroke died away. A spasm of despair followed by a shudder of surrender passed over the man clutching at the wall and he beat his head against the stone. Then he turned and let go and reached for the rope. And missed it and fell sixty-six feet to the roof of the second story.

The thousand women present let out a single scream, and still one heard the thud as the falling man struck the roof. Even those who managed to get their hands over their ears before he hit still heard inside their heads the heavy sickening thud, and felt it in every cell of their bodies.

He ought to have been instantly killed, but as a matter of fact, he survived—helplessly crippled, to be sure, but still miraculously alive. Despite some eleven operations over the years, all paid for by the community he so despised, he remained permanently bedridden and immobilized, requiring even to be fed, a duty which his wife conscientiously fulfilled, although her patient was not noted for a cheerful disposition.

The event has remained vivid in local memory, and often, hearing the clock strike the hour, New Jerusalemites pause at their play or at their busy chores to recollect for a moment those desperate hours it tolled that earlier day.

In October 1945, under "Ten Years Ago This Week," and again in October 1955, under "Twenty Years Ago This Week," the *Lariat and Northern Bee* reprinted its original account of that day when, as Grippo the Human Fly, Stan attempted to scale the courthouse tower, preserving unrevised in the interest of historical accuracy its concluding observation that he was not expected to live. Stan died in the little cottage provided for him near the jailhouse and we buried him just last week—it was his obituary I have lately had to write—after thirty-three years as a ward of the town. Anyone who supposes he was grateful for our charity not only didn't know Stan, he doesn't know human nature.

Some readers may, like ourself, be intrigued to know how many times the town clock chimed over that period. 10,571,358.

The Last of the Caddoes

I

BY THE shores of the Red River, in Texas, lived a boy named Jimmy Hawkins, who learned one day to his surprise that he was, on his father's side, part Indian. Until then Jimmy had always thought he was just another white boy.

A curious reluctance had kept Jimmy's mother from ever telling him about his Indian blood. She had felt it from the time he first began to question her about himself, about the family. She shied away from it warily, almost as though in fear. This was very silly of her, of course. Just childishness. Some old bogeyman left over from her early childhood, nothing more. She had never seen a live Indian in her life. The savages, even in Texas, had long since been pacified, not to say exterminated. Being afraid of Indians in these days and times, when the only ones left were celluloid Indians, Saturday-matinee horse-opera Indians! *Ugh. How. Me big chief Squat-in-the-Mud. Heap big medicine.* Ridiculous! It was quite plain that what she really felt was not fear at all, it was in fact a touch of jealousy, possessiveness. For it was not she but his father from whom the child got his Indian blood, and obviously she was jealous of that part of him, small as it was, that was alien to her. Not that this was not equally silly of her, of course. Not that the Indian in himself was not equally alien to her husband. Certainly he would never try to use this bond to draw the boy closer to himself, away from his mother. There was really no reason for it. And that was it, precisely. That explained entirely why Mrs. Hawkins, and, following her lead, Mr. Hawkins, had let their Jimmy reach the age of twelve without ever mentioning this trifle about himself: there was no reason to.

Yet all the while Jimmy's mother felt she really perhaps ought to just mention it. There were times, indeed, when it was as though she were being urged from all sides to tell him, reproached for her silence, even almost commanded to speak out without further delay. "But what on earth difference does it make?" she would argue. "Nowadays what difference does it make? None whatever." Though in fact it might have made a great difference to Jimmy. The boy was simply crazy about Indians: read about nothing else, dressed himself up as one, made himself beadwork belts, sewed his own moccasins; his mother might have guessed that to be able to claim he was part Indian would have pleased him as nothing else could. "But it's only the tiniest little fraction," she would rejoin. "Hardly enough to count." Or, again: "It isn't as if I had deliberately not told him. Heavens! Why on earth would I do that? What's it to me, one way or the other? The subject has simply never come up, that's all. If it ever should, why then, of course . . ." Just who it was she was arguing with at these times she never knew.

It came out unexpectedly one day when they were having one of their rows. Lately it had gotten so all they ever did, it seemed, was fuss and quarrel. Jimmy was passing through a difficult phase. Going on thirteen now, and feeling new powers stirring within him, he was forever testing his strength, trying his mother, seeing just how far he could go, how much he could get away with. This one was their third fight in two days. Jimmy had done something he knew not to do, had been scolded and punished, and had turned sullen and defiant. His punishment would end, he was told, when he confessed he had been bad and said he was sorry; the set of his jaw proclaimed that he had vowed he would sooner die. He could be very stubborn. He was getting to be more than a match for his mother, as he well knew: too big for her to switch anymore—the very threat had begun to sound absurd—almost too big for his father to correct; and he soon reduced her to that frazzled state where, as she would say, she didn't know what to do. He grew bolder and more impudent until at last he said something so sassy she slapped his face. This made dart from Jimmy's black eyes two poisoned arrows of hatred. "Oh!" cried his mother, pierced by his look, "I don't know what gets into you at times like this!" Then before she knew it: "It must be the Indian in you coming out."

Jimmy instantly forgot his burning cheek. The Indian in him! Did she mean it? Real Indian? Which tribe? What part Indian was he? How long had this been known? Why had she never told him before?

But his mother had already told him more than she ever meant to. "You get it," she said dryly, "from your father, not me." To her surprise, and her chagrin, she found herself trembling, positively seething with anger. She felt somehow as though she had been tricked into letting it out. What was most exasperating was to find herself so vexed over a mere trifle. But what she felt was not altogether anger, and she knew it. One of her heartstrings had just been tied tight in a hard little knot of fear.

Jimmy's antics, meanwhile, did nothing to soothe her temper. His disobedience, his mother's displeasure, the sentence of punishment he was still under all forgotten, he was circling round and around her doing an Indian war dance. Brandishing an invisible tomahawk, he stamped his feet, ducked his head, then flung it back, all the while patting his mouth as he whooped, "Wah wah wah wah wah wah—" Until, shaking with rage, she hissed at him, "Little savage! Treat your mother with no more consideration than a wild savage! Well, that's just what you are! So act like one, that's right! Be proud of yourself for it!" Then she broke down in tears and ran sobbing from the room.

Thus, not until he was twelve, almost thirteen, and then only by accident (or so it seemed at the time), did Jimmy Hawkins learn that he was part Indian. And that that was the part his mother blamed for all she disliked in him.

II

How big a part? Which tribe? These questions, and others, Jimmy did not again put to his mother, eager as he was for an answer to them—not after her angry outburst. His hurt pride would not let him.

She had said he got it from his father, so Jimmy went to him. But he checked himself long before he got there. Not much pondering upon the matter was needed to make Jimmy even less willing to question his father than he was to question his mother. More Indian by half than he, his father had connived at, or at the very least had acquiesced in, keeping from his son the knowledge of his Indian ancestry. There was a name for men like his father, and a punishment decreed for them. His father was a renegade, and so without further ado Jimmy drummed him out of their tribe —whichever that might prove to be.

To be an Indian, even if only in part, was to Jimmy so glorious a fate it was impossible for him to imagine anyone feeling differently. But any lingering doubts he may have had about how differently his mother felt were soon dispelled. For although she had meant never to mention it—unless, that is to say, it just came up by itself, of course—once it was out and there was no taking it back, she found herself saying again and again, whenever he goaded her to it, which was often enough as the warfare between them went on, "That's the Indian in you coming out, that's what that bit of deviltry is. Little savage!" Though each time she said it it seemed to draw tighter that hard little knot in her heart.

And it was no sooner said than something awful began to happen. Something truly sinister. Something quite uncanny and even unbelievable, and yet precisely the sort of thing that might have been expected. Indeed, it now seemed to have been a premonition of this very thing that had kept her from ever speaking out before. Overnight Jimmy began to look like an Indian. He really did. What made this sudden transformation the more uncanny was that, strictly speaking, he looked no more like an Indian than he ever had, or ever would for that matter, with his corn-silk hair and pale, almost white eyebrows and lashes, his fair, not to say pallid, skin. His only feature that might have been Indian was his glittering black eyes—brown, actually, but a brown so dark, especially being set in that pale face, as to be really black. Yet all the same he really did begin to look like an Indian—more so every day—more so each time he was reproached with being one. More sullen and sly: more Indian.

It had certainly made a change in him: Jimmy could see it for himself. And no wonder. For although it may have come out accidentally, the revelation that he was an Indian found him already prepared to be one. He knew all there was to know about Indians. All his reading, ever since he learned to read, had been about the Indians, and in the accounts of the wars between them and the white settlers he had always taken their side. Now at last he knew why. They had been calling to him, blood calling to blood.

The things about himself that Jimmy had not understood before were explained now. His outbursts of temper, his touchy pride, his moods of contrariness, his impulses of cruelty, the stubborn streak that so irritated his mother: his Indian blood not only accounted for all these, it absolved him from blame for them. If he behaved sometimes like a little savage it was because he was a little savage. It was not his fault. He was what he was. He felt a burden of guilt lifted from him. He was through forevermore with apologizing for himself. It was not his fault that he was part Indian. He could not change that. He could not have done anything about it even if he had wanted to.

Being an Indian was not going to be all fun then. It never had been: this Jimmy knew from his reading; to be one in his day and time was harder than ever, it seemed. Situated where he was, cut off from his people, not even knowing yet who his people were, he was alone, surrounded by the enemy. He would need to be very crafty, very cunning, very wary. He would need to tread softly. He would have to sleep always with one eye open. He would need to grow up very fast. At his age an Indian boy was already training to be a brave.

He no longer joined in childish games. It did not befit his new dignity. To be an Indian was a serious responsibility. He seldom smiled, never laughed anymore. He comported himself with the gravity of a sachem, spoke with the sententiousness of one of Fenimore Cooper's sagamores. He exulted inwardly to see that his new disdainful silence was more exasperating to his parents and his schoolteachers than open defiance had ever been. When stung by one of his mother's slurs upon his Indian blood, he betrayed none of his resentment; he stored these up with Indian patience, all to be repaid with interest one day.

Meanwhile the more he brooded upon it the more he resented never being told that he was what he was. And who knew how much longer he might have been kept in ignorance? Had she not lost her temper that day and let it slip, his mother might never have told him. The prospect of this appalled Jimmy. When thought of that way it was not just the pleasure and the pride of being part Indian that he would have been deprived of: that would have been never really to know *what* he was.

It had come out despite them. Blood, they said, would out, and Indian blood, more powerful than any, would out though it were only a drop. There was an unseen power at work here. The spirits of his long-denied red forefathers had spoken to him at last (ironically enough, through his mother's own mouth) and claimed him as one of their own. Only who, exactly, were they? What was he? Indian, but what kind? Heir to what renown?

There was just one person who might be able to tell Jimmy the answers to his questions.

III

That his Grandfather Hawkins was half Indian, or more, was plain for all to see, yet Jimmy saw it for the first time when next the family went for a visit out to the farm. He who had been looking all his life for an Indian to adore!

But how were you to recognize the Indian in a man who dressed always in baggy, patched old denim overalls and a tattered denim jumper out at the elbows? Who, as Jimmy had seen, let his old wife cut his hair using an oatmeal bowl as a form instead of wearing it down to his shoulders in braids? Who when he came into town came not riding bareback on a horse but in a creaky old farmwagon drawn by a team of plodding gray mules?

Sixty-five years of plowing, hoeing, picking cotton had taken all the noble savage out of the man.

"Grandfather," Jimmy said, "I've just been told that I am part Indian, and that I get it from you."

"Who told you?"

"My mother."

"Did, did she? Well, sonnyboy, our side of the family is ever bit as good as yore mother's, and you can tell her I said so. She's got a lot to brag about, now ain't she? Them Tylers. What did e'er a one of them ever amount to? Old Dub Tyler, jake-legged from all the bootleg corn liquor he's drank, in debt to everbody in town: he's something to be proud of, I reckon? That's yore other grand-daddy. So any time yore mother's in the mood to trade compliments about—"

"What I want to know is, why didn't anybody ever tell me about this before?"

"I'd of told you if you'd ever of ast me. Whether yore mother liked it or not. Think I wouldn't? Tell anybody. Not that it's anybody else's business but my own. Son, what a man is born don't matter a hill of beans. It's what you make of yoreself that counts."

"If you're not what you are then what are you?" said Jimmy. "You're not anything. Tell me now about myself."

"Tell you what?"

"Tell about your father. My great-grandfather. The Indian."

"Why, what do you want to know about him?"

"Everything! I want to know all there is to know."

"Well, he was not what you would call a big man. Neither was he a little man. More what you would call middling-sized. Bothered with stomach trouble all his life, though what killed him was not that but something else. Died of—"

"What kind of Indian was he?"

"What do you mean, what kind of Indin was he?"

"I mean like Comanche, or Cheyenne, or Apache. You know. What tribe?"

"Oh. Well, I wouldn't know nothing about that. Indin, that's all I can tell you, boy."

"What was his name?"

"His name? Mr. George P. Hawkins, same as mine."

"If he was an Indian, where did he ever get a name like that—Mr. George P. Hawkins? That's not an Indian name. Indians are named names like Rain-in-the-Face or Crazy Horse, or something like that. I expect he just never told you his true name."

"Must of been a Hawkins in the woodpile back somewheres along the line, just where and when I can't tell you, 'cause I wasn't there myself. I can tell you one thing though: I'm grateful I haven't had to go through life named George P. Crazy Horse. Yes, sir, I'm sure grateful I haven't had to go through—"

"How about your grandfather? Tell me about him."

"Never knowed the man. Dead 'fore ever I was born."

"Didn't your father ever tell you about him when you were a boy?"

"When I was a boy I never had no time to waste setting around talking about my granddaddy. And I ain't got none for it now. Maybe he was the Hawkins."

Another renegade. It ran in the family. Jimmy felt he had much to atone for.

IV

Before the coming of the white man, the northeastern part of Texas where Jimmy Hawkins lived with his father and mother was the domain of the Caddo Indians. The local tribe was one which, although he was born and raised there, and notwithstanding all his Indian lore, Jimmy had never heard of until he began delving into his pedigree.

To learn that he belonged to such an obscure tribe was a surprise, and for a moment something of a disappointment. He had rather set his heart on being a Comanche. However, he liked the name Caddo. He knew he was one: he felt a thrill of recognition the first time he read the word.

Specimens preserved in various museums, he read in the small guide book in the small town library, proved the Caddoes to have been the most talented potters of all the Indians of North America.

But who were their famous chiefs? Who were the Caddo Pon-

tiac, the Caddo Sitting Bull, the Caddo Geronimo? Who were
their most renowned warriors? Where were their great battles
fought?

The Caddoes it was, he read, who had reared the numerous
large burial mounds still to be found in that part of the state and
adjacent Louisiana (in the one on his grandfather's farm did his
own forefathers lie sleeping?), which, along with the name of
nearby Caddo Lake, were at this late date (the book had been
published in 1907) the only reminders left of this once large and
powerful tribe.

Where had all the Caddoes gone?

Like the Mohicans, the Caddoes were no more. Their numbers
depleted by their war against the white settlers, and by the diseases which the settlers brought with them, their last surviving
remnant had been forcibly removed to Oklahoma in 1854 and
resettled on government reservations, where, through intermar-
riage with and adoption into other tribes, the Caddoes had lost
their separate identity.

The little book told no more; none other told as much.

He had been orphaned of his entire nation. He was the last of
the Caddoes.

V

What Jimmy Hawkins had always known was now confirmed:
he was meant for no common fate. He had been born with a
horror of the ordinary, and had always known he was not what he
seemed to the world to be. He had often wondered who he really
was, and had felt that like the changeling prince in the fairy tale
he had been cheated of his birthright and brought up in a meaner
station of life than fate and his gifts had intended him for. The
reason, as he now knew, was that he was the last of the Caddoes:
rightful heir to all that he surveyed, with blood in his veins that
cried out for vengeance: a dangerous person, a permanent threat
to those who had wronged him. So they must have been warned
by the bad fairy (herself Indian) who was not invited to his chris-
tening but who appeared at it all the same. "You may bleach him
whiter than the snow, give him a white man's name, and bring

him up in ignorance of his people," she had pronounced in a raspy voice, shaking a bony brown finger at them, "he is what he is. What will be will be." So Jimmy had always known he was ordained, marked out, chosen to perform some bold feat; now he knew it would be something to vindicate his dispossessed, destroyed, and all but forgotten race. He awaited the revelation of what it would be. Once he knew the name of his tribe he felt the constant presence of his red forebears molding him, training him, preserving him until such time as he should be ready and his mission be revealed to him.

They taught him to see what before he had overlooked, what others, outsiders, still overlooked: the relics everywhere of their immemorial stay in the land from which they had been driven out. In plowed fields they showed him arrowheads that generations of plowmen, though their eyes were seldom lifted from the ground, had not seen. In stones that the unknowing took to be just stones he recognized the mortars in which his people had ground their maize and the pestles with which they had pounded it, the flint knives with which they had skinned their game, the tomahawks with which they had brained their foes.

He felt them most powerfully in the woods. In the green stillness he could see their spirits flitting among the trees and in the whispering together of the branches could hear their voices. He knew no fear, for they were with him. They were the lords of the forest and he their only son, their sole survivor, the last arrow from the once-full quiver of their wrath. And when at home or at school he was whipped for his disobedience, they lent him fortitude. With them at his side he could endure without flinching whatever any white man could mete out. Not a whimper could they draw from him; he sneered in the faces of his tormentors. The last of the Caddoes brought no stain of dishonor upon the spirits of his proud dead.

If to be an Indian was a career in itself, to be the last of one's tribe was a calling. To be the sole repository of a nation's history, its traditions, its laws, its beliefs, and its rituals, and to know nothing of that history, those traditions, laws, beliefs, and rituals, and to be just twelve years old, was to carry an almost crushing weight of responsibility. No wonder Jimmy was aged and sober beyond his years. That with all this on his mind he should have no time for friends, for games, or for schoolbooks.

His confirmation time was fast approaching. He would turn thirteen that summer, would enter upon his manhood, and as soon as school was out Jimmy obeyed the call he had heard to make a pilgrimage to his ancestral shrine: the Caddo burial mound on his grandfather's farm. He was to spend the summer in the country. His parents were relieved to see him go, glad of a rest. The prospect of having him always about the house, of a whole long summer of wrangling, was more than his mother could face. It was his own idea; she need not accuse herself of getting rid of him. After a few months' separation maybe they would get along a little better. Hopefully, a summer in the open, swimming, going fishing, exploring the farm, would make a happier boy of him, a better pupil when school reopened in the fall.

VI

"He don't do a thing but dig in that damn dirt pile," his grandfather reported when Jimmy's parents drove out to celebrate his birthday. "He's at it all day long every day and Sunday. Can't even get him to stop long enough to eat his dinner. If you all weren't here he'd be out there right now. Wouldn't you?" Over his shoulder the old man flung a scowl at the great mound of earth that rose like a single gigantic grave out of the field below the house.

"Well, I must say it seems to have done him good. He's so changed I wouldn't have known him. Would you, Mother?" said Jimmy's father, and turning to his wife, received a look that blazed with exasperation.

For no, she would not have known Jimmy, he was so changed, and she was in torment while his father beamed. It was not her boy but a stranger she found awaiting her, a stranger whom she had brought into the world with her pain on this day of the year. He had grown like a weed, had in just these few weeks away from her shot up half a head taller. The last of the baby fat had thinned from his cheeks, which now showed their bones, and his baby fairness was gone: he was as brown as a penny. No longer was he the soft round ungendered little sausage she remembered; his shoulders had wedged out, his little pot been trimmed away neat and flat and hard. The change in his chemistry had coarsened his skin, his hair, thickened his muscles, deepened his voice. Yet though his mother ached to be proud of his new manliness, she could not. She was no part of it. She was a little afraid of him. She felt the misgiving every mother feels when suddenly one day her son comes to present her with his bill for the many slights and indignities of his boyhood.

His manner confused and disarmed her. She had expected on his birthday to find him cocky and impertinent, and had come prepared to overlook it for the occasion. Her forbearance would not be wanted, thank you. Instead she found him subdued, withdrawn, grave. This gravity grated her as no amount of impudence would have done. How dared he treat her with such cool courtesy, as though there were no history of any troubles between them! To learn now that he had spent his time digging so fanatically in that old Indian mound instead of in the harmless pastimes she had imagined made her feel she had been betrayed and mocked.

"Must think he's going to find some buried treasure. Well, you're in for a big letdown if you do," said Jimmy's grandfather. "The Indins, why, they were all so piss-pore they never hardly had enough to eat, much less any silver or gold. What have you found? Just what I told you you'd find. Nothing but skeltons and a lot of old broken crocks."

Jimmy was used to his grandfather's disapproval of his project. The burial mound sat square in the middle of his grandfather's cotton patch. While Jimmy dug on top of the mound his grandfather chopped the cotton in the field below. Whenever the old man's progress down the row brought him parallel with the mound he would stop and rest and watch Jimmy dig. He refused ever to face the mound, he would only lour at it over his shoulder, leaning on his hoe handle with one foot crossed over the other and his behind stuck out. But if the sight of his grandson's foolishness disgusted him, the sight of his grandfather's degradation filled Jimmy with shame and despair. Commanded by the voice of his people to know himself through knowing them, Jimmy had bared the buried history of the Caddoes, delving backwards in time from their end to their beginning. He had measured the antiquity of his lineage in countless shovelfuls of earth. The handiwork of his tribe had shown him the strangeness of his heritage, his own difference. From the mound's topmost layer, where the bodies, unceremoniously interred, had been so closely packed ("their numbers depleted by their war against the white settlers") that the bones were inseparably mixed, and where the little bones of children were numerous ("and by the diseases which the settlers brought with them"), he had dug down to the splendid rotting cerements, the broken, once-magnificent urns, the weapons of flint and obsidian worthy to accompany a great chief to the happy hunting grounds, of the days of their greatness: from desolation down to grandeur that made the desolation all the keener. Then to look down and see his grandfather, the man with more of the blood of the Caddoes in his veins than any other living man, hoeing his way down the rows of scraggly cotton: it was a constant reminder of how art the mighty fallen.

"I remember digging in there myself when I was a boy," said Jimmy's father. "I never found anything worth keeping."

"Maybe you didn't dig deep enough," said Jimmy.

"Why, what all have you found?"

"Oh, things."

"What sort of things?"

"Oh, just things."

"Well, some people collect old Indian things. Mr. Will Etheridge in town, for instance. He'll pay a dime apiece for flint arrowheads. Whole ones, that is, of course. I'll speak to him about you next time I see him. You can take and show him what you've found, see if he'll offer you something for it."

A laugh came from Jimmy's mother like the sound of breaking glass. "Jimmy isn't after buried treasure," she said. "And he wouldn't think of selling any of the things he's found. Would you, dear?" she said, turning to him with a spiteful simper. "They're sacred, isn't that right? Yes. You see, I'm the only one who understands, aren't I, my little Hiawatha? I can read you like an open book."

"Are we going to fight on my birthday, Mother?" asked Jimmy.

"Why, what better day for it?" she cried, regretting what she said even as she said it. "I was only trying to be friendly, but if you want to fight, what better day for it than your birthday?"

It was a shocking thing to say. She herself was quite taken aback. She had not known she was going to say that, it had just come out by itself. Thus she was all the more taken aback when Jimmy said, "I knew you were going to say that, Mother."

"He wants to work I'll put him to work and pay him for doing it," said Jimmy's grandfather. "Chopping cotton, fifty cents a day. It ain't near as hard work as spading in the ground. Fifty cents a day. Save it up and buy yoreself something nice. Damn foolishness to work for nothing when you could be earning pay. Buy yoreself a twenty-two rifle. A banjo. Get you a bicycle, then you can carry a paper route, earn money all year round. Tell you one thing, sonnyboy: prices of goods what they are today, if you was mine you wouldn't be out there wasting time when you could be bringing in a little something towards yore room and board and yore education."

Lest his wife say it first, Jimmy's father said he believed they could manage without that.

"Do you think I've grown, Mother?" asked Jimmy.

"I think you're looking thin," she said.

"I knew you were going to say that!" said Jimmy.

"Thin and flushed," she continued, ignoring the interruption. "Not well at all. I wonder if you're not coming down with something?" Truth was, she herself felt flushed and as though she might be coming down with something. She felt terribly out of sorts.

"It's because I'm excited," Jimmy said. "It's my birthday!"

He was excited. Something was going to happen. He had no inkling of what it would be—perhaps something not at all pleasant. But something momentous, he knew. It was imminent in the air like a break in the weather. This birthday would not end without bringing about some fundamental change in things.

"Well," said his mother, "you've had enough to be used to them and you've got a great many more to come. So you'd better begin calming down."

"But this one is special! This is my thirteenth birthday. Today I become a man."

"What! Is that what you think? Ha-ha! You've got a long way to go before you get to be a man, my son. You're still just a little boy. And I advise you not to forget it."

There was a birthday cake with fourteen candles—one to grow on—and when "Happy Birthday" had been sung Jimmy blew them all out with one breath. The presents were then opened and admired. Afterwards Jimmy's father said, first submitting a glance to his wife, "Yes, I can remember digging in that old mound myself when I was your age. Though like I say, I never had any luck. So you're interested"—another appeasing glance towards his wife—"in the Indians. Well, that's natural. Most boys are. Let's go and see just what you've been up to. Mother? Let's go and see what Jimmy's dug up, shall we?" He was being the peacemaker. Show a little interest in the boy's hobby, said the look to his wife, which Jimmy caught.

"You really don't want to see," said Jimmy.

"You mean you really don't want us to see," said his mother. "Well now, I think I do want to have a look. Maybe you've got hold of something you ought not to have."

"Why, Mother," said her husband. "What sort of thing could you have in mind?"

"I have in mind," she said, fixing him with her look, "something nasty. We all know what the Indians were like."

His indignation rose with a taste as sour as gorge. Yet she demeaned only herself. They were beyond her spite, as they were beyond her understanding; nothing she might say could smirch them. And he felt slightly dizzied. Again as previously he had known the instant before what his mother was about to say. He had actually heard her words seconds before they were spoken. It was like what happened sometimes with the phonograph, when you heard distantly the opening bars of the music before the record actually began to play. It had happened several times today, so that now Jimmy had the sense of being clairvoyant. It was as though he were in some sort of occult communication with his mother's unconscious mind. But if, for all her quarrelsomeness, his mother had been delivered into his power, Jimmy did not feel like gloating. It was too uncanny.

Once today his mother had read Jimmy's thoughts. He did not want his parents to visit the mound. Not for the reason his mother suspected but because it was hallowed ground and they were infidels who would profane it, the one with his idle curiosity, the other with her hatred and scorn. But both were determined now to be taken there, his father intent on making peace, his mother on making mischief.

She hated the thing, the mound, on sight. Before, hearing of Jimmy's dedication to it, she had viewed it as no more than a red rag of his meant to taunt her with. But seeing it sitting there so squat and alien and old she hated it. Brown and bare, it rose like a single enormous grave out of the field of dazzling white cotton. That it was man-made was obvious; no one could ever have mistaken it for a natural mound. Rectangular in form, it stretched two hundred feet, was fifty feet wide, rose twenty feet from the ground. She pictured the dead savages inside it packed like sardines in a tin, and she shuddered with revulsion. Such promiscuous burial offended her as not only uncivilized but obscene. If she had her way these ugly reminders of barbarism would all be leveled to the ground. And her son was under its spell. She could see it working in the dark depths of his eyes. It was an atavism in him, a taint in his blood.

But the place had a power. Undeniably it did, if even she was forced to acknowledge it. Standing to adjust her vision inside the black shadow it cast upon the glaring cotton she could feel its solemn spell. The single grave of a whole clan of people! She felt herself belittled by its bulk and its antiquity, and despite herself, reverent. She could gauge the power it had to attract her son by the power it had to repel her. Her sight sharpened and she saw him going ahead, his pace quickening with each step, drawn to it like an iron filing to a magnet, and her heart misgave her. She felt they were hopelessly sundered. As if a snake had coiled at her feet to strike, she sensed something stir somewhere nearby. The sensation was overpowering that her approach had alerted the hostile hosts of the dead. Her courage, born of her contempt, forsook her, and for a moment she stood quaking with superstitious dread.

Jimmy's father was impressed by the size of the opening he had made in the mound. More than impressed, he was awed, dumbfounded. Starting at about the middle of one of the long sides, at the spot where, on his first visit to the mound, he had received the command to dig, he had removed a slice six feet wide and six feet deep all the way down to the base. There was nothing slipshod, nothing boyish about his excavation; it was all quite amazingly professional-looking, like a photograph in *The National Geographic*, which was where he must have gotten his ideas from, of a field camp on the site of a "dig" of an archaeological expedition. He must have dug furiously, almost frantically, and yet his cuttings had been made systematically and with care—indeed, they had been made with reverence; his findings sorted and labeled and cataloged. To house them he had erected a tent on top of the mound. He had cut in the face of it a flight of steps leading there.

On the tent floor laid out in rows were neat stacks of human bones each crowned by its grinning gap-toothed skull. With each stack was carefully preserved its owner's beaded medicine bag, his tomahawk, his clay pipe, and in those cases where it had survived intact, the pouch containing parched corn that was to have fed him on his journey to the happy hunting grounds. Being but freshly unearthed, the skulls were not bleached white but were still a waxen yellow. To some adhered coverings of pursed brown skin drawn back from toothless gums in everlasting howls. Nobody to hear them but one thirteen-year-old boy of mixed blood and divided loyalties. And his was but one of many such mounds. They were numerous throughout that part of the state and adjacent Louisiana. Sights for tourists, spots for picnickers, curio seekers. On their slopes children romped and around their bases farmers gathered their crops while a nation groaned underground and no one heard. Only he heard. To him each and every skull he uncovered screamed its plea for pity, its demand for justice. It all came down to him. He was all they had. His heart was their last war drum; on it they beat night and day.

Asked by his father what he meant to do with all these Jimmy replied that he meant to put them back where he found them.

Put them back? his father wondered.

Wasn't that what he would do? One of those might be his great-great-grandfather.

In her hands Jimmy's mother held a clay jug, one of the few he had managed to salvage unbroken. Perfect in condition, perfect in form and in decoration, it demanded to be picked up and handled, demanded it even of a person in whom it produced an aversion exceeding what she felt in looking at the grimacing yellow skulls. It seemed fresh from the hand that had made it centuries ago. The design was of diamonds in bands that coiled about it shrinking and expanding in conformity with its shape, a treatment that must have been suggested to the potter by his own procedure in coiling his rope of clay. If, as has been said, the soul of a people is to be found in its pottery, then the soul of the mound builders, as expressed in this piece, was one of boundless self-assurance, superb and haughty, implacable and utterly without remorse, possessed of some inner harmony that gave them a careless mastery of life. Unconquerable, the spirit of the people who could produce one such thing!

She tore her eyes from it to look at her son. He stood gazing at the vessel in her hand with an expression that shrank her heart. There was nothing of pleasure, nothing of fond possession in his look—rather the reverse: a look of his belonging body and soul to it, and an ineffable sadness: the look a priest might give to the chalice of the mass or the reliquary of the founder of his order. A shudder of revulsion shook her soul, she dashed the jug to the ground, where it burst like a grenade, and as Jimmy drew back—for he had already heard the words she was about to utter—she hissed, "A snake in your mother's bosom, that's what you are! A snake in your mother's bosom!"

They stood staring into one another's eyes in mute wonder. She was merely aghast, but he was both aghast and enlightened. What was to have happened had happened. On his thirteenth birthday an Indian boy becomes a brave, a man, and is given his man's name. The spirits of his ancestors, speaking through their enemy's own mouth, had just told him his.

VII

Snake-in-His-Mother's-Bosom, in whose new name was contained his mission, returned home in September after his summer in the country most unwillingly. He dreaded ever to see his mother again. He was not afraid of his mother, he was afraid for her, and thus for himself.

He knew now that his mother's telling him about his Indian blood had been no accident. She had been tricked into it against her will by her enemies, the spirits of his dead tribesmen. And he knew why. If he had not known before, he knew now, after excavating the mound—that hive that like hornets had lived and died all for one and one for all. Digging down through layer upon layer, generation upon generation, he had come to know the importance to them of preserving the tribal continuity, the sacrilege it would be to them should ever the chain be broken, especially in its last link. He knew now how inexhaustible was the Indian patience in waiting for revenge, the refinements of Indian cruelty in exacting it. He had not read these things written on buckskin or bark or carved in stone. He had seen them in the grin of Indian skulls, in the incisions on Indian jugs, in those geometric designs endlessly repeated that always came full circle, returning in the end to their source. His mother's crime against them was to have brought him up in ignorance of them. For this she must be made to pay, and Indian justice decreed that her punishment was that her son be a snake in her bosom, Indian subtlety that out of her own mouth must come the discovery that he was theirs, that she herself must bestow upon him his tribal name, that out of her very mouth must come— That was what he dreaded. What message would they next transmit through her to him? Not knowing what she was saying, what would she say next?

One thing his mother was determined never to say again was that he was a snake in her bosom. She regretted saying that. It was a terrible thing to say. Dreadful! She had meant to hurt him, and could see that she had; but not nearly as much as she had hurt herself. What made it doubly awful was that it was also rather laughable. Stiff, stagey, like something out of an old-fashioned play, like "Never darken my doorway again!"—not at all her usual way of expressing herself. And this comical old-fashioned stiffness somehow made the memory of it all the more embarrassingly painful. Her excuse was, she had not really meant to say it. She had gotten carried away and it had just popped out. If only she could have kept her vow never to repeat it! Before he had been back home two days, however, she did, provoked by his sullen refusal to answer to his name.

But that was not his name. Not anymore. He was Jimmy Hawkins no longer and never again would he answer to that name. When called by it, at home or at school, he would await silently and with a maddening little smile the question or the command that followed, but he would not answer to that name though beaten for his surliness until the principal's arm ached, until his father begged him to be allowed to quit. Hostile as he felt towards his mother, she was still his mother, and even the last of the Caddoes shrank from his terrible new appellation. But his people had spoken. Snake-in-His-Mother's-Bosom they had called him: Snake-in-His-Mother's-Bosom he must be. That the name fit him he had to admit. It fit him like a skin. And painful though it was, there was also strong medicine in the name. It encased him in an armor of scales. It enabled him to slink in silence. It gave to his brain the serpent's subtlety. It equipped him with a forked tongue for speaking to the enemies by whom he was surrounded. It armed him with fangs.

Because he would respond to none other, his mother was often goaded into calling him a name that was painful to her. Thus things went from bad to worse.

They could not be together for half a day now without a quarrel breaking out. Though she charged him with being the one who always started it, in fact it was she herself. In dread of what she might say, he wanted peace, no more quarrels. Yet he was Snake-in-His-Mother's-Bosom. And of course when riled he struck back. But she began it. The spirits egged her on.

It was as if, that day in the country, his birthday, they had lured her, using her very hatred of them as bait, to their mound, where, like a host of germs entering the bloodstream through some scratch, they had stolen inside her. Now she was like a person unconscious that a fatal disease is quietly eating him alive, as cancer is said to be painless and give no warning until its host is already past cure. In this case the organ invaded was the soul.

To watch them play with their victim was both horrible and fascinating. That he was himself a part of their scheme he knew, but was powerless to prevent. Besides, he rather enjoyed it. By making him remind her continually of them they rubbed her where she was rawest. Drop by drop the cup of her irritation would fill, then at some trifle brim over. Then she tore at her hair as though there were bats in it. Then she would not have peace. Then nothing so irritated her as his efforts to appease her. "You're good at starting trouble, aren't you?" she would taunt him. "But when the going gets rough you cry off. Soft! Can't take it, eh?" She would not let him give in to her. He shunned her; this enraged her. He fleeing, she pursuing, their arguments swept up and down stairs and through all the rooms of the house, doors banging, windows, walls, and furniture shuddering at the violence. He could not shake her off; she clattered after, attaching herself to him like a tin can tied to a dog's tail. When she had him cornered then he turned. Then he bared his fangs. They parried words. She always won, always had the last word: *they* put it in her mouth. And when she had said something at last that chilled him into silence, then she would quit the field in dubious triumph. For days, weeks—the torture was fiendishly drawn out—all their quarrels would end on the same double-edged phrase. So it had been from the start, with "That's the Indian in you coming out!" So it was later with "A snake in your mother's bosom, that's what you are!" So it was for a time with "I brought you into the world just to torment me!" Then, wrought to a pitch of outrage which that phrase had grown too worn to express, she would utter a new and more reckless one, something that left them both appalled, then retire to savor the bitter taste of her triumph. So she was led on from one Pyrrhic victory to another.

As he grew more morose she grew more cutting. "Aren't you the little joy to your mother, though? Mother's little joy! Other women's children bring sunshine and laughter into the house, but you, sullen creature—! You're a stranger in the house. You came into the world just to torment me, you snake in your mother's bosom, you little savage, you!" And he would glower at her out of those hooded cold black eyes, remote, hostile, alien, lashing her on to ever more bitter recriminations, drawing the net ever closer about herself, until in a fit of rage one day she said, "You will be the death of me!"

So ended the worst quarrel they had ever had, with both of them left gasping for breath. This time she feared she had gone really too far. Ah, but she had certainly given him something to think about! That she could see. As in the days when she used to wash him, her words had wiped his face clean of its black scowl, leaving him pale and blinking. In tones still more ominous she repeated, "You will be the death of me!"

VIII

Under cover of darkness Snake-in-His-Mother's-Bosom fled from home that night, never to return. He went to seek for himself a new home, new parents, a new name. He knew where to find them. Where not to be found by the ones he was leaving behind.

To postpone the discovery of his flight he left a dummy of himself in his bed as jailbreakers do. It looked so much like him lying there in his bed it made him feel it really was himself, the old him with all his troubles, with that heavy curse upon him, that he was leaving behind. By the time his trick was found out and chase given, he would be beyond recapture.

His mother would fume and rage when she found him gone. Doubting prophetess, eager victim, she would pursue her appointed executioner and be angry when he eluded her. Then having done her duty she would give up the search. His mother would receive condolences from family and friends, and look sad, and be secretly glad, and never know how much she had to be glad for.

The route taken by Snake-in-His-Mother's-Bosom was the same one along which the last surviving remnant of his people had been driven in 1854. His destination was the same as theirs. Across the Red River in Oklahoma among those Indian tribes with whom the earlier Caddoes exiled from Texas had found a home, and lost their identity, the last of the Caddoes hoped to find for himself a new home, a new mother and father, or many mothers, many fathers, lose his identity, and thereby evade his terrible fate. A Comanche, a Cherokee, a Choctaw, or a Creek: when Snake-in-His-Mother's-Bosom had been adopted as one or another of those and been given his new name then the Caddoes would truly be no more.

No more! The night around him groaned at the dismal thought. The moon veiled her face behind a cloud and through the treetops passed a long low sigh of woe. Over the dark land of the Caddoes the sentence of irrevocable doom rolled out in the muffled drum of the owl.

The road to the river and the ferry to Oklahoma, the road he was on, would take him within two miles of his grandfather's farm. Could Snake-in-His-Mother's-Bosom pass so near and not pay a last visit to his ancestral burial mound? At this season, early spring, before time for the planting of crops, his grandparents slept late. He could go and pay his respects and still get away unseen. Although it was from their prophecy that he was fleeing, the last of the Caddoes must not go forever from the land of his fathers without taking leave of his tutelary spirits.

He arrived shortly before daybreak. The house was still asleep as he passed it going down to the mound. In the field still stood the stalks of last year's cotton. A multitude of empty cottonbolls murmured in the wind. Day broke as he stepped on top of the mound. He advanced to the center and set down his suitcase. Looking at the ground he seemed to see into it, down into the depths where he had dug, down to the bottommost layer where the old first fathers lay in their lavish decay, smiling serenely, confident of the continuity of their kind, having gone into the grave before the white man's coming. Above them in successive layers of decline, those who had followed after: children laid on top of their parents, their children on top of them, and now on top of all himself, the last of the line, come to forswear his allegiance and bid them good-by forever.

He prepared to deliver his farewell speech, and the silence grew attentive. He was about to begin when a sound, a rustle, at his back made him turn. From a hole in the ground quite near him a snake was emerging slowly like something being squeezed out of a tube. Out and out it came: its final four inches were rattles. It was an old snake. Its skin was dull and lusterless, its markings blurred, and it was half blind with a film clouding its eyes so that it groped its way with its tongue flickering constantly, tasting the air for unseen danger. It hitched itself along in angles as the knight moves on a chessboard. It passed within mere feet of him while he stood rigid and unbreathing. Yet he was not afraid of being bitten by the snake. No snake would bite him. He was of the clan of snakes. He was a snake himself. It was something else that he feared. This was the time of year when the ground's warming up roused snakes from their winter's sleep and brought them out. But in the emergence of this old, decrepit, possibly dying one coinciding with his visit here he feared some omen.

Every few feet the snake paused and half coiled itself to strike and reared its head and peered blindly about, its long forked tongue quivering like an antenna. Presently it came up against a stone. At once it began stroking its jaw against this stone. He could hear the rasping of its scales.

And suddenly with one long stroke, at the part dividing its nostrils, the snake's skin split and out of its dull wrapper popped a bright new head with keen new eyes that blinked at the raw daylight. Then rapidly it peeled itself its entire length, turning the old skin inside out as a finger comes out of a glove. Its glassy little scales tightly woven in a pattern of diamonds, it resembled nothing so much as a belt of Indian beadwork. A shiver of pleasure ran down from its head to its rattles as it felt the air for the first time on its new skin. It gaped, showing its fangs, coiled and reared itself high and slowly looked about with lordly menace. Then quick as a fish it flashed away and was gone.

Snake-in-His-Mother's-Bosom knelt and picked up the cast-off skin. Rising, he saw his mother's face appear over the top of the mound. He felt himself instinctively coil, his lips fly back to bare his fangs. "Ah-hah," said his mother's smirk, "I knew where to find you, didn't I? You can't get away from me."

Beneath his feet all was silence. Silence and sly toothless grins.

Snake-in-His-Mother's-Bosom surrendered himself with a sigh to his fate. He could not get away from her—foolish ever to have thought he could. He was what he was; what would be would be. The snake might shed his skin, but only to grow another one the same as before.

In obedience to his victim's nod, Snake-in-His-Mother's-Bosom took up his suitcase and followed her down the steps and across the barren field to the car. In its rearview mirror he watched the mound diminish and finally disappear. The snake-skin rode on his lap. Now he must wait. Must wait for their next, their final command. It would not come soon; they sipped their pleasures slowly. Many times yet he would have to hear his mother say that he would be the death of her. So many times that when the final order came it would be almost welcome, a release. Distant and ghostly, it sounded already in the echoing silence of his mind. Over and over, like a phonograph record when the needle cannot find the starting groove. "Kill me at once then and be done with it!" his mother's voice was saying. One day the needle would find the groove. Then out would come the command loud and clear and with the sudden shock of long-expectedness. Then Snake-in-His-Mother's-Bosom would strike, accomplish his mission and fulfill the prophecy; and then at last the ghosts of the Caddoes could lie down at peace in their many-tiered mound and haunt the land and him no more.